THE ACCOMPLICE

An Eddie Flynn Thriller

Steve Cavanagh

ORION

First published in Great Britain in 2022 by Orion Fiction,
an imprint of The Orion Publishing Group Ltd,
Carmelite House, 50 Victoria Embankment
London EC4Y 0DZ

An Hachette UK company

3 5 7 9 10 8 6 4 2

ISBN (Hardback) 978 1 4091 9873 4
ISBN (Trade Paperback) 978 1 4091 9874 1
ISBN (eBook) 978 1 4091 9876 5

Typeset by Born Group
Printed and bound in Great Britain by Clays Ltd, Elcograf S.p.A.

MIX
Paper from
responsible sources
FSC® C104740

www.orionbooks.co.uk

Praise for Steve Cavanagh

'This guy is the real deal. Trust me' Lee Child

'A terrific writer. He has talent to burn' Don Winslow

'A brilliant, twisty, ingeniously constructed puzzle' Ruth Ware

'If you read a thriller as good this year, it's only because you've read this one twice' Mark Billingham

'Trust me – it will keep you guessing until the very end' Ian Rankin

'Steve Cavanagh must have sold his soul to the devil at the cross-roads outside of Rosedale, Mississippi in exchange for becoming one of the world's best crime writers. Steve is 5/5' Adrian McKinty

'Top notch thrills and courtroom drama' Shari Lapena

'A dead bang beast of a book expertly combining his authority on the law with an absolutely great thrill ride. Books this ingenious don't come along very often' Michael Connelly

'Bristles with dramatic courtroom tension, suspense, intrigue and more twists and turns than a moonlit country road' S. A. Cosby

Steve Cavanagh was born in Belfast, Northern Ireland, and for twenty years he practiced civil rights law. All of his novels have been nominated for major awards and many are international bestsellers. His third novel, *The Liar*, won the CWA Gold Dagger for Crime Novel of the Year 2018. *Thirteen* won the Theakston Old Peculier Crime Novel of the Year 2019. *Fifty-Fifty* was a Richard and Judy Book club choice, and was also selected for the BBC Between The Covers book club. *Twisted, Fifty-Fifty* and *The Devil's Advocate* were all *Sunday Times* Top 10 bestsellers.

To find out more, visit Steve's website or
follow him on social media.

www.stevecavanaghauthor.com

 /SSCav1

 @SteveCavanagh_

 @SSCav

For Tracy.

"In the evening ... he comes up the stairs very softly, for he walks in his socks, then he opens the [children's] doors without the slightest noise, and throws a small quantity of very fine dust in their eyes, just enough to prevent them from keeping them open, and so they do not see him. Then he creeps behind them, and blows softly upon their necks, till their heads begin to droop. [My brother] he is also called Ole Luk-Oie but he never visits any one but once, and when he does come, he takes them away on his horse, and tells them stories as they ride along ... he is also called Death."

– "Ole Luk-Oie", from *Hans Andersen's Fairytales*,
by Hans Christian Andersen (1888).
A legend of the Sandman.

PROLOGUE

PAIGE DELANEY

The SWAT leader called it.

Ten seconds.

Once the count reached zero, they had a hundred yards of well-tended lawn to clear before they reached the back door. Paige Delaney eased herself up from the wet leaves, pulled down a thin branch from a pine tree to get a better view of the house. A chalk ball moon sat over the silhouette of a brick colonial-style mansion set in Old Westbury, New York.

Delaney filled her lungs, breathed out slow. Listened to the count over the comms.

Ten . . .

She liked numbers. In her tenure in the FBI as Special Agent in Behavioral Science Unit 2, she had come to trust numbers more than people. And the figures in this case were extraordinary.

Nine . . .

For fourteen months and twelve days she had been hunting the man the papers first called the Coney Island Killer. Of course, he had given himself another name. He had talked all about it in one of his letters to the FBI, which he copied to the *Washington Post*. He called himself the Sandman.

Eight . . .

On average, Delaney worked fifteen-hour days. The taskforce she ran with special agent in charge, Bill Seong, was made up of two hundred police officers and federal agents. The taskforce had interviewed over a thousand potential witnesses. Spoken to seventy-one suspects. And compiled case files that ran to sixty-three boxes spread over two evidence rooms in the New York field office.

Seven . . .

Then there were the big numbers. The ones that made the front pages.

Seventeen victims. Men and women.

The first victims had been found half buried in the sand on Coney Island beach. They had been shot, stabbed and mutilated. A heavy police presence at the beach had caused a change in the killer's pattern. The remainder of the victims had been killed in their homes. Mostly it was a single victim. Sometimes he killed more than one person in the house.

Six . . .

Delaney's profile of the Sandman highlighted two consistent patterns with every killing. One everyone knew about. And the media loved to post those gory details. After the victims were killed their wounds, mouths and empty eye sockets were filled with sand. The killer took the eyes with him. The whole of New York seemed to hold its breath at night, waiting for another attack.

Five . . .

Only Delaney and a select few in the taskforce command knew the second profile marker. This couldn't be leaked to the press. The killer took a personal item from each victim. This might help catch and convict him someday, and so this was a closely guarded secret. Mostly, it was jewelry.

Four . . .

Eventually, the numbers started to work against the Sandman. You can't commit the perfect murder every time. Sooner or later, he would make a mistake. Delaney had been sure of this, and she had been right. Three days ago, they found his latest victims. The Nielsen family. Husband and wife, kids sedated during the killing. The children said during the night they felt someone blowing on their necks, then a sharp sting and then they fell asleep.

A bloody thumbprint had been found on the wife's torso, just beneath her right arm.

Three . . .

Within two days they had a match on the thumbprint, but not from any criminal databases. Daniel Miller, forty-five years old, had to give his ID and fingerprints when he registered for his trading license under the Banking Act. The next fifteen hours had gone quickly as Delaney built up a picture of Miller's life, his private equity business, his background and most importantly his current location. He was not on their list of suspects, which they had narrowed down from several thousand potentials.

Two . . .

It was coming up on ten o'clock. There were a few lights on downstairs in the Miller residence. The kitchen, lounge and hallway.

Delaney drew her Glock 19. Leaned forward. Her muscles tense. Palms already greased in sweat. She was ready to be free of the smell of pine and rotten leaves. Ready to burst out of the tree line. Ready to get her man. They estimated two occupants of the house – Daniel Miller and his wife, Carrie.

One . . .

She didn't wait for zero.

The roar of a Ford Crown Victoria sounded somewhere in the distance. The sound of that engine was like a starter pistol. By the time the SWAT leader called *GO*, everyone was on their feet, boots tearing up the lawn, hauling ass to the points of entry. There were a dozen agents and NYPD ahead of Delaney, even wearing their heavy assault gear, helmets and Kevlar. She wasn't going to win any foot races tonight, but that didn't matter. Others would go in first. Officers and agents who trained to kick down the doors of hostile buildings.

By the time Delaney put a foot on the patio, and passed the swimming pool, the SWAT team was already inside, the back door hanging loose off its hinges. She heard a voice. A scream. Female.

Delaney waited at the back door; weapon drawn. There were five other FBI agents with her – the search team. Laminated cards hung off their lanyards alongside their FBI IDs. The cards were pictures of key search items – items of jewelry known to have been taken from the victims. Some of them would be easy to spot because of their rarity. Like the Tahitian black pearl necklace taken from Stacy Nielsen three days ago.

A call came over the comms.

'*He's not here. House, grounds and garage are clear. The wife is in the kitchen. Property secure.*'

Delaney swore, entered the house through the back door. A large utility room led to a vast kitchen. The twelve-foot-high arched ceiling accommodated a huge window that would flood the space with light during the day. Now, it only seemed to let in the dark. A wine glass lay on its side on the marble counter top. The red wine pooled on the counter and slowly dripped onto the white tile floor.

There was a woman with short, dark hair sitting on a couch at the far corner of the room. Carrie Miller was shaking her head, crying, looking up at two armed NYPD SWAT officers standing over her, asking her questions. She wore a white tee, gray sweat pants and cream house socks. As Delaney approached, she noticed the woman's perfect oval face, clear skin and bright green eyes glazed in tears.

'I don't know where he is. He hasn't been home in days. He-he s-said he was going away on business, p-please, what is this about I—'

'Mrs. Miller, I'm special agent Paige Delaney. I know how scared you must be feeling right now. I'm sorry for the intrusion. We have a warrant to search your property and arrest your husband, Daniel Miller.'

It's hard to gauge someone's reaction to this kind of news. Right then, Delaney wasn't sure Carrie was taking this in.

'Mrs. Miller, what I'm going to say will upset you a great deal, but it's important for your safety that you know the truth.'

Before she laid the motherload on Carrie Miller, she paused and searched the woman's eyes. Carrie already looked grief stricken – traumatized. The tears were stripping the make-up from her face. She sniffed and wiped at her cheeks, smudging her lipstick against her white teeth. There was something about trauma that was a great leveler. Delaney had sat on a lot of couches with a lot of women and given them all bad news.

Carrie looked like those women.

Her marriage had made her rich. Delaney knew Carrie came from a poor Midwestern family, had come to New York to become an actor and somewhere on that journey she had met Daniel Miller.

Did it matter whether those women Delaney had held and comforted on all those couches touched up their smudged lips with a ten-buck stick of Maybelline or a ninety-dollar stick of Christian Louboutin? Carrie's purse sat open on the glass coffee table and Delaney was pleased to see a cheap brand of lipstick. It didn't look like the money had changed Carrie. That showed character. She thought Carrie would need every bit of that fortitude to get through this next chapter in her life.

It was not unusual for serial killers to carry out their crimes while simultaneously leading relatively normal lives. The BTK killer, Gacy, the Green River Killer, and many more serial murderers were married men. Once the shock and disbelief subside, and the wives accept who their husbands really are, a different kind of internal struggle begins. In time, Carrie, just like those women, would ask the same question again and again. How could they not know they were married to a monster? Then guilt would kick in. Unwarranted guilt, but it would feel real and hurt just as bad. Not only would those women suddenly realize they had no future, but any happiness they had enjoyed in the past would disappear. Every kiss, every embrace, every shared moment would turn poisonous. And then the *real* pain would kick in with this question – what was it about them that attracted someone who was so evil? If that didn't rip Carrie apart in the next couple of years, she might get through it. Delaney sure hoped so. She glanced at the ten-dollar lipstick in Carrie's purse and thought she might have a better shot than most.

'May I call you Carrie?' asked Delaney.

Carrie nodded in agreement, her lips parted as if to let the fear and dread flood inside, making her shake.

'Carrie, we think your husband is the killer known as the Sandman.'

What do you say to that? How do you react? Delaney thought that *any* reaction would be okay. It's not something that can be easily processed. But she knew this *was* a process. And the first step was denial: *you've got the wrong man. I know my husband – don't be ridiculous – he's not a violent man – he's such a good father, he provides for us, takes care of us. I'm sorry this must be a mistake . . .*

Carrie Miller's open mouth trembled, and she searched Delaney's face.

But she didn't say anything. She didn't protest her husband's innocence. It reminded Delaney of her tenth birthday. That same day her father died. He had been in hospital for a month with a brain tumor, inoperable and terminal. He was in a coma, and she had been to see him that morning. In the afternoon there was a small party – three of her best friends and some cake. After everyone left, her mother was putting on her coat to go back to the hospital when the phone rang. Delaney would never forget her mom's face. It looked like the tears were freezing her expression. Carrie had that same look. A woman who knew something terrible was going to happen, even had time to prepare for it, but when it did happen, the pain was worse than she had expected.

'Could we get Carrie a glass of water?' said Delaney to one of the SWAT, and he moved to the cupboard, found the glasses and filled one from the faucet then handed it to Carrie.

She held the glass in both hands, brought it, quivering, to her mouth.

'If you know where he is, I need you to tell me that location,' said Delaney.

'I don't know where he is,' said Carrie. 'And I don't care. I don't ever want to lay eyes on him again.'

Delaney squeezed the radio attached to her stab vest, said, 'Any news on the search, Bill?'

Her message was answered straight away by agent in charge, Bill Seong, 'Come on upstairs. Master bedroom.'

She took the grand staircase two steps at a time. Found the large master bedroom at the end of the hall on her left. Inside were two lounge chairs, a mirror, a king-size bed in the center of the room and a flatscreen on the wall.

'Here, in the closet,' said Bill.

There were two doors off the master. A private bathroom and a walk-in closet that was the same size as her apartment in Manhattan. The closet had mahogany shelves, drawers and wardrobes built into both sides. His and hers. Bill shone his flashlight at a rack of white shirts, tightly packed together.

'Check the cuff on this one,' he said.

There was a stain on the cuff. It looked like a splash of dark liquid. Even though the shirt had been laundered, the rust-colored mark was still there. Delaney had seen enough bloodstained clothing in her time to know this looked suspicious.

'Bag it,' said Delaney.

Bill clicked his fingers at a tech behind him, who started opening an evidence bag.

'That's not all,' said Bill, pointing at an open drawer with his flashlight.

Delaney took a look at the drawer and saw an array of jewelry resting on black cloth. Some of the items looked familiar. One in particular.

Stacy Nielsen's black pearl necklace.

'Jackpot,' said Bill, with a smile.

'Is this the right shirt?' said the tech.

Delaney turned. It was the right one. White with a stain on the . . .

For the first time, Delany realized it wasn't a man's shirt.

It was a woman's blouse.

She turned back to the jewelry drawer. It was on the 'hers' side of the closet.

Clutching his radio, Bill spoke over the comms, 'Any sign of the van on the property?'

'Not in the garage,' came the answer.

'Shit,' said Bill.

'We've got the jewelry and his DNA,' said Delaney. 'We don't really need the van.'

'I want it all,' said Bill.

A few of the witnesses who had been in the vicinity of the crime scenes around the time of the murders had reported seeing a dark-colored panel truck nearby. The FBI had identified some eleven thousand registered owners of dark-colored panel trucks in New York. A good thing it wasn't a white truck that had been spotted as there were fifty-five thousand of those in circulation. Along with local law enforcement, they had gone house to house with the dark-colored van owners, eliminating names from the database on a set criteria.

The truck wasn't at Daniel Miller's office. And it wasn't at his home.

Bill's phone rang. He saw the caller ID, handed the phone to Delaney who stepped out into the hall to answer.

'Bill Seong's phone,' she said.

'Where's Bill?' said Drew White, the assistant district attorney in charge of the Sandman case.

'He's busy. We're in the middle of a search here, Drew.'

'Tell me you got the truck.'

'We've got something better. We've got the jewelry,' said Delaney.

'Well, that's good news. I'm afraid I have some bad news. Want to know why Daniel Miller wasn't on our list of potentials for the truck search?'

Delaney covered her other ear, focusing on White.

'He bought it second hand and didn't register it?' asked Delaney.

'Nope. He was on our list, goddamn it. We could've got him two months ago.'

'Jesus, why was he eliminated?'

All around Delaney was the sound of cupboards and doors being opened and their contents emptied on the floor, heavy boots stomping around her, men talking, and despite all of it she only heard White's voice.

When he'd finished talking, he hung up. Delaney felt sick.

She went downstairs, Bill followed.

'What did White want?' he asked.

Delaney said nothing, so he asked again. She continued downstairs without another word. Went through the hallway, into the lounge and stood in front of a shaking Carrie.

'Carrie Miller,' said Delaney. 'I'm arresting you on suspicion of multiple homicide . . .'

BREAKING NEWS – THE SANDMAN NAMED
Breaking news this hour on the Sandman case out of New York. The FBI-led joint taskforce has confirmed it has definitively identified the serial killer who terrorized the city for over a year. Taskforce lead, Special Agent William Seong, held a press conference where he stated they now hold forensic evidence identifying forty-five-year-old Daniel Miller, a hedge fund manager from New York, as the Sandman. Alerts have been set up at every bus station, train station, ferry terminal and airport in the country. People are to be on the lookout for Miller, who is described by Special Agent Seong as armed and extremely dangerous. For more on this breaking story, we're going live now to our crime and justice correspondent, Shimon Prokupecz, who is in Federal Plaza . . .

CNN NEWSHOUR

INDICTMENT IN THE SANDMAN CASE
The District Attorney's office for the Southern District of New York has confirmed that six months after her arrest, Carrie Miller, wife of the alleged serial killer, Daniel Miller, has been indicted by a grand jury on six counts of homicide. Assistant district attorney in charge of the case, Drew White, told reporters that they believe Carrie Miller not only knew her husband was the Sandman, but she also acted as his accomplice in at least six murders. Mr. White stressed that these charges reflect the evidence, which directly links Carrie Miller as an accomplice to the murder of these six victims. Each count on the indictment carries a life sentence . . .

The New York Times

THE MOST EVIL WOMAN IN AMERICA
Her husband is the most wanted man in America. She is the wife of the alleged serial killer Daniel Miller, better known as the Sandman. She is due to stand trial next month on six counts of homicide. The District Attorney's office for the Southern District of New York says she acted as an accomplice, knowing her husband was a serial killer and actively assisting him in his crimes and even helping him evade capture. She denies all charges, but this hasn't stopped speculation about what she knew, and what she didn't know, about her husband's reign of terror. We spoke to Carrie Miller's former co-workers. They describe a woman as cold as the grave . . .

The National Enquirer

Killer Carrie's Neighbors and Friends Speak

The trial of Carrie Miller, known as the Sandman's wife, begins next week and with speculation rampant about what Carrie Miller knew of her husband's murderous activities, we spoke to her neighbors and high school friends on condition of anonymity, and asked them what's it like knowing someone who may have been responsible for multiple homicides, and were there any early signs that Carrie Miller was in league with a serial killer?

'I just always thought she was strange. Quiet, you know,' said a close neighbor.

'I've known Carrie for fifteen years. We were best friends in high school. I was her maid-of-honor at the wedding. Jesus, even thinking about that now gives me the creeps. If you're asking me could she kill someone, I have to say I don't know . . .'

'I don't trust her. I never did. Not from the moment she moved in. You get a sense off of her, you know, just pure evil. I can't even look at her house anymore.'

There has been no trace of the Sandman since he went on the run from police. But there has been speculation recently that a deal is on the table for his wife. In exchange for information that could lead to the capture of the Sandman, Carrie Miller may walk free. We asked lead prosecutor Drew White if there was any truth to that rumor. 'The victims require justice. There is no deal.' The trial will begin next week as planned . . .

The Washington Post.

CHAPTER ONE

EDDIE

It began with a stranger.

It always does.

This stranger, the one sitting in a brown leather chair in the reception area of my firm, didn't look like the others. Not at first. He had long legs wrapped in blue, pin-striped woolen pants to go with the rest of his suit. The white button-down shirt was a blend of silk and cotton. A thick, deep-blue tie completed the outfit. His curly brown hair was swept back and his beard neatly trimmed. He looked like a model in a catalogue selling that suit. And he could've been, but for the one similarity with the rest of the folks who sit in my reception. He was slumped in the chair. His long legs stretched out before him as if he'd just walked fifty blocks in a pair of brand-new shoes. As well as the fatigue, it was the look in his eyes that seemed so familiar.

His gaze shifted around the room, but his eyes were unseeing. They were searching for something. The man had the look of someone who was carrying a heavy burden.

Trouble is money. And you don't come to me unless you're in the very worst kind. Lately, the office cash flow had taken a hit because of the shutdown that came with the pandemic. New York was recovering now, the vaccines had helped, and things looked brighter here. I studied the man for a moment and thought he looked vaguely familiar. Denise, the office secretary, walked past the man in the good suit, hitting him with a smile while she did so, opened the glass door of my office and shut it behind her.

I drained my first cup of coffee of the day and got up to fetch a refill from the machine in the kitchen.

'Sit down,' said Denise, with a smile.

She was holding a hot cup of coffee, but I noticed that it wasn't her mug. She set the coffee down on the desk in front of me, said, 'Here's your second cup.'

Denise was an experienced legal secretary. Smarter than most lawyers, but fiercely organized and with a good head for business thrown in. A worker with a heart the size of Lake Michigan. Typing one hundred words a minute and half running my law firm were Denise's main duties. Those duties did not extend to getting me my coffee. I didn't like other people getting me coffee, or lunch. I looked after myself. Denise had never brought me so much as a glass of water before.

She stood there, smiling.

'Do you need a raise?' I asked.

'No, I'm fine. I know you've said before you're not a hundred percent in the morning until you've had two cups of coffee.'

This was true, but I couldn't remember when I'd said this to Denise.

Next thing, Harry Ford came into my office carrying a large bundle of papers that filled his arms. A former judge, my old mentor, and now a consultant who helped out with the thornier legal issues in our cases. Harry dumped the files on my desk, sat his ass down in one of my clients' chairs.

Bloch, our investigator, followed Harry. She wheeled two chairs into my office, and sat on one, leaving the other free. Kate Brooks, my partner in Flynn & Brooks, came in with her own chair and folded her legs beneath it as she sat. Bloch and Kate had known each other from childhood and enjoyed that kind of shorthand that worked through looks, gestures and half-smiles. Bloch took her cell out of her jeans, turned it off. Kate, in her business suit, took her phone from her jacket and turned it off.

They were all staring at me.

'Is this an intervention?' I asked. 'I'm not drinking, ask Harry—' I said, but Denise cut me off.

'Drink up,' she said.

'What is this? And why do I get the impression it has something to do with the suit in reception?' I asked.

Bloch pursed her lips and threw a look at Kate that must've been a cue.

'We're taking a new case,' said Kate.

'We?' I asked.

She nodded, said, 'This one will need all of us at the top of our game. Bloch and I read the file over the weekend and Harry read it yesterday. It's the big one, Eddie.'

I stood still.

I liked getting work. Helping people was the job, and it was good most of the time. If we had landed a big case, I would've expected Harry or Kate to have told me before now. Bloch never said a lot, although we were friends. She just didn't say much to anyone.

'If we've landed a big case then why do I feel like this is an ambush? And why is Denise getting me coffee?'

'Because I like to get coffee,' said Denise.

'No, you don't. Who is the suit outside? Is he the client?'

'No,' said Harry. 'He's the client's lawyer.'

I craned my neck around the gathering, took another look at the man. That's where I'd seen him before – on TV.

'He's Otto Peltier?' I asked.

Harry nodded.

It explained the suit, the haircut. He glanced back at me, wiping his lips with manicured fingers. Most criminal lawyers in Manhattan had never heard of Otto Peltier before last year. His clients lived in the high-class areas of New York and Otto practiced in the high-class areas of law. Real Estate, Tax, Wealth Management, Divorce and Probate. In other words, he saved his clients enough money on their taxes so they could buy a boat, or a house, and then he made sure they held onto it through their divorce, and, finally, made certain that the government didn't take a big slice of the inheritance when they'd died. So it was a real surprise to the criminal lawyers of New York when Otto Peltier landed the biggest criminal case in the city. It showed on him. I could see the strain around his eyes.

Otto represented Carrie Miller – the Sandman's wife. Last year her property was raided by police and FBI, after they identified Daniel Miller as the Sandman from his fingerprint and DNA left at a crime scene. A year later they were still looking for the Sandman. Some felt that because they couldn't catch the real murderer, Carrie Miller was a good substitute. It made the feds, and the cops, look as though they had accomplished something. And they needed a win, because the city and most of the state had lived in fear of this man for a long time. Putting away a killer was the right political decision for law enforcement.

'Wait a minute, he wants us to ride on his coat tails in this case? I don't sit in second chair,' I said.

'He's not asking us to do his donkey work or hold his hand,' said Kate. 'He wants us to take over the defense.'

'What? Why?'

'He was holding out for a deal and the DA hasn't played ball. Otto Peltier is not a trial lawyer. He needs a team with trial experience,' said Harry.

'That's very generous of him and the right thing for his client, but the problem is we don't represent the guilty. The DA says Carrie was an accomplice in six of the Sandman's murders. I won't put a killer back on the street—'

'She says she's innocent,' said Kate.

'They all say that,' I said.

'I think she's telling the truth,' said Kate.

Of all the lawyers I'd ever met, Kate was maybe the smartest. If she believed Carrie Miller, then there had to be something there worth fighting for. I was beginning to get interested. Then I stopped.

'Wait, doesn't this case start in a couple of days? Why is he dumping the case now? Maybe he's messed up the defense and we're going to walk into a lawsuit from the client if we take this to trial.'

'I don't think so,' said Harry. 'He doesn't have anywhere near the experience needed to run a murder trial, but I've looked over the case papers and he's done everything right in pre-trial prep. All appropriate motions filed. I don't know what the jury is like but how bad can it be? The case is ready to go in two days. That's enough time for us to be ready. We've parachuted into cases before. And it's not like there's no defense. There's a decent fight in this one, Eddie.'

My hands covered my face. I needed the darkness, a little silence and another damn cup of—

'Drink your coffee,' said Denise.

I brushed my fingers down my cheeks, opened my eyes and saw everyone staring at me. There was another reason I didn't want this case.

'The Sandman is still out there. If we get involved, we are one step closer to a madman. There's a risk—'

Kate cut me off. I could see the passion in her eyes. She wanted this case. Since we became partners, Kate had focused on representing women who had suffered sex discrimination and sexual harassment at work. At her last firm Kate was the victim of unwanted advances from a partner in that practice and she'd been taking down misogynist employers since. These cases were personal. With every woman Kate helped she was saving not just that person, but a part of Kate that got hurt and hadn't fully healed.

'We all know the risks, but I don't see why he would target us,' she said. 'We're saving his wife. The biggest risk is the media taking a dump on our firm if we don't prove she's innocent. If we do, that's another female victim who has gotten justice because of us. You know this is important to me.'

I nodded.

'Let's hear the man out,' said Kate.

'Okay, bring him in.'

Denise asked the man to come in. I didn't have the biggest office, so it was a little crowded. That look was still on his face – someone in trouble who needed our help. I reached for my chest; felt the Saint Christopher's medal I wore beneath my shirt.

Soon as he sat down, Peltier forced a smile. Even though he needed us, he still felt like he should sell me the case. He introduced himself, then said, 'Congratulations, Mr. Flynn. You now have the most high-profile murder trial in America.'

'I don't want to be rude,' I said, 'but this is all news to me. I get the feeling my colleagues were anticipating some resistance on my part. See, first, I don't take a case unless I believe the client is innocent. I've been burned before, and I don't need any more ghosts in my head. Second, I'm the suspicious type. I'm still not sure why you would hand this case over to another law firm. I know lawyers who would wrestle their own grandmothers for a case like this.'

Peltier crossed his long legs, his face cracked into a smile as he said, 'I can give you more than one reason to say yes. My client, excuse me, *your* client, is willing to give your firm two *million* reasons. The agreed fee for the case is three million. I take a third of that for the preparation work, the rest is yours. So, do we have a deal?'

That number blazed Kate's eyes. This was the big one. This was the hottest case in the country. With a payday that most lawyers only get to fantasize about. A once-in-a-lifetime case. The one we all chase, the one that will make our careers. Far as my firm was concerned, we'd just won the lottery. Only a fool would turn it down.

Which is why I said, 'No.'

CHAPTER TWO

EDDIE

'Look, no disrespect to you or your client, Mr. Peltier, but this just doesn't feel right to me,' I said.

'I understand. Perhaps I have not made myself clear to your colleagues,' he said. 'I was hoping to broker a deal with the DA. In exchange for my client's cooperation in the Sandman case I wanted them to drop the charges against her. At first, I thought they were just playing hardball. Taking us to the door of the court before they made a deal. Unfortunately, they are not bluffing. The case will begin in two days. And while I am a talented lawyer and negotiator, I don't have your trial experience. Carrie is innocent, and I intend to make sure she gets a fair hearing. For that to happen, she needs the very best representation.'

He spoke clearly, confidently. Good eye contact, natural hand movements. No tells. No indication he was lying. Apart from the fact that he wasn't telling me the whole story.

Something had caused a change in Peltier's tactics for Carrie Miller's defense. There had been a development which had meant he couldn't try the case. I was sure of it. No lawyer would pass up a trial like this.

'What was the last pre-trial motion?' I asked, fixing my stare on Peltier.

The question caused the skin around his eyes to tighten.

'Prosecution motion for inspection and seizure of a number of files from Mr. Peltier's office,' said Kate. 'All the files and papers pre-dated Mrs. Miller's arrest, am I right?'

Peltier nodded, slowly.

I swallowed the last of the coffee. Denise, who was standing

18

behind the assembled group, folded her arms. She knew me well enough to tell when my brain was finally kicking into life.

'We're not getting off to the best of starts, Mr. Peltier. You haven't lied, but you haven't told us the whole truth either. That stops. Right now. I'm going to ask you some questions. If you lie, this meeting is over and you can take your case along with your expensive suit into the street. Do I make myself clear?'

'I was intending to divulge everything once you had agreed to take the case, and then our conversation would fall under attorney-client privilege,' he said, with a smile.

He had been holding back, and this was a decent excuse. Attorney-client privilege is the basis of the profession. Anything your client tells you directly, or through another party, is private. You don't reveal it to anyone, and no one is allowed to ask you about it or look at your notes or any client documents. For the DA to get access to Peltier's files there must have been a damn good reason.

'What led the DA's office to your old files?' I asked.

'Payments detailed on bank records, from Carrie Miller to my firm, for legal advice,' he said.

That was the truth. No question about it.

'What was in the files?'

'To give that information I am breaking attorney-client privilege . . .' he began.

'It's already broken if the DA has the files. What were they looking for?'

'They were looking for any information in my possession that implicated Carrie Miller in the murder of six of the Sandman's victims.'

Another honest answer. And something I had anticipated.

'And what did they find?' I asked.

He answered straight away. No hesitation.

'They found notes I'd made of a number of meetings with Mrs. Miller. And her diaries, which she wished me to hold for her. Before you ask, those meetings were about potential divorce proceedings on the grounds of cruel and inhuman treatment. Mrs. Miller told me that she suspected her husband was a serial killer.'

'She knew?' asked Kate.

'She did not *know*. She *suspected*,' said Peltier, gently.

'And she did nothing about this, is that right? She didn't go to the police?' asked Harry.

'No, she did not. There were several clauses in the prenuptial agreement which would have been triggered by a police report if the allegation turned out to be false, that is. If the allegation were made and not proven, Mrs. Miller would forfeit her right to a share of the marital property and assets. In other words, she would be throwing eight million dollars away with a phone call.'

'Eight million, that would've been her share from the divorce?' asked Kate.

Peltier nodded.

'This changes the case,' said Harry. 'The DA can give the jury eight million reasons for Carrie to keep her mouth shut and help her husband escape the police.'

Harry was right. Carrie Miller couldn't make the case that she knew nothing of her husband's crimes, all she could say is she wasn't sure. She would have a hard time convincing any jury of that fact.

There were a lot of serial killers who carried out their crimes while happily married. Far as I could remember, none of their wives knew or even suspected them. None of them were charged as an accomplice. Every talking head, on every news channel, was discussing this case. Oprah did a special on it, even though Carrie refused to appear on the show. The question on everyone's lips was – *How could you not know you were married to a killer?* In some ways, we engage with stories like these because we want reassurance. That there was some clear sign or indication that these men were killers, and their wives ignored it. The public want to know that they would've spotted the signs, that they would not have been so easily duped. In reality, the wives of killers never suspect a thing.

That's disconcerting on a number of levels.

First, it confirms the incredible ability of these killers to mask their true nature from everyone, including those closest to them. Second, it makes people uneasy. If it could happen to those women, couldn't it happen to anyone? How well do you know your partner, your brother, or your father? But the public always think it's the woman's fault. That she was blind to the truth.

That had it been them in the same situation, they would've known.

Psychological barriers in jurors are often impossible to break down. All the DA had to do in this case is strengthen the juror's preconceived belief that Carrie Miller knew her husband was a killer and helped cover for him. And Carrie's so-called suspicion only helped the DA. An easy win even for a mediocre prosecutor.

While the case against Carrie Miller looked a lot stronger if they could prove she knew he was a killer, that wasn't the real reason Peltier had to find her alternative representation.

'Mr. Peltier, you could have saved a lot of time if you had just been honest about this. We would've found out if we had agreed to take the case.'

'Of course, but by that stage it would've been too late. You would've already agreed to take the case and been added to the court record as counsel for the defendant.'

'I don't follow,' said Denise. 'Just because the DA has your old files doesn't mean you can't represent Carrie Miller.'

'There is a consequence of the DA having my files,' said Peltier.

I knew what it was, straight away.

'You can't be her lawyer anymore. You can't act as a lawyer in this trial at all,' I said.

Peltier let out a long sigh.

I said, 'Carrie Miller told you she suspected her husband was a serial killer. That makes you the star witness for the prosecution.'

CHAPTER THREE

EDDIE

While Peltier followed in his Mercedes, Bloch drove us out of Manhattan in a cream Grand Cherokee Jeep. The midday traffic wasn't so bad, and Bloch cruised the big SUV along the blacktop. Harry sat up front so Kate could argue with me in the back. Forty-five minutes took us to the end of the Grand Central Parkway as it flowed into the Long Island Expressway. A sheet metal sky hid the low November sun. It was getting cold, but not yet cold enough for me to break out my overcoat.

Kate said, 'I think Carrie is just another victim of the Sandman. It's important to me that we show the world the truth. Give her a voice. I believe her. I think you will too.'

'I'll talk to her, but if I'm not convinced – we walk away. Agreed?'

'You know this is not the way normal lawyers practice, right?'

'If someone admits to what they've done then I've got no problem representing them. I'll tell their story to the court and ask for the appropriate sentence. Sometimes that's probation, sometimes I wish them all the best as they go to prison. Everyone makes mistakes, and it's good that they admit it, but I decided a long time ago I'm not going to be the one responsible for putting a dangerous person back on the street.'

'But you're not the one doing it. The jury decides. Everyone is entitled to a defense, that's the way the system works . . .'

Kate was a hell of a lawyer already, even though she hadn't been in practice very long. In a few years she would be the best, but the law hadn't kicked her in the guts yet.

'The system can be manipulated. Usually by us. Look, I said I would talk to Carrie Miller. If I think she's telling the truth, then we'll take the case.'

'I don't understand you, sometimes,' said Kate, turning away to look out the passenger window. I hoped she never would come to understand my reasons. In the justice game it's the lawyers who really wear the blindfolds, not the statues of Goddess Justicia standing atop the courthouses with a sword in one hand and a set of scales in the other. Criminal lawyers don't ask their clients if they're guilty. They tell the clients when they should fold their cards and plead, and when to fight. But if you win a case for a guilty person – that victory has a price, and I don't mean legal fees. A little bit of that lawyer dies. Do it enough times and you're a zombie. Then one day you get a client off and they walk straight out of court and kill somebody – and that's when the kick in the stomach arrives.

About five years ago I was in that same situation. Only I was able to stop the guy before he finished off his victim. I had put him back on the street. It was my fault. Everyday I pay for that mistake. I had learned to carry that pain without sharing the load with a bottle of Jack.

I turned away from Kate, stared out at the trees that lined both sides of the expressway. Bloch took us to the exit and quickly into a residential area of Old Westbury. I had driven through this part of Nassau County maybe twice in my life. Never stopped by to take a look around. Each time, there were film crews nearby. If you're shooting a movie and you need a mansion location, you come to Old Westbury. With the exception of the Silicon Valley suburb of Atherton, California, it was probably one of the most affluent areas in the country. Tree-lined streets, with vast houses that sat way back off the curb.

Carrie Miller lived in a small, gated community on Meadow Road. There were maybe twenty people outside the gates. News channel vans lined the sidewalk, but it wasn't just reporters making up the crowd. Five or six people stood holding banners. They were chanting something. I cracked open the window to hear it.

GUILTY BITCH!
GUILTY BITCH!
GUILTY BITCH!

The banners weren't much better. Bloch hit the horn and the reporters and protestors turned to give us the once over. I hid my face with my hand. The crowd moved aside. Otto's Mercedes pulled in behind us and the gates parted.

Soon as they saw Otto's car the lights flared on the TV cameras and the chants grew louder. He had been filmed and photographed at the pre-trial hearings and it was well known who he was representing. They crowded around his car. One of the protestors, a woman with a thick pink scarf around her neck, spat on Otto's windshield. He hit the wipers and followed us through the gates, slowly, making sure he didn't accidentally run over a protestor or a reporter.

'Jesus, that's tough to live with,' I said.

'Otto told me Carrie is barely hanging on. She's had hundreds of death threats and last month she got a letter signed by every one of her neighbors asking her to move out.'

The development had houses of various sizes, although they were all mansions to my mind. Harry looked at one house with a pool to the side and whistled his admiration. Yet, this was the poor side of Old Westbury to some residents. Old New York money that needed a palatial home with grounds and gardens moved out here. The Vanderbilts, the Phippes, the Whitneys, Du Ponts and others who had more money than sense. And they built grand, twenty-bedroom palaces that looked like they'd been plucked from rural England, possibly with an inebriated lord still inside, and lovingly deposited in Old Westbury. The homes on this side were modest by comparison, but I would never be able to afford one – not even if my lottery numbers came up.

Bloch stopped outside a brick house in a colonial style with a red front door. We got out just as Otto parked his Mercedes behind the Jeep. I took a moment to admire the neighborhood. The properties were set wide apart, their football-field lawns adding to the sense of distance and space. Carrie Miller's house backed onto a clump of oak and copper beech trees.

Otto leaned over his car, examining the body work.

There was a deep scratch all along one side of it.

'That looks bad,' I said.

'Doesn't matter, really. It's the third time this month. It's nothing compared to what Carrie has to deal with. She's almost a prisoner here. The reporters and the protestors normally go home around ten, when it gets really cold. I usually schedule my appointments at six a.m. or after ten at night, when there's no one at the gate.'

'How has Carrie dealt with all this?' I asked.

Otto dropped his head for a moment, when he looked back at me I could see the picture written on his face.

'For the first two weeks she hardly spoke. She cried all the time. Lost her voice. I called a doctor and he gave her some pills that basically knocked her out for a few days. After that she was able to talk. The pills only numbed things for a while. She was just devastated, Eddie, in every way possible. She was betrayed, and alone, hated by the entire country, facing a multiple-homicide charge – look, at one point I thought she was just going to check out. I had to give her meds to her daily. I was frightened to leave the whole bottle. You know what I mean?'

I nodded.

'But she's still here. She's strong and she has a reason to keep on going. She wants people to know that she's innocent. In some ways, I think the trial is what has kept her here. She wants to fight it. But whatever strength she had is starting to leave her. The strain is back, now that the hearing is about to begin. You'll see.'

'And what do you think of her? Really?'

'I remember my first month of law school. You read cases and you know the law can work wonders, but it can crush innocent people just as easily. It's a terrible thing, the justice game. She reminded me of that. And this is why you're here. You're a much better trial lawyer than me, and I don't want law students to read about her case in twenty years' time and pick apart all the ways I failed her.'

Even with the thousand-dollar suit and the top-of-the-range car, and all the power and money Otto projected, right then he was scared. Scared in case he let Carrie down. That's what trial work can do to you. In fact, you should be scared. It's a good sign. It means you care, and it means you'll do the work, and you'll fight hard. Lawyers care about the innocent clients. The ones who need the system to work. These are the cases that keep us up at night, covered in sweat. This was Otto's first taste of that kind of work.

'I know you won't let her down, Eddie,' he said.

He led the way up the path of marble paving stones. We followed, and by the time we got to the entrance the door had been opened by the woman I recognized as Carrie Miller. When I'd first seen her picture on the news, she was coming out of the court building at 100 Center Street into a hail of reporters and camera flashes. It was a familiar sight, but this picture was different. I've led clients out of that same building in similar media-hungry circumstances. Usually, my client would wear a hat, or sometimes put their coat over their head, unwilling for their image to be captured in this moment of high drama when they were at their most vulnerable.

Carrie Miller had strutted through the phalanx of reporters in a navy business suit with her chin high. A look of determination in her eyes. It was because of her confidence perhaps that the reporters broke their lines to let her through to a waiting car. There was a certain poise in her movement, in her look – something approaching grace.

Standing at her front door, now, all of that was gone. Whatever image she had been advised to portray to the media – the reality was very different.

She wore violet jeans and a black tee. She could barely raise her head to look at Otto. Her shoulders slumped, arms wrapped around her fragile frame and her eyes were locked on the floor, only occasionally glancing upward with great effort. The skin around her neck was blotchy and red with scratches, and her mouth turned down. It looked as though an elemental force was dragging her lower and lower, into the earth. Even her dark hair had thinned and traces of gray shot through it.

'Carrie, these are the lawyers I told you about, and this is their team. Miss Kate Brooks, Harry Ford, their investigator Miss Bloch and this is—'

'Eddie Flynn,' she said, locking her eyes on me.

I could see the strain and the look of the lost in those green, bloodshot eyes.

'Please, come in,' she said, and turned to lead us inside.

A curved staircase with a brass rail dominated the entrance hall, and I followed my team into the room on the right. A lounge with two couches facing each other. The room looked minimalist, with only a white marble table separating the couches, and a fireplace in the back wall. A single picture of a gold bull hung on one wall, the other taken up by a large window overlooking the front lawn. It was a masculine room. If I didn't know Carrie lived here, I would've assumed it was a bachelor's place.

There was a display unit for a large TV, but no television sat upon it. I didn't ask where it had gone. If I had to see my face on TV every night, and listen to people who didn't know me call me a murderer, then I'd throw the damn thing in the garbage too.

Carrie and Otto took one couch, Harry, Kate and Bloch the other. I remained standing.

'We have some questions before we take the case, Mrs. Miller,' said Kate. 'We need to know before we jump into this that you have a solid defense.'

'I didn't hurt anyone. And I didn't know I was married to the devil, if that's what you mean, Miss Brooks,' she said. Her voice sounded strained, low and broken, as if she had been crying for hours. From the way she appeared now, I guessed that might just be the case.

'We understand that you discussed your suspicions concerning your husband with Mr. Peltier. Can you tell me what made you suspect your husband?' asked Kate.

'Well, that's the thing,' said Carrie. 'When I think about it, there were strange occurrences, but Danny always had an explanation. It all seemed innocent once I'd talked to him about it. It was more of a feeling. I'm not paranoid, maybe I should've been, but I just had to talk to someone and tell them what had happened and what was on my mind.'

'So, you never truly believed your husband was the Sandman,' said Kate.

'I'm not sure. For a time, I thought he was. Even now, in some ways I still can't believe it.'

Kate looked at me. I could feel her eyes. Carrie was speaking from the heart. But there was something else behind that voice, and it wasn't the sound of shale in her raw throat, it was different. Like she was hiding something. It was only a sense. A gut instinct.

'Mrs. Miller,' I said, 'did you hurt or kill anyone with your husband?'

At first, she said nothing. Her eyes closed, softly, her brows clinched as if she were suddenly in pain. Like the question was poison in a wound that had to be expelled.

'No, I did not,' she said, in one long breath.

'Did you know that your husband was a murderer?'

A glaze of tears spread over her eyes. She blinked once, and a single tear broke from each eye and chased one another across her cheeks, and along her jaw to her chin where they met, became one, and fell to the floor.

'I didn't know for sure. I suspected him. I also suspected I might've been crazy for thinking that way.'

'During the times when you suspected him, did you ever do anything that might have helped him stay out of the police investigation?'

She answered straight away. 'Not knowingly. Not deliberately. If I had known for sure he was a killer, even for one second, I would have called the police.'

'The jewelry they found in your drawer, which belonged to some of the Sandman's victims, where did you get it?'

'Danny gave it to me.'

'The bloodstain on your shirt sleeve, do you know how it got there?'

'I didn't know it was there until the police told me. I have no idea how it got there. I can only assume it came from Danny.'

'Did the fact that you might lose eight million dollars by calling the police have anything to do with the decision not to involve them?'

She leaned forward, wiped away a tear with delicate, trembling fingers and let her heart out.

'Not even one bit,' she said. 'Otto told me it would be unwise to make an allegation I couldn't prove, but I didn't care. If I had known for sure I would have called the cops. Believe me, I've been over this and over this in my mind. I was stupid. I listened to Danny. Have you ever been betrayed, Mr. Flynn?'

I nodded.

'It hurts. But nothing hurts like this. I'm not talking about what has been said about me in the newspapers or on TV, or those people out there with banners, or the thousands of rape and murder threats I got on social media. All of that is a nightmare beyond anything I could imagine, but part of me thinks I deserve it.'

I shook my head, said, 'You don't deserve that, Carrie.'

'Maybe I do. I trusted Danny and I doubted my own mind. Because of that, because of *me*, people died. And I blame myself for that, every day. Because if I had been smarter, braver, I could've saved some of those people. They are dead because I didn't speak out. And that's something that will eat me alive for the rest of my life.'

I saw then, in her eyes, what she was hiding.

Pain and guilt.

Carrie Miller had been lied to and manipulated by an evil man. A man whom she had trusted and loved. I couldn't imagine the emotional toll that would take on a young woman. And on top of all of that, her husband's filth had somehow stained her. She was in the middle of a storm of hate, guilt and pain. Even sitting on her couch, I could feel those winds swirling around her, threatening to tear her apart. There was no rest from this. Her mind was in perfect torment for every single second of every conscious moment. This woman was in a psychological torture chamber. The world's media, her friends, her neighbors, and even Carrie herself, were slowly tightening the screws that sent hot pins into her brain.

I knew pain and loss. I had known people who had been crushed in a vice of grief. It destroyed them, and when grief sat heavy with me, as it often did, I battled through. Because I knew if I didn't it would drown me.

Carrie Miller was suffering like no one else I'd ever met.

I had listened carefully as she had spoken.

It's hard to describe the truth. It has a weight. A density. It makes a sound when it drifts through your breastplate, hits your soul and then falls into your guts. You feel it. It haunts the air and it's so thick and undeniable you almost feel like you can take a bite clean out of it. Mostly, you just know it when you hear it.

She was telling the truth. And I knew then I would fight for her. Because no one else would.

Sure, there would be a line of lawyers willing to take this case to help their own careers, or simply for the money.

I didn't care about money. As I stood watching her fall to pieces on her couch, I knew then I had to help her. I wanted to believe she could get through this. More than anything else, I wanted her to believe that.

We all hurt sometimes. The dark touches all of us sooner or later. If I could get Carrie through this, if I could save her, then it was possible that anyone could be saved. Even me. I didn't become a lawyer to win cases. I became a lawyer to help people. It's human instinct. Maybe the best part of us. No matter what kind of catastrophe you see on the news – a fire, building collapse, earthquake or terrorist attack – there are always people running toward that danger, trying to help.

She needed someone to stand beside her. To hold her hand.

She needed Kate and the rest of us.

Right now, Carrie Miller was in a burning building and I was outside, ready to climb the ladders and get her out.

I looked at Bloch. She smiled at me, winked. Harry gave me the thumbs up.

I nodded at Kate.

Kate said, 'Mrs. Miller, we're delighted to be your new legal team.'

CHAPTER FOUR

THE SANDMAN

Lots of people lead two lives.

A bloodthirsty, remorseless CEO in a penthouse office can be a gentle, loving parent and spouse at home; a caring, dedicated psychotherapist by day could be a destructive, obsessive partner by night; a soldier who won't hesitate to take a life on the battlefield but flinches at the sight of blood from the cut on their child's knee. People don't just put on a different set of clothes for each life, they put on a different persona. The situation and environment help reinforce this change of personality.

For those few people who are not like the rest of us – the ones who are driven to prey on their fellow humans without remorse or regret – the change can be even starker.

For this man, one of those few, had shed his outer skin like a beast from a nightmare, being born into the world by tearing through the flesh of its host with sharp claws. He had given this version of himself a name. And when he worked in his beast's skin, he thought only of himself by that name. It carried fear into others. It had power. And he wore it proudly.

His name was Sandman.

He had been in hiding for a year, avoiding the FBI and the NYPD.

He could hide no longer.

Now, he had a purpose. A mission. One that could not fail.

The low red sun was descending below the dilapidated roof of Grady's Inn when the Sandman pulled into the parking lot. There were any number of hotels in the area. This part of Queens was close to JFK, so it was practically cheap-hotel city. Grady's Inn happened to be cheaper than any of the others and you got what you paid for. It had once been a grand mansion, but the family had their entire fortune wiped out on Black Friday 1929, when the New York Stock Exchange crashed heralding the Great Depression.

From the look of the building, the Great Depression was still going on. Only those who were desperate, or broke, or both, would stay here.

Money wasn't a problem for the Sandman.

Security cameras – they were the problem.

Grady's Inn had been a premier hotel for fifty years, but time and lack of care had let the place fall to near ruin. The New York Department of Justice had kept the place going for a number of years by block booking rooms to sequester juries. That had helped keep the place afloat, but all of that had now stopped since the serial killer Dollar Bill had stayed here, and killed here, while himself serving on a jury. Now, the only guests were those who couldn't afford a Holiday Inn and didn't care or didn't know about the hotel's recent bloody history.

There were two other vehicles in the small lot, which had maybe twenty spaces. The old station wagon had been there for a long time, judging by the dirt on the windshield and the four flat tires. The other, a Toyota, probably belonged to the night manager.

The Sandman lifted his bag clear from his black panel truck. Every law enforcement agency in the United States was looking for this truck, had been for a year. Changing the license plates regularly had kept it in use and out of their gaze. He put on a ball cap and took another moment to admire the building and the surrounding woodland. The paint had cracked on every timber siding panel, every window frame. The roof tiles were old slate and looked as though they could slide right off with a breath of wind, as some of them clearly had already, allowing grass to grow in tufts from the roof cladding.

A dark house. Big and empty.

It suited him perfectly.

He ascended the steps and walked through the grand entrance hall to the reception. Wood paneling covered the walls, making it an imposing space. The mounted deer heads didn't help lighten the décor either. The guy behind the reception desk sat on a chair reading a paperback. Even when he noticed the Sandman approach, he didn't get up. Not right away. He lowered the book to reveal a pasty complexion, oily hair and a thin smile.

'Can I help you, sir?' he asked.

'I'd like a room.'

The man thought about this, and it took a moment before he realized the Sandman wasn't joking.

'How long will you be staying? We don't charge by the hour,' said the man.

'I'll take it for a night.'

'That'll be fifty-three dollars,' said the receptionist, pushing a guest registration form across the desk.

The Sandman selected a pencil from the mug, began filling out the form.

'I'll need to take your credit card for the room, and it's our custom to hold fifty dollars on your card for extras, if you don't mind?'

'Not at all,' he said, and removed a credit card from his wallet and handed it to the receptionist who swiped it through the machine, printed a guest slip and asked for an address and another signature.

While the man tapped at the computer screen, the Sandman turned over the slip, wrote something on the back, then flipped it over, wrote down the address in Old Westbury, and signed it. The Sandman handed the slip back, said, 'I'm just going to go grab some dinner. Is it okay if I leave my bag in your luggage store?'

'Sure, I'll take it for you, sir. I'm Tom, by the way. The manager.'

'Thank you, Tom,' said the Sandman, handing over his rucksack. He then left the hotel, got into his van, turned the key in the ignition.

He checked his watch and couldn't resist running his index finger around the bronze casing. A Panerai Submersible 1950, it had been an expensive and much-loved gift. There were only another two hundred and forty-nine pieces made. The watches were identical when they left the factory, but the casing took on its own individual patina over time, with exposure to the elements. The watch meant a lot. It had been a thoughtful gift because it was just like him – precise and unique.

It was exactly two minutes to eight in the evening.

Thirty minutes, give or take.

That would be the FBI response time.

He put the truck in first gear, drove out of the parking lot.

CHAPTER FIVE

DELANEY

Two minutes to eight.

Delaney ended her day at the FBI office in the exact same way it had begun. Every morning, and every evening, for the past year, Delaney checked for updates on the Sandman. The FBI had access to criminal databases all over the world. They were updated more or less regularly depending on the region. Some, like the IFRS, Interpol's Face Recognition System, was refreshed every few minutes with new biometric data. For others, it was every few hours, daily or even monthly. Didn't matter to Delaney. She worked the numbers. Thirty-one databases to check. Every morning. Every evening.

As she ran through her checks, she put away a pint of cold coffee. Like she did every morning. Every evening. No cream. Five sugars. Just the way God intended.

She punched a number into the phone on her desk. One more way to multitask. The phone rang once, twice, three times. That's all she was required to do. Let the phone ring three times, then hang up. From the age of eighteen, whenever Delaney spent a night away from home, she had to call her mom when she got back to where she was staying, no matter what time of the night, and let the phone ring three times. Just so Colleen knew she was safe. Mothers worry, but Irish mothers are world heavyweight champions of worry. Just as she was about to hang up the phone, her duty to her mother done, albeit a little prematurely, she heard the phone being answered.

'Paige, is that you? The number you're calling from is restricted. You're not back home, are you?' said Colleen, in a breathless Dublin brogue that she had stubbornly failed to lose despite forty plus years living in Boston.

'It's me. I'm fine, Mom. I just—'

'You know I can't get to sleep until I know you're home safe. Don't be lying to me, now. I'm too old, and you're not half as good a liar as you think you are, young lady.'

'Mom, I'm fine, I'm just leaving the office right now—'

'Well, that's no good now, is it? Ring me when you're home safe. Not before.'

Delaney heard a faint rattle on the other end of the line. It wasn't the connection; it was her mom clutching her rosary beads. She knew better than to argue.

'I'll call when I'm home. I love you.'

'I love you too, sweet pea.'

She hung up, returned to the monitor.

Thirty-one databases.

And just like this morning there were no hits or leads on Daniel Miller's bank accounts, nor his credit cards, nor his license plate on that panel truck, nor had his face been picked up on a facial recognition security camera. The Sandman maintained his number-one slot on the FBI's Ten Most Wanted list. Tidying her desk for the next day, Delaney found her task list. She normally scrunched up the list and threw it in the shredding pile at the end of her shift. If any items on the list still had to be completed, she stayed late until they were done.

There was one job left.

Delaney dialed the number and waited for the call to connect. It went straight to voicemail, just like it had the previous three times she'd called. Carrie Miller's trial began in two days. The witness list was long, and the labor had been divided between the NYPD and the FBI. Any witnesses that Delaney had a relationship with, it would be her responsibility to check, making sure they're ready for trial and giving them updates on when they would likely have to answer their subpoenas.

She'd gotten a hold of every witness, except one.

There was always one.

Chester Morris. He worked as a doorman for Le Blue Hotel on 4th Avenue in Brooklyn. After Carrie Miller's picture first appeared in the press, Chester came forward and spoke to NYPD. He said that at the end of his shift one night he stopped at the diner on the corner of 4th and 6th Street for a take-out burrito. As he left with his food, he noticed two people standing at the front door to the apartment building next to the diner. A male and a female. They stood under the awning, huddled close together even though it wasn't raining. The man looked as though he was fumbling with his keys, trying to open the door. He saw the man working the lock, with a key, or something else. Chester walked on toward the bus stop and didn't interfere.

It wasn't until the next evening he heard on the news that two women in that same apartment building had been murdered by the Sandman. While the two people outside the building concerned him, the police were only looking for one man. Not a couple.

Only after Daniel and Carrie Miller's pictures made the front page did Chester make a call to the NYPD to tell them he'd seen those people outside that apartment building the night of the murder.

It was important evidence, and Chester would be a good witness. Of course, Chester wanted something in return for testifying at the trial. He had a pending assault charge that could pull his ticket as a doorman if he was convicted. Bill Seong and Drew White had made a deal with Chester promising the assault case would go away if he co-operated. Somehow, the media had gotten wind of Chester's deposition, and there had been a few articles about it.

Now, he wasn't answering his phone. Delaney left a message. He was probably on shift, dealing with a guest.

She stood up from her desk, stretched her back. It was five after eight. She had done enough for the day. As she reached for her cell phone, she heard the ping of a new message. And then a chime signaling an email on her computer.

The message was an alert from the financial fraud team at American Express. She checked her email. It was a back-up notification, to make sure she had seen the first text. Before Delaney could call the bank, her phone started to ring. It was the White Collar Criminal Investigation Division in Quantico.

'Special Agent Delaney, it's Agent Rudnick here at CID. Got a hit on your boy,' said the voice.

For a time, Delaney couldn't speak. She had waited for a break for so long, and now, here it was right in front of her. This was *the* call. Since Daniel Miller had gone on the run, the FBI had been monitoring his bank accounts and credit cards. They hadn't been frozen, simply observed for any activity. It was thought that Miller, who was independently wealthy, had a large amount of hard cash to keep himself under the radar. But cash runs out.

'Where?' asked Delaney, expecting an alert to come from a car dealership in Suriname, a private air charter service in Colombia or just buying some groceries in El Salvador. She was sure he had fled the country and was now holed up in a backwater town far away from the reach of the FBI.

'The Sandman just used his American Express at Grady's Inn Hotel and Bar in Queens.'

CHAPTER SIX

DELANEY

The parking lot of Grady's Inn was lit up by police cars. Headlamps, flashing blue and red lights and even some large spot beams were making the place look like the fourth of July. She had been to the hotel before, on the hunt for the serial killer Dollar Bill, who had been sequestered here as a jury member. If anything, the place looked even more run down than last time.

Delaney pulled up and parked by an old station wagon with four flat tires. There was one other civilian car in the lot – a Toyota. At least the hotel wasn't that busy, and if the Sandman tried anything there wouldn't be a hotel full of people to worry about. Around thirty cops were standing outside the hotel with either shotguns or assault rifles in their ready hands.

Bill Seong escorted a man in black pants, a black waistcoat and white shirt out of the hotel. The duty manager, probably. Behind them came a lady in her fifties wearing sweats and an apron, the only cleaning staff the hotel needed with so few guests. An officer took the manager and the maid to a nearby SWAT van and escorted them inside.

'Is he here?' asked Delaney, with a heaviness to her voice. She could already tell they had missed him.

'Tom, the duty manager, says he checked in around forty, maybe forty-five minutes ago. He left his bag; said he was going to get something to eat.'

'He left his bag in the room?'

'No, he left it with the manager.'

'Is it him? Is it Miller?' asked Delaney, a sick feeling in her stomach. The last thing they needed was someone to steal Miller's credit cards. It had to be him, the Sandman.

'It's him.'

'Is there security footage?'

'Their security cameras work off of a VCR which broke down five years ago and they haven't been able to find someone to fix it and they can't afford a new system. There's no video. The manager gave a rough description and it's the right age and right height.'

'Did you show him a photograph of Miller?'

'I did. He said he could've been the guy. He was wearing a cap. We don't know how Miller might have altered his appearance in the past year. But don't worry. It's him.'

'How do you know for sure it's the Sandman?'

'He used his American Express and he left us a note. Come on, we've got to clear the perimeter,' he said, handing Delaney a clear plastic evidence bag with a guest registration slip inside. Then he took her arm, and gently turned her around and led her away from the building.

She looked at the guest registration form.

He'd signed it *D Miller*. Used the Meadow Road address in Old Westbury. She turned the slip over.

Written on the back were two words.

Tick – Tock.

As she thought about the significance of those words, Delaney glanced over her shoulder at the hotel, then back to the parking lot, filled with police vehicles.

'We need to put some men in the hotel, hide these cars and set up a perimeter with unmarked vehicles. He could be back any second,' she said.

'He's not coming back,' said Bill. 'I went into the storage room, then turned and walked straight back out when I heard it.'

'When you heard what?'

'Miller's bag. It's ticking. The bomb disposal team will be here in five.'

Delaney's shoulders slumped.

'He didn't run out of cash. He didn't make a mistake,' she said.

Bill nodded, called out to the force in the lot to move back, clear the area.

'No, he didn't,' said Bill. 'He wanted us to go straight to the bag and then – *boom*.'

'Why now?' asked Delaney, more to herself than Bill.

'Maybe because his wife goes on trial in a couple of days.'

The bomb disposal unit rolled into the lot as the police vehicles started to move out and form a wide perimeter. Grady's Inn enjoyed a lot of grounds around it. Mostly badly kept lawn and trees that went all the way back to another four-lane highway. The closest building happened to be a Baptist church, and it was well out of range of any device that could be hidden in a backpack. Still, the police made sure no one else drove into the lot and they got the only two members of staff to a safe distance. Even with all that legwork, there were still too many cops around and Bill sent a third of them to go patrol the area, and another third to go find whatever road cameras covered the approaches to the hotel and secure the footage for the hour around his arrival and departure. If they were lucky, they might be able to pick up a license plate. They suspected he was regularly changing the truck plates if he was still driving it.

All of this was discussed at the mobile NYPD command vehicle, set fifty feet from a row of blast screens that were rapidly being erected in front of the hotel. Nothing they could do about saving the building if the device went off, the screens were there to catch debris and glass from the explosion.

The unit sent in their robot, and Delaney set in for the wait. These things take a long time, and they feel even longer. It's a strange sensation, waiting for an explosion. Something like a bored tension. Delaney had experienced it a few times in her life. She had joined the feds after she mustered out of the US Army. Tours in Iraq and Afghanistan were enough to make her realize a career change was in order. Sitting in a base, in the supposed downtimes between missions, gave her that unusual, apathic strain. There was no downtime – not really. At a half-hour's notice she could be back in the shit and even in the base there remained the ever-present threat of a mortar attack, or a suicide bomber rolling into the compound in a Semi filled with ordinance. It was during those periods of agonized waiting that she began to appreciate how her mother felt. That was also part of the reason for quitting the military. During Delaney's tours, Colleen would visit the little parish church in Dorchester, daily, light a candle and pray to Saint Mary for her safe return. When Delaney came home from her tour, the priest told her Colleen almost burned the place to the ground with those candles.

This waiting was similar, but it didn't make her sweat so much. Not like Fallujah. And it wasn't the heat back then. It was the pressure cramping her shoulders and creeping up the back of her neck to boil her brain. She stood with Bill, leaning on the hood of his Range Rover while she ground her teeth. Not much happened for forty minutes or more. A team of forensic techs arrived with coffee to wait it out until they got the all-clear. A bomb technician suited up in heavy, blast-proof armor and slid through the gap in the blast shield, headed for the hotel. Another half hour passed before Bill got word over the comms.

'All clear. It's a false alarm. There's no device in the bag,' said the technician.

Delaney exchanged a curious look with Bill as they started walking toward the hotel. They entered just as the armored technician was coming out.

'If there's no device in the bag then what was the ticking sound I heard?' asked Bill.

The tech shrugged, said, 'There's no metal in the bag. No plastic explosive, no liquid. It's . . . well, you had better see for yourself.'

The bag was now sitting on the counter of the hotel reception. It was open at the top. Wearing gloves, Bill lifted the bag from the counter and set it on the floor. Delaney glanced up, saw the forensics team on their way in. One of them had a camera and he was already lining up to take a picture.

'Get a photo of the top of the bag,' said Bill, stepping back out of the way of the shot. The camera flashed a couple times, then Bill knelt down, Delaney beside him, as he pulled the zipper all the way around and spread the bag wide open.

She knew why Chester Morris had not answered his phone. Chester wouldn't need to worry about testifying against Carrie

Miller, and he sure as hell wouldn't need to worry about getting that assault charge dismissed.

Chester's eyes were missing. His head had been severed at the base of the neck by something very sharp. The clean cut told that tale. His mouth lay open in a scream no one would hear. Something dark filled his mouth and his ocular cavities, but it wasn't blood.

It was sand.

Delaney had seen a lot of terrible things in her time.

People ripped apart. Tortured. Murdered. Both the terror and the agony of their final moments writ large on what was left of their faces. She stood back, took a deep breath and cracked her neck before she returned to look more closely at the head.

That's when they heard the ticking.

'Jesus, there must be some kind of device in his head,' said Bill, but before he could say more, Delaney interrupted.

'That's not a mechanism. Listen,' she said.

They stood still, holding their breath, and heard it again. A rapid, tapping rhythm. Removing a torch from his belt, Bill shone it inside the bag. The sudden burst of light sent something small and black darting across Chester's front teeth. It wasn't a shadow. An insect of some kind.

'Crickets,' said Bill, exhaling. He had been holding his breath ever since he'd heard the ticking.

'Those aren't crickets,' said Delaney. 'Too small. And they don't make that kind of sound.'

'We should haul in Carrie Miller,' said Bill. 'She must've fed information to her husband and now he's taking out key prosecution witnesses. I'll call the DA, and we'll get round the clock protection for every witness in the trial.'

'Bill, we need more than that. Chester had been on the morning news, for God's sake. I told you months ago we should've brought in—'

'No way. I won't have it.'

'Well, everything we've tried so far has failed. If there's one person who can bring in the Sandman, it's Gabriel Lake.'

'You really believe that?'

She nodded, said, 'He's the only person I know who can think like they do.'

'And there's a reason he can think like a killer, isn't there, Paige.'

She opened her mouth to say something but he cut her off.

'I can't do it,' said Bill. 'He's dangerous and I don't trust him.'

She shook her head. There was no convincing Bill.

Delaney and Bill left the forensic technicians to examine the bag, and the head. Both the small insect-like creatures in the sand and the sound they made was somehow familiar to Delaney, but right then she couldn't place it. After two hours they could accomplish no more. The Sandman was taunting them. Taunting Delaney and Bill. She had spoken little to Bill after they had the conversation about Lake. He wouldn't listen. Men like Bill Seong could only see the political fallout if shit went south. They were thinking about themselves. Their own careers.

Lake came with more baggage than a 747, but with that came results.

He was a manhunter. Pure and simple, and right now they needed him more than ever.

Exhausted, Delaney made for her car in the lot. She noticed the old station wagon beside her vehicle – the rear door was open an inch. There were some blankets in the back seat. Probably made a good rest spot for one of the city's many homeless. She drove back toward the city with the promise of sleep lying ahead of her. The release of that tension she'd felt waiting for the bomb disposal team, coupled with the blow from losing her witness, had sapped her energy levels close to zero. This was what the Sandman wanted. He was killing at will, and toying with the police and the FBI. Delaney felt fearful for the days to come.

The Bureau had a dozen properties scattered across New York. Even a few in Manhattan, like the apartment where Delaney had spent her time working on the Sandman case. They were safehouses, mostly, but occasionally they were used by agents on secondment. She had requested this building because it was one of the few with basement parking. The apartment itself was no great shakes, and the parking space was worth as much as the property that came with it. She opened the barrier with her fob, drove down the ramp and found her space in the dimly lit basement lot.

She killed the engine. Sighed, rolled her shoulders and then let the back of her head sink into the headrest.

As she closed her eyes, she glimpsed something thin and black being whipped over her head, down past her line of vision and then . . .

She heard the ripple of plastic teeth grating as the zip tie was pulled fast around her throat, cutting off her air and making her eyes bulge wide, her mouth gaping, her throat locked to the headrest. Her fingers clawed at her neck, and her legs thumped against the footwell, scraping her ankles on the side of the foot pedals.

In her rearview mirror she saw a figure in the back seat. A strong hand took hold of the top of her head, and another plunged something sharp into her throat. As the hand moved away, she glimpsed a needle from a syringe, wet with her blood.

Her legs wouldn't move. Her arms fell limp and a wave of nausea and dizziness swept over her. As her eyes fell closed, she thought she could hear a telephone ringing, once . . . twice . . . three times . . . and behind it, the rattle of rosary beads.

Hot breath grazed her neck.

And then a voice.

A real one, not part of a drug-induced hallucination. A low, gravelly baritone that sang her to sleep almost instantly.

'Mr. Sandman, bring me a dream. Make her the cutest that I've ever seen . . .'

CHAPTER SEVEN

EDDIE

I closed the Carrie Miller file on my desk, leaned back in my chair and listened to the night. As a kid I watched a nature show in school on VHS. It was about the Amazon rainforest, and I remember the narrator saying that when the sun went down, the forest got busy.

It was the same for Manhattan. The noise from traffic and people was always there during the day, and I guess it was probably the same in a South American rainforest, but you damn sure noticed it more at night. Someone was singing an old Irish folk song, but I couldn't tell which one because some people close by were screaming over the top of the chorus about who was going to pay for a cab. Car horns trumpeted, engines droned, and tires howled.

After spending five hours reading about death and looking at pictures of the Sandman's victims I needed to stop for a minute and bathe in life. New York was the best place for that. It was a different kind of jungle. Just as crowded, just as filled with light and sound. And perhaps just as dangerous.

There were predators here that stalked the dark streets. Mostly they hunted the weak and the poor, but some, like the Sandman, hunted everyone. That's what made him so scary. There was no pattern to his attacks. Location, timing were all over the place and there was no victim profile. It didn't matter if you were walking the street at four a.m. or at home behind locked doors – you were not safe.

While he had been on his killing spree, the city had quietened. Then the murders stopped. After the Covid lockdown, and the prevailing theory that the Sandman had gone into hiding, probably even left the country, most people thought it was safe to go outside again and to be alone in their bed at night. The fear was still there, but it had dissipated, and normality had slowly returned to the steel, glass and concrete canyons of Manhattan.

As I closed my eyes, I caught flashes of some of the images I had looked at in the crime scene photographs. Mostly women. Eyes ripped out, sand poured over their faces, filling those twin holes where once there had been a soul, filling their throats and mouths too. It stuck between their teeth and on their lips and gums. Their wounds had turned the sand pink. Except the sand in their mouths, which had remained pale and alien.

The file was subdivided into different sections for each victim, according to the indictment. Six in all had been linked to Carrie. I thought that if the DA got a conviction on these charges the feds might try to tie in the other Sandman murders to Carrie. But that was a worry for another day. I had the crime scene reports and the depositions from neighbors and family, which gave me all I needed to get a snapshot of the six victims in this trial, their lives, and the visceral knowledge of how those lives had been taken.

Margaret Sharpe was a thirty-two-year-old marketing director who lived in East Harlem. She liked vintage clothes and home baking. She cycled to work every day on a lilac and white polka-dot bicycle with a wicker basket mounted over the front fender which she used to carry home her groceries. She had just met a young lady in her gym named Petra who also liked to cycle and bake. They had recently celebrated their six-month anniversary. Petra found Margaret dead in her apartment the morning after the attack. They cycled to their jobs together, most days, and when Margaret hadn't answered her phone, Petra used the spare key to Margaret's apartment. She had been murdered on May 21 last year. Later, Petra confirmed that the vintage sterling silver rose earrings found in Carrie's closet had once belonged to Margaret.

Penny Jones and Suzanna Abrams shared an apartment in Brooklyn, on 4th Avenue. Penny was a twenty-one-year-old singer-songwriter who played eight gigs a week and waited tables at Katz's Deli whenever she could get a shift. Suzanna was older, but no wiser. She poured Guinness and whiskey in an Irish bar two blocks from the apartment and made more in tips most nights than Penny would hit in a week. Trouble was it all flowed back into the bar, one way or another. Especially when Penny got a rejection. She had written a novel and was trying to land a literary agent, which felt like getting punched in the face every time she opened her email.

Two young women enjoying life and trying to make it in the greatest city in the world.

Their neighbor noticed their apartment door open on the morning of May 29, got no answer when he called for them. He went inside, then ran back out and called 911. Penny and Suzanna were each found in their bedrooms. Mutilated, filled with sand. Their bedroom doors were both closed, and there had been no sign of a struggle in the apartment itself. It was remarkable that two healthy young women did not appear to have been able to put up a fight against their attacker. A witness named Chester Morris had spotted a male and female at the door of Penny and Suzanna's building the night of the attack, May 28, and it looked as though the male might have been trying to jimmy the lock. Morris had identified Daniel and Carrie Miller as the couple at the door. Penny and Suzanna were each missing a ring: Penny, a rose gold ring with two red garnets; Suzanna's a silver ring with a gray gemstone. Both were found among Carrie's jewelry.

Lilian Parker was quiet and kept to herself. A freelance designer who mostly worked from home, in Tribeca. Her body was found in the alleyway behind her apartment building, which was unusual for the Sandman. She was forty-one and a keen violinist, although her neighbors had no clue about this. Her violin was found with the strings wrapped in cotton wool to dim the sound. A neighbor in the apartment next door, Teresa Vasquez, said she saw a man and woman hanging around outside the building on the night of the attack, June 3. The description matched Daniel Miller and Carrie Miller. Teresa Vasquez, like Chester Morris, had only come forward after Carrie Miller's very public arrest. A cameo brooch that Lilian wore everyday was not in her apartment and not on her body. It was Lilian's mother who told the police that it was missing. This had led to a review of the other killings with relatives of the victims and an identification of various pieces of jewelry that were taken by the Sandman. If it had not been for Mrs. Parker, police and FBI may not have known the Sandman took trophies from his killings.

The Nielsens lived in a grand brownstone in the East Village. A good Samaritan had noticed their front door lying open at around six a.m. The first officer on scene was relatively new to the job. His supervising officer led the rookie inside and told him to check upstairs. The supervisor ran up the staircase when he heard a dull thump from the floor above. The rookie was out cold on the landing, outside the master bedroom. At first, he thought the rookie had been knocked out by an attacker, but he soon saw what had caused the collapse. Tobias and Stacy Nielsen were tucked up together in bed. The sheets pulled up to their necks. Mouths and eye sockets filled with sand. In the room next to them, eight-year-old Elly Nielsen lay asleep clutching a teddy bear. Her adopted brother, Robert, was in his bedroom. He was only five. The children were alive and unmolested, save for having had a sedative administered by injection. They didn't see the man who pricked their necks in the dark, but one of them, little Robert, said he felt someone's breath on his cheek.

The rookie took a month off work on sick leave and quit when that had run out. He took an overdose of painkillers within a week of resigning and was buried with full NYPD honors. I wondered, if he had lived long enough for the feds to find Daniel Miller's home, and Stacy Nielsen's black pearl necklace in Carrie Miller's closet, would it have given him some element of closure? Would it have saved him?

This was only a handful of the victims the Sandman had murdered. These were the latest murders and ones that the DA could evidentially link to Carrie Miller. I had stood in Carrie Miller's house, we'd talked, and I could not equate that person with someone who could put two children to sleep and then casually murder their parents.

I had dealt with monsters before. So had the lead FBI analyst on the case, Paige Delaney. In fact, Delaney had worked with me on the Bobby Solomon case where we came across a killer who had worked his way onto the jury in Bobby's trial. I had been lucky to survive that case, and the seven-inch scar on my thigh still itched in the winter and felt raw in the summer. She had also given me some pointers in the Avellino trial, where Kate and I had first met, as opponents. Delaney hunted killers for a living. I represented people who were accused of homicide. It was no wonder that we'd met, seeing as how we were both dealing with the worst kind of horrors in the same city. I liked Delaney. She was smart and diligent. A woman I had loved and lost, named Harper, had been a mutual friend of ours.

Last time Delaney and I spoke was at the anniversary memorial for Harper. She talked about our friend and the warmth and affection she felt was genuine. While Delaney spoke, I had listened, nodded, and we'd parted with an embrace. I couldn't talk about Harper. Not yet. Not to anyone, not even Harry. At one time I thought the two of us might have had a future together. The scars on my body were not the only old wounds that I would carry around for the rest of my life.

I got up out of my chair and approached the window. The blaze of neon from the club across the street fell through the window, washing the room with a deep red. Noises from the street seemed to fade away in the glow, as if the riot of color muted everything else.

Bloch, Kate and Harry all believed in Carrie Miller. I couldn't discount that. And when I had looked her in the eye, and asked if she had killed those people, she had told me the truth. I knew it. The evidence against her was circumstantial, but it all added up. I had learned not to discount my instincts, no matter what the prosecution said.

I thought that perhaps she knew more about her husband's dark life than she was willing to say. Maybe she had known about it all along and had been living in fear – slowly drowning in the guilt of her silence. I knew there was a point when she suspected him, and she didn't act on it. And that was torturing her. It meant that she cared. Killers don't have empathy, and they can't fake it. All four of us believed Carrie. That counted for a lot.

It was just the rest of the world that thought she was a killer.

The DA would make two arguments. First, that she intended the victims to be murdered and she encouraged or aided her husband's conduct. If the DA couldn't prove intent, there was a fallback argument – that she was an accomplice. In this case, he had to prove her knowledge that her husband intended to kill, and she provided the means, opportunity or simply aided his crimes. The last was easier to prove. If she was found guilty of either one, she would never see another day from the outside of a prison cell.

A final piece of prosecution evidence gave us a big problem. It was one I hadn't asked Carrie about. Not specifically. No doubt the grand jury would have found this crucial when considering whether she should be indicted. One thing was certain about this case. Daniel Miller was the Sandman, and he had killed all of those people. No question.

And Carrie Miller had lied to cover it up.

The question I needed answered was why she'd protected him.

My cell phone began to vibrate on my desk.

I checked my watch, a gift from my daughter, Amy, many years ago. The face was all scratched up, and the battery needed replacing every few months now, but there was no way I would part with it. She had one just like it, or at least she used to until hers stopped working. Her stepfather, Kevin, had bought her a new one for her fifteenth birthday. He wasn't officially a stepfather, not quite yet. My ex-wife, Christine, was due to be remarried in a few weeks and the news hadn't hit me as hard as I'd expected. I had accepted that Christine had moved on. It felt like old grief. Most of the time I was fine, it only hurt when I bumped right up against it, unexpectedly. I was more concerned about Amy than Christine. It felt like I was losing my daughter.

I swept up my phone, double checked the time on the screen with my watch.

Coming up on two in the morning. Calls at that time of night are never good.

It was our investigator, Bloch.

'Are you okay?' I asked.

'I'm on my way to the FBI resident agency out by JFK. A statewide alert just went up. One of the occupants of Paige Delaney's building called the cops. Paige's car was in the basement parking lot, all four doors open and the alarm going off. Her cell phone and side arm were found in the car . . .'

I wanted to speak, but I couldn't. My breath had frozen in my chest.

'He's back,' said Bloch.

CHAPTER EIGHT

EDDIE

The FBI's Manhattan field office sits at 26 Federal Plaza. There are five satellite offices scattered around New York, known as resident agencies. The Jamaica resident agency, out toward JFK, was in a modern glass-covered building on Kew Garden Road. It took up one floor and shared the building with a twenty-four-hour fitness center, a nursing agency, a bartending school, a hair salon and an insurance brokerage.

Security was light.

Bloch waited for me outside, wearing a black tee under a black sport coat, skinny blue jeans and steel-toe-capped boots. I still wore my navy suit, but I'd lost the tie and left my white cotton shirt open at the neck.

'Lawyers should wear ties,' said Bloch.

'I do things a little differently.'

'I've noticed.'

'Any update?'

She shook her head.

We approached the glass revolving doors and shuffled through them without a problem and took the elevator to the FBI satellite office. All the security was on this level. Metal detector gates, bag scanners, body scanners – the works, all before we got to the reception area. It was pretty small. Four hard plastic chairs. Two on either side of the door all facing a formidable desk ahead with a formidable woman behind it. She was in her sixties and carried the benefit of those years in her eyes. Swiveling her chair toward us, she glanced over the top of her thick black spectacles and drew her lips together.

'Can I help you?' she asked.

'We're friends of Paige Delaney. Could we speak to one of the agents on duty? My name is Eddie Flynn.'

'Take a seat,' she said, then disappeared through a side door. I didn't tell her that I was representing Carrie Miller, because they would escort me from the building in a flash.

I hadn't realized there was someone else in the waiting area, on one of the plastic chairs on the other side of the reception door. He had his head between his knees, which explained why I hadn't spotted him. As we approached the reception, we could only see the back of the chairs. He had dark brown, slightly curly hair and his fingers were locked together at the back of his neck, as if he were in a brace position. We sat down on the seats on the opposite side of the door. He sat up, rubbed his face and then took a moment to appraise us.

He was pale and thin, with light stubble on his cheeks. His blue shirt and black suit looked as though a larger man had slept in them and this guy had stolen them off his back that morning. The collar of the shirt was way too big, and the jacket hung off his shoulders like a tablecloth. The man looked ill, and I guessed he'd lost weight recently. His brown eyes were a different story. They were keen, and never seemed to linger very long on either Bloch, or me. They were moving over us rapidly – taking in every detail.

The side of his mouth twitched before he spoke.

'Did I hear that right? You're friends of Delaney?' he asked.

I couldn't place the accent. East Coast, but I couldn't tell from where exactly.

'That's right. Are you a colleague?' I asked.

The guy didn't look like an FBI agent, unless he was undercover.

'I used to be,' he said. 'How do you know Delaney?'

'She helped us out on a couple of cases. And she saved my life once. Or helped save it. That counts for a lot,' I said.

He nodded, but the look in his eyes said he wasn't satisfied.

'You're not a cop,' he said to me. 'But your friend used to be.'

Bloch shrugged.

'My name is Eddie Flynn. I'm a lawyer and this is my investigator, Bloch.'

'Where did you serve?'

'All over,' said Bloch.

She wasn't being rude. She was just being Bloch.

Before the man could introduce himself, an FBI agent appeared from the door behind the reception. Everything about him was neat. Tie, shirt, suit, hair. Crisp and fresh. He came around the desk, took a sideways glance at the man in the chair, but said nothing, and approached us with his hand extended in greeting.

'Mr. Flynn, I'm Special Agent Bill Seong. We appreciate you coming down, but we can't give out any information at this time. We acknowledge your concern and we'll let you know more when we can, but at this moment you'd be better going home. There's nothing you can do.'

'We just thought we might be able to help. Bloch here is a great investigator. If you need another pair of boots on the ground—'

'No, thank you. Bloch's reputation speaks for itself, but we're fine. We have every agent in the state looking—'

'How do you know it was the Sandman who took her?' asked Bloch. There was no small talk with her. Straight to the jugular. Every time.

Bill paused, mid-sentence, his mouth open. His mind making calculations before he spoke.

'That information has not been released to the public, yet.'

'It's all over the radio. How do you know it was him?' she asked, again.

I saw the man on the chair look up at Bloch with interest.

'I can't say, but we know it's him for sure. And we think she's alive, for now.'

Nodding, Bloch stood up. She was a good three inches taller than Bill.

'Delaney is a friend of Eddie's. He's real concerned.'

'She's a friend of mine too,' said Bill, the muscles in his jaw working.

'Then let us help,' said Bloch.

'We can handle this on our own.'

Bloch nodded, then turned away and headed back down the hall.

I guessed our meeting was over.

'Bill, just let me take a look at—' said the man in the chair.

'No. None of you are getting involved in this. We'll get her back. Just stay out of it and let us do our job,' said Bill, then disappeared back through the door behind reception.

The man stood up, hoisted a faded brown leather satchel onto the crumpled shoulder of his suit, and approached me.

'I was hoping they'd let me in. It would make things easier. I'll just have to do this the hard way. So, do you want to find Delaney?'

I nodded.

'I've heard of you, Mr. Flynn. People say you're a smart guy. And if you're a friend of Delaney's then I guess that makes you okay in my book. I think I know where we can start looking,' he said.

'Where?'

'You got a car?'

'Yeah, you want me to follow you?'

'No, I need a lift.'

'Who are you?'

He held out his hand. I took it, surprised by the strength of his grip.

'I'm Gabriel Lake,' he said. 'I hunt serial killers.'

CHAPTER NINE

EDDIE

I'd taken a cab to the FBI office, knowing I'd meet Bloch there. She fired open the Jeep and I got into the front passenger seat, Lake in the back behind me.

'Where are we going?' asked Bloch.

'A lot of NYPD units got called to a hotel tonight,' said Lake. 'Bomb disposal and FBI too. The usual alert signals that go to law enforcement statewide when there's a terrorist threat didn't go out, so my guess is it was something else that needed SWAT, fifty cops, a bomb team and the feds. I think it was the Sandman. Grady's Inn is like ten minutes from here.'

Plugging her phone into a jack, Bloch then began searching for the address on her navigation system.

'I know the hotel,' I said. 'I've been there before.'

Two cop cars were parked in the lot of Grady's Inn, along with two other vehicles. I hadn't been back to the hotel since that night I'd met Joshua Kane, a killer who'd worked his way onto a jury in one of my cases. The building had fallen into further decay since then. The roof had bowed deeper, more paint had flecked from the walls and window frames and the grounds surrounding the place were heavily neglected, the grass and weeds standing four feet tall.

Bloch brought the Jeep to a stop in the small lot, then got out and walked over to the police cars parked across the entrance to the hotel.

'You want to go with her?' I asked.

'Nah,' said Lake, 'I'm not too popular with law enforcement.'

'Me either. So, you track serial killers for a living?'

'I used to.'

'Is that how you know Delaney?'

'She trained me at the Behavioral Analysis Unit. Delaney was my mentor, but she is more than that. We're friends. She stuck by me . . .'

I glanced over my shoulder when Lake stopped talking. His eyes seemed to recall another time, another place, when fear and pain were all that he knew. The light from the dash threw an orange glow on his face, as if he were standing in front of a cold flame.

'Sorry,' he said, his voice shivering, the words heavy in his throat. 'She means a lot to me, Mr. Flynn.'

I nodded. Delaney is good people. If she went out on a professional limb for Lake, then that made him, for all his slight eccentricities, good people too.

He cleared his throat, gazed through the windshield and said, 'She's coming back.'

Bloch got into the driver's seat, took out her phone.

'I trained one of the uniforms in advanced driving a few years ago. He's cutting us in. The Sandman checked into this hotel earlier today. Swiped his card, put his bag with reception and then left. The feds thought it was a bomb. They heard ticking. Turns out it was some guy's head in the bag. I think Bill Seong knows who it is, but these cops don't. There are eighty patrol cars, almost every precinct, driving the city right now looking for Delaney.'

She held her cell phone higher, as if she were looking for a signal.

'One of the patrolmen snapped a picture of the head in the bag when the forensic techs were setting up. Don't be surprised if it's on the front page of the *New York Post* in the morning and a cop buys a new car in the afternoon.'

'Was it him, the guy you trained, did he take the picture?' I asked.

'No, but cops have a way of covering for each other. Whoever it was, once they'd sold the picture, they then shared it with the precinct WhatsApp group. And that group shared it with another group. That way if there's an internal affairs investigation about who took the photograph and sold it to the *Post* – every damn cop in the city will have that image on their phone.'

'Cops cover for cops,' I said, shaking my head.

'Not all of them,' said Lake.

I wanted to ask him what he meant, but a sharp *ping* signaled a new message on Bloch's phone, and that took priority.

She opened it to reveal an image.

The inside of the bag was yellow canvas. The blood stains had turned dark red. At the bottom of the bag was a man's head. His eyes were missing. In their place were pools of bloodstained sand. In his mouth too. Black dots scattered across his face, and at first, I thought they were dried droplets of blood. Bloch pinched the screen, drew her index finger and thumb apart to widen the image. They weren't blood drops.

'Bugs,' I said.

'No,' said Lake. 'They're not bugs. They're Hymenoptera – insects. Beetles. Can I take a closer look?'

Bloch's eyebrow shot for the ceiling as she handed her phone to Lake in the back.

We turned around to see him enlarging the picture further, then zooming back out and in again.

'I'd say about a centimeter long, maybe under. There's yellow hair on these. Very distinctive. It explains why they thought the bag was ticking, I suppose.'

'What are they?' I asked.

He handed Bloch her phone, leaned back in the seat.

'They make a loud clicking sound. With enough of them together it might sound like a clock or mechanical timer. For years people didn't think it was the beetles making that sound. They thought it was the wood they infested, cracking. But we know now, they make the sound at certain times of the year. They like old houses, with old timber frames. Most people hear them at night when they're up and the house is quiet. They say they got their name during Irish wakes. The Irish have a vigil – someone stays with the corpse at all times, even at night, for three days. That's when they hear the clicking – during the death watch.'

'Deathwatch beetles,' said Bloch. 'You know a lot about insects.'

'You spend your time looking for serial killers and you pick up a few things. These insects don't feed on the dead. The Sandman put them in the bag with the guy's head. He wanted them found.'

'Why?' I asked.

'It's a warning,' said Lake. 'That sound is an omen of death.'

None of us said anything for a moment.

The silence was broken up when Bloch's phone chimed again and again as more images came through.

These were background shots. One of the front of the hotel, with a bomb disposal tech in a protective suit that made him look like a deep-sea diver. He was walking through the blast screens. The other shots were dramatic images of the massive police presence in the parking lot, giving an impression of the scale of the response. Flicking through them, Bloch hesitated, then went back and looked at the previous image, then forward again to the last one.

She handed me the phone, got out of the car without a word and went to take a look at the parking lot.

Lake and I got out and followed her as she approached the station wagon with flat tires and a thick layer of dust on the windshield. She reached for the rear passenger door. It was open.

'They found Delaney's car in the underground parking lot of her building. Doors open, alarm going off,' she said. 'An intruder couldn't have gotten in there without a key-card or fob. All of those lots are secure because they cost a fortune. So how did he get into the lot? He couldn't drive in.'

I checked the photos she had been studying. In both pictures the station wagon was in view. In one, the rear passenger door was slightly ajar. In the other picture, the door was closed.

'Next to the station wagon, that's Delaney's car,' said Lake. 'Now we know how he got into the underground parking lot. He had been hiding in the station wagon the whole time, and when the attention was on the bomb disposal squad he slipped out and into the back of Delaney's car.'

'But how would he know she would park next to the station wagon?' I said.

'He wouldn't,' said Bloch. 'The station wagon was at the rear of the lot. With the bomb squad here, every cop had their attention focused on the building. They're not watching what's going on in the parking lot fifty feet behind them. He took his time, chose his moment, and snuck into Delaney's car. She just made it easy for him. We need to go check out her building.'

'I know where it is,' said Lake.

CHAPTER TEN

EDDIE

Only buildings that went up in the last forty years or so have underground parking. There aren't that many, but more than you might first imagine. The FBI had secured a lease on an apartment in a building in Midtown, on the east side.

There were two patrol cars parked across the entrance and exit to the underground lot. No way past them. This was a crime scene, and Bloch's reputation wouldn't get us past the cops at the ramp leading to the basement parking lot.

One of the patrol officers reached for his radio, spoke into it then got in the car and reversed it. The other patrol vehicle did the same, clearing the entrance for a gray Sedan that pulled onto the ramp, and drove down into the lot past the barrier which had been locked open. I didn't see the driver, but one of the men in the back was Bill Seong. Soon as the car passed, the patrol vehicles put their roadblock back in place.

'That was Seong in the back of that car,' said Lake.

'Let's get inside,' I said.

Bloch parked up the street and we made our way back to the building. The residents' entrance was two glass doors. Outside, affixed to the wall was an intercom with a number pad and instructions beside it.

'What's Delaney's apartment number?' I asked.

'1011,' said Lake.

When the FBI are first notified one of their agents is missing, there are standard checks to be done. Cell phone. Apartment. Witnesses.

A team would've been inside Delaney's apartment tonight. Once they found it empty, they would've spoken to her neighbors to ascertain when they last saw her, and if they'd seen anything suspicious that night.

I dialed 1012 on the keypad. A ring tone was answered quickly by a male voice.

'Yes?'

'This is the FBI, we spoke earlier. Would you mind buzzing the door, please?' I said.

A buzzer sounded, Bloch pushed open the front door, and we were in. The elevator took us down two floors to the parking lot. One basement parking garage is much the same as any other. Exposed steel beams and strip lighting. Yellow and white paint on treated concrete floors and somewhere there was always a puddle of water with a constant overhead drip feeding it. And the smell. Burnt motor oil and old garbage.

There were a bunch of forensic techs in blue hazmat suits swarming over Delaney's car. Twenty feet away, Bill Seong stood in a huddle with five other agents. All males. All in the same navy or black suits. Same haircuts too, apart from one guy who had shaved his head.

I was hoping he wouldn't see us, and we could get closer to Delaney's car for a better look. In part because I wanted to see if there were any more warnings left behind by the Sandman, but mostly I needed to know if there was any blood on the seats or dash. It was cold in the lot, but I could feel the sweat on the back of my neck. I didn't want to lose another friend. Bloch and I moved quietly toward Delaney's car.

'Hey, Bill,' cried Lake.

Bloch swore under her breath, gestured toward Lake.

'I like him,' I said.

'How did you . . . You can't be here. Get these people out of here, right now,' said Seong.

The feds who had been standing around moved toward us with purpose.

'Wait, we know how he got into the building,' said Lake. 'He hid in the back of Delaney's car. Daniel Miller got you all riled up with the bomb threat at the hotel. It was a distraction. He had been hiding in the old station wagon and with everyone's attention on the bomb squad he snuck into the back of her car.'

Seong said nothing, but I could see his wheels turning. By the time the first fed reached to put an arm on me he told them to wait. Then beckoned us over.

'If you know so much, then tell me what this means. This is the live feed from Delaney's car over there,' said Seong, holding up an iPad. I glanced across the parking lot, saw a camera set up on a tripod, pointed directly into Delaney's vehicle. On the iPad was the live feed. There was something sitting on the dash. It took me a second to realize what it was.

The object was maybe a foot tall. It had been set between the windshield and the dash. At first, I thought I was looking at two whiskey glasses, stacked on top of one another and housed in a wooden frame.

I looked closer.

It was an hourglass. The top bulb had little sand in it now. There was a steady stream of grains falling through the opening into the symmetrical bulb below.

'How long is left?' I asked.

'We think maybe ten minutes. Our guess is it's a four-hour sand timer. There have been no demands. No contact. No note in the car. Just this goddamn timer,' said Seong.

'How did he get her out of this building?' asked Lake.

'We're not sure. We've checked the camera in the lobby, and he didn't go out that way. The only camera in the lot covers the entrance and exit and no vehicles left after Delaney drove in. It's possible he sedated her, dragged her behind him as he hugged the wall up the ramp, beneath the camera's viewpoint, ducked under the barrier and carried her into a car parked on the street. That's our best guess.'

'You can't drag a body along a New York street for what, ten, twenty feet, and not be seen by half a dozen people. He takes risks, but that is just way too risky for Miller,' said Lake.

'You got a better idea how he got her out of here?'

Together, Bloch and I took a walk to the ramp. A security camera high up on the left side of the wall. Someone directly beneath, their back to the bricks, could skirt up and out without the camera picking them up. But not with a hostage, conscious or not.

'I don't like it,' I said.

Whether Bloch didn't hear me, or chose to ignore me, it didn't matter. She clicked a pocket flashlight on and started to look around the lot. I left Bill and the rest of them and followed Bloch. Nearly every space was taken. Forty, maybe fifty cars.

'I'm sure they checked the lot,' I said.

'They would've performed a quick sweep. No more,' said Bloch.

While Lake argued with Seong, Bloch and I walked the lot. Our gaze followed her flashlight to the dark recesses behind and between the vehicles, where the strip lighting could not reach. The smell of motor oil, gasoline and damp filled the space.

A steady *drip, drip, drip* from the ceiling sounded like an old clock, ticking down the seconds.

Nothing stood out. Bloch shone a light between each car but didn't linger. She spotted a twenty-year-old Porsche, and checked the interior, then moved on. We finished one side, then crossed over to the next aisle. Bloch stopped at the car parked opposite Delaney's. It was an older model Toyota pick-up with a tarp covering the flatbed at the rear.

'You mind telling me what we're supposed to be looking for?' I asked.

'An older car without an alarm . . .' she began, then stopped. Bloch held up a hand, calling for silence.

'You hear that?' she asked.

I listened, but I could only hear the steady drip from pipes. Louder over here. I looked up, trying to see where the drip was coming from, but I couldn't tell.

'I can't see how he got Delaney out of here,' I said.

'I think the fed was half right,' said Bloch.

'What do you mean, half right?'

'I think the Sandman hugged the wall, ducked the ramp and went onto the street on foot. But Delaney . . .'

'Shit. You think she's still here.'

She bent low, shone her torch beneath the pick-up.

'Lake! Seong! Get over here,' she called.

I dropped down to my knees. Beneath the flat bed of the pick-up there was a pool of dark liquid that curled into the drain. There was a drip coming from the back of the truck. It didn't smell like oil.

By the time I got to my feet, Bloch had already torn away the tarp covering the bed of the pick-up. Paige Delaney lay on the steel floor.

I'd seen a lot of hurt. The very worst of what human beings can do, but the shock of seeing someone I knew ripped apart made me flinch. I closed my eyes for a second and looked away.

A huge wound in her stomach had drenched her in blood from her knees to her neck. He had taken her eyes.

Bloch called for a paramedic, she had one hand on the stomach wound, the other at Delaney's neck. She took her hand away from her throat, said, 'I can't find a pulse.' I climbed in beside her, helped keep pressure on the wound. Soon as I laid my hands on her stomach, I knew we were too late. She was cold to the touch.

A lot of things seemed to happen all at once. The underground lot became flooded with noise. I heard the calls and footsteps of a handful of feds running over to the pick-up. One was screaming into a radio for a paramedic, Seong was barking orders, the *drip*, *drip*, *drip* of Delaney's life's blood faded away.

Her hands were bound behind her back. Through the blood, I could see a large circular bruise on her neck and in the center of it – a needle mark. She had been sedated. I prayed she never woke from that.

Bloch started chest compressions as I leaned down on Delaney's stomach. The panic all around us seemed to slow down time, and I watched Seong reach into the flatbed and pick up an envelope. His name was on it. The rest of the feds were either barking orders at Bloch or talking on the phone.

Every time Bloch pumped Delaney's chest, fresh blood spilled over the back of my hands. I glanced to my left and saw Lake. He had leaned against an exposed steel beam, but it wasn't enough to keep him upright. His back slid down the beam until he sat on the floor. His hands covered his face and I could see his body heaving with grief.

I heard the sirens in the distance. Breaking through the night.

But I knew they were too late.

CHAPTER ELEVEN

Extract from the Journal of Carrie Miller

May 22

It's Danny's birthday today.

I'd really wanted to make the evening special for him, to show just how much I love him and to maybe recapture some of the chemistry we had when we first started dating. God, I make it sound like we've been married for ten years. We're almost a year into our marriage and I'm already worried and panicking (slightly) that I've failed at this. Like I kinda fail at everything.

What do you get the guy who has everything? I've even Googled that exact question. In the end I found a calligraphy artist online who sent me a framed vellum sheet with 'I'm happiest when I'm with you,' in beautiful old handwriting. I wanted him to know that I didn't need his money, or this house, or the fancy car, that all I really wanted was him – his time. One year together means it's a paper anniversary, so I had that gift covered, but I couldn't give it to him on his birthday. I needed something else.

He's always surprising me with thoughtful gifts that are just perfect. I wanted to give him something really nice too. I found a watch dealer, because Danny has some nice watches, but they're a bit flashy and I wanted something for him with a bit more class. The Panerai Submersible watch the dealer suggested was just gorgeous. The color of the brass would deepen over time and I hoped our relationship would do the same. Danny is so special to me. I wanted him to have something special too, something that no one else would have and the watch was just right on the money.

After it was delivered, I remember having just a touch of fear. I'd remembered something my grandma used to say whenever my gramps

67

complained about her old wind-up watch that always ran slow. She forbade him from buying her a new one – said a watch puts a time limit on a marriage. Like a ticking bomb.

My grandmother also thought Elvis was alive and working in a Walmart in Reno.

I bought the damn watch.

It was worth it to see the look on his face as he opened the box at the breakfast bar. He put it on while I made eggs this morning. This is the Danny I love. When we're together I have such a feeling of warmth. I feel safe.

But we seem to be spending less and less time together. I thought that when we got married it would be just the opposite. I've tried to make the house more comfortable, you know, putting my own stamp on the place here and there. Nothing major, just soft touches to make it more homely and warm – a space he would never want to leave.

It didn't work last night. I heard him come in at four a.m., found him in the guest bathroom showering. After I got him some fresh towels he apologized for waking me up. I was going to grab his suit and shirt for him, but he said he'd already bagged it up for the dry cleaners – said the clients he'd been with had smoked cigars all night. He'd wrinkled his nose and laughed as I toweled his hair. Part of his job is making connections with investors, and I reminded myself he was doing all of this for me. He once told me he would give me the world, and I believed him.

This morning, after he ate his eggs and he sat at the kitchen bar, admiring his watch, he told me to close my eyes and open my hands. He had a surprise for me. Typical Danny. Even on his birthday he's thinking about me. I felt something in my hands and when I opened my eyes I saw a beautiful pair of antique earrings. Silver, each one in the shape of a rose. My favorite flower. Simple and stunning. No presentation box. He said he found them in a little store and couldn't resist. They were perfect.

He was perfect.

When I met Danny, my life changed.

Ever since I was a little girl, sitting on my parents' couch in our little house in Cleveland watching Showboat, Guys and Dolls *and* 42nd Street, *I wanted to sing and dance. Like so many others, I came* to New York with a big dream and little money. Shared terrible apartments with people I barely knew, worked three jobs, and racked up an impressive number of failed open auditions. When I didn't get the job of Chuckie the Chicken for a children's playday, I decided the entertainment business wasn't for me.

I quit the three waitressing jobs, got a better position as a customer sales agent in a leather goods store at the corner of East 26th and Madison, and started making my rent on an apartment that wasn't so crammed with strangers. I didn't have to feel around the cushions on the couch, looking for lost nickels so I could buy some noodles. And that was my life for a year, until Daniel Miller saw me through the window, stopped and came inside. He didn't want to buy a briefcase, or an overnight bag, or even a wallet. He wanted me. Said I was the most beautiful woman he'd ever seen, and he would regret it until his dying day if he didn't ask me out to dinner that night.

He said his name was Daniel Miller that day, in the store. Like it meant something. I would learn that his name did mean something to rich people in the city. He managed a private hedge fund, and he made a lot of money doing it. He was tall, well-built, handsome, charming, and on our first date that night I wondered what was behind that gorgeous smile. I didn't know he was rich when we first started dating, but on our fourth date, when he booked a jet to take us to Vegas, I kind of figured it out. It wasn't the money that made me fall in love with him. It was the way he made me feel. Like I was the most important person in the world.

My life up to then had always been uncertain. My father couldn't hold down a job and he would fight with my mom a lot. Alcohol played a part for sure, but lack of money was the root of it. I was nineteen and tending bar when he drove his truck through a barrier on the highway. Mom was in the passenger seat. He was drunk. They both were. And they never made it out of that truck. Losing my parents made me try for an acting job in New York. Life seemed fragile and chaotic.

But Danny gave me security, warmth and certainty. I would wake up every day knowing he cared for me, that I didn't have to worry about money, or a place to stay, or anything really.

I don't have to work anymore, but I volunteer at the animal shelter to keep me busy when Danny is not around.

I got home around four-thirty this afternoon and showered. Daniel was still at the office. I'd just come back down to the kitchen in my sweats to start a birthday dinner when the doorbell rang. I opened the door to a young man in a suit with a clipboard and pen in his hand.

He said his name was Detective Mike Stone. He asked if Daniel Miller lived here and was I Mrs. Miller?

I said I was.

He asked what kind of vehicle Danny drove.

I started to shake. A wave of panic rising up through me with memories of the cop who came to my house to tell me my parents had died in a car wreck. Just then, Danny pulled into the driveway and I ran to his car and threw my arms around him. He was confused as to what was going on, then I told him the guy was a cop and he'd been asking about Danny's car and I had put two and two together and made five. I'd panicked.

Danny knew what had happened to my parents, and he understood immediately how I'd reacted. I was still shaken up, so he explained what had happened to the bemused cop who suddenly looked really embarrassed. He apologized, said he just wanted to check if Danny owned a dark-colored van. Danny said it was owned by one of the companies he owns.

The cop then asked where Danny had been last night.

He said he was home, with me. The cop looked at me. I was still choked up. I couldn't really speak, I just nodded and managed to mumble, that he was home with me.

The policeman thanked us both, apologized again for scaring me and then quickly left.

It was only when we got back inside the house, and I'd had some water and calmed down, that I thought again about what Danny had said. I asked him why he'd told the cop he was home last night when he'd been out late.

He said he had seen how upset I was and he just wanted to get rid of the cop so he could look after me, and that whatever the cop was looking into it had nothing to do with Danny.

He came over, held me close, until the warmth of him had made everything feel okay. I was safe.

I was loved.

CHAPTER TWELVE

EDDIE

It was eight-thirty in the morning by the time Bloch and I stumbled out of the FBI office in Federal Plaza into the morning sun. I had a headache, and we were both hungry. Our hands were clean, but both Bloch and I had wet cuffs on our shirts, faded pink now that we had washed our friend's blood off them. In the men's bathroom that morning, I'd seen a copy of the *New York Times* under the arm of an agent. He put it on the shelf above the sink while he washed up.

All of the newspapers today would have front page news on the murder of an FBI agent by the Sandman. Except one. A copy of his letter had found its way to the *New York Times*. The slogan at the top of the banner on the *Times* reads, *All the news that's fit to print*. This phrase has been on the gray lady for one hundred and fifteen years. It never looked more out of place than today. They had printed his letter in full. It was short, and to the point, and should not have gotten the attention.

I am a killer. My wife is not.
Let her go or more will die.

On the street outside the FBI office, a man in a wrinkled shirt, creased pants and jacket, shaded his eyes from the morning sun and stared at us as we came out of the building. If I hadn't known those clothes looked that way the night before, I would've sworn he had slept in them. None of us had slept. Gabriel Lake raised a hand, said, 'Can I buy you folks some breakfast?'

Eating in a Manhattan diner is one of life's great pleasures. Lake said he knew somewhere nearby. Two blocks brought us to an old-school diner. They had booths and laminated menus and a big guy behind the grill with five-day-old stubble who swore a lot and spoke in a language I couldn't place. In other words, it was perfect.

Bloch ordered the grilled cheese with a side of eggs and chorizo. I took a chance on the pancakes and bacon and Lake ordered hot water with lemon.

'I don't do caffeine,' he said, and then proceeded to interrogate the waitress about the muffin he was thinking of ordering. Where had it come from? What was in it? Were those ingredients organic? The wait staff in diners don't make a lot. They are there to serve with a smile solely so they can make their tips, and consequently, their rent. Lake wasn't trying to piss her off. He genuinely wanted to know all this stuff. The waitress's name was Halina. She watched Lake's fingers tapping on the table as he talked, punctuating her answers with a forceful thump of his thumb when he liked what he heard. The booths were pretty full, and there were customers waiting at the door to be seated. Halina cocked her hip, put a fist on it, and started tapping her foot. She had reached the end of this conversation, even if Lake hadn't yet realized it.

'And are the poppy seeds grown organically?' asked Lake.

'Gee,' said Halina, 'I don't know what to tell you, pal. The muffin didn't have no fuckin' birth certificate.'

'*Halina*,' called the big guy at the grill. 'Shitting Christ, be *nice* to the fucking customers.'

And off she went with our order.

'I'm beginning to see why you weren't cut out for a career as a federal agent,' I said.

'Sorry,' said Lake. 'I'm trying to be more careful about what I put into my body these days. That's all. It's not a thing.'

'It kinda looks like a thing.'

'It's *not* a thing.'

He leaned back in the seat, his gaze fell and a pained look came across his face.

'Delaney thought it was a thing, too,' he said, quietly.

'We didn't know her that well,' I said. 'Something I regret now. She was good people.'

He nodded, and raised his index finger on his right hand, as if he was about to make a point, then put his palms on the table as the waitress came over with our drinks. Coffee for Bloch and me, hot water and lemon for Lake.

He examined the contents of the cup carefully, stirred the sliced lemon with a teaspoon and let it cool.

'I was going to ask you,' he continued, 'if you told Bill Seong you're representing Carrie Miller?'

Bloch tensed.

I said nothing. I hadn't told Lake. And I knew Bloch hadn't told him.

'Oh, I have a contact at the courthouse. Keeps me up to date with subpoenas, motions – any developments in Carrie Miller's case. I hear you filed your appearance with the court office last night,' he said.

It was going to be common knowledge soon enough.

'No, I didn't tell him,' I said. 'I thought if I did it would close a door. Any information on Carrie Miller's husband might help her case. Seong didn't ask us, and we didn't tell him. Our concern last night was for Delaney.'

'I know, that's okay. I agreed to help out in the case as a consultant. Delaney wanted me on this, and I guess Seong's conscience is getting to him, so he has reluctantly agreed. I wanted to know what Carrie's defense is going to be.'

Tipping off the people who want to send your client to jail for fifty years isn't the smartest idea. I put cream and sugar in my coffee, stirred it and took my first hit.

'She's not an accomplice. Simple as that. I can't say any more,' I said.

'So, she's saying she wasn't a participant. Fair enough. Is she saying she didn't know her husband was a killer?'

Bloch put her boot heel on top of my shoe and pushed down hard.

'It's okay, Bloch,' I said, then turned to Lake. 'Look, I'm sorry, I can't say.'

'I understand. So, she *did* suspect him. Do you mind if I talk to her?'

'I do mind. You interrogate my client, then you share that information with the FBI and you're a new prosecution witness. No thanks.'

'It won't be like that.'

'Why do you want to talk to her?'

Conversation stopped as Halina arrived with three plates. My pancakes and bacon, Bloch's grilled cheese with chorizo eggs, and a muffin for Lake. Bloch took a pack of anti-bacterial wipes from her jacket, opened it and wiped down her cutlery, all the while never taking her eyes from Lake. He had taken the paper wrapping off the base and was now dismantling the muffin on the plate. Looking through it. Smelling it. Satisfied, he put a piece in his mouth.

Bloch dried her knife and fork on a napkin and plunged it into her eggs.

Lake caught Bloch staring at him.

'You're weird,' said Bloch.

'Least I don't disinfect my cutlery,' he said. 'Anyway, look, whatever Carrie Miller tells me will be confidential. I promise not to share it with the Bureau.'

'Is that a pinkie promise?'

'Don't be like that. I give you my word I won't share anything,' he said.

'If you gave me a signed affidavit to that effect, I'd still tell you to get lost. You haven't answered my question, why do you want to talk to Carrie anyway?'

'Because I've read the Sandman case. I looked over the files, unofficially, talked about it with Delaney. I know what happened. I don't know Daniel Miller. Your client was married to him for a year, she's got the kind of information I need if I'm going to catch him.'

'Sorry, I can't.'

He wiped at the stubble on his chin, ate some more muffin.

'You know, it's in your interests that I catch this guy,' he said.

'Delaney should be alive right now. I want that son of a bitch as bad as you do, but I'm guessing you're talking about something else,' I said.

'There's a case against Carrie Miller, but it's not who they want. They're gonna say she was an accomplice, but really, she's the support act. They want the main event. If I catch him, you can make a deal.

Her old lawyer, Peltier, was holding out for a deal. My courthouse contacts said he was always asking for meetings with the DA. Carrie Miller is much more valuable as a prosecution witness against her husband than a co-defendant, but that value is only realized if the Sandman is in custody.'

He was right. If the Sandman was put on trial, the DA's attitude to Carrie Miller would change overnight. The city was under huge pressure from the media to get a result for the victims' families. Putting Carrie Miller on trial helped alleviate that pressure, but they would do anything to nail Daniel. Even if it meant making a deal with Carrie for her to turn state's evidence against her husband.

'That might work, but there's no time. Carrie Miller goes on trial tomorrow. The case might take a week at most. It took the FBI fourteen months to identify Daniel Miller as the Sandman, and now, a year later, they still haven't caught him. What can you do in a week that they can't?'

Lake leaned back in his chair, rubbed his hands together.

'For a start, he's now active again. We don't know where he's been for a year, but we know now he's back in New York. You see that letter to the *Times* today?'

'I saw it. He's saying Carrie is innocent and he's going to kill more people if they don't drop the case. That's not going to get Carrie much sympathy with a jury.'

'Maybe not, but it's helpful to me,' said Lake.

'How?' asked Bloch.

'Well, now I know his motivation. He doesn't want Carrie going to jail. It helps me get into his mindset.'

'Why is he coming out of hiding now?' I asked.

'It was all over the papers that there might be a deal in the case. Right up until Assistant District Attorney White eight-sixed it and said he was going after Carrie. That's what triggered him.'

'But why come out of hiding at all?'

'Isn't it obvious? He loves his wife. Serial killers have a complex psychological make-up. They might not give a shit about tearing a random stranger to pieces for their own gratification, but that doesn't mean they can't care about someone. There's an inherent narcissism and self-loathing in a lot of serial killers. If they find someone who makes them feel good, even feel loved, that helps normalize them. They start to crave that feeling. It's not exactly love, but it's the closest thing they can get to it. Daniel Miller loves his wife. Or he at least thinks he does, and he's going to take a lot of risks to help her. That's our advantage, but I might need some help to do this, if you could spare Bloch?'

She looked up from her plate, cocked an eyebrow at Lake, then went straight back to her eggs.

'I can't spare my investigator. I told you, I've got a major trial in the morning.'

'If we catch him there won't be a trial. The DA will be falling all over you to make a deal. Look, I don't ask lightly. I could work a lot faster with another pair of hands. And I know Bloch by reputation. I . . .' He trailed off, looked over my shoulder.

He took a sip of hot lemon, his eyebrows clenched, as if he was trying to say something that didn't come easy.

'Look, I have a problem trusting people . . .'

'You have a problem ordering a muffin.'

He nodded, a smile building at the corner of his lips.

'It's a thing, but this is different. Catching monsters is what I do. I could do it faster with Bloch.'

'And why would you trust me?' asked Bloch.

'Because you tried to help my friend. And you're not a cop anymore.'

I watched Bloch put down her fork, wipe her lips with a napkin before she spoke again.

'The name Lake is kind of familiar. When I was working in a sheriff's department in Port Lonely, I heard about a fed named Lake who took out a meth cook house in New Jersey single-handed. Twelve guys with shotguns, AKs, AR-15s. Half of those guys were ex-military. Well trained and well paid to kill anyone who set foot in that house. I heard this guy Lake was shot twice during the firefight. That you?'

Lake met her eyes, his jaw working silently like he was revving up his mouth to spit out a response.

'That's not how it went down and I'm no hero.'

She returned to her eggs, said, 'Lake is okay,' like it was the Declaration of Independence.

Delaney had been willing to put her faith in Lake. Now Bloch was doing the same. I knew better than to doubt either one of them. If they were willing to trust this guy I couldn't ignore that.

'Lake may be okay, but that's not the issue here. No disrespect, Lake, but the FBI and the NYPD had two hundred officers and the entire resources of two law enforcement agencies looking for Daniel Miller for almost two years. What makes you think you can catch him in under a week?'

I was serious. I didn't want to lose Bloch on a hopeless chase when I needed her on the Carrie Miller trial. I liked Lake, but even if he could shoot his way out of a drug den, he wasn't a miracle worker. He seemed to take the point. He looked at me like he was weighing me up. Judging my character, searching my eyes. Finally, he nodded.

'I think I understand the Sandman more than the other agents. He's an opportunist killer, in many ways, but it also looks like he has a careful plan. It's weird. I think he's highly intelligent and can adapt to his environment and the situations he finds himself in with a real clarity of thought that most killers can't even contemplate. It's like chess. He may not know exactly which piece his opponent is going to move, but he has half a dozen strategies in his back pocket ready to go. I can catch him because I work smarter and harder than the feds and cops combined, plus I have a significant advantage.'

'What's that?'

'Unlike the feds, I know how to catch people like Daniel Miller. And I won't make their mistakes. You see, there's a secret that's increasingly difficult for the Bureau to hide. It's embarrassing. It's really a national scandal. They don't want me talking about it, and they sure as hell don't want anyone else to find out.'

'What is it?'

Pushing aside his plate, Lake put both elbows on the table, leaned forward and said, 'What if I told you everything the FBI knows about serial killers is wrong?'

CHAPTER THIRTEEN

THE SANDMAN

It was almost three-thirty in the morning. The Sandman circled the block in his van one more time. Letting his mind wander. Driving helped him to think. It would take the feds a few days to figure out what happened to agent Delaney.

He had to be careful. Her kidnap and murder could have gone sideways any number of times, for any number of reasons. But experience had paid off. That and planning, risk analysis and clear thinking.

The result was a powerful message to law enforcement. And the whole damn city.

The Sandman is back. He can get to anyone. At any time. And the cops should leave Carrie alone.

He thought carefully about every move he made. Every murder had been planned, considered. The risks of capture evaluated and minimized.

He didn't fully understand why he chose certain victims. Sometimes it was clear. Certain women stood out as if they were glistening idols. They were different to the ordinary crowd. The way they walked, or carried their heads high, or even just the way the sun caught their hair, or their skin was particularly fine. With others, it was because of their ordinariness. It was the way they didn't stand out. How they were almost invisible to those around them. A brunette wrapped in a long towel, carrying a surf board across the hot sand at Coney Island beach. Or the blonde who stood on the corner holding a sign, handing out flyers for the restaurant just up the street. But no matter how someone drew his attention, his decision to select them as his next victim came down to a single aspect.

Ultimately, it was the eyes that drew him in.

Beautiful, clear eyes. They sparked something. Something more than anticipation. A heat, which grew into a strange desire.

Not quite rage. Not quite love.

But deeper and darker than both.

It always ended the same way though. He blew gently on their necks, put them to sleep with the needle and then he could go about his work undisturbed. That work sent them to sleep forever. In many ways, he felt as though he was releasing them from this world into an everlasting, undisturbed dream.

He had seen many dead bodies. Something elemental changed when life departed. Blood no longer flowed. They grew cold quickly. The body lost its wonder and became so much dead meat.

Only the eyes retained the reflection of life.

He was fascinated by the human eye. Had been forever. Once, he remembered reading a very old book of crime stories that said a hundred years ago, coroners and medical examiners retained the eyes of murder victims and examined them closely, believing that the image of the killer was somehow still embedded in the back of the eye. Nonsense, of course, but the tale intrigued him.

And so, when his victims were safely dead, he removed the eyes and kept them. At times, in his special place, he would remove the eyes from their jars and hold them in his hands. They were glassy at this stage as the preservative solution had hardened them, like gumballs. He stared at them, wondering if his face was still in there, somewhere.

The sand he used on his victims served two purposes. It would, according to the old stories, make sure they never woke. And it helped hide any traces he may have left behind. He poured the sand into their gaping mouths, red stomachs and hollow eye sockets. Watching the grains stick in their bloody gums and on their teeth. Their bodies a lifeless vessel, and at the same time he felt the power and strength flood into his body.

The Sandman returned his thoughts to the road, and drove past the alleyway on the south side of the block and pulled up at the curb. He felt a mild thrill. It was exhilarating. A rush that began in his stomach and travelled up his spine, into his brain. It was memory. A sumptuous memory that somehow made his body relive the physical intoxication he had experienced that night.

The night he had murdered Lilian Parker and dumped her body in that alleyway.

He got out of the van and made his way across the street. This part of Tribeca was a real mix of cultures. There was a bail bondsman on the corner, next to an artisan coffee shop and a high-end bookstore that mostly sold first editions. Across the street from the bookstore was an all-night laundromat that sat between a dollar store and a ladies' designer clothes store. The evidence for the increase in gentrification of Manhattan continued, and it was curious to see the parts of the city where the old and the new sat side by side.

The door to an apartment complex which sat above these stores was sandwiched between the clothes store and a bakery. He opened the front door with a key and stepped into the hallway.

While surveilling Lilian Parker last year, the Sandman had taken the loft space in the building opposite hers on a monthly lease. It was too small for an apartment, but it suited small businesses who needed a space but couldn't afford to rent in the rest of Manhattan and didn't care what the place looked like. The windows overlooked the street and were high enough on the seventh floor to provide a great view of Lilian Parker's apartment.

A few days after the murder, he had allowed the lease to lapse. But not before making a copy of the front door key, and the key to the loft, just in case he needed to return. Something he often did. He wasn't consciously planning for the future, more like creating options. And tonight was the first time he had been in this building in a year.

While he had one plan for success, he had five more ready if anything went wrong. The Sandman always gave himself options. It was this type of critical analysis and hypothetical problem evaluation that had given him an edge in his day job and made him rich.

He climbed the stairs. There was no elevator in this building. With his hand on the iron rail, he inhaled the familiar odors of the place; the old lady on the second floor who always seemed to be boiling cabbage or burning butter; the damp corner of the third-floor staircase that had rotted through the wooden paneling, turning it dark green; the metallic smell of the rails and the musty odor of old wood and dust which was thrown up with each creaking step of the climb.

He reached the top floor. Put his key in the lock, turned it slowly. Having completed a few cycles of the block, he knew the lights were out in the apartment. The current occupant was Peter Durant. An up-and-coming artist of some repute. The tenant who had taken the loft before the Sandman took his tenure last year had been an artist too. It wasn't that surprising really. In the summer, the loft was flooded with light for most of the day from its two large dormer windows.

The door opened a few inches and the Sandman stopped. Held his breath.

No noise inside. The floorboards were at least as old as the stairs and every inch of them creaked like crazy. He guessed he had managed not to disturb Durant by opening the door. He eased it open further, wincing at the sound from the old hinges, then closed and locked it behind him.

He let out the breath he was holding and turned around to take in the room by the moonlight.

An easel was set up by the window. A table beside it filled with paint bottles, used paint pallets, rags, brushes in glasses of muddy water and pallet knives stained with paint. The room to the left was a bathroom. To the right, a small walk-in closet that was just wide and deep enough to take a thin cot bed. This door was ajar, and he could see a pair of feet jutting out against the open door.

It had been small enough for the Sandman to use as a sleeping area, but Durant was probably a good few inches taller. The Sandman moved around the easel to take a look at the painting first.

It was a self portrait. Not very well done, but he guessed that it was still a work in progress. The painting showed the artist stripped to the waist, wearing only a pair of blue jeans. The musculature was well rendered, but Durant wasn't going to win any prizes even though he captured and used light well.

It was the sort of thing Carrie would love.

He heard noise. Bedsprings groaning. The rasp of rusty door hinges.

'Who the fuck are you?' said a voice.

The Sandman moved to one side and saw Durant in his sweat-pants, bare-chested, standing in the middle of the room. There was paint on his hands, up to his elbows, and flecks covered his stomach and wide chest. If he spent as much time working on his brush strokes as he did lifting weights, he might just get somewhere.

'I'm an admirer of your work,' said the Sandman as he moved around the picture and walked casually toward Durant.

The artist tensed. His hands balled into fists.

'How did you get in here?'

'The door was open,' said the Sandman, taking another step forward.

'Woah, stay back. You need to tell me exactly who you are and what you're doing here.'

'Please, Mr. Durant, relax. I was hoping to discuss a commission.'

'I don't do commissions, now get the fuck out of my apartment.'

He stepped forward, shoulders tensed, right hand in a fist, cocked and ready to unload. The Sandman guessed Durant was six foot four, maybe six five. Two hundred and fifty pounds, easy. There was a jagged scar on his forehead, and his nose had been broken some years ago and not set accurately. None of these imperfections appeared in the self portrait. The Sandman added vanity to what he knew of Durant. That, and the man was clearly a brawler. The scar could have been caused by a few things, but judging by it's angle he guessed it was a broken bottle.

Little raised white scars sat up like maggots on Durant's knuckles.

Casting his gaze behind Durant, he saw two empty bottles of Jack on the floor.

He caught the scent of it on the artist's breath, too.

'Last chance to walk out,' said Durant, taking a step toward the Sandman, who stood very still.

'You go now, or you'll be carried—' Durant didn't finish his sentence. His jaw dropped slack and his eyes widened as he looked down.

The Sandman's arm was extended. In his hand was a skinning knife. The blade was not visible, only the hilt, which touched the skin of Durant's muscular abdomen.

'Do you know what Damascus steel is, Mr. Durant?' he asked.

Durant said nothing. He didn't even breathe. He just stared at his stomach with a look of abject horror frozen on his face.

'They say it is so sharp you don't even feel the cut.'

Taking a step back, he removed the blade from Durant's stomach and dark blood began to erupt from the wound. His breath returned, but not for long.

The Sandman planted his feet, bent his knees, dropped his shoulder and then thrust the blade upwards, using his legs and turning his hip to put power into the strike. A similar movement to a boxer executing an uppercut. The knife was supposed to slip under the chin, through the roof of the mouth and into the brain, killing Durant instantly and before he could scream.

He missed.

There was a sound that gave him gooseflesh. A shrill, scraping and cracking noise. That sound was quickly followed by the *tinkle* and *pitter-patter* of broken teeth bouncing off the polished hardwood floor.

Durant's body dropped suddenly, wrenching the knife from the Sandman's hands. He bent low, put his right foot on the top of Durant's forehead, yanked the blade free from where it had lodged, quite solidly, in his face.

He wiped the knife on Durant's sweatpants, then took a moment to examine it. There was no sheen on the blade, but it had a distinct pattern. It appeared as if someone had cut a slab of silver and blue marble in two, revealing the ripple effect in layers. It was not true Damascus steel, but it was perhaps the closest thing to it. He put it away and looked down at the dead man on the floor.

He grabbed Durant's ankles, dragged his body back into the bathroom. Stepping around the corpse, he got behind it, lifted Durant by the hair into a sitting position, then bent low and locked his arms over the chest. Then he stood and tipped the corpse into the bathtub.

As he washed his hands in the sink, the Sandman hummed a familiar tune.

He dried his hands on the towel and moved to the window. A perfect view of the building opposite. He pulled up the single chair in the room so he could sit while he looked out over Manhattan.

Teresa Vasquez lived in the apartment next to the late Lilian Parker. This view was just as good for watching her as it had been for Lilian last year. Vasquez would die today. He hadn't decided when, but the opportunity would come. He couldn't take the risk of Vasquez testifying against Carrie in the murder of Lilian Parker.

For a moment, all thoughts of killing Teresa Vasquez left him. His mind drew a powerful memory. One Sunday morning that felt like a lifetime ago. Lying in bed beside Carrie, her head on his chest. The smell of her hair. His fingertips gently brushing her shoulder. The only sound was the soft rustle of the sheets as she slowly rubbed her feet together. She did that when she was tired. It was one of those thousands of little things that he loved about her. It was those things he clung to. Those memories were important. He was good at remembering details, facts, patterns. His emotional memory was different. There were snatches of images from his childhood. So fleeting and abstract that he sometimes wondered if he had invented them. His time with Carrie became imprinted on his brain like a movie reel. He could recall almost all of it. And those intimate moments were a cool drink of water for his mind. So vital and unique.

He enjoyed killing. The sensation of taking life sent shudders of pleasure through him. It was only now that he was apart from Carrie that he realized how powerful his feelings had become for her. He wanted her. He wanted to lie in that bed, with her head on his chest, her feet kneading the sheets. He wanted the smell of her, the warmth and the sensation of belonging to her, and she to him. He knew it from the first moment he saw her.

He loved Carrie Miller. She was the only person he had or would ever love.

And that made her the most important woman in the world.

Worth fighting for.

Worth dying for.

Carrie should never have been put on trial. That was something he had not expected to happen. He could not let her be separated from him again. There would be a time, in the next few days, when they would be reunited. When her trial was over and her worries behind her. When he had killed Chester Morris, cut off his head and put it in that bag, when he had killed Delaney, it was for a different reason than the mere pleasure of the kill.

Now, the Sandman killed to protect Carrie.

He killed for one reason. The purest reason.

He killed for love. And there was a lot more killing to be done.

CHAPTER FOURTEEN

KATE

Harry pulled his tiny, convertible, racing-green sportscar to a halt at the gates to Old Meadow Road at eight fifty-nine in the morning. He was a good driver, thought Kate. He needed to be. This was a European car, probably British. It had wood on the dash. Real wood. And the roof leaked. The tires were too small, the engine was too loud, and with the low profile it felt like Kate had just spent half an hour on the freeway with her ass on a skateboard strapped to a lawnmower engine. Harry had told her the car was vintage. A classic. Kate had grown up in New Jersey. And in Jersey, a car being described as a classic was another way of saying the exhaust was about to fall off the damn thing, if the chassis didn't break in half first.

There were only a few protestors outside the private road, and they hadn't seen this car before, so they didn't give Kate and Harry any hassle. Kate opened the electronic gate with the key fob Carrie had given her last night, and Harry drove through and then on to Carrie's house.

Kate got out of the car as soon as Harry cranked up the hand-brake. It was a two seater, but there was a small space between the back seat and the trunk. He reached over the back of the seat and retrieved a piece of two-by-four. Harry got out of the car, then bent down and wedged the length of wood between the brake pedal and the seat.

'If the handbrake doesn't work, then why crank it on?' asked Kate.

'It makes me feel better,' said Harry.

'How old is this car?'

'It's about as old as I am,' he said.

'*That* old?' she said, with a smile.

'Apart from the handbrake, this car is in perfect working order. Just like its owner. It's *fast*, chic and it handles well.'

Harry took a while getting up. One hand on his lower back, which had been giving him problems lately. Kate came around to his side of the car and gently laced her arm over his to steady him as he rose. He didn't complain. Instead, he gave her one of his smiles when he got fully upright. Harry was still a good-looking man, and he was charming, but it was the kind of smile a father gives to his daughter.

'Fast, huh,' said Kate.

'We go a lot faster when we're going downhill these days.'

She retrieved the files from the trunk and together they made their way toward the front door of Carrie Miller's house.

'How do you want to handle this?' she asked.

'I was about to ask you the same question. This is your case. I'm just the consultant.'

'Come on, Harry. You were a judge for twenty years. How would you do it?'

He considered this for a moment, said, 'I think we go slow. Let's get her talking first. Easy, open questions. When she's loosened up, we can get to the more difficult stuff.'

As they reached the front door, they realized it was open. Just an inch or two of a gap. They paused. It was likely Carrie Miller had seen them pull into the driveway from her kitchen. She probably went straight to the front door and opened it for them, like she had the day before.

But neither Harry nor Kate touched the door.

Not yet.

'Mrs. Miller? Carrie?' called Kate.

They listened. Heard nothing.

Harry called out this time. Waited.

Silence.

From his jacket, Harry slid an old Colt 1911 from the worn leather shoulder strap. Racked a round into the chamber, held the gun low and pushed the door with his finger tips. It swung all the way open. Harry raised his hand, indicating that Kate should stay outside.

'I'll be behind you,' she said.

Harry tutted, shook his head, then stepped into the house. Inside, there was no sound from a radio or TV. Kate called out. No answer. No one in the living room, and no one in the kitchen. Harry moved quicker now toward the stairs. A sense of urgency rising in them both. They called out again. Nothing in return. The bedrooms and bathrooms were empty. No sign of a struggle. Nothing out of place. Bed made neatly. A set of white silk pajamas were laid on the pillow.

Kate moved quickly back down the stairs, leaving Harry in the main bedroom. She went outside.

No one around the back at the pool. Daniel Miller's sportscar was still in the garage beside Carrie's. These were the only cars Kate had seen on the property during her first visit. She set down the case files on the porch, took her phone from her purse and called Carrie Miller's cell.

It was switched off.

'She knew we were coming this morning, right?' said Harry as he reached the bottom of the staircase in the hallway.

'I told her last night. Maybe she took a cab to the store?'

'This isn't the type of neighborhood where people use cabs, or Ubers. If she was going somewhere, and didn't want to drive, she'd call for a town car. But why? Why not use her own car? And why isn't she here?'

'I'll call Peltier,' said Kate.

He picked up straight away.

'Otto, we're out here at Carrie's house. Both cars are in the garage. The front door is open and she's not here.'

'I don't like the sound of that. Have you tried her cell phone?'

'It's turned off.'

'Shit, do you think . . .?' But he didn't finish the thought. The lawyer sounded rattled. There was genuine concern in his voice.

'Do I think the Sandman took her? I have no idea what's going on.'

'Maybe we should call the police?' he said.

'No,' said Kate. 'Not yet. There's no sign of forced entry. And it's a condition of her bail she resides in this property. If the cops think she jumped bail they'll get an arrest warrant.'

'An arrest warrant is one thing, but Carrie could be in danger. I saw the papers today. The Sandman killed two people yesterday. One of them an FBI agent.'

Kate had spoken to Eddie last night, after Delaney's body was found. He also got a brief mention in one of the news articles she'd read that morning. The *Post* recorded that Eddie Flynn and two private investigators, Melissa Bloch and Gabriel Lake, were at the scene of the murder last night, but it wasn't known if they had any official involvement in the investigation. There was even a picture of the three of them coming out of Delaney's building.

'I know, she was a friend of Eddie's. He's been up all night with the FBI.'

'Oh my god, this is so terrible. I'm so worried, Kate. This is not like Carrie. I think we have to call the police. I'd never forgive myself if something has happened to her . . .'

Kate didn't know what to think. She heard the genuine concern in Otto's voice. He seemed to put the same passion into his cases as Kate did. It was one of the things that first warmed Kate to Otto.

'Maybe she just went out for a breath of air around the development. The case is all over the news again. Her husband is back and killing people. That might be a lot to take in for her.'

'I suppose that's right. She's been through hell. When she was indicted, every one of her friends dropped her. She is utterly alone and of course she's completely innocent. The one thing she had was that Daniel was out of her life. She thought he'd be gone for good. Into hiding. This must be devastating for her.'

'Then there's no need to call the cops and make everything worse by having her arrested for breach of bail. She'll come back. Let's give her some time before we call the cops. I'll have another look in the house and I'll call you back,' said Kate, then hung up.

'The closet is still full of clothes. There's a set of pajamas on the bed. Maybe she did just go for a walk around the neighborhood and lost track of time,' said Harry.

'Yeah, I'm sure that's all,' said Kate, gripping her cell phone tightly, then letting her teeth dig into her lip. She didn't like this situation. An innocent woman, in charge of all her senses, about to go on trial for multiple homicide, does *not* miss an appointment with her legal team. That just doesn't happen. Even if her serial killer husband made a sudden reappearance in New York last night.

Harry stepped out of the house, put his gun away and shielded his eyes from the sun as he looked around the grounds and took in the view of the neighborhood.

'She must be on the road somewhere, there's no way she'd make it past those protestors on foot. If she wasn't going far then that might explain leaving the door open. I went out last week and left my apartment door open by mistake,' said Kate.

Harry looked at her, incredulous.

'The latch on the door is faulty. Unless you really slam it, the door won't close properly. I told the super, but he hasn't gotten around to fixing it. I thought I'd closed it last Tuesday, but when I got back my door was open and my TV was gone.'

'You never mentioned this,' said Harry. 'I'm old, but I wouldn't forget a thing like that.'

'I didn't tell Eddie either. Since it happened, I haven't been able to sleep. My neighbor suddenly has a TV with a really good sound system. And he likes to play it loud.'

'Why didn't you . . .' said Harry, then stopped. Because he already knew the answer.

'*Ah*, you didn't want Bloch to find out,' he said.

Kate nodded, said, 'I have to live in that building. It's just a TV. It's not worth it.'

She picked up the case files and put them into the trunk of Harry's car.

'Let's take a drive. See if we can spot Carrie,' said Kate.

Harry closed the front door over but didn't fully shut it. They got in the car and Harry drove around Meadow Road. There was no sign of Carrie. Kate suggested they take a look around Old Westbury anyway. They passed the antique stores, high-end furniture showrooms and boutique salons. There were three car dealerships in the area. Ferrari, Land Rover and Mercedes. It was that kind of place. No sign of Carrie, so after a half hour or so Harry turned around and headed back to the house. Two news crews were setting up outside the gates and more protestors had arrived. Around fifteen of them now, and they were starting their chants.

KIL-LER CARRIE, LOCK HER UP!

KIL-LER CARRIE, LOCK HER UP!

Soon as they pulled off Meadow Road, Kate saw the car in the driveway.

A midnight blue 1965 Mustang. The driver's door opened and Eddie Flynn got out. Kate exited Harry's car, made her way over the gravel driveway toward him.

Kate was about to explain when Eddie said, 'Peltier called me to see if I was alright after last night, and to express his remorse for Delaney. He asked if I knew where Carrie Miller might be. Don't tell me she's jumped bail, please.'

Crunching through the gravel, Harry joined Kate. They exchanged a look.

'Hard to say,' said Kate. 'Doesn't look like she's packed anything. She hasn't taken her car. There's a set of night clothes laid out on the bed, like it's just been made this morning. No sign of a break-in either. The only strange thing is she isn't here, and her front door was open when we arrived.'

'Does she have a maid service?'

'Not that I know of,' said Kate.

'Let's take a look inside.'

Kate followed Eddie into the house. He looked around downstairs. The lounge, kitchen, everything was immaculate. They went upstairs. He checked the closet, the guest bedrooms, the two guest bathrooms and then the bathroom attached to the master bedroom.

An electric toothbrush sat in a charging point above the sink. It was the only toothbrush in the bathroom – there were none in the cabinets. Eddie took a piece of toilet paper, lifted the toothbrush and grabbed the bristles with the paper, examined it then threw it in the toilet bowl. Kneeling he placed his hand flat on the shower basin, then got up and looked at the tub.

He nodded, then Kate followed him downstairs to the hallway.

'What do you think?' he asked.

'I don't know,' said Kate. 'There's no struggle. She left in a hurry, that's for sure.'

'You're right,' said Eddie. 'Her toothbrush is dry. So is the tub and the shower basin.'

'What does that prove?' asked Harry.

'It proves she probably didn't leave this morning. You remember her last night. Even in the depths of whatever hell she's living through she is at least looking after her appearance. I'd at least expect to find some dampness in the toothbrush or the shower.'

Kate folded her arms, looked down at the tiled floor of the hallway.

'The silk pajamas on the bed were the ones she was supposed to wear to bed last night. She must've left after dark, when there were no protestors at the gate. The first reports of the Sandman at Grady's Inn made the ten o'clock news. All I know is she's been gone overnight.'

'Shit,' said Harry. 'She's jumped bail, hasn't she? Trial starts tomorrow. The nerves kick in around now. I've seen it before. Problem is, we don't have a defense if we don't have a client.'

'We need to find her. Where's Bloch?' asked Kate.

'She's with Gabriel Lake. They're going to try and hunt down the Sandman.'

'You mentioned him last night. Who is he again?'

'He's ex-FBI. Used to work with Delaney. He's smart, but a little unusual.'

'And this unusual guy and Bloch are going to find the Sandman?'

'Well, give them a chance. They just started,' said Eddie.

'So where is Carrie?' asked Harry.

Kate thought back to yesterday. She had never seen anyone who looked so tortured, so defeated and broken, as Carrie Miller. The options were not good.

'If she saw the news she was probably frightened out of her skin, and ran,' said Kate. 'The other possibilities are no better. If she didn't run, maybe he came and took her. Or maybe she's not running at all and she's lying in some hotel bedroom or at the bottom of a . . .'

She didn't finish that thought. Didn't need to. She saw that Eddie and Harry had already considered it. No one has infinite strength of mind. What Carrie has been through, and survived, others would not. It's not a failing. It's an illness. And for some, suicide seems like the only way out.

The only sound came from the protestors, five hundred yards away on the other side of the gate. Harry and Eddie looked at one another, but said nothing. They were fearful for Carrie, and somehow that made Kate even more afraid.

Her phone began vibrating with a call. The number on the display was familiar.

'Kate Brooks,' she said, answering.

'Miss Brooks, this is Center Street clerk's office. You're required to attend before Judge Stoker at noon for an emergency hearing in the Carrie Miller trial.'

Kate felt a dull pain in the back of her neck. The beginnings of a stress headache. What brought it on for Kate was knowing she'd just been ambushed. She knew exactly what the emergency hearing was about, but she asked anyway just for confirmation.

'And the nature of the hearing?'

'Bail,' said the clerk, and told her which courtroom and floor to attend before hanging up.

Kate dialed Peltier's number.

'You talked to Eddie, after we spoke. Who else did you talk to?' she asked.

'No one,' he said.

'I just got a call from the clerk's office. There's a bail hearing in Carrie's case at noon. The DA thinks she's jumped bail. The only people who know she's missing are Eddie, Harry, you and me.'

'I told you, I spoke to no one else. I don't want Carrie arrested. I swear I didn't speak to anyone other than Eddie,' he said.

'Okay, I'm sorry. We'll talk later,' she said, then hung up.

'Who did he talk to?' asked Harry.

'Nobody but us, he says. The way he sounded, I think he's telling the truth,' said Kate.

'Then how did the courthouse know there's an issue with her bail?' asked Harry.

'There's only two explanations,' said Eddie. 'Either Otto told the police, or they knew already.'

'But how could they know?' asked Kate.

'Because I think there was a lot more in that warrant than just seizing Otto Peltier's old files. The FBI are bugging his phone.'

CHAPTER FIFTEEN

Extract from the Journal of Carrie Miller

May 29

I still felt really bad about telling a lie to the police officer last week. I hadn't meant to. I was just so upset and freaking out and I just wanted him to go away. But even after I'd asked Danny about it, I still felt awful.

I decided to ask him about it again the next day. Told him I felt guilty. Was it a crime to lie to a cop? I wanted to call the precinct and speak to him, get this all straightened out. He told me there was no need. He went to his laptop, found the local news website and clicked on a story. I read it and felt better. The police were carrying out routine checks on the registered owners of certain types of panel trucks. It was believed the Sandman might have used a vehicle similar.

Danny said he didn't want to get involved in that case. He didn't own a van, not really. There was a van registered to one of the companies he owned, but he wasn't even sure they still had it. He invests in a lot of small businesses and flips them for profit from time to time. He said there would be no point in wasting the police's time over it when really what the cops needed to do was go out and find the actual killer. I said I agreed with him. There was no point now, and I felt a lot better about the whole thing.

Things between Danny and I were great in the days after the cop's visit. He even came home early a couple of times and we cooked together, had some wine and more than a few laughs. It was easy and fun and warm. Like the early days, when we just started going out.

Until last night. He didn't get home until after three in the morning. Showered in our bathroom and came to bed with his hair wet. I pretended to be asleep. He got up and was out of the house before I woke this morning. Probably wanted to avoid the inevitable argument.

When he got home later I decided not to be that nagging wife and just mentioned, casually, that he was working so hard and he looked a little tired. That's all I said. But I saw that flicker of irritation passing over his features nonetheless.

After dinner he seemed more like my Danny. I guess maybe he was just tired and hungry. He insisted I put my feet up with a glass of white wine while he loaded the dishwasher. When I was settled on the couch, glass in hand, he came over and put a ring box on the coffee table in front of me.

He said he loved me and he would never stop showing me how much I meant to him. Inside were two rings. One was a rose gold ring with red stones, the other was silver with a smoky gemstone in the center. I tried them on. The silver one was a little tight, but it fit. They were gorgeous. He knows my taste so well. I told him he doesn't have to keep buying me jewelry, that what I really wanted was him. Danny time. We kissed, and he went back into the kitchen to finish cleaning up.

I turned on the TV and found our favorite movie was already playing on TCM.

I made him watch it when we were dating and he loved it just as much as I did. It has kind of become our thing. My favorite movies are Pretty Woman, Dirty Dancing, Beaches (I cry every time) and this one. Because it scares me to hell.

He came back into the lounge, saw the wine and the movie playing and said he was sorry, but he had to go out and meet a client. Said he'd just finished a project, but he was already planning for the next one. He leaned over the couch, kissed me on the cheek. I told him I didn't mind. It was okay.

It wasn't okay.

He put on his coat as I settled in to watch The Night of the Hunter, with Robert Mitchum.

As he passed by the couch, Daniel glanced at the screen, and sang in his husky baritone, 'Leeaaannning, leeeaaaning, leaning on the everlasting arms . . .'

In the movie, Mitchum plays a pastor and serial killer who finds out the proceeds of a bank robbery are hidden somewhere on the property of the robber's widow. Mitchum befriends and marries the widow so *he can find the money. He murders his new bride with a switchblade, then discovers that one of the kids has hidden the money in their ragdoll. Lilian Gish plays a tough old lady who takes in the orphaned children to protect them from the murderous pastor.*

It's my favorite scene. Dark, past midnight. Mitchum sitting on a tree stump in the garden, singing that old Christian hymn, 'leaning on the everlasting arms . . .', while Gish sits in silhouette on a rocking chair, behind the porch screen, a shotgun cradled in her arms. To show she is not afraid, she actually joins in the song. Until one of the children approaches with a candle, lighting up the porch screen and obscuring Mitchum's menacing figure with the glare. When Gish leans forward and blows out the candle, Mitchum has vanished into the night.

Ever since I first saw that movie, I couldn't get the song out of my head. Here was Mitchum, a stone-cold killer, singing in such a beautiful baritone voice. And a hymn, no less. He was someone who sent people into the everlasting arms, via his switchblade. He was so badass, evil and unafraid that he sat outside that house – singing. It gave me the chills every damn time.

I didn't hear the front door close. Didn't hear the garage door open or the sound of Daniel gunning the engine on that sports car of his. I just saw the reflected red glow on the TV. Turning around, I looked through the window, watched his tail lights disappear down the lane like two great red eyes, receding into the night.

I watched the movie, fell asleep on the couch for an hour or so and my phone woke me up.

A few days ago, I'd read all about the Sandman case. I was curious after the cop's visit, and now my phone sent me an alert when there were new articles. I clicked on the alert. There were two news stories.

The Sandman had killed two women last night in their apartment. The police were appealing for witnesses. Second news story was more on the Sandman's previous victim. Margaret Sharpe. There was a picture of her in a red and white checkered summer dress, wearing vivid red lipstick, her hair all curled up in a fifties kind of style. She was smiling.

I dropped my phone.

Picked it up and pinched the image of Margaret Sharpe with my fingers, enlarging the picture.

She wore a pair of silver earrings shaped like a rose.

CHAPTER SIXTEEN

BLOCH

Lake said he had a car, but it was in the shop for repair.

Normally Bloch wasn't much for conversation. She liked cars and had modified her modest family Jeep to the extent that it had largely become a different vehicle. Mainly this involved reinforcing the chassis, the drive shaft and all of the wheel components to cope with a newly installed V6 pushrod engine with two superchargers. The bodywork she left alone, so that when she put her foot down your jaw hit the floor in shock around the same time your spine fused to the seat.

'What kind of car do you drive?' asked Bloch.

'Oh, a blue one,' said Lake.

This was going to be a tough week. They took Bloch's Jeep into Tribeca. Lake had suggested they start there.

'What's in Tribeca?' asked Bloch.

'Lilian Parker's apartment. I want to check it out.'

'Why that victim?'

'The witnesses who are set to testify against Carrie Miller. Chester Morris is already dead. That leaves Teresa Vasquez who saw a man and a woman hanging around outside the building the night Lilian Parker was killed. Then there's the witness in the Nielsen case, but I'm not ready to go there yet. The Sandman will be targeting those witnesses, so he might be in the area. That's reason number one. Reason number two, I need to get a first-hand look at the scene – get a better sense of who this guy is.'

'You're writing a profile?' said Bloch as she pulled into traffic. 'I thought you said the FBI's methods for catching serial killers was all wrong.'

He smiled at her from the passenger seat, or at least pulled his lips into something resembling a smile.

'There are multiple schools of thought on psychological profiling and repeat offender behavior. I have my own way.'

'And what is that?'

'You ever heard of George Metesky, the Mad Bomber?'

Bloch nodded, made a left turn. The entire field of criminal profiling and its public fascination was spawned by one man in a double-breasted suit. This was the first case of modern offender profiling. It has been the example set for the discipline for more than sixty years, and the circumstances of the case remain fascinating for those studying patterns of violent repeat offending.

'You know the tale they spin in training. The real story is more interesting. In November 1940, a bomb was found on the windowsill of the Consolidated Edison utility company with a note wrapped around it calling Con Edison crooks. It was initialed F.P. Another bomb was found close to the plant in September 1941. In December of that year the police got a letter from F.P. saying he wouldn't plant any more bombs for the duration of the war as he was a patriot, but after that he would make Con Edison pay for what he called their *dastardly deeds*.

'He made good on his promise, and from 1951 to 1956 he planted more than thirty bombs, some at Con Edison and the rest at New York landmarks like Radio City Music Hall, Grand Central Terminal, the Paramount Theatre at Times Square, and more. He injured around twenty people, but never killed anyone. The NYPD thought it was just a matter of time before that happened so Captain John Cronin brought in a criminologist and psychiatrist named James A. Brussel—'

'Who wrote the first offender profile,' said Bloch. 'It was pretty accurate.'

'It was wrong in some places and general enough to be accurate in others, but it was the description of the Mad Bomber that caught the media's attention. Brussel made two predictions. He said that when they caught the man, he would be wearing a double-breasted suit *and* the bomber would wear the jacket buttoned up.'

Bloch smiled at the memory. She had been seated in a class with other officers while an FBI instructor had told this same story at the beginning of an afternoon course on how the Bureau uses profilers to catch serial offenders.

'He was right though. When they caught George Metesky he was wearing that suit, and it was buttoned up,' said Bloch.

'That's some real Sherlock Holmes shit, right there. And the newspapers loved it. Serial killer profilers wear that story like a badge of honor. But here's the thing – the profile didn't help the cops catch Metesky. Not one bit. They guessed correctly it was an ex-employee with a grudge. Metesky got his lungs scorched in a furnace, so he had a grudge alright, but Con Edison hid their old worker compensation files from the cops. A company clerk named Alice Kelly found Metesky's file and saw he had used the same phrases in his complaint letters to the company as he had in his correspondence with the cops. But Brussel, he thought Metesky was a meticulous individual given his dedication to bringing down Con Edison. Plus, he thought his handwriting made him a pristine man in appearance and comportment. That's why he thought Metesky would be wearing that suit. It was a lucky guess based on a bogus theory about handwriting, but it shouldn't have been. There was enough information there to tell anyone without a degree in psychiatry that Metesky would be wearing that suit, and that he always buttoned it up.'

'I don't see how.'

'Think about it.'

Bloch pulled up at a set of traffic lights, engaged the handbrake and took her hands from the wheel for a moment and let them lay on her lap.

Sixty seconds passed, and the light turned green. She said, 'I don't get it. Tell me.'

'First bomb was in 1940,' said Lake. 'The target – Consolidated Edison. The Mad Bomber had a grudge against the company. He'd lost his job because he got hurt and couldn't work. He waited ten years or more, to 1951, to start another bombing campaign, which meant he was still sore at the company, and he was still too sick to find another job. If he had been able to move on and find new employment, he wouldn't have been leaving bombs around the city and crying out for justice against Con Edison. In the 1950s fashion changed. Most men wore suits, and the new cut was narrow lapels, short slim-fitting jackets and skinny ties. In the thirties and forties men wore double-breasted suits. Metesky was wearing a double-breasted suit because it was the last suit he'd bought while he was still working. He couldn't afford the new style.'

'Okay, so how did Brussel know he'd wear that suit buttoned up?'

'That's easy, you ever wore a double-breasted suit?' asked Lake.

Bloch shook her head.

'There's like another foot of fabric over the stomach. The jacket folds over itself before you can button it once on the inside, and then two buttons on the outside. It's designed to be worn buttoned at all times. If you don't button up it feels like there's a parachute hanging off your shoulders. The jacket just flips inside out. If you watch any movies set in the thirties or forties, everyone wearing a double-breasted suit has it buttoned up.'

'What's your point?' asked Bloch.

'All of the evidence needed to catch Metesky was there already, staring straight at the investigators. They didn't need a psychiatrist or criminologist. My point is you don't need a profiler to tell you which way the wind blows, you just lick your finger and stick it in the air.'

The Jeep pulled up at the curb in a parking spot just in front of an alleyway on their right.

'This is the place?' asked Bloch.

'This is it.'

A brown Ford Sedan was parked up just in front of them. Two guys in the front. Street clothes and earpieces. One of them was drinking something from a thermos cup.

'The FBI are here. Protection detail for the witness, Teresa Vasquez,' said Bloch.

'That's fine. We won't interfere. The Sandman dumped her body in that alley. Let's take a look there first.'

'And what exactly are we gonna do?' asked Bloch.

'We're going to lick our fingers and stick them in the air.'

*

Surprisingly there are few large, open alleyways in Manhattan. Most of them are gated. This one was open. Bloch watched Lake lead the way. He walked slowly, but confidently. There was a little swagger to his step. Yet he didn't seem to be aware of it. He was not a self-conscious man. If he were, he'd shave that stubble, iron his shirt and get his suit pressed. She got the sense that all of his focus was outside of himself. As if he could talk intensely on a complicated subject for hours without realizing his ass was on fire.

The alleyway was perhaps fifteen feet wide but didn't feel so spacious. The iron fire escapes on the buildings either side narrowed the gap. Bloch looked up toward the oyster-colored clouds. At the top of the buildings the ironwork fire escapes seemed thin, inky traces against the paper sky. Apart from three dumpsters and some garbage and cardboard boxes piled beside them, the alleyway was empty. Even though it wasn't jam packed with garbage it sure smelled like it. The alley went on for fifty feet, dog legged left for another twenty. The red brickwork was dirty and chipped here and there, and there were even some fly posters stuck to the wall. One for a rock band advertising a gig that happened three years ago, and some others that the elements had torn down off the brick, leaving only ripped fragments of paper clinging to the wall.

It was a sad place to die.

'They never found Lilian's cameo brooch,' said Lake. 'And it was her mother, Joan Parker, who informed police it was missing. That cameo belonged to Joan's mother, Lilian's grandmother. The rest of the victims' families will have the jewelry returned after the trial. It means so much to Joan and they can't find that piece.'

'I read her statement. Daniel Miller probably still has that brooch hidden somewhere.'

Bloch had brought her iPad from the car. She switched it on and opened the zip folder. Denise had scanned every document in the Carrie Miller case onto the firm's computer system. Every piece of evidence, every motion, every scrap of paper was indexed so that it could be accessed in seconds. Double tapping on the file marked

'Lilian Parker,' Bloch brought up all the witness statements and photographs of the scene. Lilian had been found atop a dumpster, on a hot night – June 3 last year. She was dressed in jeans, boots and a white tee. He left her like all the others, mutilated and with sand poured over the body and into the empty eye cavities.

No one had heard anything. None of the occupants of the buildings on either side of the alley. Several stated they had their windows open because it was so hot, and they complained about the smell of garbage, and the noise from the damn cats, but the heat was worse than the shrill baying of alley cats.

Lake stopped at the dumpsters, which were gathered in a row on the left, just before the alley turned.

He looked back the way he had come, then bent down, checked the ground. Standing up, he checked his surroundings again. There were two ground-level exits into the alley. One for each building. Both were fire doors, with no way to open them from the outside.

'The alarm was working on the fire door for Lilian Parker's building,' he said.

Bloch nodded, then raised her head. There was a ladder, hooked up, ten feet off the ground, leading to the first rung of the fire escape. In order to get down the side of the building from Lilian Parker's floor, Lilian would have had to pass by at least twenty-one windows. Three on each floor. And some of them were open that night. It didn't seem likely to Bloch that Lilian, nor anyone else, could've gone down the fire escape without either being seen or being heard, no matter what time of night.

'How did he get her into the alleyway?' asked Bloch.

Nodding, Lake said, 'That's a real good question. She didn't come from her building. Fire doors didn't open because there were no alarms, and she didn't come down the fire escape. You can't get a truck into this street with the garbage, so he didn't capture her somewhere else and move her body here. She came into the alley from the street?'

'Had to be that way,' said Bloch, nodding.

'This guy takes risks, but *calculated* risks. Grabbing Lilian Parker off a busy Manhattan street and dragging her into an alleyway doesn't make sense. Somebody would've seen or heard something.'

There were two distinct patterns in the method and execution of the Sandman's crimes. In the beginning, victims were found on Coney Island beach, half buried in the sand. After the fourth victim was found, the twenty-four-hour police patrols along the entire length of the strip forced a change in the Sandman's pattern. He began targeting victims in their homes. Except this victim.

'Let's go upstairs,' said Lake.

The building supervisor was unlike any Bloch had ever seen. His name was Dennis, he was neatly dressed, didn't smell, didn't have the crack of his ass on display every time he turned around, and he was polite and co-operative when Lake told him they were here to assist the FBI with their investigations. Bloch didn't think Dennis was going to last in this job.

He led them up to the seventh floor in the elevator, took out his keys and began to work on the door locks for Lilian Parker's apartment. The door had at least four locks, with four different keys needed to open them. All told, it took Dennis close to a minute to unlock the door. A cat flap was built into the bottom of the door, but it was way too small to be a point of entry.

'So, any idea when I can get rid of the furniture and lease this place out again?' asked Dennis.

'Shouldn't be too much longer. The Bureau is not insensitive to your business needs, Dennis,' said Lake. 'Thank you for your co-operation.'

That was Dennis's cue to leave.

This was a studio apartment. Everything in one room. Soon as Bloch stepped inside, she saw the bed in the corner, a couch and TV opposite and behind that some cupboards, a fridge and what looked like a camping stove. The single door off the room led to a small shower and toilet. No bath.

She looked again at the locks on the door, this time from the inside. All were pretty new and looked solid. Bloch knew a little about lock-picking, from a burglary case she'd handled many years ago. Lilian had all the best lock brands, and they were accurately fitted. Even for a talented lock-pick, it would take at least five minutes to get through those locks, and it would be damn hard to do that without making any noise.

Lilian Parker had not led an extravagant lifestyle. There was little in the apartment of any value. A litter box sat just left of the TV, which was at least ten years old, and what little furniture there was in the room had been scratched up. A cat tower in the kitchen, with mirrors, string and chew toys hanging from its platforms. There was more cat food than real food in the kitchen cupboards. The cat tower hadn't stopped the pet leaving scratch marks on the base of the bed, the nightstand, or the little coffee table. Two ceramic cat bowls on the kitchen floor.

'Her neighbor, one floor up, took the cat,' said Lake. 'Just in case you were wondering.'

Bloch nodded; she *had* been wondering. She couldn't abide animals being abandoned and was glad the cat had a new owner. Hopefully someone who would love it as much as Lilian had.

She approached the window, checked the street below. Even at this hour, there were people all around. It was a busy part of the city – one that never got quiet.

'What do you think?' asked Lake.

'I don't know. I wish he'd tried to kill her in this apartment. Somebody would've heard him trying to get through her door.'

Bloch and Lake didn't speak for a moment. They looked at each other. And their minds were one.

CHAPTER SEVENTEEN

EDDIE

There are some people in this world who lack empathy.

I don't know what it is about the way judges are appointed, but the lawyers with little capacity for empathy have a head start when it comes to getting on the bench. I can count the judges I would trust to look after a dog on one hand. His Honor Judge Leo Stoker was not one of them. I wouldn't trust him to babysit an alligator. He caught a big case as a young DA – the prosecution of a number of low-level mob guys, mostly Albanians. He put fifty-eight of them away within eighteen months, and even though they were immediately replaced on the street, and his actions were like a flea bite on the ass of the Albanian mob – it sure looked good in the newspapers and on TV. That was the way things worked in New York – if you couldn't manage to do something truly great, appearing as if you have done something great is just as good, if not better.

Stoker rode that wave all the way to a judicial appointment. He had ten years on the bench behind him, and seemed content to cruise along, sending as many people to prison as possible. Clearing cases was all a judge had to do. That was their function – to get as many folks through the system as fast as possible, and while most took at least some time to make sure that due process was followed, Stoker had never been burdened by any notions of justice. He punched his ticket at nine a.m. Cleared his case docket. Went home and drank. Played golf on the weekends.

Stoker never married, which was unusual. To get enough time and cases under your belt as an attorney usually left at least a couple of broken marriages behind – but not Stoker. It kind of made sense, as marriage is supposed to be everlasting devotion to another – something Stoker was incapable of comprehending. The word in the backrooms and corridors of Center Street was he liked high-priced call girls and had a couple of detectives from vice on his payroll to make sure his activities never caused him any public embarrassment. His public profile was important to him, and he would be seen out in restaurants with girls half his age who looked like catalogue models.

He liked to keep it quiet that these girls *did* come out of a catalogue.

His corruption was not only professional, but personal.

He sat now in Center Street, looking down at me and my team from on high. His fingers were laced together, a streak of oil or wax through his neat black hair swept it back from his eyes. His tan never waned, no matter the time of year, and the paler spots around his eyes gave away his tanning-bed regime. His skin always had a sheen to it, as if he sprayed not only his hair, but his whole face with lacquer.

'Mr. Flynn, I will get to you in a moment. Mr. White, I understand you have a motion at this time?'

Drew White was one of the outstanding assistant district attorneys in the city. He was also one of the city's outstanding assholes. He was on his feet, buttoning his suit jacket. I never judge anyone by their physical appearance. White stood now, a little over five foot two. Nobody mentioned the two-inch elevated heels he wore, at least not to his face. The criminal defense attorneys, and most of the women he worked with, were all too happy to wait until they made it to a bar after work to make fun of him. He had a reputation for being very hands-on with the younger assistant district attorneys, but only if they were female. I'd heard that the DA's office had quietly promoted or let go of no less than five female assistant prosecutors who had the audacity to complain that they were being harassed by White. These were only rumors, but Kate had made it her business to try and find these women. Suing companies and institutions for sexual harassment was Kate's real passion, and she was damn good at it. The rumors included an attempted rape at a DA's Christmas party. He had apparently spiked the drink of a young female prosecutor, six months into her job. Two secretaries who had spotted him leaving with her managed to haul her out of the cab before White could take her somewhere private. The gossip was that there was worse still, and only a rape kit that had been mysteriously lost by forensics had saved his ass from a charge.

Before White spoke, he turned and looked at me, Harry and Kate, making sure the judge couldn't see his face.

As his eyes passed over Kate, his gaze lingered. He smiled at her. Just briefly, but it sure wasn't friendly. It was the way a drunk guy smiles at a cheeseburger at four o' clock in the morning. It was a hungry, creepy look. Then he turned and began to introduce his prosecution team to the judge.

'Euuugh,' said Kate, 'is that a new prosecution tactic or something? Make your opponent feel physically sick?'

'Is that how young men flirt these days?' asked Harry. 'For a second I thought he was having a stroke.'

'Your Honor,' began White, 'it has come to my office's attention that Carrie Miller has breached her bail terms. As you know, she is technically under house arrest. She is not at her property. We would ask that the court revoke bail.'

'Is this true, Mr. Flynn?' asked Judge Stoker.

As I got up to answer the judge, I reminded myself of the few legal rules I was unwilling to break. One was telling the judge a bare-faced lie. At least one that he might actually know is a lie.

'My co-counsel, Kate Brooks, and my firm's consultant, Harry Ford, were unable to locate her at the property this morning. I would like to know how this came to the attention of the District Attorney's office. We were in the process of locating our client when we got the call to attend at this hearing,' I said.

'That does not concern you, Mr. Flynn. I believe there is only one course of action here – I'm revoking bail and issuing an arrest warrant for your client. Any other motions, Mr. White?'

'Yes, Your Honor, I would like to adjourn this hearing for a short time and reconvene in an hour for a Parker hearing.'

'Granted,' said Judge Stoker, getting up off his seat and disappearing into his chambers before I could open my mouth to object.

Shit. A Parker hearing. I turned to Harry, and his face had fallen. Kate was shaking her head. I felt the weight of this case falling on me. We'd had a defense, and a client, not twenty-four hours ago. Now, this thing looked like a stone-cold loser.

A Parker hearing decides if the defendant can be tried in their absence. They were going to try and push the case on, with or without Carrie Miller.

We kicked our heels in the corridors for an hour and fifteen, and in that time, we made thirty plus calls to Carrie's cell and home number. Kate had called Peltier and he provided us with a list of her friends, and the few who answered the phone hadn't heard from her or seen her either, and they were pretty specific that they didn't want to ever see or hear from her again. Ever since it had become public knowledge that Carrie was married to the Sandman, no one wanted to know her or even admit to having met her. She deleted all her social media accounts to protect herself from abuse and harassment, but she had not expected her friends to stop taking her calls – even her bridesmaid, who she had known for thirty years.

I put my back to a cool marble pillar, let my head fall against it. The chill from the stone didn't ease the ball of tension in the back of my neck. It got worse as I saw White striding up the corridor, leading Bill Seong, and half a dozen prosecutors, none of them were over six feet tall but they all made White look even smaller than he was as he cockily headed the pack. He looked like a mascot. Kate sat on one of the pine benches that lined the hallway and as he passed her I saw that look again. It wasn't exactly overt, but it wasn't really subtle either. Kate grimaced. I joined Kate on the bench and White came over.

'Ready to get your ass kicked, folks?' he said.

Kate gave him a hard stare, said, 'My father's cousin, Albert, was a little shorter than you. He had a wife, eight kids, ran a grocery store in Edgewater, New Jersey. Nobody who went into his store left without taking home plenty to eat. Didn't matter if you went in with a fifty-dollar bill or a nickel. He never let anybody go hungry. When he died, his funeral procession stretched over eight blocks.

Albert was exactly five feet tall, but he was a giant of a man. You, Mr. White – you're truly a small man.'

'Fuck the both of you. After I win this motion, this case is as good as over. Good luck.'

He turned and went into court. I was left with a horrible feeling that he was right. The evidence was stacked against Carrie, and if you never met her, or spoke to her, you'd buy that she was guilty right away. But talking to her – it wasn't that she was convincing. She had no real argument to blow the prosecution evidence away, it was just that when she spoke you knew she was telling the truth. It's hard to put it any other way. Without her testimony, this case was practically unwinnable.

A Parker hearing isn't that complicated. The judge needs to be satisfied that two things have happened – the defendant has absconded of their own free will, and the defendant was warned that if they didn't show up for trial the case would proceed in their absence.

To do this White called three witnesses. Bill Seong confirmed to the judge he had been out to Carrie Miller's property in Old Westbury, and she was not at home, in breach of her bail conditions. Second, an assistant district attorney named Sandra Collins testified that she had called all of the medical and psychiatric hospitals in Manhattan, and those local to Carrie Miller, she had also contacted Central Booking, and so far as she could tell, Carrie Miller had not been admitted as a patient nor had she been arrested. Collins gave her answers in short order and seemed to squirm in her chair when White stared at her, especially when his gaze fell on her legs.

I asked Collins and Seong the same two questions and got the same answers from each of them.

'Carrie Miller's husband is wanted by the NYPD and the FBI for multiple homicide, correct?'

They both said yes.

'It is possible that Carrie Miller has been abducted by her husband, isn't that right?'

Both agreed.

And that was about the best I could do.

'I have heard the testimony,' began Judge Stoker, 'and I would ask the clerk to note for my written judgement that I personally gave the defendant a Parker compliant warning when she was granted bail. She was warned and she confirmed that she understood that her trial would proceed in her absence if she absconded from bail. To that end, I am satisfied that she has absconded on her own free will—'

'Your Honor—' I began, but he cut me off.

'No, Mr. Flynn. There is no evidence that your client has been abducted. I have to take an evidence-based approach. The case will proceed in her absence. We are adjourned.'

White looked over again. No lick of the lips. No sneer. No flirting this time. He simply gave a satisfied smirk and left the courtroom.

Harry sighed, said, 'The one chance we had in this case was Carrie's testimony. If she told the jury her story, the way she told us, they would believe her. Without Carrie Miller, there is no defense.'

I glanced at Kate, who was stuffing her loose pages back into her leather satchel, along with the iPad and her pen. Her lips were drawn tightly together, and there was a thump as she shoved each item into the bottom of her bag.

'We need Bloch,' said Kate. 'She has to go find Carrie Miller and get her ass to court.'

I followed Harry and Kate out of the courtroom. In the hallway, Bill Seong was waiting for me.

'Eddie, can we have a word in private?'

I nodded, and we made our way to a quiet corner of the hallway, beside a barred window. The glass had turned tobacco brown from the grease, dirt and grime of the city. I looked around, saw the groups of lawyers and their clients, standing and sitting, talking, drinking bad coffee, waiting for their cases to be called. It was hard to tell who was the lawyer and who was the crook. Made me think the windows might have gotten grimy from the inside – there seemed to be a lot of dirt walking these halls.

'I got a call from my protection detail in Teresa Vasquez's building. Since Chester Morris was targeted, we have placed all of the witnesses under close personal protection. Bloch was seen entering Lilian Parker's building with Gabriel Lake. You and I don't have a beef, so this is a word of warning – your people are not safe around Lake.'

'Why not?'

'Just trust me.'

'But you trusted him enough to put him on the case, like Delaney wanted. What's wrong with Bloch working with him?'

Seong's eyebrows knitted together, but not in anger – in confusion.

'Delaney wanted Lake in on this case. I said no. Delaney's murder hasn't changed that. He begged me last night to let him in as a consultant, and I refused.'

'But he told us he was working . . .' I didn't finish my sentence. The other shoe dropped. Lake had lied to us. He was on a mission all of his own.

'You can't trust this guy, Eddie. And he's dangerous.'

'Bloch's pretty dangerous herself.'

'I can't say a lot. It's classified. Files are sealed. All I'll say is this. He once kicked down the wrong door. Stumbled onto a heroin stash house all by himself, with no back-up. There was four million in cash and fifty pounds of H in that place, and it was well guarded. Ten men. And three of the guys there were ex-military. The commission who investigated the incident found that it was self defense. Word got around. The guy was a fucking super cop. A hero. The Bureau quietly pensioned Lake out of the service on medical grounds because there was another story. It sure started as self defense in that house, but it didn't end that way. At some point, Lake had a chance to get out. He stayed, and he took down all of those men, even though he was badly wounded. The last one, he put two in the guy's chest. Then he reloaded, emptied the full clip into the man's face. He executed those men. He's a killer, Eddie. I don't want Lake near any of my people, and you shouldn't have him near any of yours.'

I thought of the nervous man I had breakfast with. The guy who tapped the table when he spoke, who couldn't even order a muffin. I decided I would tell Bloch, just in case, but what Bill said and my impression of Lake didn't quite fit together. I thanked Bill, he didn't need to tell me anything, but I decided I would make up my own mind about Lake and let Bloch do the same.

I looked around for White. I wanted to talk to him about the bug on Peltier's phone. Mark his card. Let him know I wasn't going to let that slide. Tapping a defense attorney's phone was a career-ending move, even if he managed to get a warrant for it from an amenable judge. It was as low a play as I'd ever heard. If that got out, White wouldn't be able to get a job sweeping the floor in a law firm.

Harry, Kate and I stepped outside, into a hail of reporters. They were all crowded around White, like blue sharks feeding on a dead seal. When they saw us, some broke off and ran toward us. White turned around, waved a hand and departed into a car that was waiting at the curb.

A young female reporter in a blue pin-striped suit and Coke-bottle glasses was the first to reach us. She shoved a digital recorder into my face, but misjudged it and hit me in the mouth with it as she said, 'Do you think Carrie Miller has absconded with her husband? Oh, God, I'm so sorry . . .'

'It's okay,' I said, checking my lip. No blood, no foul. Before the rest of the journalists made it this far, I said, 'What's your name and number?'

'I'm Betty Clarke, with the *Sentinel*,' she said, handing me a card.

'I can't make a statement right now, but we'll be in touch. If we can work something out, I can offer you an exclusive once all of this is over.'

'What do you mean work something out? Our paper doesn't pay for stories.'

'Good, we don't want money. We just want a few tips.'

With that, Harry and Kate and I battled our way to the street. Once the reporters realized they weren't getting anything they soon left us alone.

I approached Ray, who ran a hot dog stand outside the court-house and used to give me some advertising at a good rate since I got his nephew out of Rikers Island.

'Three dirty water hot dogs, please, Ray,' I said, and handed him a fifty.

Some vendors grill their dogs. The best are kept warm in a small steel vat in their cart filled with what looks like water from the East River, but really it's a blend of cumin, chili, onions, and God knows what else.

'I don't want a hot dog,' said Kate.

'This is our lunch. We've got a ton of work to do. Trust me, you need this.'

Ray loaded us up with three dogs, mustard, ketchup and onions for Harry. Just mustard for Kate and me. We each took a soda, found a bench in the middle of Foley Square, watched the traffic go by. Ate our dogs, drank our Cokes. And I filled them in on what Seong had told me, then I called Bloch to make sure she was okay. She answered straight away.

'We have a situation. I need you. Have you caught the Sandman yet?' I asked.

'Believe it or not, I'm looking at him right now,' said Bloch.

CHAPTER EIGHTEEN

BLOCH

'He didn't attack her in the apartment because he couldn't get in,' said Bloch.

Bloch opened the door, examined the lock faces. There was some scratching around them, but it was hard to tell if it was from an attempt to pick the lock or just a nervous tenant.

'But it's just as difficult to grab someone on the street and drag them into a dark alleyway without being seen or heard,' said Bloch.

'He wouldn't have done that. My guess is he persuaded her into that alley,' said Lake.

'Bullshit. No woman in New York is going into a dark alley with a stranger.'

'There's something which might make her walk into that unlit alley. The witnesses, they didn't hear a struggle or a scream, but they did hear—'

'Cats,' said Bloch.

Their eyes were locked on each other. But they weren't seeing. Their minds were elsewhere, caught now in the electric current of a breakthrough. There was something important, something absolutely vital that Bloch could almost taste, almost touch, it was right there, just in front of her . . .

Lake moved toward the kitchen, bent down and picked up one of the cat bowls. The red one said 'Poochie' on the side of the dish. The other, a blue one, said, 'Mr. Paws.'

'The neighbor, one floor up, took the cat. That's what the file says. But there was more than one . . .' said Lake.

Bloch took a look at the bowls, then opened up the iPad, looked again at the photos taken in the alleyway. She swiped away from the close-ups, looking for a broader angle.

'There,' she said. 'The flyer on the wall.'

She pinched the screen to enlarge it. Beside the old band poster was a flyer that had been partially torn. She couldn't read all of it. It was black and white, and printed in block capitals.

—ST CAT

And below that a cell phone number. Lake took out his cell, dialed the number and hit speaker.

The phone didn't ring. Straight to voicemail.

'You've reached Lilian Parker; please leave a message and I'll get back to you as soon as I can.'

'He stole her cat. That's why she went into the alleyway. She heard it. Motherfucker was holding that cat, luring her in there,' said Lake.

'He would have to know she loved cats for that to work,' said Bloch.

'He knew her?' asked Lake, but even as he asked the question, he was shaking his head. The Sandman, so far as they knew, didn't target anyone in his circle. There was no evidence of any link between Daniel Miller and Lilian Parker. That had already been checked by the FBI, exhaustively. Lilian Parker didn't get any visitors to her apartment.

'No, Lilian Parker didn't have male visitors. No one came in here. Wait, he was . . .' began Bloch, but the thought took hold in her legs, and she approached the window that overlooked the street and the buildings opposite.

'He was watching her,' said Bloch, taking in the scratched-up furniture, the cat tower, the litter box. 'Lilian Parker loved cats. Anyone looking through her window, into her apartment, could tell that in a heartbeat. If they saw the locks on her door, they'd know there's no way of sneaking inside without the keys.'

'That meant he had a vantage point,' said Lake. 'And not one he wanted to reveal either. I bet he's linked with one of the apartments across the street – something identifiable, like a short-term lease.'

There were two buildings opposite. One was commercial office space. A tower forty-stories high and all glass. It was the same story on every floor. Bloch saw office workers at their desks, bunting for sales conferences hung on the windows, meeting rooms with multi-colored chairs surrounding white desks, men on the phone, their ties already loosened by the stress of the morning and interns milling paper through Xerox machines. The Sandman would not have chosen this building as an observation point – way too exposed. The other building, much smaller, about the same size as the apartment complex they were in now.

The top floor of the building opposite looked perfect. A loft space. Big window, almost directly opposite this one. Perhaps just a little higher, giving a better view of the apartment they now stood in. And there, at that window, Bloch saw a man staring back at them.

Her phone rang.

'Is that someone looking at us?' asked Lake.

'Teresa Vasquez has the apartment next door to Lilian Parker. She would have the same view,' said Bloch.

If someone wanted to keep an eye on Teresa's movements, the same vantage point that worked for Lilian Parker's apartment would work for looking into her neighbor's.

It was Eddie calling. She picked up.

We have a situation. I need you. Have you caught the Sandman yet?' said Eddie.

'No, it couldn't be . . .' said Lake, staring hard at the man in the loft apartment across the street.

He was so far away it was impossible to make out any features. He was white, wearing dark clothing.

He was holding something black in front of his face. Something which caught the light.

Binoculars.

He seemed to tilt his head.

'Believe it or not, I'm looking at him right now,' said Bloch, staring at the face in the window.

Lake moved forward, his nose an inch from the window. His breath misting the glass.

The man in the loft lowered the binoculars, turned away.

And ran.

CHAPTER NINETEEN

THE SANDMAN

He lowered the compact binoculars, blinked, then brought them to his eyes again.

Gabriel Lake was in Lilian Parker's apartment with the investigator, Melissa Bloch. The photographer at the *New York Post* had taken a photograph of them coming out of Delaney's building last night along with Eddie Flynn.

Nothing to worry about, he thought. He turned his attention to the apartment next door, and Teresa Vasquez. Teresa was in her early twenties and worked when she could. She had a part-time position at the New York Public Library working weekends. During the week she fried chicken at Popeyes.

She had left her apartment that morning, accompanied by two FBI agents, to get some groceries and the morning paper before returning home. That had been useful as it allowed him to observe her protection detail. There were two agents in a car on the street, outside her building. They took charge of her at the front door from two agents who had escorted her downstairs from her apartment. The agents in the car were in their thirties, both in street clothes – blue jeans and dark hoodies. The two agents in her apartment were in suits. One younger with dark hair and a veteran with gray hair.

This was a sweet deal for the protection detail. No one was going to walk into a crowded fast-food joint, jump over the counter and shoot Teresa in the head. Similarly, the New York Public Library was a reasonably secure building, with metal detectors and security screening at the entrance. The danger points were getting Teresa from her apartment to her workplace, and then back again.

He would wait for an opportunity.

One would come. It was only a question of when.

He was good at waiting. He had practice. For years he had suffered with insomnia. Once he lay in bed, in the dark, his mind wandered over every possible terrible thing that might happen to him or his family. It had begun when he was around seven years old. He would get up once his parents had gone to bed and get into his closet. Sitting on the floor of the closet, surrounded by clothes hanging from the rail, he would read fairytales with a flashlight.

He read until it was almost dawn, then crept back into bed and fell asleep, exhausted. This pattern continued until he was too big to sit in the closet, and so he stayed in bed to read. The tales he came back to again and again were those involving sleep. It was a part of so many stories – *Hansel and Gretel, Sleeping Beauty, Snow White, Goldilocks and the Three Bears, The Princess and the Pea* and more. And then there were the stories of a figure who visited children who would not go to sleep – the Boogey Man, Wee Willie Winky, Ole Luk-Oie. These tales were there to encourage children to stay in bed. The Sandman, who would sprinkle his dust in your eyes and make you fall asleep, that was his favorite.

These stories, he knew, did not make him a killer. That was in him already. He fantasized about killing the family cat for years and would attempt to hurt it whenever he got the chance to do so unobserved. The cat, Lucy, always managed to get away unscathed. It hated him before he ever hurled a kitchen knife at it. Perhaps it sensed his nature when others could not. It would hiss at him and arch its back whenever he walked into a room. The cat feared him. To him, this was natural. He knew he should be feared. He learned not to question his impulses. There was no explanation required. A shark doesn't need to explain itself. It is a shark.

He was a killer.

And that summer night on Coney Island beach when he first came across a woman, drunk and asleep on the sand, he realized his true calling and gave in to his nature. The sensations he felt that night still echoed through his memory and even his very limbs. His body physically shook with power.

And afterwards, he went back to his special place and put the woman's eyes in a little tin box, lay down on the floor and slept like he had been awake for a hundred years. Nothing changed that feeling that came with a kill. Not even when he met Carrie. The sensation of seeing her for the first time, talking to her, stroking the small hairs on the back of her hand. She was the first woman he had been close to who he did not want to kill, merely to possess. But what surprised him most was his desire to be possessed by her. For Carrie to call him her man, her partner, her husband.

She was the one. His true love. And he would tear this city apart to save her.

He told himself it wasn't too late. If he could rescue her from this nightmare, then she would be his forever. No one would stand in his way. And if they did, he would teach them what fear really felt like.

The FBI were afraid of him. He remembered the sweet smell of it on Delaney's skin.

The two plainclothes agents in the unmarked sedan were fearful too. Not so the young, nonchalant protection officer who was now standing in the apartment belonging to Teresa Vasquez. The easy-going officer sat on her couch and read *Cosmopolitan* while Teresa fixed coffee for him and his older, wiser partner.

Movement to his left caught his attention. He lowered the binoculars, and saw Lake standing in Lilian Parker's apartment, his face against the glass.

Lake was looking straight at him.

For the first time in years, the Sandman felt a mild chill over his body. A cool tingling sensation at the bottom of his spine that worked its way up, sending gooseflesh over the back of his neck – his hair standing up.

Fear.

A very old feeling. Not one that had touched him for decades.

Lake and Bloch weren't looking at the street or the other buildings. He could feel their eyes on him.

He turned, moved quickly toward the front door. Lake and Bloch swiveled and ran from the apartment.

No doubt about it now. They had spotted him.

He trotted down the staircase, his feet thumping on each step like a drum roll, his pulse threatening to match the beat, sweat on his palms making the leather gloves sticky. He was not afraid for his own safety. There was not a man alive that he feared in a confrontation. No, he was afraid of losing the life that lay ahead of him. A life with Carrie, far away from New York, and the FBI, and the cops. A new beginning someplace where no one knew their faces, and no one would ever think to look for them.

He had never envisaged anyone discovering him in that loft apartment. In all of his forward planning, this was an eventuality he had not accounted for. Yet, it was an opportunity. One he could use. Thinking clearly and adapting was what had kept him alive and out of custody for so damn long.

The lobby of the building was empty, and he barreled through the door and out onto the street where he turned left, sharply. No sign of his pursuers. Just before he got to the end of the block, he slowed to a walking pace. Behind him, he heard a car blowing its horn, the screech of rubber against the blacktop. A clothing store on his right had a curved window, and by stepping to the side he was able to see a little behind him and to the left.

Lake and Bloch, followed by the two FBI agents in street clothes, reached the entrance to the building.

The Sandman turned the corner, and then ran, in a loop of the block. He'd exited the building on the east side, had run around the south side and was now reaching the end of the west side, but he didn't slow down. He increased his pace, ran across the street to Lilian Parker's building. He found the door unlocked and he was able to slip inside and up the stairs unnoticed. When he reached the seventh floor he pulled the silenced Swiss-made pistol from his shoulder holster and knocked on the front door of the apartment belonging to Teresa Vasquez.

Stepping to one side, he watched the peephole closely. There was a chink of light visible in the corner of the refracted reticule. About three millimeters, if that. It was the tiny reflection of light from the window of the apartment.

He breathed out.

Rolled his shoulders.

The light disappeared.

Keeping his body out of view of the peephole, his left shoulder tight against the door frame, he angled the pistol with his right hand so that it aimed squarely at the door, in the center, and he squeezed the trigger, released it and feathered it again, rapidly, emptying the clip. He heard a scream, and something heavy hit the floor. Reloading as he moved back, he then took two deep breaths, shot out the lock then charged forward with his right foot raised and kicked open the door.

The cheap wood broke clean off its hinges, and the door landed on top of a body on the floor. It was one of the agents, the cocky young one in the suit. No sign of the gray-haired agent. The Sandman stepped into the apartment and saw the bedroom door was open. He found Teresa Vasquez huddled in a corner on the other side of the bed, her hands over her mouth, stifling her screams. Her face wet with tears.

The Sandman shot her four times, then turned and moved quickly into the hallway, then to the window that led to the fire escape.

Within two minutes his boots slapped down onto the alley where he had murdered Lilian Parker. He took off his jacket and turned it inside out. The reversible lining was yellow, and not to his taste, but it was different to the description of his clothes that Lake and Bloch had no doubt given the agents in blue jeans. From the pocket of his cargo pants he pulled out a surgical Covid mask and a cloth baseball cap, put them on. Took off his gloves and put them in his pocket. He reached behind him, loosed the hilt of the gutting knife strapped to his lower back. He might need that blade in a hurry. The gun he kept in his shoulder holster.

When he stepped out of the alley he glanced, quickly, to both sides of the street, and saw no pursuers. He could hear the police sirens though. They would be here any minute.

His van was parked a few blocks south of here anyway, so it made sense to get to it now before the area was swimming in cops.

He waited at the crosswalk beside a lady in a floral dress, wheeling a bright blue baby carriage. The baby couldn't have been more than a few months old, and it was awake and gurgling softly, tucked up behind a blue blanket. A yellow pacifier hung off a clip on the light blue bib. He was chubby, with red cheeks and the beginnings of golden curls in his hair. The child gave a big toothless smile that beamed those baby blue eyes at him, as bright as the dawn.

'He's adorable,' said the Sandman.

'Thank you,' said the mother. She was short, with wavy blonde hair, sunglasses and a heavy backpack. New parents always bring half the house with them when they venture out with their kids, he thought.

'How old?' said the Sandman.

'Baby Josh is four months now, yeah.'

The mother looked tired, despite the effort to hide it behind her Ray-Bans. She shuffled her feet, her Converse sneakers squeaking on the greasy side walk. She checked the traffic, looked at the crosswalk signal. It still read 'Don't Walk.'

'They can be a handful at that age,' said the Sandman.

She simply turned, smiled and nodded. While the Sandman had been perfectly charming, and the woman had no reason to be afraid, he could tell she was fearful of him. Her palms were on the handle of the carriage, her fingers raised, and shaking ever so lightly. Some people can just get a sense of him right away, no matter what kind of mask or pretense he might use. He had seen it before.

On the other side of the street, about fifty yards to the right of the crosswalk, Lake, Bloch and two federal agents came around the corner, and stood, shielding their eyes from the sun as they looked around for the fleeing Sandman.

He pulled his cap down. He would cross the street, turn left and get clear of the area. All he had to do was make it across the street and turn his back. They were not looking for a man in a yellow jacket and baseball hat. They were not looking for a man with a woman and baby in a carriage.

For now, he would stand beside the woman, and make idle conversation, and then cross the street with her. No matter how uncomfortable it might make her, he needed her to disguise his appearance: make it look like they were together.

As well as these calculations, the Sandman decided what he would do if Lake or one of the agents recognized him as he crossed the street. The options were plentiful.

He stood almost at the center of a traffic intersection. Two lanes of traffic passed in front of him from left to right. West to east. Beside him, twenty yards to his right, two lanes of traffic were stalled at the lights. When the traffic in front of him stopped, the traffic on his right would get a green light and they would pass from north to south.

The red lights brought the vehicles passing from the left to a stop at the crossing. The pedestrian light turned from an orange 'Don't Walk' to a green 'Walk' and the Sandman stepped into the road in time with the mother. They were side by side. The two lanes of cars twenty yards to his right began to move.

From beneath the brim of his cap, he watched Bloch and Lake on the other side of the street. If they recognized him, or he attracted their attention, he needed a distraction so he could get away.

It would give him no pleasure to harm a child, but it would not cause him any pain either. If the investigators or the feds saw him now, he would shoulder the mother out of the way, turn the baby carriage to face the moving traffic on his right and push baby Josh toward it.

The investigators, the feds, would all run for the baby carriage. If he pushed it fast enough a car or truck would have no time to stop. They would probably catch a glimpse of the carriage right before they hit it.

Baby Josh made a *goo-goo* sound and kicked at his blue blanket with his little feet.

From below the brim of his cap, he watched Lake.

A countdown started on the crossing lights.

15 . . .

One of the feds looked his way.

14 . . .

The Sandman stepped closer to the carriage.

CHAPTER TWENTY

BLOCH

As soon as Bloch saw the door to the loft apartment lying open, she knew the Sandman had left the building. Still, she took no chances. He was cunning, this one. Bloch drew Maggie from a shoulder holster – a Magnum 500. Her weapon of choice. It held only five rounds. If you knew how to use that gun, you only needed to fire it once. Didn't even matter if her target was behind a cinderblock wall.

She heard Lake coming up the stairs behind her, threw her palm at him to tell him to be quiet and keep his distance.

Then she went inside, checking the corners. A painting of a man stood in the center of the room on an easel. Beyond the picture, blood spotting on the floor that led to a blood pool and a trail. Someone had been badly hurt and then dragged along the floor.

She found the body in the tub. The man had no shirt on, and his face was ruined. Bloch turned and ran out of the apartment.

'He's gone, we've got a body in the tub. Probably the occupant of the apartment,' she said.

And then they were hammering down the stairs again, out into the street. They looked around, all four of them now. The feds in blue jeans had seen Lake and Bloch running and had decided to lend a hand.

A third fed crossed the street and came toward them, an older guy.

They stood on the corner, looking around. Bloch didn't need to study Daniel Miller's picture in the case file. His image had been in every newspaper, on every news station, on every channel, and on every news website for two years. If she saw him, she would know him, even if he did try to change his appearance.

'Any sign of him?' asked Lake, panting.

The two feds looked around, all of them trying to catch their breath, scanning the faces of the pedestrians on the street. Couples walking hand in hand. Men in suits marching along the sidewalk at speed, joggers, two women in gym clothes in conversation, and the rest of the teeming life that inhabited Manhattan.

'Better check on the witness. I left her with my partner,' said the older agent as he came alongside Bloch. He had gray hair, a slash of a mouth and keen eyes.

'Shit,' said Lake.

Lilian Parker's building was across the street. And they all focused on it for a moment.

The traffic in front of them thinned for a red light, just on their right at the crosswalk. There were still some cars in front of them, blocking their direct crossing of the street. A woman was standing on the opposite sidewalk with a baby carriage, talking to a man beside her in a yellow jacket and ball cap. Something about the man drew Bloch's attention. It looked like they didn't know each other, but they were making polite, yet stilted conversation. The man wore a blue surgical mask. A lot of people in the city did the same, to protect themselves from Covid or the traffic fumes.

Lake moved toward the crosswalk. The feds followed. The older agent said his name was Miggs, and he was really struggling for breath. Bloch decided to walk with him.

Lake and the two feds continued to scan the faces of passers-by.

Bloch looked at the man in the yellow jacket.

The crosswalk gave the signal to walk. Almost instantly, it began the digital countdown on the crossing display. That's when Lake's head snapped toward the man in the yellow coat.

Bloch felt a tingle of adrenaline making her fingertips prickly. She was already sweating from the run and breathing harder. Yet just looking at the man in the yellow jacket put her on edge. She had holstered her gun when she left the apartment, now she found herself putting her hand inside her jacket.

The man in the yellow coat reached up with his left hand, started pulling down the zipper of his coat.

She didn't know why, but her breath caught in her throat when she saw him reach for the baby carriage.

CHAPTER TWENTY-ONE

THE SANDMAN

While Lake's gaze did not linger, there was another set of eyes on the Sandman. He felt them. Their heat and intensity. An innate, primal instinct. Something left over from when the human race lived in caves, hunted for food, and were in turn prey for larger predators. The instinct was to look up, and lock eyes with the watcher.

He resisted. Instead, he allowed a quick glance by tilting his head upwards.

The woman who had been with Lake – the investigator, Bloch.

13 . . .

He put his right hand on the baby carriage.

The mother tightened her grip. Her knuckles white, fingers burying into the soft rubber sleeve of the steering handle.

10 . . .

Josh giggled and kicked the blanket right off his feet. His little round legs bicycling the air, his impossibly small, perfect toes stretched to meet the heavens.

He could feel Lake and Bloch looking at him now. He couldn't risk exposing his face and kept his head down letting the cap hide him. The hairs on his arms stood up and a prickle of fear caressed the back of his neck. He brought the zipper down further, past the grip on the pistol hidden in his jacket.

8 . . .

He heard the rumble of a Semi truck coming behind him and to his right. He glanced over his shoulder. Splashes of brown mud were on the side walls of the tires and the rims. The tire itself weighed around one hundred and ten pounds. The truck, with the trailer attached, weighed between thirty-five thousand and fifty thousand pounds.

Josh had that thin gossamer golden hair. His skull as fragile as fine china. He imagined the carriage hitting the front of the truck and then flipping over. The child suddenly airborne, then landing under the wheels . . .

6 . . .

He took one step closer to the mother, ready to push her out of the way.

CHAPTER TWENTY-TWO

BLOCH

Bloch hesitated when she saw the man in the yellow jacket talking to the mother pushing the carriage. Maybe they were friends. Not close friends. The way the man acted, putting his hand on the carriage, it was proprietary. Even though the mother tensed. If a stranger did that, wouldn't she react?

She wanted to see his face beneath that baseball cap.

Bloch shook her head.

The man they had seen was wearing black.

This instinctual response to the man crossing the street was a distraction. He wasn't the Sandman.

'I can't get my partner on comms. Julian was with the witness,' said Miggs.

'Shit,' said Lake, and then bounded into a sprint, across the street, the feds behind him. Bloch increased her pace, but stayed with the older agent, Miggs. He was breathing hard now, but it wasn't from the physical exertion. They made it to the other side of the street, and he stopped, knelt down, breath ragged, clutching his left arm.

'Call a paramedic,' Bloch shouted, and Lake swung around, pointed to Miggs and one of the feds got on his earpiece.

Gripping Miggs by his shoulders, Bloch tried to steady him. It was no good, he lay down on the sidewalk, unable to speak. His lips were moving. Mouthing a name.

'Julian.'

'I'm sure he's fine. Take it easy,' said Bloch.

'I-I shouldn't have left him . . .'

'Don't try to talk,' said Bloch.

She was aware of passers-by stopping, crowding around her and Miggs. She heard their whispered gasps, and their muttering, *'heart attack,' 'has he been shot?' 'what happened to him?'* and then, somewhere close by — a woman let out a scream.

Bloch looked around, but she couldn't see past the people surrounding her. And she couldn't leave Miggs.

'I shouldn't have left him . . .' said Miggs, then clutched his arm tighter, grunting.

Cradling his head, Bloch said, 'He's fine. He's absolutely fine. Don't worry.'

She heard the crackle of the radio. Loud voices. Agents in urgent conversation. Then, his expression changed. His eyes shut tightly, squeezing a tear loose. And she knew. Right then, that Miggs had heard his partner was dead. Reaching down, she pulled out Miggs's earpiece.

When she looked back at him, he was staring straight up, past her. His vision skyward. There was no breath. No heartbeat.

Bloch started CPR. She opened his airway, blew into his lungs, and as she rose again, to start compressions, she glanced up. Through a gap in the crowd, she saw a man walking away. His back to her. Far in the distance now.

The man in the yellow jacket.

Bloch looked around, saw that the woman was sitting on the curb, hunched over, crying.

In the center of the crosswalk, lay an overturned baby carriage.

CHAPTER TWENTY-THREE

THE SANDMAN

His plans, even those made on the spot, always accounted for eventualities. As much as it confused him at times, he felt like he understood human behavior. It was something he had to work at, because he often had unnatural reactions which made his friends and family uncomfortable. He had to fake grief when his grandparents died. It was hard to cry. He found that if he dug his nails into the soap in the bathroom, he could fake it easily by rubbing a little of the soap from beneath his fingernail into the corner of his eye. It stung, but it was better than the looks he got from his parents. He tried hard to learn what so-called normal behavior was expected of him, and in turn, it gave him an advantage. Having studied human emotions, and how people responded to certain situations, he found that he could predict their reactions.

He did not understand why the mother let go of the carriage.

He saw her hands in the air, free of the handle, as she reached for the baby. And then, her hip shoved into his, unexpectedly, throwing him off balance. She grabbed baby Josh into her arms, screamed as loudly as she could and ran to the other side of the street.

The child began crying.

Bloch and Lake were already across the street, lost in a crowd. He skipped off the road onto the sidewalk and gave the mother a wide berth as he ducked down the street ahead, walking quickly away.

The witness was dead.

Carrie was a step closer to freedom.

He checked his phone, saw a dozen notifications. He had alerts set for Carrie Miller. He checked each one, it was the same news report. Carrie had disappeared, breaching her bail conditions and a warrant had been issued for her arrest. The judge had ruled her trial would proceed in her absence.

The screen on his phone cracked with the pressure from his grip. He tossed it in a nearby trashcan.

Where the hell was Carrie?

She must have run. The pressure was too much for her to take. No matter, he would find her when this was all over. And then they would be together. Then, their new life could begin.

He needed to make sure she was acquitted, even if she wasn't there for the trial.

And right then he thought of a way to make sure of it.

CHAPTER TWENTY-FOUR

EDDIE

No one was really sure what breed of dog Clarence was. Harry had adopted him from the street, or Clarence had adopted Harry, one or the other. He wasn't a large dog, but there was some Labrador in there for sure, and probably a few other things too. He wore a high-tech collar with a GPS signal built in and synced to Harry's phone. His brown leather leash was too thin and too long for sure, but he never strained at it while we were out walking the streets. Clarence never wanted to be too far from Harry. It was past eleven, a big potato moon filled the night sky, and the sidewalks were quiet. Which is when Harry walked Clarence and I came along for the air and the talk.

Clarence stopped outside the entrance to Trump Tower on Fifth Avenue, cocked his leg, sending a stream of urine toward the front door.

'Good dog,' said Harry as we walked on, toward Central Park.

A vapor cloud hissed from a nearby manhole, but it didn't bother Clarence. He was a city dog, used to the vagaries of life in Manhattan, like jackhammers, the constant roar of traffic and horns and people. Lots of people. It had been a hard two days and I was bone tired, but there was no chance of sleep. My mind was a hot rod at six thousand rpm, spinning its wheels on a drag race start line.

Bloch had come by the office earlier and told me to add four more names to the Sandman's body count. Two FBI agents, one of them dead from a heart attack. A local artist who happened to occupy an apartment the Sandman wanted to use, and Teresa Vasquez – one of the witnesses in Carrie Miller's case. Bloch had slouched in my clients' chair. That's not like her. Normally she sits up straight, arms on the rests, hands relaxed, eyes keen.

'You look tired,' I'd said.

She nodded.

'I was talking to Bill Seong at the courthouse. He wanted to warn me about Gabriel Lake. It seems Lake lied to us. He's not consulting on the case for the feds. Whatever he's doing he has no authority, and in fact Seong thinks he's dangerous. Turns out he went a little crazy during the shootout in that house, didn't even try to escape. Instead, he killed everyone in that property. Made sure of it, you know?'

As I spoke, her boot heels went flat on the carpet tile, and she pushed herself up a little straighter.

'I heard about the house, that doesn't worry me. He's been through hell. You can see it. But he won't hurt us,' she said. 'He lied about the feds because he needed access to the Sandman evidence, which we have because of Carrie's case. And there's only one reason he lied to us.'

The economy Bloch put into her speech made some people cold toward her. It was an unfair judgement. If I was walking into hell the first person beside me would be Bloch. You can't buy that kind of friendship. Her ferocity was only matched by her quick mind. I knew the reason Lake had lied to us, and Bloch had come to the same realization, just as fast.

'He doesn't want to catch the Sandman,' I said. 'He wants to kill him.'

'If we find him, I'll make sure that doesn't happen.'

That was good enough for me.

'Go see Kate before you turn in,' I said. 'We got our asses handed to us in court today. She needs to know that it's not her fault if this all continues to go to shit. She's at home working.'

Swiveling the chair around, Bloch got up and headed for the door.

'Go easy on her. She really is having a rough time. On top of everything else, she thinks her asshole neighbor—' And then I stopped talking when I saw Bloch's expression harden. I shouldn't have told Bloch.

'Her asshole neighbor did what?'

'She thinks he stole her TV.'

Without another word, Bloch left. A shiver went through me. I would not want to be Kate's neighbor. Bloch left straight away and I sat in my chair, thinking. That is until Harry showed up with Clarence, asking if I wanted to go for a walk to clear my head.

Now, I glanced up at the night sky, framed by the canyon of buildings. Harry and Clarence walking beside me.

'I hope Lake is as good as Bloch thinks he is,' I said.

'So do I,' said Harry. 'But I have a feeling no matter how good he is, Daniel Miller is always going to be one step ahead. He's clever, this one. Maybe smarter than any killer we've met so far.'

'Maybe, but is he smarter than Lake and Bloch combined? I don't know. I wouldn't bet against those two, but I'd prefer it if we had an extra pair of legs chasing down Carrie Miller.'

'Any word from Peltier?'

'He's looking for her, or so he said on the phone tonight. He's more a part of her world than either of us. You know, rich? Who knows how rich people think or where they would go?'

'She wasn't always wealthy. Remember that,' said Harry.

We reached the park and Clarence's tail began to wag. It was late for a stroll in this part of the city, but Harry wasn't afraid. He'd taken to carrying personal protection lately. New York, just like the rest of the country, was on edge. It felt like there were two Americas, and battle lines were drawn. Crime was up in the city, especially armed robberies. But two guys out for a walk with a dog were not easy targets, and I wasn't worried about a gangbanger with a switchblade in his trembling hand.

'Wherever Carrie is, she's not thinking straight,' I said. 'I don't think she's with her husband either. You saw her that evening. She trusted him, loved him, and all along he was really a monster. How could you ever trust anyone again after something like that? This guy changed her life when they met. Gave her everything she ever wanted – the big house, the car, and never having to worry about money again. And it was all a lie.'

'Maybe it wasn't *all* a lie,' said Harry. 'Maybe Miller really loved her. Maybe he thought being married would change him.'

'I know what you mean. People don't just wake up with an idea to kill fourteen people. Men like that have evil growing in them for a long time. Once they start maybe they can't stop, even if they want to. When she and I talked . . . actually, it doesn't matter.'

'No, go on. What were going to say?' asked Harry.

'On top of the betrayal, and the public hatred, she's carrying around a lot of guilt. She blames herself for part of this. She knows if she had picked up the phone to the FBI, people would still be alive today.'

'The last victims were the Nielsens,' said Harry. 'That's a lot to carry around. Knowing you could have stopped those murders – saved those kids' parents. People have jumped . . .'

'Go on, say it.' I said, 'I've thought about it too.'

Sighing, Harry stopped, bent down and stroked Clarence's head.

'I don't need to say it. If the coast guard found her body in the river it wouldn't surprise me. We've seen all that stuff on TV – the most hated woman in America. Her friends talking about her on the news. Jesus. What a nightmare.'

'I just hope that she's still out there, somewhere,' I said.

We walked along in silence for a spell, in our joint hope that Carrie Miller was still alive somewhere, hiding beneath the same ceiling of stars. There were not too many people in the park. There never was at this time. Some folks were visible ahead, or on other paths in the distance as they walked beneath the beautiful cast iron street lamps. We wandered in silence, taking pleasure from Clarence's enjoyment of being away from the noise and bustle of the city.

'Where are we?' I asked.

Harry stepped toward a lamp, put on his reading glasses and used the flashlight on his phone to read the base section of the metal housing.

'What the hell are you doing?' I asked.

'This park is over eight hundred acres, built long before phones and GPS existed. The park employees needed to be able to pinpoint the lamps and their location, for lighting and maintenance. Every lamp in the park has a four-digit number. This one is 7238. First number is the cross street, so we're close to 72nd Street. The last two digits tell us what side of the park we're on. Odd numbers are west side, even numbers east side. That's why people say all—'

'All the odd people live on the west side,' I said.

Right then, I felt something. It was a sensation I'd felt many times, right before I finally realized something important. Something I'd missed.

It started as heat, in my chest, then rose to my throat. Like a spark that was hopefully going to travel all the way to my brain.

But not right now. There was something important, something absolutely crucial about Carrie Miller's case that I wasn't seeing. It was right there, and then it was gone. It would come again.

'You looked like you were about to say something,' said Harry.

'I thought I was. Doesn't matter, it will come to me. Let's get back. We need sleep or we're never going to get through tomorrow.'

'It's the DA's opening statements. Kate is practicing hers now. I heard it earlier, it's good. There will be time for maybe one witness tomorrow. Not a whole lot for us to do.'

'We're doing a lot more than that. Tomorrow decides if we win this case or not. So far we've been reactive. Time to change that up. In the morning we're going after Drew White and Judge Stoker. They need to know they're in a fight.'

CHAPTER TWENTY-FIVE

KATE

'Alexa, pause playlist,' said Kate.

She thought she'd heard something. Kate stood in the little kitchen area of her apartment. While she was making great money now in partnership with Eddie, and could afford a nice place, she still had another few months left on her lease. It would be easier to move when the lease was up, which meant another three months living in one room. Bed, small couch, kitchenette and breakfast bar. There was a separate bathroom, with no bath. Just a shower and a toilet. And neither of them worked very well.

At least she kept it clean and free of roaches and pests. In truth, she was working so hard this was simply becoming a place to crash late at night, and no more. She sure felt like crashing right now, but wanted to go over her opening statement in the Carrie Miller case one more time. When Otto Peltier called the office about taking on the case, she had been the one to take the call. Eddie was at court. She had seen Carrie on TV and knew some of the details. More than that, when she saw Carrie, she recognized something in her expression.

Before Kate started working with Eddie, she had been an associate at a large corporate law firm. It was the dream start for a young lawyer. All that she could have hoped for. She soon discovered that like a lot of things in America – dream jobs, dream cars, dream lives – well, they're not all that they're cracked up to be. In her first week, one of the male partners started leering at her. During a drinks reception on the Friday of that week, one of the other female associates told her she was leaving the firm, because she couldn't handle the constant pressure for sex from the partners and senior associates. Kate ended up going through months and months of grinding her jaw, taking deep breaths, and doing her best not to think of herself as a victim. Yet her work was marginalized and she was told, in no uncertain terms, that if she 'was a little more friendly with the guys' her career prospects would start looking up.

Kate left the firm and ended up suing them. And that started her passion project – representing women who had suffered sexual discrimination and harassment in the workplace. This was her mission. And when she saw Carrie, she had recognized that look. She had seen the same look in her own tiny, cracked bathroom mirror. It takes a lot to recognize that something wrong has happened. Kate found it hard to admit to herself that she was the victim of harassment. The emotions that came with it were complex – anger, pain, revulsion and, strangely, guilt. She constantly second-guessed herself until she was sure that she had done nothing to encourage this behavior. Once she realized she had been wronged, it took her some time to accept that it wasn't her fault. Carrie was a victim too. She would have all those emotions and more. She had been hurt really bad. And Kate would do whatever it took to help her.

She put down her pen at the breakfast counter as her Alexa device muted the music.

Thump—bang—bang—thump

At first Kate thought it was coming from the hallway, but as she listened she realized the noise was coming from the asshole in the apartment next door.

'Alexa, continue playlist,' she said. 'Volume up.'

Her little apartment was filled with the music from her favorite artist – Taylor Swift. She liked Beyonce too, but Taylor had a special place in her heart, and it helped her think while she worked.

More banging came from next door and she cut the music. It was louder now.

Bang—bang.

This time, it was her front door.

Kate got up and looked through the spy glass.

Bloch was outside her apartment.

When Kate opened the door Bloch picked up a large flatscreen TV and carried it inside without a word.

'That's my . . .' But Kate wasn't sure she wanted to finish that sentence. She remembered hearing the loud thumps coming from the neighbor's apartment.

Bloch set the TV on the empty stand.

Stepping around her, Kate wanted to get a closer look and make sure it was her TV. It was the same model and had the same scratch on the lower left corner where the knife she'd used to open the box had scraped the frame.

There was something else on the TV, in the opposite corner.

'Is that blood?' asked Kate, pointing to the spots on the top right of the screen.

Fetching a wash cloth from the kitchenette, Bloch wiped at the dark red marks.

'Your neighbor needed some persuasion before he decided to come clean about stealing your TV. Make sure your door is locked when you leave the place next time,' said Bloch.

One thing was for damn sure, Bloch wasn't a victim. And never would be.

'You want some coffee?' asked Kate.

Smiling, Bloch took off her jacket, sat down on the couch, said, 'Sure. Any *Columbo* reruns on tonight?'

The two women had been childhood friends. When they weren't terrorizing young boys in their neighborhood in east New Jersey, they were in Kate's house watching *Columbo*.

'I've got them all on TiVo. You want to watch *A Stitch in Crime*?'

'Is that the one with Leonard Nimoy?' asked Bloch.

'That's the one. You get the coasters and napkins.'

Kate's apartment wasn't much bigger than her office at the firm, and she was obsessive about keeping it clean and tidy. Any kind of mess in a space so small made everything look dirty, and that drove Kate crazy.

'I'll get the coffee,' said Kate. 'Or would you prefer—'

'Milk and cookies,' said Bloch, and the two of them shared a warm smile that reminded them of rain-filled Sunday afternoons, curled up in blankets on the living room floor of Kate's parents' house, with cold glasses of milk and plates full of Oreos.

Two hours later, close to midnight, Bloch left the apartment and Kate went over her opening speech to the jury one more time. She was trying to redirect the jury's anger. Explaining how all of the evidence shows that Carrie was another victim of the Sandman, and nothing more. She wanted them to know that her client had suffered and will continue to suffer. It was a hard argument, but one that needed to be made right away.

Having made some notes with her favorite Muji pens, Kate brushed her teeth, changed into her cotton nightdress and climbed into bed. Sleep took her quickly.

She woke suddenly, in the dark, a few hours later. Alexa was playing a song. At first, coming bang out of a deep sleep, she wasn't sure what was going on. She sat straight up in bed, unsure and startled as the world of sleep and consciousness seemed to collide.

The song was old. At first it sounded like a Disney track. Orchestral instruments recreating, in musical form, the sound of a cascading, magical waterfall.

And then she heard the percussion. It was like bells, or maybe a xylophone, and then the male harmony group.

'Mr. Sandman, bring me a dream . . .'

She froze as a chill swept her entire body like an arctic blast.

And then something dark, a shadow, grabbed her and held her down, one hand covering her mouth. A weight sat on top of her, and hot breath warmed her neck before she felt the needle prick her skin. The smell of leather gloves filled her nose as she struggled to breathe.

She tried to turn, to push him off of her, to fight back. But her limbs felt strange. Like they weighed two hundred pounds. She could barely lift them. Her eyelids were heavy too, and then the room started to move. It felt like she was falling into the bed, and she would never be able to climb out of it.

He was talking to her. It sounded as if he was very far away.

'You have beautiful eyes. I think I'll keep them.'

She felt herself being lifted, and then placed down. She was lying on something black. The smell of rubber. A noise threatened to engulf her in panic, and yet she was so sleepy she couldn't move. It was the sound of a large, thick metallic zipper.

She realized, in horror, as the zipper closed over her, that she had been placed in a body bag.

It was then that her eyes closed into a darkness deeper than the blackest night.

CHAPTER TWENTY-SIX

EDDIE

Eight-thirty in the morning is not a usual time for me to be up and in the office, and I hadn't slept well the night before. Too much on my mind. Every time I closed my eyes I could see Delaney in the back of that pick-up, I could feel the warm slick of her blood on my hands, and terrible dark pink pools of bloody sand in her eye sockets.

My office door opened, and Denise came in carrying a brown paper sack. She emptied the bag on my desk. They were cheap, burner cell phones still in their hard, transparent plastic clamshell packages. Five of them.

I picked up one and pulled at the plastic. No dice. I picked up a heavy pair of scissors and promptly broke them in two while trying to cut through the hard, packed edge of the packaging.

'Can you get me a pick ax, or a blow torch so I can open these?' I said.

After a heavy sigh and a roll of her eyes, Denise disappeared into the kitchen and came back with a can opener. She clamped the device on the side of the packaging and started to turn it. The can opener sliced through the tough plastic seal, and she opened up the clamshell, in seconds, and gave me the phone.

'Have I given you a raise yet today?'

'Not yet,' she said, with a smile.

'Pick a phone.'

'In a minute, I need to check our email first.'

'Is there any coffee left in the pot?' I asked, but she was already out of my office, on her way to her desk.

'Get your own damn coffee,' she said.

'I always do. I only wanted to know if there's some left.'

It took me a lot longer than Denise to open the packaging for the phones, but by the time I prized the last one free, Harry and Bloch stepped into my office.

'Let's swap numbers for these burners. With the DA tapping Peltier's phone, I wouldn't put it past him to put a trace on ours. The authorities want the Sandman so bad Drew White could get a warrant for my high school records if he really wanted to. Don't use your own phone, or the work phones. These are the new work phones. Wait, where's Kate?'

No matter what time I got to the office, which was, in fairness, normally after nine, Kate would already be there.

'I swung by her place this morning and there was no one there. I tried her cell but no answer. I thought she was already on her way to the office. I'll call her again,' said Bloch.

'Denise! Come on in and pick up a phone,' I said.

She came in with a stack of today's mail. I hadn't seen real office mail since we started the firm. Kate always went through it in the morning. The envelopes were all various sizes and shapes, mostly white or brown, but sticking out of the bottom of the pile in her arms I saw what looked like the kind of envelope for a greetings card. There was no mail stamp on it, which meant it had been hand delivered. It was addressed to me.

She dumped the pile on my desk and began sorting it, then she saw the envelope, looked at it front and back and gave it to me.

'Your birthday?' she asked.

I shook my head, opened the envelope while Bloch helped Harry navigate the new phone, and Denise started ripping open the mail.

Inside the envelope was a single page, folded in half. It had been torn from a yellow legal pad. I recognized the handwriting and the gel ink Kate liked from those Japanese pens. It was part of Kate's draft opening speech to the jury in Carrie's case. I turned the page over.

A message was scrawled in red, in block capitals, over Kate's notes.

I HAVE HER.

SHE IS ALIVE, FOR NOW.

IF YOU TELL THE AUTHORITIES, KATE DIES.
IF CARRIE IS CONVICTED, KATE DIES.
IF YOU GET AN ACQUITTAL FOR CARRIE, I LET HER GO.

CHAPTER TWENTY-SEVEN

EDDIE

Sometimes you get hit. Hard.

My office seemed to lurch to the right, as if the building had broken in two and tilted, violently, throwing me off balance. Spots formed in front of my eyes, and I tasted the pancakes I'd had for breakfast. Saliva flooded my mouth. The note left my hand, drifted to the desk.

The desk.

I lurched for it, grabbing the sides with two hands to steady myself.

The same words were banging through my head like a snare drum, *'not Kate, not Kate, not Kate, not Kate . . .'*

I couldn't speak. I couldn't think. I needed to get a hold of myself, or I would be sick.

Harry picked up the page in both hands. He'd seen my reaction, and his eyes widened as he read, his lips moving soundlessly, mouthing the words, making them real, the page shaking so much in Harry's hands it was almost vibrating. His legs gave way and his ass hit my clients' chair. If that seat hadn't been directly behind him, he would've ended up on the floor. As he read, Bloch leaned over, and read the note, even as it slipped out of Harry's hand.

Bloch covered her face with both hands. And stood there. Unmoving.

'Bloch,' I managed to say, reaching out for her, fighting down the nauseous sensation, getting my breath back.

'Bloch, we're going to get her back,' I said, but she didn't hear me. She wiped her face and ran out of my office.

'Oh, Jesus,' said Harry, and crossed himself. He bent over, laced his hands together and started to say a prayer.

I heard something. Cracking and smacking on something hard. I managed to get out of the office, feeling a little steadier on my feet. The door to the ladies' room was open. Hearing the same booming cracks, Denise ran inside. I followed her in. She stood with her back to the stalls, hand over her mouth, watching Bloch.

Each punch took another piece of white bathroom tile off the wall. Her hands moved quicker, like she was working the heavy bag. A pile of broken tiles was forming at her feet and a small cloud of plaster dust billowed with each strike.

I grabbed her from behind, trapping her arms, and, gently, I pulled her away from the wall. She resisted at first, and I got the impression she could retaliate if she wanted to, starting with throwing the back of her head through my nasal bones.

She didn't of course.

Panting for breath, she let me hold her. Physical contact was not easy for Bloch. But right now, with her blood up, either she didn't notice, or her engine was running too fast to feel it.

Gradually, her breathing deepened and the pace slowed.

I relaxed my grip, slightly. Just enough to test whether she would break free and start pounding the wall again. She didn't. I released her, stood back.

Grabbing a handful of paper towels, Denise ran cold water over them and stood, cleaning first Bloch's bloodied knuckles, and then, with great care, she dabbed at the powder covering her face.

A tear had ridden through the layer of dust on her left cheek, leaving a deep track in relief, like a scar.

Denise wiped it away, and then the two women embraced.

'What the hell is going on?' said Denise.

'The Sandman has Kate. You can't tell anyone. Not the cops, nobody. He says if we don't get an acquittal for his wife, he's going to kill Kate.'

Shutting her eyes tight, she held Bloch close, whispered something to her.

Bloch nodded and they parted. Bloch sniffed once, said, 'I have to meet Lake. I'll call you from the car,' and left.

Harry stood in the doorway, said, 'Bloch's gone. Is she okay?'

I shook my head.

'I didn't think so. Goddamn it. What are we going to do? We have to tell the cops.'

'No, he'll kill her,' I said.

'So, what *are* we going to do?'

I raised my hand to wipe the sweat out of my eyes and noticed my fingers were trembling, and it wasn't from the exertion of holding Bloch. My nerves were shot to shit. I couldn't think.

Tile fragments cracked underfoot as Denise went back to the sink, ran more water over fresh towels and gave one to me and one to Harry. She leaned on the stall, folded her arms, and dabbed at the tears streaking her mascara.

'This isn't a law firm,' said Denise. 'I worked in law firms all my life. This, right here, this is a *family*. I couldn't bear it if something happened to Kate. What the hell are we going to do?'

Harry and I stared at each other.

Finally, Harry said, 'Looks like we don't have a choice.'

CHAPTER TWENTY-EIGHT

BLOCH

In Bloch's line of work getting a few cuts and bruises was something she accepted. It was common enough, and she had bandages in her glove box. Sitting in traffic, she wrapped up both knuckles. Blood still seeped through the cut on her right hand, but it wasn't too bad. It would do for now. She wasn't used to displays of emotion, or anger. It took something out of her, but she had never been in a situation where her best friend was in real danger. For Bloch, these were uncharted waters. She needed to keep her cool. Keep her head – so she could use it.

Waving at her from the sidewalk, Lake approached Bloch's Jeep as she pulled up at the curb and buzzed down the passenger window.

'Get in,' she said.

'But we're right here. This is the Nielsens' street.'

'Get in. We need to go somewhere else first.'

He hesitated, but only for a moment, then got in beside her and put on his seat belt.

'What I'm about to tell you goes no further,' said Bloch, gunning the engine as she pulled out. 'If the cops or the feds find out about this, I'll know it came from you. And then I'll hurt you. Do you understand?' she asked.

'What's wrong?'

'Last night, the Sandman took my friend, Kate Brooks. She's Eddie's partner. He sent us a note this morning saying that if we don't get an acquittal for Carrie Miller, he's going to kill Kate. He'll do the same if we go to the cops.'

'Oh my god, I'm so sorry. Where does your friend—'

'We're going to her apartment right now.'

148

They were only twenty minutes from Kate's building and for twenty minutes neither of them spoke. But Lake said a lot.

He stroked his leather messenger bag, which he held on his lap, then drummed his fingers on it, pulled at the straps, rubbed his wrists, tapped his feet, sucked his teeth and tugged at his ear lobe. The man was a ball of anxiety, even more so today. And while Lake let those anxious feelings show, Bloch simply drove the car. She only moved her head, pumped the gas and turned the steering wheel. Her teeth were clamped together, and occasionally she could feel a vein standing out in her neck, but she kept all her fear and worry inside. Letting it simmer and boil. And when she could hold it no longer, she would find something to let it out on. If that something happened to be a person, God help them.

She hadn't been surprised that Kate had been burgled the other night. The only surprise was that it hadn't happened before. There was an illusion that once you were several stories above the street in Manhattan, you were safe. This was not true. Even the most secure apartment buildings had regular spates of burglaries. If you lived in the city long enough it wasn't a question of *if* you would get robbed, but simply *when* and how bad it would be. Unlike Lilian Parker's building, Kate's apartment complex was not secure. There were any number of ways out of the building, into alleyways, or down fire escapes. You could walk straight out of there carrying a body and there wasn't a single camera to catch you. Also, the street outside was quiet in the small hours of the morning. The Sandman would've had very little trouble accessing Kate's apartment and kidnapping her without being seen.

When Bloch pulled up, Lake simply nodded, followed Bloch into the building and up to Kate's apartment. Her front door was closed, but both locks had markings around the keyholes.

'He used a key drill,' said Lake. It was a small, valuable device that used a soft, heavily muffled motor to operate what were essentially lock picks. Some people called them magic keys.

Bloch pushed at the door with her fingertips, and it opened.

One of the drawbacks of using magic keys was that they tended to bust the lock, preventing the door from closing.

Inside, the curtains were drawn, but they were only thin and cheap, and light was still able to penetrate the room. Throwing them open, Bloch let the sunlight burn through the dust motes dancing in the air. While they swirled in the sunbeams, Bloch surveyed the apartment. Nothing out of place, apart from the unmade bed. Kate never left that bed unmade in the morning.

'Anything I should be looking for in particular?' asked Lake.

Bloch didn't speak, she was concentrating. Taking in every detail, referencing her memory to highlight anything strange or unusual. While she took her time, and examined the place thoroughly, she could see nothing out of the ordinary.

Apart from one thing.

Kate's legal pad was on the breakfast bar, and a page had been ripped out. The page he had used to write the note to Eddie. Finally, she approached the unmade bed. The comforter had been pulled back as if Kate had just leapt straight out. Or been hauled out of it.

Bloch took the comforter, which Kate always insisted on calling a duvet, and drew it back. She decided she would make the bed. It seemed like a stupid thing to do. But Kate was fastidious about keeping the place neat. Bloch picked up her pillow, drew it to her face and inhaled. Kate's scent. Not perfume, or hair products, it was Kate. And she had known that smell since she was eleven years old. She swallowed. Suppressing that spasm in her throat that threatened to erupt into a torrent of loss and fear that would overwhelm her. Instead, she made the bed. It was only a small and totally inconsequential action, but it had weight for Bloch. Because it would mean something, somehow, to Kate.

As she leaned over and smoothed out the comforter, her fingers touched something hard. The cover was a gray pattern of close-knit, interlacing lines with some yellow streaks. It was difficult to spot something lying on the bed, particularly if it was clear plastic, but that is exactly what Bloch found.

It was thin and cone shaped. The protective plastic cover for a syringe needle.

'Check the kitchen drawer below the coffee machine,' Bloch said. 'You'll find plastic sandwich baggies. Bring me one.'

'What have you got there?' said Lake, coming close.

'The bag,' said Bloch.

Lake seemed to know that he wasn't going to get anything else from her until he got the bag. He walked around the counter, found a supply of baggies in a cardboard container and handed one to her.

She opened it and scooped up the plastic cover from the bed.

'Oh my,' said Lake. 'He missed this.'

'He took her in the dark,' said Bloch. 'He would have had one hand out, to put over her mouth. Moving slowly and silently toward her. He would know these walls are thin, and stifling a scream was key. The syringe would be in his other hand . . .'

'Smart,' said Lake.

The question each of them wanted to know the answer to was would the Sandman have risked putting his two hands together, right at the last moment, to take the lid off the syringe and expose the needle? The cap was right on the bed, so he had done it last minute. It was likely he grabbed Kate with one hand, holding her down, covering that scream, and he took the lid off the syringe by biting down on it with his teeth and then spitting it out, onto the bed.

'This came from the Sandman. If he's taken Kate, then that means she's being held somewhere. Wherever that is, there's a good chance that is where he's been hiding all this time. There might be fibers, trace chemicals, something on this that might give us a clue as to that location,' said Bloch.

'I'll take it right now to my guy. I have a friend who is a private forensic tech.'

She sealed the bag, held it and stood up straight, staring at Lake.

'My best friend's life is on the line. Why should I trust you after you lied to us?'

The dust motes whirled through a sunbeam, contrasting how perfectly still Lake had become. No twitching, scratching, nervous movement. His engine, which was always going, had suddenly stalled. Bloch knew he was debating his next move. He would either double-down on the lie, in which case Bloch would dump his ass on the floor and get her own tech, or he could come clean.

His gaze never wavered from her, as if he were calculating her likely response.

He held up his hands, palms facing her, fingers spread. 'Okay, you got me. I'm not working for the feds.'

'So why did you lie?'

'Because I don't want to arrest Daniel Miller. I want to kill him. And that doesn't help your case with Carrie one bit. I needed an incentive so I could get another investigator to help me, and so I could have access to the FBI file on the murders. Your files. I'm sorry I lied. If I had told you the truth you wouldn't have let me in, and like I said, I have a problem trusting people.'

'So why shouldn't I cut you out of this investigation right now?'

He licked his dry lips, stared at the floor for a second, and when he spoke, his voice crackled. His tone went high, then low – splintered with a grief that he couldn't hide.

'Because my friend is already dead. And I can't let that go. I can help you catch him and get your friend out alive. There's another life on the line now. That's more important than revenge. I give you my word I won't kill him.'

Bloch paused for a second, taking it all in. Then she nodded.

'Is that okay? Is that it? We're good? Seriously?' he asked.

'You want a parade? Let's go check on the neighbor.'

Kate's neighbor was unlikely to open the door for Bloch after their altercation last night. She decided it would be better to go straight in.

She put her back to the wall opposite, took two big steps forward, at speed, and the third put her right foot through the hinges of the door. Kate's neighbor sat on his couch, beer in one hand. The other hand didn't look usable. His pinkie finger was in a splint. A large Band-Aid covered his nose. Deep violet bruising surrounded his fearful eyes.

He started whimpering as Bloch grabbed him by the shirt, hauled him to his feet then planted him into the nearby wall.

'Did you see or hear anyone in the hallway late last night, after I left?'

'I already said I wasn't going to the cops,' he said.

Bloch pulled him away from the wall, then slammed him back into it.

'I'm not talking about this. This isn't about you. I don't have much time and I need to know if you saw or heard anyone, or anything, last night after I left.

'Go on, hit me,' he said, then held up his broken pinkie finger. 'What else could you *possibly* do to me?'

Lake took hold of the man's broken finger, said, 'I could think of at least nine other things.'

'Please . . .' said the man. 'I was in the emergency room. I didn't see nothing.'

'You didn't see a stranger in the hallways, a strange car parked outside, or—'

'Music,' he said.

'What music?'

'I got home from the ER around one a.m., couldn't sleep. Then I heard your friend playing some old-timey music. And then I went to sleep. That's it. That's all.'

Kate was not into classic songs. She liked Beyonce and Taylor Swift.

'What kind of old-timey music?'

'It was kinda like that song they play in *Back to The Future*. You know, the movie. After Michael J. Fox goes back in time.'

'Let him go,' said Lake.

Bloch released him, and they backed out of the apartment.

'What is he talking about?' said Bloch, in the hallway.

'I know the song. It's a close harmony, acapella-type thing. It's called "Mr. Sandman."'

CHAPTER TWENTY-NINE

EDDIE

The world's media was outside the Criminal Courts Building. I saw trucks from the BBC, Bloomberg, France 24 and some I couldn't even read. They were all jostling for position with the rest of the US networks. The Sandman was big news. And his wife going on trial attracted a lot of attention.

Harry and I used the side entrance to the courthouse, the one reserved for DAs and courthouse employees. We knew the security detail well enough for them to let us in without much hassle. We went up to the eighth floor in the elevators and saw a tightly packed crowd of reporters in the hallway. Nothing to do but put our heads down and push through.

Somehow, Harry got to the door of the courtroom before me, he must've been able to push around the crowd from the sides, and he grabbed my hand and hauled me inside just as the court usher closed the door behind us.

I've walked into a lot of courtrooms, in a lot of high-pressure trials, but this was different. I could feel the weight of the air as I breathed. My left hand wouldn't stop shaking. The thought of Kate, maybe bound, definitely frightened, wondering if we were going to save her . . .

I felt like I wanted to throw up.

For years, I practiced alone. Just me. No secretary, no employees, no associates, no partner. Because sometimes the heat from my cases put me in the crosshairs of dangerous people. And I didn't want anyone around me to get caught in the crossfire. Those close to me are always looking over their shoulders. Part of the reason Christine and I broke up was my line of work. I made the choice to protect my family by distancing myself. I didn't want that life for my wife and child. By the time I realized I'd made the wrong choice, and I should get a regular lawyer job, it was too late. I'd lost them both.

Then came Harper. A woman I'd loved. And I never got to tell her. She died because of me. Because I tried to help someone. I still woke up in the night, breathless, sweating, from a dream where I am running to Harper's house, and she's still alive.

But I know it's too late. That I'll never make it.

And now I'd made the same mistakes all over again.

Kate was in the hands of a madman because of me.

I felt dizzy. My hand shot out to one of the benches to steady myself.

That's when I felt Harry grabbing me around the waist. Slipping his shoulder under mine.

'Come over here, to the corner,' he said.

We ambled to the end of the gallery, away from the clerks and the rest of the courtroom staff. In trials with a large media presence, the court officers usually let the lawyers have the room to themselves for a while before the proceedings begin. There's nothing about this in the rules, it's just become a convention.

I sat down on the bench. I didn't want to sit near the defense table. I couldn't. Not yet. The world was shifting, my stomach was turning and I couldn't focus. Couldn't breathe.

'Eddie, take it easy. You're having a panic attack,' said Harry.

'It's my fault. I should never have partnered up with Kate. Harry, she's so young. I can't—'

'I'm feeling it too. She's like a daughter to me. So, you have to get it together. There's a way out of this. We can save her.'

'I can't—'

'You *can*. We can. This is not your fault. It's no one's fault. But you have to fix this. Kate is alive and we have to keep it that way. You've got to get a hold of yourself and get your head in the game. Because if you don't, Kate is not going to make it.'

I closed my eyes, put my head back.

It felt like all the mistakes I'd made in my life were stacking up around me, ready to topple over right onto my head.

I thought about what Kate would do if the situation was reversed – if I was the one who was trapped and Kate had to fight to save me.

The answer was clear. I admired Kate. She was smarter and stronger than almost anyone I'd ever met. I knew exactly what she would do. She would grit her teeth, remember that she was from Edgewater New Jersey, and that nobody fucks with Kate Brooks.

I held that thought, breathed it in. I had no doubt now that wherever she was, she was going to fight back. She was going to survive. I just had to be as strong as she was.

A deep breath. I drank in that feeling, that strength that I was drawing from Kate. I stood, and together Harry and I made our way to the defense table.

There was another convention in US courts – retired judges did not go back into legal practice. It was more or less observed, with only a few examples of judges going back into battle for old clients after they had retired from the bench. Harry had no intention of getting back into real practice. He was a consultant at the firm. That was it.

Or so he thought.

'I can't do this on my own. I need your help,' I said.

'I'm right here, Eddie,' he said as we took our seats at the defense table.

'No, I mean, I need you to take second chair.'

'But I shouldn't . . .'

'There's no law that says you can't. We'll file your papers this afternoon. You're under my insurance until then, as I'm lead counsel.'

'Eddie, it's been twenty years. I don't know—'

'You can cross-examine better than me. I need you. I can't do this alone.'

I spread out the Miller files on the desk in front of us and two iPads with all the files in digital form. He gazed down at my trembling fingers. From his briefcase, Harry took out a yellow legal pad, a Pelikan fountain pen and a bottle of blue ink. He set the pen on the page, looked at it. Looked at me.

He nodded and took up the pen. Made a horizontal stroke at the top of the page, and then a vertical line, cutting the page in half.

Right side for notes of what the DA or witnesses said, left side of the page for his counterpoints. It was advocacy 101.

Harry reached out and placed his hand over the top of mine, gripped my quivering fingers. When he spoke, his voice cracked with the strain.

'Let's win this one for Kate,' he said.

CHAPTER THIRTY

EDDIE

'Where is he?' I asked.

'He'll be here. He wouldn't miss it,' said Harry.

The prosecution team had arrived. Drew White and a host of assistant DAs, all male, all in their late twenties, all looking to make a name for themselves with this case. The District Attorney's office boasted a wide selection of capable and intelligent female assistant district attorneys, and not one of them had been given the opportunity to shine in this case. White had carefully selected his support team. All guys, all friends, all of them willing to overlook and, if need be, cover up any misconduct White may commit while trying the case. None of them thought of the victims. All they cared about was writing the name of this case on their resume before they sent it to a Wall Street law firm that paid starting salaries in the mid-to-high six figures.

Behind the prosecution table was a row of cops and feds. Bill Seong sat at the end of the aisle. It was his case really, and it could have gone to federal court. I had a feeling if they caught the Sandman, Seong would insist the US Attorney's office deal with it under their federal jurisdiction. But this wasn't the Sandman. This was the next best thing. And Seong was smart to let the local DA handle it. This case was a risk-free experiment. A free run at the evidence with no consequences for him. If the case bombed and Carrie Miller got an acquittal, Seong could wash his hands of the whole thing and blame the locals in state court. Then he could make sure the same mistakes would not be repeated in the Sandman trial in federal court. If White managed to get a conviction, Seong could take full credit.

'He's got to be here somewhere?' I said.

Harry got up and turned, scanning the faces of the crowded benches behind us. A hand went up at the back. I stood and saw, at the very corner of the courtroom, Otto Peltier with his hand in the air. We'd talked on the phone after the hearing yesterday. He had been the one fighting for Carrie for a long time and he was invested in this case. Plus, as long as Carrie was missing, so was his money. I liked Otto, but I also couldn't help thinking he wouldn't be putting all this time and effort into finding Carrie if she had already paid him the million dollars in legal fees. He had been out yesterday checking around motels, small hotels and hostels in Brooklyn, Queens and the Bronx. Anywhere that took cash for a bed and didn't ask questions. The kind of place someone with Carrie's profile might hide. He'd put two hundred miles on the car and made more than a hundred phone calls – a lot of work, but there was a seven-figure pay-out in the wind.

So far, no sign of her.

'I'll go talk to him,' said Harry.

'Don't mention Kate.'

'I won't, but he's going to ask where she is.'

'Tell him she's out with Bloch chasing down a lead. Ask him for a list of the places he's tried.'

I watched as Harry made his way to the doors of the courtroom, and beckoned Peltier outside.

I waited.

There's a lot of waiting in court. You're at the mercy of the legal system, and the judge's golf schedule. I folded my arms, bracing my hands. Anything to stop them shaking. The clerk caught my eye, held up a hand to indicate five minutes.

I checked my phone. No new texts. I was waiting on Betty Clarke from the *Sentinel* coming back to me with some information. Since Bloch was out with Lake, I needed another source. I'd done some research on Betty. She was five years into the job at the *Sentinel* as their crime correspondent. Now that I thought about it, I'd seen her hanging around night court. You see a lot of hungry journalists there, hoping that a drunken celebrity might be rolled in so they can get a scoop to sell themselves to the *New York Times* or the *Post*. Having asked around, I found out Betty was well liked, even trusted. And that meant she had access. Sometimes it's a smarter career move for a reporter not to publish a story. There's always a bigger one, and making friends always helped unlock the kind of doors that might have big skeletons hiding behind them.

I sent her a text.

Any luck?

And waited.

My phone vibrated.

I've got something but waiting for confirmation.

I tapped out a reply, hit send.

We're tight for time. Please get it asap.

I heard the doors opening over the hum of the excited crowd. Harry strode up the center aisle and took his seat beside me.

'All good,' said Harry.

I got up and approached Stoker's clerk, an old timer called Jerry. The last judge he'd clerked for was a drinker. Sometimes he showed up to court too drunk to sit upright. That is until Jerry poured a pot of coffee into him and stalled all the lawyers to buy him time. In other words, Jerry came from the kind of loyal stock that was rare in support staff. He was Stoker's first choice once Jerry's judge retired.

'Jerry, I need to get in to see the judge,' I said. 'It's a personal matter. I don't want the DA in there with me.'

'Is that even allowed? Is it do with the case?' asked Jerry.

At this point, Harry came over and said hi to Jerry. They knew one another well. Jerry even acted as dealer in an illicit card game that Harry ran for senior judges.

'Eddie needs a minute with the judge on his own. I know it sounds unusual, but it's fine. Tell Judge Stoker he has nothing to worry about.'

Normally, counsel in a trial cannot speak to the judge without opposing counsel present. It stops any kind of implication of impropriety and actual or perceived bias. It's not written down anywhere, it's one of those conventions.

'Well, if you say it's okay, Harry. I don't think His Honor is going to like it one bit, though,' said Jerry.

'That wouldn't surprise me. How's it going with him anyways?' asked Harry.

'He's a fair man,' said Jerry, with a resigned sigh that translated 'fair man' into 'raging asshole'.

'Keep it together, Jerry. Good seeing you,' said Harry.

And with that, Jerry led me through the rear door of the court-room, along a hallway and into the chambers of the orange-tanned Judge Stoker, who was seated behind his desk. If anything, he looked an even deeper bronze this morning. Perhaps he was anticipating the myriad international news reports and wanted to make sure he looked his best. Or what he thought looked good, at least. To me he looked as if he had been dipped in a barrel of varnish before falling into a buffing machine. It all looked so unnatural. And yet, that was the way of some men. To hide the darkness in their hearts, they wore a disguise. Except they weren't exactly sure what normal looked like, nor what it felt like. And so they made some extreme choices.

'Good morning, Your Honor, I'd like to discuss a private matter, if I may?'

'You'll have to wait until Jerry brings in the DA.'

'He's not bringing in the DA. Like I said, this is a private—'

'Jerry, where's the DA?' said Stoker, cutting me off.

'Judge Ford said it's okay for you to talk to Mr. Flynn on a private matter.'

'He's not a judge anymore, Jerry,' said Stoker. 'I'm the judge in this case.'

'You're a fair man,' said Jerry, and left the office, closing the door behind him.

'Jerr—'

'Your Honor, this is a potential criminal misconduct issue with the District Attorney's office. If you bring him in here, you're going to tip him off and that's an abuse of process and possibly perverting the course of justice. I do not come into a judge's chambers asking to speak with them privately without good cause.'

Stoker leaned back in his chair, his bushy eyebrows twitching on the slab of oak that passed for his forehead.

'What's going on?'

'The District Attorney's office has a wire tap on the defense team. He's listening in on our calls. This violates attorney-client privilege and work-product privilege. I want it to stop, and I want all the records from those phone calls he has taped.'

'What? I mean, say you're right about this, which you are most definitely not – a judge would've signed off on a warrant for that wire tap.'

'When you were a junior member of the judiciary, how many times did the NYPD come to your house at three a.m. and shove a fifty-page affidavit and a draft warrant under your nose? How many times did you read that affidavit cover to cover, and the warrant, line by line? You're not telling me the DA isn't smart enough to sneak this by a judge who's not paying attention.'

Leaning forward, Stoker thumped his elbows onto the desk and locked his thick fingers together, like it was a stance. A position for him to lodge a blistering attack.

'Do you have any evidence to back up this very serious allegation?' he asked.

'No, I have none whatsoever,' I said.

'If you do come across solid undeniable evidence that your phones are tapped then file a motion and I'll deal with it then.'

'I can't file a motion because I'd have to serve it on the DA's office. I'd be tipping them off.'

'Mr. Flynn, our justice system is not perfect, but we have rules of procedure for a reason.'

'Just grant me this one thing, if I find solid proof our phones are tapped you'll make a ruling that I get those records.'

He smirked, said, 'If you get me that evidence, I will make that order. Now, stop wasting my time. We have a trial to run. Your client show up yet?'

'She's not in court, but I am confident we can get her here before the trial concludes. I can say no more on that . . .'

'Of course, because of attorney-client privilege. I see . . .'

I got up and left.

In the hallway, on the way back to the courtroom, my phone vibrated. A text message from Betty.

The text gave me a name.

A time.

A location.

And Betty had confirmed it was accurate.

I started running.

Back into court, I jogged down the steps from the judge's bench, and right to the defense table. My phone was in my hand. Harry got up, and as we passed the prosecution table I said, 'If the judge comes out, tell him I had to make an urgent call.'

Drew White's eyes widened, and I noticed he turned in his chair and met the gaze of Bill Seong. They both knew I was up to something, but they had no idea what that might be.

Harry and I moved swiftly to the exit, through the doors and out into the corridor.

'Where's Peltier?' I asked.

'He's in the coffee shop across the street, waiting to be paged by the DA.'

Assistant District Attorney Drew White insisted his witnesses wait outside the court building, so that they do not hear any part of the trial before they are called to provide testimony. They are given a pager and told to go get coffee. Peltier had attended court this morning to see us before the trial started. Now he was off campus.

I dialed his number and he picked up straight away.

'I have a source, I can't say who it is, but Carrie Miller is going to meet her private banker at the Commodore restaurant at one-fifteen. Private table at the back behind the fish tank. We need to talk to her and bring her in. You ready for that?'

'I'm ready. I'll be there,' said Peltier, and I ended the call.

Harry and I went back into court, took our seats just as Jerry called out, 'All rise,' and introduced Judge Stoker as the presiding judge. White didn't take his eyes off me until the jury came in, and it was at this point I knew we had a problem on the jury.

Eleven of the jurors looked okay.

But it only takes one to poison an entire jury room. I wasn't the only one who had spotted our problem juror. Harry scratched at the flop of white hair on his head, leaned over and said, 'Look at juror five. The one in the floral dress.'

Juror five was a white lady in her late sixties. She wore a blue patterned floral dress, wore her silver hair pulled back so tightly you could see it stretching the skin around her small, black eyes. Large, thick glasses framed those eyes, and made them seem even smaller. Her lips were pressed tightly together, pinched as if she'd just licked napalm off a cactus. She held a small beige purse in front of her like a riot shield, both hands on the handle. You didn't want to mess with juror five. She had a build that could make a college linebacker jealous. And she looked mean. Pissed. Except when she looked at the prosecutor. When her gaze fell on Drew White her features softened, but only for a second. Then, she shifted in her seat, moving a little to the left, and gave the juror on her right a filthy look. This juror was an African American lady about the same age as juror five.

'That lady looks like she just wants the world to burn,' said Harry.

'Don't marry her, is my advice.'

'You know I like getting divorced, but she wouldn't have me. Did you see the look she gave juror six?'

'She isn't throwing any dirty looks at white jurors,' I said.

'Doesn't seem like the shy, retiring type either. She'll be real noisy in the jury room.'

I brought up the juror list on the iPad. There were some rudimentary notes below each juror, which Peltier had made during jury selection.

'Her name is Ethel Gorman. Former manager at an abattoir in Jersey. Never married. Spends her spare time fundraising for her local church and the NRA. She's a registered Republican and firmly against face masks and the coronavirus vaccine.'

'She's a . . . what do you call it? A Karen?' said Harry.

'She's like the alien queen of the Karens,' I said.

I looked at the list of alternate jurors. First alternate was Clay Dryer. He sat beside the jury box with the other two alternates.

He was about the same age as Ethel. He'd lost most of his hair, apart from a thick white band that surrounded the shiny dome. He wore glasses in a red frame, had a checked shirt, navy blazer and chinos. There was something around his wrist, just in front of his watch. A bracelet of brightly colored beads with a leather tag hanging from them. I was close enough to the alternates to make out the lettering on the tag. I couldn't read all of it, but I read enough to know it was a single word – Grandpa.

Peltier's notes said Clay was a retired carpenter, married fifty years and had seven grown children. He and his wife now looked after the grandkids while their children and their spouses worked. They enjoyed taking large family vacations. He owned three dogs. All seven kids, their spouses, and his thirteen grandchildren, came to a set of cabins upstate where they spent the summer together as one big family.

'We have to eighty-six Ethel and get Clay on the jury,' I whispered.

'Agreed. We can't take any chances. Ethel will be a firestorm in that jury room. Jesus, this is a shit show, and Kate . . .'

His voice faltered as he pointed to the jury list on the screen.

'Kate's relying on us. How do we bump Ethel? We can't object now.'

I had to put my head down into the work. This trial. The witnesses. The DA. The judge. Now, the jury. My mind was focused on destroying the case against Carrie Miller. Because it had to be. It was the only way of saving my friend. I had to put away the fear, the torturous anxiety, and laser my attention on doing the one thing within my power to bring her back.

But sometimes, like just now with Harry, I caught myself thinking about her. Where the hell was she? Was she hurt? Was she afraid? What was going through her mind?

Across the aisle, Drew White stood and moved around the prosecution table to take his place in the well of the court, facing the jury, and began his opening speech.

'Ladies and gentlemen of the jury, my name is Drew White. I am the person who is going to guide you through the prosecution evidence against Carrie Miller. This is an unusual case. I can't think of one quite like it. And like all unusual cases, it requires special attention. Your attention. By the end of this trial, we believe there are two reasonable opinions that can be formed. The first is that Carrie Miller actively participated in the murders along with her husband, Daniel Miller, better known to most people as the Sandman. She had the same intention as her husband – that intention was to kill. And knowing her husband was a killer, she intentionally aided his crimes. We have evidence to demonstrate her intentions and we will prove she gave aid to her husband. In other words, she is an accomplice. And that makes Carrie Miller a murderer.

'If, however, you are not sure beyond all reasonable doubt that she shared her husband's intention to kill, there is an alternative charge, that she facilitated his crimes. Both charges carry life sentences. One thing is clear, ladies and gentlemen of the jury, there can be no doubt whatsoever that Carrie Miller knew her husband was a killer. She did not contact the police, nor the FBI. Instead, she confided in her lawyer. And what did she do after receiving legal advice? She kept her mouth shut, and she aided and abetted her husband in evading capture, and allowed him to kill again and again and again. Carrie Miller is not here today. She has jumped bail. She's on the run. From justice. From you. You may ask yourself why an innocent woman would go on the run? The answer is simple. She is guilty. We can all see that. Your job is to make that official.'

CHAPTER THIRTY-ONE

BLOCH

There are several private labs in New York. Some of them have links to databases managed by law enforcement, some don't. Bloch parked outside a modern building in an area slap bang at the edge of Soho, the Civic Center and Tribeca. Lake went inside, and ten minutes later he came back out.

'Thirty-six hours,' he said. 'They'll check for fibers, DNA and any other traces left on the syringe cap. They're good. If there's something there, they'll find it.'

'They had better. We need the break,' said Bloch, and pulled into the street. She brought up her cell phone on the dash of the Jeep, dialed a number that read 'Parks.'

Parks was one of the agents in blue jeans who had been guarding Teresa Vasquez. He and Bloch had talked after the ambulance came and took away Miggs.

'Bloch, how are ya?' said the voice.

'I need to know if you got anywhere with the landlord for the artist's loft.'

'No, he said there was a short-term lease taken out the same month Lilian Parker was murdered. The guy paid in cash, there was nothing signed and no ID or bank details taken.'

'I'm sorry again, for the agents who died yesterday,' said Bloch.

'We appreciate what you did for Miggs. If we get anything else, I'll let you know.'

Bloch hung up. The Sandman had been watching Teresa Vasquez's apartment from the same place he'd watched Lilian Parker. The artist who had been the current tenant of that property could've lain up there dead for days or even weeks before anyone discovered him, and considering his eyes had not been removed, nor were any of the other Sandman signatures present, the murder and the location of the apartment would never have been linked to the Sandman nor any of his victims.

The Nielsens had lived in a relatively quiet suburban street in the East Village. Unlike most New Yorkers, they could afford a house. A brownstone that sat on the corner. Once, this house held a family. Now it remained empty. It was to go on the market once the trial was over, but the realtor didn't expect it to get many offers. The house had stood for probably ninety years. It would have held a myriad of families in that time. Every year, its value would have increased.

And now, no one wanted it.

If anyone did buy it, Bloch expected that to be someone who played the property market. No family would buy the house just yet. Evil had visited this place and left its mark.

Houses have memories. There probably isn't a single building in the city that hasn't been host to some kind of horror, and people were happy to move in soon as the blood was cleaned up. But some crimes are so terrible they leave a stigma in their wake that can't be washed away with thick bleach and baking soda.

Bloch pulled up a few houses away from the Nielsen place. Killed the engine. Checked her mirrors, then began scanning the cars parked on the street. No panel vans. Three cars were parked outside the building where Daisy Broder lived. Bloch had read her statement in the file and found out all she could about her. After all, Mrs. Broder was a prosecution witness and Eddie needed ammo. Bloch had found out plenty. None of it helped the defense.

Mrs. Broder, as she was known, was in her late eighties at Bloch's best guess, and in the very prime of life. Every morning she rose at six a.m., did her stretching, ate a bowl of organic muesli followed by two pots of coffee, pancakes and a rack of bacon. After breakfast she headed out into the neighborhood to one of her many jobs. She taught Spanish at the local community rec, had a part-time job as a cashier in the 7-Eleven two blocks away, and in her spare time she took classes at the local gym. Spin class, yoga, and line dancing were her favorites.

Popular with the kids in the neighborhood, Mrs. Broder's was always the first place they called at on Halloween because she had the best candy. She never shied away from answering their questions when they saw the number tattooed on her arm. It was faded and small, because she got it when she was not much older than they are now. Her memories of her early life in Poland had never faded.

Mrs. Broder had been sitting in her apartment, across the street from the Nielsens', when she saw a man and a woman walking by, late one night. Nothing unusual in that. When the same couple passed by again, Mrs. Broder paused her Arnold Schwarzenegger movie and came to the window. This time, the couple stopped outside the Nielsens' and stared at the house. Mrs. Broder later told the police it seemed as if the couple stood outside the house for a few minutes, looking it over. As if they were studying it. At one point the man turned and stared at Mrs. Broder. She felt a chill when he looked at her. Something inside was warning her about this man. She had met evil men before, especially as a young girl. And that same sense enveloped her, and she found that she had to move away from the window.

After the murders she told the police about the couple, but they didn't seem interested. They were not looking for two people. Just one man. Things changed when the FBI and the police identified Daniel Miller as the Sandman. Mrs. Broder was contacted by the NYPD and asked if the couple she saw that night were Daniel and Carrie Miller. She said it looked like them.

And now, Bloch stood outside the Nielsens' property, gazing up at the second-floor apartment across the street belonging to Mrs. Broder.

'You think she could identify somebody from that distance?' asked Lake.

'I'm not sure,' she said.

Bloch stared at the window, trying to estimate how far away Mrs. Broder would've been. It was difficult to concentrate. She had an urge to jump into the car and move. To search. Just to drive the streets looking for Kate. That would be pointless, but at least she would be moving.

She took a moment to breathe. She needed to think. Wherever the Sandman was hiding, that's where Kate would be. She needed focus, not movement. She checked around, found the nearest street-light then took pictures with her camera phone, emailed them to Eddie, just in case. He could make mountains of very little, and it was better that he had at least some pictures of the street.

'Let's go look in the house,' said Lake, and produced a chain from his pocket with a bunch of keys on a ring at the end of it.

'Where did you get the Nielsens' key?' asked Bloch.

'These are my keys,' he said.

Before he did anything else, he examined the lock. The same circular tool mark on the lock face.

'He drilled it again,' said Lake, then selected a key from the chain and tried to insert it in the lock. It took a bit of jiggling, but he got the thing in there and turned it with little effort, opening the door. Drilling the lock with this special tool didn't destroy the mechanism, but it made the lock so loose and buttery that you could insert a nail file into the slot and it would still work.

'After you,' said Lake.

Bloch stepped into the hallway of a family home. It was the kind of picture you see listed on the homepage of high-end real-tors' websites. White walls, pastel colors, wooden parquet floor. All of it tastefully decorated. A picture of the family sat on the coffee table of the lounge on the left. Bloch took a moment to study it.

A beautiful little boy and girl. Not far off each other in age. They both had those super-wide smiles with not even a hint of self-consciousness – just full of mirth, happiness and love. Only kids smile that way. Lost in the moment. Robert was five. Elly was eight. This picture couldn't have been taken long before the Sandman came into their lives.

And behind them, their parents. Tobias Nielsen was clean shaven, with a million-dollar smile you could put on a toothpaste billboard. His eyes were clear and bright, and even at forty-five, free of lines.

He owned restaurants in the city and bought and sold real estate on the side. Every year he threw a party for friends. He and his wife, Stacy, were real New York socialites. Stacy had been even more beautiful. Long auburn hair caressed the side of her cheek, as if it was igniting the coral glow from her skin. Even her imperfections seemed to enhance her good looks. A scar bisected her right eyebrow, ruining the symmetry of her face, but it didn't in any way detract from her allure. Somehow it only added to her glamour and enhanced the faultless perfection of her other features.

She had died younger than Tobias. At thirty-four, the Sandman had ended her.

Moving through the lounge, Bloch found the large kitchen and noticed the back door. Built from solid oak with two heavy deadbolts. One at the top with the bar going into the ceiling, and one at the bottom with a bolt hole in the stone floor. Even if the Sandman had drilled the mortice lock, there was no way past those deadbolts. Bloch opened the back door and stepped out into a narrow, covered alley. A Perspex canopy, affixed to the back of the building leading on from the brownstone, covered the trash cans. A brick wall on the right, she followed the alley left as it wound around the house and back onto the street. The mortice lock on the back door had no tooling marks. The Sandman had accessed the property from the front. There was nothing else of interest on the rest of the first floor, and Bloch followed Lake upstairs.

The second floor had a playroom, bathroom and large studio. Stacy had been an architect who worked mostly from home. The third floor had another bathroom, two children's rooms opposite one another. They made for the main bedroom down the hall.

The king-sized bed was still in the room. In the center of the mattress was a huge stain. It was an oval shape, like the abdomen of a giant black spider.

Bloch went to the window and looked out. She could see straight into Mrs. Broder's little apartment. She took the iPad from her backpack, fired it up and skimmed through the crime-scene photos for the Nielsen murders, looking for the pictures taken of the victims as the police found them.

Looking at the faces of the dead is hard. Studying the faces of those who had died violently was something else. It was nothing new to Bloch. She had been trained to look past the horror so that she would be able to see the evidence. Every murder told a tale.

After he had sedated the children, he pulled the comforter up under their chins. They were found with their eyes closed and, at first, the cops thought they were dead. At least the first responder did, the officer who had subsequently taken his own life. The girl woke first and stumbled out of her room to find a cop in her house, staring at her parents who had been murdered in their bed. The shock traumatized them both.

Tobias had a bullet wound on the left side of his nose. The exit wound was on top of his head, suggesting he had been lying down when the shot was fired, and the shooter was in an elevated position. Stacy had multiple stab wounds. According to the medical examiner, any number of them could have been fatal in a matter of seconds. They were found in bed, the comforter covered their bodies, eyes missing, sand in those sockets and in their wounds.

'Why a family?' asked Lake.

The FBI analysts, including Delaney, thought they had an answer.

He was upping the ante.

Taking greater risks and showing the world his power.

Bloch could see the logic in that, but somehow it didn't quite fit.

'He let the children live. Made sure they wouldn't interfere. He shot the father in the head, but used a blade on the wife. I get the impression the couple were the target. The children were just part of the job,' said Bloch.

'Why this family?'

'I don't know,' said Bloch as she began to pace around the room, thinking.

'This is not an easy house to access,' said Lake. 'He went in the front door. That's a busy street and he risked being spotted. Actually, Mrs. Broder *did* spot him, and a female, casing the place.'

Something Lake said seemed important. When he'd spoken just now, Bloch had felt a prickling sensation over her skin, sending goosebumps running along her flesh.

'Say that again,' said Bloch.

'What?'

'Just repeat what you said.'

'Ah, ahm, this house is pretty secure and visible from a lot of windows. He was taking one hell of a risk in—'

'No,' said Bloch, frustration creeping into her voice.

'Take it easy, let's just think this through,' said Lake.

'I can't take it easy,' said Bloch. 'He took my friend. We have to move quicker. You said something else. You said something about this house.'

'Oh, he had to go in through the front – a major risk for—'

'That's it,' said Bloch, moving out of the room and quickly down the stairs.

'What? What is it?' he asked.

Bloch said nothing, she just went straight into the kitchen and waited for Lake to catch up.

'If you were going to break into this house, how would you do it?' asked Bloch.

'Well, only real way is the front . . .'

Lake stood still.

'The front door is the *only* way in,' he said. 'The back door has better cover but he didn't even try to enter that way. There are no tool marks on the locks. The deadbolts on the inside of the kitchen . . . Shit, you can't see the deadbolts from the outside. He knew about them. Miller had been in this house before . . .'

But Bloch wasn't listening. She was on the phone to Eddie.

CHAPTER THIRTY-TWO

EDDIE

'Mr. Flynn, do you wish to make an opening statement at this time?' asked Judge Stoker.

The courtroom had flooded with silence. After the murmurs that erupted from White's opening, and Stoker's question to me, it had now settled into an almost liquid quiet. A dense nothingness in the air. A total void of sound. Or so it seemed to me.

My head was whirling. A thousand problems were thundering through my brain.

'Eddie, we're not helping Kate. Just go talk to the jury,' whispered Harry.

'And what am I going to say?'

'Just tell them what Kate told us.'

I got up, took a long drink of water and put the glass back down. My heels were like a snare drum on the floor – the noise filling that pool of void, sending ripples of sound along the four walls of this place. I looked down, found that I was standing in the center of the courtroom, facing the jury. The judge on my left, the rest of the courtroom on my right. I looked at the faces of each jury member. There were some, like Ethel Gorman, who couldn't hide their disgust. It was written on her cruel lips and her small black pin eyes.

'The prosecution will talk a lot about the victims in this case. And this is only right. It's Mr. White's job to give a voice to the dead in this courtroom. To let them speak through him. And to show you who killed them. Ladies and gentlemen, there are two problems faced by the prosecution. The first is that the man who killed these victims is not in this courtroom. He's still out there.

Still taking lives. And the FBI and NYPD can't catch him. The FBI and NYPD have rarely faced this much public pressure to bring a criminal to justice. Because they have failed to do so, they are offering you his wife instead. You will hear the evidence against Carrie Miller, but really this is evidence against her husband, Daniel Miller. There is no evidence to link Carrie Miller to these murders. There is no evidence that proves Carrie Miller knew her husband was a killer. There is no evidence that proves she ever assisted or aided him, knowingly. Carrie Miller is a victim of the Sandman. She has had her life torn apart. She will never trust another man. Not for as long as she lives. Imagine finding out that your partner is a killer? Imagine what that would do to someone?

'Ladies and gentlemen, the prosecutor will try to ride two horses in this case. He's going to try to prove that she was involved in these murders, but that is going to fail. When it does fail, he is going to try and show that she knew about the murders, and colluded in those murders, even lying to the authorities.'

I paused, took a moment to drink in the expressions of the jurors.

They weren't buying it.

I realized in that moment it was because, deep down, I didn't buy it either.

Carrie Miller was carrying around something heavy. Something dark that latched onto her heart. And whatever that was, it had caused her to run from this trial. Run from me, Kate and Harry. But when I'd spoken to her and she told me, face to face, that she hadn't killed anyone, I had believed her. Deep in my soul, I *knew* that was true. And yet, here I was, delivering an opening statement, doubt about my client's innocence running rampant in my own mind. I had made a mistake taking this case. Now, with Kate's life in the balance, I had no choice. I had to make this jury believe me. I had to win. Not for Carrie.

For Kate.

'I'm not going to tell you Carrie Miller didn't have suspicions about her husband.'

I paused again, let that one float around the jury. Some of them shifted in their seats. One or two leaned forward, just a little.

'At what point does a suspicion become a legal obligation to tell the police you think your husband might have hurt someone? That's a question that's never been in front of a jury before. Her husband lied to her. And she believed him. If that's a crime, you can lock up every married person in New York.

'Carrie Miller isn't here today. She might not be here for the rest of the trial. That's okay, because she doesn't have to prove anything. It's the prosecution's job to prove their case. And when it comes right down to it, they don't have a case against Carrie Miller. I believe that soon enough – you will see that too.'

I turned and started walking back to my seat. My phone vibrated. With my back to the judge, I checked the caller ID. It was Bloch.

'The People call Doctor Farley Climpton,' said White.

The medical examiner. White was going to start this case with a horror picture. Several of them. Lurid photos of the victims. The jury would carry some of these images around in their minds for the rest of their lives. And with that terror in their guts, he would then proceed to point the finger at Carrie Miller and tell the jury she was responsible. Looking at those photos inflicts trauma and the jury would need to blame someone for their psychological injury – and the blame rested easy on a defendant.

'Take over a minute,' I said to Harry, then carried on walking right out the door.

I answered the call in the hallway.

'What have you got?' I asked Bloch.

'We're getting closer. Daniel Miller knew the layout of the Nielsen house. We need to find the link between him and the Nielsens.'

'We need to move faster. We have to find her—'

'Don't you think I know that? I don't know what I'd do if—'

'Stop it. That's not going to happen. We won't let it happen. Did the feds get anything from the landlord of the loft apartment?'

'No records. Short-term lease, paid in advance.'

'That doesn't sound right. No one leases out a property in this city without getting information on the tenant so they can go after them if it all turns sour.'

'The feds said there was nothing.'

'The landlord is lying, and I think I know why. There's someone you can go talk to. A lawyer for slumlords named Archie Bunsen. He's not going to want to give you anything, so you might have to lean on him. Just so you know, Bunsen has protection. His personal bodyguard is a former wrestler called Moonman. He's six-five, maybe five hundred pounds. A steroid freak. Super strong and mean as hell. Be careful—'

'What? You think I can't handle him?'

'No, I meant be careful you don't hurt him too bad.'

CHAPTER-THIRTY-THREE

EDDIE

Bloch and I talked for a half hour.

After I finished the call, I dialed the office and Denise picked up.

'I need you to take three hundred dollars out of petty cash and buy two hundred bucks' worth of lunch vouchers. Then I want you to hire a limo and a driver for the afternoon,' I said.

'Wait, what's the hundred for?'

'I'll tell you later. One more thing. I'm going to text you a number. Call it. Tell them exactly this. Do you have a pen?'

'Go.'

'*We have a mutual friend, and we'd like to give him a special treat for the lunch he has arranged. He's a little shy, but he likes wigs. Neon blonde, the more artificial the better. We'll pay an extra grand right now. Also, he's Covid secure so she'll need a mask.*'

'Is that it?'

'That's it. Put the money on the office credit card. Have you got that?'

'What the hell are you doing?' asked Denise.

'I'm practicing law. Trust me. Once you're done with that, grab a clipboard and your notebook and come meet me outside Center Street at the lunch break.'

If Denise said she would do it, you can take that to the bank.

I walked back into court. As I took my seat alongside Harry, Doctor Farley Climpton was on his feet with a laser pointer in his hand. It was aimed at a six-by-five foot blown-up picture of Stacy Nielsen as she lay dead beside her husband.

'The wounds on Stacy Nielsen's chest, like the other victims, were made with an incredibly strong, and incredibly sharp object.

Again, this was probably a leaf-bladed knife of unknown origin, more than likely an exotic weapon, possibly handmade. The blade was strong enough to pierce her chest plate. Again, no metal shards were found in the wound after the sand filling the wound cavity had been sieved, and the fissure searched by x-ray.'

I leaned over to Harry, whispered, 'Any surprises?'

He threw a glance at the jury.

Ethel Gorman was wringing a handkerchief so tightly her hands were shaking. If I listened carefully enough, I thought I might even hear her teeth grinding together. The rest of the jury looked the same as most others who have to deal with a case like this. Half of them looked at the floor, only glancing up when they absolutely had to, and then back down again. The others covered their mouths, shook their heads, and grimaced as the images were displayed.

'That good, huh?'

He nodded.

Harry had a stack of notes in front of him from the medical examiner's testimony.

'Do you want to take this guy?' I asked.

A half smile gave me my answer.

'Doctor Climpton,' said White, 'did you find any defensive wounds on Stacy Nielsen's body?'

'There were none,' he said.

'Just so that I understand this, Doctor, there were no defensive wounds on Margaret Sharpe, Lilian Parker, Penny Jones, Suzanna Abrams, nor on Tobias and Stacy Nielsen? No defensive wounds on any of the six victims?'

'Correct. There were none.'

'And were all of the female victims attacked with a knife?'

'Yes.'

'Were all of the female victims sedated?'

'Yes, by injection into the neck area.'

'Were there any scratch marks or needle marks anywhere else on the body that would indicate a struggle?'

'None.'

'In your extensive experience of dealing with victims of stabbing or knife crime, is it unusual not to have any defensive wounds?'

'Highly unusual.'

'Again, based on your extensive experience, can you offer any explanation for this?'

He cleared his throat. Took a sip of water.

A tell.

District Attorney White would have prepared Climpton's testimony carefully. Coaching him. Pushing him as far and as wide as he was willing to go. This last question was the outer limit, and I could tell Climpton wasn't happy. He was stretching his testimony to give the DA what he wanted. Like a fifty-five-year-old truck driver in an advanced Pilates class, the stretch would be painful.

'It is possible,' began Climpton, 'that the reason we don't have defensive wounds is because the victims were restrained by another person during the attack.'

White turned to the jury, repeated the answer, slowly, in a triumphant tone. Then he turned to me, said, 'Your witness.'

'Just a moment, Your Honor, we do have questions for this witness,' said Harry. Then whispered to me, 'How do you want me to handle this?'

Harry and I had already talked strategy. There are any number of ways to take apart a witness, and many more tactics when facing a professional witness like Climpton who had plenty of trial experience.

'That crack about a third party restraining the victim went way out of Climpton's comfort zone,' I said.

'Agreed. Either we go Joe Frazier or Larry David. I'm thinking Larry.'

'Larry David, all the way,' I said.

Harry took hold of his legal pad, and his pen, and walked around the defense table beaming a big smile at the witness.

Cross examinations are like short cons. You need the right style for the right mark. Option one with Climpton was to go Joe Frazier, a legendarily powerful hitter who liked to fight in the pocket. Boxers use the ring and the space between them and their opponents in different ways. Angelo Dundee, a legendary cornerman, once said that Ali liked to fight in a room, Tyson liked to fight in a closet, and Frazier liked to fight in a phone booth. The Frazier style of cross examination is to get right into the witness's face and throw hard fast questions in the hope one will knock them out.

Harry went with the Larry David.

'Doctor Climpton,' said Harry, adjusting his glasses, 'before we begin, I'd like to thank you for your testimony and the respect and courtesy you have shown not just for the victims, but for their families. I know you're doing your professional duty here today, to the very best of your ability, but your enthusiasm, commendable as it may be, has got the better of you. Let's correct those mistakes. Just a moment, let me check my notes here . . .'

The classic Larry David opening. Harry hadn't asked a question. He had complimented a professional who worked for the city, and after that he had told the witness he had made some mistakes, and Harry was going to help him correct them. Then, the pause. To let Harry check his notes. Of course, he didn't need to read his notes. He needed to give the jury time to absorb what he'd said and to recognize that Climpton didn't seem to be arguing with him. The witness didn't have a question to answer, so like all pros he waited for one. Meanwhile, the jury thinks Climpton has accepted some mistakes. And those mistakes were not malicious – the witness was *too enthusiastic*. It's a way of using the witness's authority against them, which is probably more powerful because it makes them a defense witness, instead of the DA's witness.

This style referred not to Larry David himself, but to his TV show. It was all about getting the witness *to curb their enthusiasm*.

'Doctor, you stated for the record, that apart from the trauma to the ocular area there was usually only one or two stab wounds on the female victims, in the stomach or chest area?'

'Yes.'

Professional witnesses have been on this ride before. They know to keep their answers short, snappy. Don't elaborate, don't speculate. The more they said the greater the chance of the defense being able to slip a crowbar between those words and start breaking them up into worthless little pieces.

'Lilian Parker and Penny Jones all had single stab wounds to the chest?'

'Correct.'

'And those wounds proved fatal?'

'Yes, instantaneously, I would say.'

'And this second attacker you mentioned, how would they restrain the victims exactly?'

This was an open question. It allowed Climpton room to say whatever he wanted, and back it up however he liked. In any cross-exam, open questions are a bad idea. They carried enormous risk because you had no control. The witness would say something more than 'yes' or 'no.' Probably a lot more. This is why the Larry David method carried so much risk.

'From behind, I would say. Restraining their arms from behind,' said Climpton.

He was still on shaky ground. Not where he wanted to be, and it was the DA who had put him there.

'The victim would struggle against the second attacker's grip?'

'Most assuredly,' said Climpton.

'I don't want to put the images of the crime scenes before the jury again, to spare them, but I will if I must. It depends on your next answer, Doctor. My question is, in any of those crime scene photographs we've had to look at, did any of those scenes show signs of a struggle?'

Climpton bit his lip.

Harry had put him in a tight position. If he disagreed, Harry would bring out the photos, and go through them in detail, pointing out that all the furniture was upright, there's no blood spread around the room and nothing is broken. And the jury would have to go through this again because Climpton insisted on it. They would blame him for it, and when he tried to argue his point in the face of what the photos clearly showed, they would doubt his credibility even more.

'No,' said Climpton, swallowing that one in case Harry put him through hell with the photos.

'There were no signs of bruising on any of the victims either?'

'No, there was no bruising.'

'These women were fighting for their lives. They would have tried to break free, yes?'

'Yes.'

'The victims would have cried out, too?'

'I don't know,' said Climpton, trying desperately to avoid walking this path.

'But you've just told this jury that the victim's arms would be restrained from behind. The second attacker would need to use both hands to do that. So there would be nothing to stop the victim screaming, would there?'

Climpton was now looking at the DA as if he had sold him a used car with a hole in the exhaust and no engine.

'No, I guess not.'

'Penny Jones and Suzanna Abrams were murdered in the same apartment, not twenty feet from one another, isn't that right?'

'Right.'

'The prosecution doesn't have any witnesses who heard a victim screaming, do they?'

'Not to my knowledge.'

'Isn't it more likely that a single attacker moved silently and swiftly through these victims, administering an instant killing stroke as they lay asleep in their beds?'

'I wouldn't say it's more likely . . .' said Climpton, then saw Harry's expression change. I could see it registering with Climpton. Like he'd just looked up to see a piano about to fall on top of his head.

The mistake here would be to allow Climpton to elaborate, spin some bullshit to muddy the point and call it a draw.

'Doctor, we saw the photos. There were no signs of a struggle. There is no evidence from the injuries inflicted that there was a second attacker, in an effort to be helpful to the victims in this case you have made a mistake, isn't that correct?'

'I can't tell from the injuries who wielded the knife. It could have been the defendant, with her husband holding the victim down, and covering their mouth.'

About the best Climpton could do. He breathed out, took a sip of water.

Harry walked over to the witness stand. He could reach out and touch it if he wanted.

He asked, 'So now you're saying Carrie Miller wielded the knife, not her husband?'

'It's possible.'

'How long have you been a medical examiner?'

Larry David wasn't working. Climpton was wriggling too much. Harry was moving in, like Joe Frazier. I saw his play, took hold of the iPad and searched for a document. A section of Climpton's report.

'Fifteen years,' said Climpton.

'And you've read your reports on the victims in preparation for your testimony today?'

'I have.'

Harry reached out a hand, and I got up and gave him the iPad with the relevant section of Climpton's report open on the screen.

'This is from your report on Stacy Nielsen. At the concluding paragraph, *"The blade pierced the skin easily and passed through the breastbone with great force in a single stroke. This suggests the perpetrator is physically strong. Perhaps much stronger than your average male."'*

Climpton swallowed, but kept his head very still. Maybe he had been sweating before now, but I noticed his forehead was glazed in perspiration.

'You go on to say, *"This corresponds with the wounds found on the other victims. A violent blow delivered with enormous power."'*

'Yes, well . . .'

'Carrie Miller couldn't weigh more than a hundred and ten pounds. She didn't cause those wounds, did she, Doctor?'

A Joe Frazier uppercut.

'Ah, I suppose not,' said Climpton.

'Just so we're clear, and the jury is clear, there is nothing in your expert opinion to suggest that Carrie Miller was a second attacker in any of these murders, isn't that right?'

Climpton had done his best for the DA. And he wanted out of that witness box. You could see it. He was practically squirming in that seat like it was covered in fire ants.

'In hindsight, having taken stock of everything – no. I can't say that she was a second attacker here.'

Frazier wins by knock out.

'Thank you for clarifying your position, Doctor,' said Harry, and he walked back to the defense table.

As White got up to re-examine, he noticed Climpton was already halfway out of that chair. Smart and experienced, he knew he wasn't going to get any more out of Climpton. The man was done.

'No re-examination,' said White.

Harry sat down, whispered, 'Don't get excited. There's still plenty of time to lose this case.'

Stoker looked at the clock. 12:45 p.m.

'We'll stop to allow the jurors some lunch. Back at two-fifteen. Mr. White, is that enough time to prepare your next witness?'

'We'll be ready, Your Honor,' he said. 'The question is will Mr. Flynn be ready?'

'We'll find out after lunch,' said Stoker.

CHAPTER THIRTY-FOUR

EDDIE

Harry and I took a table at the Commodore restaurant. I don't eat in places like this. I get by with deli sandwiches, pancakes and if I'm in a hurry a dirty-water hotdog suits me just fine. Restaurants with table-cloths and wine lists make me nervous. I'm never sure what piece of cutlery I should be using or whether I'm holding it the right way. It was a table for four, at the back of the joint, close to the kitchen. The table that's reserved for clientele you don't want eating in your restaurant.

Like a lot of New York restaurants, the Commodore resembled a luxurious bunker. The windows were heavily tinted. Small electric lamps burned on the tables, and every ten feet or so, industrial-style light bulbs hung from the ceiling. Some folks thought this made the place intimate. I just thought places like this made it impossible to read the menu. Still, it smelled like a good restaurant. The scent of roasting meat smothered in fragrant herbs would normally give me an appetite. Today, I was too worried to eat. This was strictly business.

The maître d' got us settled and offered water. Still or sparkling. Harry said he'd like a beer, because he didn't trust water, and gave the maître d' the old W.C. Fields line – 'Have you seen what it does to the inside of pipes? I'll stick to beer.'

I asked for a Pepsi.

'When are you expecting the rest of your party?' he asked.

'Soon,' said Harry. 'In the meantime, do you have steaks?'

'Of course, the waiter will be over to take your order in a—'

'Just tell him to throw us a pair of steaks. Medium. Thank you.'

There's a hierarchy in restaurants like this. A whole other class system that operates not just on the floor, and in the back, but with the customers too.

The maître d' smiled like he wanted our mothers to roast on his grill, and left.

'Do you think this is going to work?' asked Harry, folding a napkin over his lap.

I took a napkin from the table and tried to mimic Harry's flick of the wrist before he draped it, expertly, across his thighs. I nearly dropped the thing and decided to leave it on the table.

'It has to work. All we have to do is rely on the FBI.'

'Famous last words,' said Harry.

A tall man entered the restaurant. At first, I didn't notice him. I noticed other people noticing him. Heads turned when Otto Peltier came into a room. The good looks, the height, the shoulders and, of course, the suit. He made his way to our table, took a seat.

'Gentlemen,' he said, by way of greeting.

'We've ordered steaks. You want something?' asked Harry.

The maître d', who I thought might instruct the kitchen to spit in our food, seemed to have a personality transplant as soon as he laid eyes on Peltier.

'Mr. Peltier, it's so good to see you,' he said.

'Thank you, Charles. I'll just have the chicken salad and the Italian still water, please.'

'A wise choice. I'll bring it right out with the rest of the . . . order. If you fine gentlemen need anything else, just let me know.'

As the man left the table, almost bowing to Peltier, Harry shook his head.

'You can have my steak with that, if you like,' I said. 'I don't have an appetite.'

'When I was in Vietnam,' said Harry, 'in deep country, our platoon was ambushed by the VC. Two of my best friends died that day. My lieutenant, a twenty-year-old veteran, told us all to eat double rations that night. Eat while you can, he said. The body and the mind are linked. When that steak comes you better tuck in, Eddie. You'll need it.'

While Harry spoke, I noticed Peltier's hands adjusting his knife and fork, aligning them perfectly. Then he folded his arms. As if to resist the temptation to fiddle with the cutlery further.

'Do you think she'll really show up?' he asked.

Harry and I exchanged glances. I turned and looked over at the fish tank. I'd always found tropical fish soothing. It was something to do with the way they swam and the light dancing off their tiny, luminescent scales. I always wanted one as a kid, but all we could afford were a couple of goldfish in a bowl that never lived long. Even the names of these fish were exotic. This tank had graceful clownfish, who always looked like they were dancing as they swam; blue angelfish with their feather-like fins; a shoal of tiny neon tetras, which were just flashes of bright light that shimmered and danced in the water like green and red flames. There were others, but I'd forgotten what they were called.

The lamp gave Peltier a golden glow. Maybe it was his skin, I couldn't tell. I got up from my seat, said, 'I'll go look out front.'

As I passed through the gloom of the Commodore, I took my time to examine the faces at the tables. The men wore suits, or at least jackets and ties. It was that kind of place. Business people wrapped in conversation, ladies with shopping bags from Maison Goyard and Alexander McQueen tucked by their feet, couples hunched over the table in whispered conversation, and two guys in dark suits leaning back in their chairs and studying the menu like it was written by James Joyce. The two suits were at a table by the window, with a view of the front door. Both cradled their heads with one hand, the other holding the large leather-bound menu awkwardly, as if it were about to tip over. They were covering their earpieces. Feds. They may as well have worn tee-shirts and baseball caps with the FBI logo.

I pushed through the front door onto the street. It was a cross street in the low thirties, just off Madison Avenue. A newsstand on the corner. I picked up a copy of the *Wall Street Journal* off the stack. As I leaned over, I saw a black van parked on the corner. There was a guy beside me in a beige mac with a copy of *Time Magazine* in his hand. He flicked through it, but wasn't really paying attention. I paid for the paper, turned and clocked another panel van across the street with a lone driver at the wheel.

There were two guys in high-vis yellow vests and hard hats drinking 7-Eleven coffee from Styrofoam cups and talking about the Yankees game. I'd never seen two construction workers with cleaner boots, pants and soft pink hands.

They stopped talking when the woman in the white pant suit got out of a cab. She had long neon-blonde hair. It was a wig, obviously. The suit looked like silk, and she wore it with four-inch heels and a purse that probably cost more than my car. A Covid facemask obscured her features, but I caught the whiff of expensive perfume as she entered the Commodore. Between the wig and the mask, it was difficult to get a good look at her. She appeared to be hiding her appearance.

I waited a beat.

Checked my watch.

Thirty seconds was my guess. They would wait until she got seated before they arrested her. Then Peltier, then Harry.

And then me.

CHAPTER THIRTY-FIVE

EDDIE

The guy in the mac suddenly lost interest in the copy of *Time Magazine*. He dropped it and moved quickly inside. At the same time, the construction workers dumped their coffees and followed the guy in the mac into the restaurant, pulling Glocks from the back of their pants as they went. The rear doors of the panel van across the street were thrown open and Bill Seong and DA Drew White leapt out along with two other feds.

I ducked inside the Commodore.

There was some commotion up ahead as the guys in the hard hats darted between tables.

The woman in the blonde wig and the mask was already at the back of the restaurant, oblivious to the scene behind her.

Otto stood up when he saw her approach.

She was one of those women who didn't exactly walk. She glided. Her purse swung on her arm, the white jacket and pants bloomed and swayed with her movement.

She walked right past our table.

And walked around the fish tank.

I turned and saw Seong dart into the restaurant, followed by White. The DA wasn't going to miss the opportunity to see Carrie Miller arrested along with her whole legal team.

'Flynn, hold it. You're under arrest. Harboring a bail jumper,' said Seong.

I stood still, said, 'I'm not harboring anyone. And I'm not meeting anyone. Go on back and see for yourself.'

People say a lot of shit before they get arrested. They threaten the cops, either physically or say that their lawyer will sue them,

190

or sometimes it's just abuse followed by a lot of resistance, trying to hit out and scramble away from the law. The feds and the cops have seen it all. Every arrest is different. And anything can happen.

But this was a new one on Bill.

I could see him putting the brakes on. He put both hands out, as if he were about to break his fall. He looked at me like I'd just handed him a winning hand of four aces in a poker game when he already held three of them.

'What the hell is this, Eddie?' he asked. 'That's Carrie Miller up there, right?'

'You'd better get a hold of your men,' I said.

The guy in the mac had his gun drawn and pointed at Harry and Peltier. Otto was on his feet, hands in the air.

Harry didn't give one shit. His steak had arrived, and he was ignoring the shouting from the FBI agent. Just cutting into his meat and enjoying his beer.

The construction guys had followed the woman in white behind the fish tank. I could see them in their shooting stance, bellowing instructions for Carrie to get on the floor.

The whole restaurant had erupted. People were frightened, and most of them were trying to leave, maybe without paying.

As Seong made his way to the back he was trying to calm everyone down. I followed him. I didn't want to miss this.

Seong came around the fish tank to the table behind it. He immediately grabbed the arms of the high-vis guys and got them to lower their weapons. I came around the corner and saw the lady in the wig on her knees, cowering on the floor. She had removed her mask and now it was clear she was *not* Carrie Miller.

Betty Clarke from the *Sentinel*, with her connections in the court office, had texted me the lady's name, but I couldn't remember it. All I knew from what Betty told me was she came from an agency called Classical Companions, she charged two hundred an hour for the pleasure of her company and that she would be here to meet a regular client at the Commodore. It was the client I was interested in.

The schmuck paying the two hundred had his hands raised, and his mouth open, on the other side of the table. As Seong got his men under control, the schmuck's expression switched from shock to indignant rage. Now he looked more familiar.

The client, and schmuck, Judge Stoker, lowered his hands, screamed, 'What is the meaning of this?!' just at the same moment Drew White came around the corner and realized that between him and Seong, they'd been set up.

'Your Honor—' began White, but it was drowned out by Stoker.

'What the hell are you doing? I'm having lunch with my . . . girlfriend,' said the judge, and took his date by the arm to try and settle her down.

'I'm so sorry, Judge,' said White. 'We had information that Carrie Miller would be here in this restaurant right now. We're sorry, we saw this lady, you know, the wig, and we figured it was Miller in disguise . . .'

'What kind of information? Who told you this?'

'I did, Your Honor,' I said. 'Only I didn't tell the district attorney. I called Otto Peltier and told *him*. Carrie Miller was never coming to this restaurant. We knew you'd be here. I got a tip from the court staff that this was your regular lunch place. I didn't know you'd be with your girlfriend. For that I'm sorry, but, Your Honor, this proves that my phone and the phones belonging to the entire defense team have been tapped by the DA's office.'

I lied, but only a little. Of course we knew he'd be here with his escort. We'd paid extra for her to wear the wig and the mask so she'd look like a lady in disguise and the feds would jump on her thinking she was Carrie Miller. The whole performance was for Stoker.

'Is this true?' asked Stoker.

Rubbing his temples, Bill Seong closed his eyes and probably wished he was anywhere else on earth rather than right here. White said nothing.

'Mr. White, either you answer my question, or I will be holding you and every cop and federal agent in this restaurant in contempt. You can answer me now, or you can go to the cells and think about it there . . .'

'Yes, Your Honor. There is a warrant which permits a wire tap—'

'Well, that warrant is now struck down, do you hear me? And you hand over to Flynn every document, tape and digital recording you've got. And you . . .' said the judge, now looking at me with that almost purple face.

Stoker was going to put on a show. Do a little shouting and threaten me and White. But he couldn't make any kind of official complaint because his girlfriend charged by the hour, and not just for lunch. He wouldn't want any of this on any kind of record. Likewise for White. He'd just put the FBI through an expensive surveillance operation to catch the judge's call girl. He wanted to forget this asap.

'I know you played the DA, but you *used* me,' said Stoker. 'So you'll get your records, but you can kiss goodbye to any kind of motion for a mistrial. If you find something in the wire tap records then file a motion, but right now, *no way*. You set this whole thing up. You can't manufacture your own mistrial. And if either one of you tell the jury the DA is bugging the defense lawyer's phones, then there *will be* a mistrial. I'll have no choice but to declare one. But if that happens, I will report both of you to the bar ethics committee and you'll lose your license. Do I make myself clear? The jury cannot hear about any of this. Got it? Do you *both* understand?' said Stoker, a thick vein standing out in his neck. I thought the guy might have a heart attack right there.

White apologized again.

I didn't.

'Your Honor, there's one more thing,' I said.

'What?!' he yelled, sending flecks of white spittle over the table and the feds that were standing closest to him.

'I need you to dismiss juror Ethel Gorman.'

'You've got to be fucking kidding me, Flynn? *Now* you're going to ask me this? We're not in court. And why the hell would I do that?'

'Because she's sitting right over there,' I said, pointing to the table in the corner where Ethel Gorman sat, her mouth open, a half-eaten oyster on her tongue and her eyes wide as a truck's headlights. We all squinted through the gloom, but it was Ethel.

I'd met Denise outside court and pointed out Ethel as she came through the exit taking her cigarettes out of her purse. Denise approached Ethel and told her she had been selected at random for today's mystery-shopper lunch prize. She had two hundred dollars to spend, right now, in a high-class restaurant called the Commodore. She would be taken there, and then back to Center Street in a limo, and all she had to do was tell Denise what she thought of her lunch afterward and fill out a comment card in order to take home the one-hundred-dollar market research fee, paid in advance. From the look on Ethel's face, she was beginning to realize there is no such thing as a free lunch in Manhattan.

For what seemed like a long time, no one moved. And no one said anything.

Then I heard Harry behind the fish tank. He was coughing, politely, and I guessed he was trying to get someone's attention. Then I heard him hollering at the maître d'.

'Excuse me, can we get this order to go?'

CHAPTER THIRTY-SIX

Extract from the Journal of Carrie Miller

June 4

It was after three in the morning when I heard the front door close.

I waited to hear his footsteps coming up the stairs. It was hot in the bedroom, but that wasn't the reason I couldn't sleep.

Over the past weeks I'd been driving myself crazy. Ever since that cop arrived at the front door asking about Danny's van. In the past few days he's been out super late every night. And I've been lying here, thinking. Panicking.

Thinking the same thoughts over and over again.

He loves me.

He was out the night of Margaret Sharpe's murder.

He has never been violent to me. I've never even seen him angry.

He gave me a pair of earrings the day after her murder that were exactly like hers.

That was a coincidence. Had to be.

He lied to the police about being home that night.

He had an excuse for that.

He made me tell the same lie.

He was concerned and just wanted rid of the cop who upset me.

He was out the night of the last two murders. Those girls killed in their apartment.

He has to work late and meet his clients, some of those he talks to on the phone are in different time zones.

He took a shower when he got home.

He had an excuse . . .

THIS. IS. DRIVING. ME. INSANE.

I listened for the sound of him coming upstairs.

There was only silence in the house.

Then, I heard door hinges whining downstairs.

That was strange. There was only one door in the house with squeaky hinges. A door that Daniel never opened.

I threw off the covers, padded downstairs in my bare feet.

I had to know.

I went into the kitchen and saw the door to the basement open. The light was on. I slipped through the open door and quietly walked down the basement stairs.

My breath caught in my chest.

My life, the fairytale, was over. It ended that night in our basement. The walls I had built to protect myself from those thoughts had cracks. Fissures that had widened with every late night, every missed dinner, the earrings, and now this . . .

I was on the other side now, staring back at my past life from a new place, watching it disappear.

Nothing would ever be the same again.

Daniel stood naked in the basement, pouring soap into the laundry machine. He saw me standing at the base of the stairs and it startled him.

He said I'd almost given him a heart attack. I didn't give him a chance to settle down, I demanded to know what the hell was going on.

Before he answered, he poured the remaining soap powder from the cup into the machine, closed it and pressed a button to begin the cycle. I'd never seen him do laundry before.

He said he'd had dinner with a client who had spilled red wine all over him and he had to get his clothes in the wash right away or they would be ruined.

His shoes were on the floor, and he was barefoot.

I asked him if his client had spilled red wine on his socks, too.

He looked at me. There was something in his eyes I'd never seen before. It reminded me of the way Mitchum looked in our movie, right before he stabbed his wife. It's a cold, blank look.

He said he may as well put everything in the wash, while he was there, and tried to laugh it off. There was no mirth in that smile or in that hollow laughter.

I started backing away from him. I didn't like this. I ran up the stairs, into the kitchen and put my back to the counter.

I couldn't breathe.

Daniel came up the stairs, turned the lights off in the basement and shut the noisy door.

He stood there for a moment, looking at me. He wasn't smiling anymore. He wasn't embarrassed. His face was blank. Like he was looking at nothing – like I didn't even exist. He took one step toward me, and I flinched. Pushed myself back against the counter.

He apologized again and said he was going upstairs to take a shower.

I watched him go. When he was safely upstairs I went into the downstairs bathroom, locked the door and sat on the toilet seat. I cried and rocked on that seat. I don't know how long I was in there, but at some stage I must've curled up on the floor, because when I woke up, that's where I was. The sunlight brightening the room through the window. I got up, sore from sleeping on the tiles, and opened the door. I looked out at the garage.

Daniel's car was gone.

I poured a glass of water and found my phone upstairs beside my bed. There were four new alerts, all from different media sites.

A woman had been found dead in an alleyway in Manhattan this morning. Her eyes had been removed. She was thought to be the latest victim of the Sandman.

I put my face in my hands and cried.

CHAPTER THIRTY-SEVEN

BLOCH

The law offices of Archie Bunsen were not exactly welcoming for new clients. A steel door with a buzzer beside it on 110th Street. It looked more like a bunker than a law practice. No sign above the door. The words 'Bunsen Law' were written on a slip behind the clear plastic button for the buzzer.

Lake pressed it. Waited, and Bloch hung back, content to let him do the talking.

The steel viewing slot ripped open with a clang and a face filled the slot. A big face. Maybe the size of a dinner plate. The man had a perfectly trimmed pencil-thin beard that went around his jaw as if it had been drawn on with a Sharpie. His cheeks were so round and fulsome they looked as though they were trying to crush his nose.

'Wat du want?' said the face.

'We'd like to talk to Archie Bunsen, please,' said Lake.

'He ain't here,' said the face, and slammed the viewing slot shut.

Lake banged on the door, shouted, 'Eddie Flynn sent us.'

Silence.

The slot slid open slowly.

'Wat du want with Archie?'

'We want to talk, that's all.'

The slot closed. The door stayed closed.

'That's okay. We can tell the FBI to come and talk with Archie instead,' said Lake.

The door opened.

The face had a body to match. Bloch guessed this was Moonman. The guy was over six-five and four-hundred pounds. Not all of it fat. The face sat on a pair of well-developed traps that curved to his rounded shoulders, giving the appearance of rolling hills of muscle. Even if he did weigh as much as a Volkswagen, he could probably lift the same amount.

He turned around in the narrow hallway, not without some difficulty, and led them to a door at the end. He knocked on it, said, 'Peeps here to see you. From Eddie Flynn.'

The door opened to reveal an office that looked like it had been robbed. Papers and files were strewn over the desk, the floor, on chairs, stacked high on tables, and paper stuck out of metal file cabinets groaningly full and unable to close. Behind a vast, ornate oak desk was a small, balding man in a yellow shirt, a pair of brown braces over his shoulders and a cigarette hanging from his mouth. The shirt could've been white once, but the whole room was bathed in a saffron-colored haze from the one window on the left, which had a thick layer of nicotine on the glass. Bloch had smelled cigarettes from the hallway. An ashtray on the desk hadn't been emptied in months. Cigarette butts had been stuffed into it, row upon row, until they stood proud of the lip of the ashtray like thick orange porcupine needles.

'What's up with Eddie?' said the man. His voice sounded like nuts and bolts rolling around in a bucket of wallpaper paste.

'Are you Archie?' asked Lake.

'You can call me Mr. Bunsen.'

'We need some help. A loft in Manhattan was leased last year by one of your landlord clients. The FBI has been in touch with the landlord and he said he has no paperwork on the tenant. It was a short lease and the guy paid in cash. Eddie says no landlord in the city would lease so much as a hole in the wall without some kind of collateral and bank account information. You handle the paperwork for all the . . . *landlords* in that area and—'

'You mean *slumlords*, don't ya?'

'I didn't say that,' said Lake.

'No, but Eddie did. I don't mind. I'm a plain speaker Mr . . .'

'Lake, Gabriel Lake. This is my friend, Bloch.'

'She don't say much.'

'She doesn't have to. The FBI came up short on a paper trail, but Eddie knows you handle all the paperwork for your clients, and you might have some documents that could help us.'

'And why would I give my client's paperwork to you?'

'We need to find that tenant, urgently. Any paper trail of his is important to us.'

'I'm sorry, I can't divulge any client information without a court order.'

'Eddie told us you might say that. He said he would appreciate your help with this.'

'I'm afraid I can't be more helpful. Now, if you wouldn't mind, I'm busy.'

'We know you keep two sets of books for your landlords. There's all kinds of ways around rent control and keeping some of their income away from the IRS. We wouldn't want that to come to the attention of the FBI now, would we?' said Lake.

From the way Lake folded his arms, Bloch thought he was expecting this threat to be met with a little co-operation. He had underestimated the lawyer. Lake may be a good investigator, but he was shit at this.

'You're not in any position to make threats, Mr. Lake. You and your little friend should leave now before you get hurt.'

Before Lake could say anything in reply, Moonman took one step toward him. It was a big move. In more ways than one. This wasn't just someone stepping into your personal space, it was more like a buffalo getting ready to charge, or a planet moving within twenty feet of your house. Lake glanced at the big man and smiled. The smile was not returned.

He put his hand on Lake's wrist, gently at first, then looked toward Archie for confirmation he should throw them out on the street. The hand looked like it was wearing a catcher's mitt, but it was just one big goddamn set of fingers.

'Tell your friend to keep his hands to himself,' said Bloch.

'Oh, she speaks. Is this your muscle, Mr. Lake?' said Bunsen, suppressing a laugh. 'You're in a whole lot of trouble now. You should've brought somebody bigger.'

Lake stood between the giant and Bloch. She had remained still the whole time. Taking in the room, her hands clasped in front of her. So when she moved, and moved fast, it all seemed to happen in the blink of an eye. She dipped her right hand into her jacket, and suddenly there was a huge gun in that hand, in front of Lake's face, pointed directly at the big guy's head. The Magnum 500 is a weapon of such size and power it tends to make a dramatic entrance in every situation in which it is introduced.

'That big enough for you?' asked Bloch. 'The paperwork. I don't have time for this. You already know what we're looking for because your client would've called you when the feds paid him a visit. Get it now.'

'What is she going to do? Shoot him?' asked Archie.

'Your friend's head is the size of a basketball. I don't think she could miss it from fifty feet away,' said Lake.

'I'm not going to shoot him,' said Bloch as she opened the hand holding the gun. Her finger was still in the trigger guard, and the barrel swung down, and the mahogany grip tilted up, as she closed her fist on the chamber of the weapon, reversing it so the butt was now a hammer. Like an old gunslinger move.

She drew back her arm, flicked it forward and the butt of the pistol sank into the flesh around the top of Moonman's wrist. He immediately let go of Lake, and his huge mouth opened to suck in air as he cradled his forearm. Stepping back, he stumbled and fell flat on his ass.

'You're starting to piss me off,' said Bloch. 'A heavy ballpeen hammer weighs around two pounds. This gun weighs almost six pounds. If you don't get us the paperwork now I'm going to break your friend's other arm. Then I'm going to hammer your head up his asshole.'

There was something in Bloch's tone that resonated with Bunsen.

His chair squeaked, loudly, as he leaned forward and got up, moving swiftly to a file cabinet. He hauled it open, started looking through the file dividers inside, his fingers tripping through the pages.

'If you bring a gun out of that file cabinet, I'll put a big hole in your wall. The hole will go through you and the file cabinet first,' said Bloch.

Bunsen's fingers stiffened, then began again. He grabbed a thin navy-colored file from the cabinet and handed it to Lake.

He opened the file and saw only a few pages. A lease with a signature he couldn't make out, and a bank statement. The lease and the bank statement were in the name of a company – Shoreline Limited.

'Is this all?' asked Lake.

'That's all we got.'

'Good enough,' said Bloch.

Lake got into the passenger seat of Bloch's Jeep with the file in his hand while Bloch started the engine. Opening the file on his lap, he scanned the documents with his finger, found what he was looking for and started typing on his phone.

'Shoreline Limited looks to be a shell company of some kind according to the SEC databases. No accounts have ever been filed,' he said. 'Company director is Daniel Miller – no surprises there. Wait, there's a company address, but it's not Miller's home address.'

Traffic wasn't too bad in the Holland Tunnel for a change, and within the hour Bloch pulled into an industrial complex in Bayonne, New Jersey. The area was a honeycomb of warehouses, factories and haulage depots. The address Lake pulled up from the SEC database was an old brick building surrounded by a rusty chicken-wire fence. It had once been some kind of warehouse or garage, judging by the wide and tall double oak doors on the front. Every window in the building had been broken. Kids in need of target practice, guessed Bloch.

They got out of the car and examined the chain securing the fence. Not new, but not that old either. The lock on the chain was certainly in good shape. No rust anywhere.

'This is a decent place to hide,' said Lake.

Bloch went to her car, took a crowbar from the trunk and gave it to Lake. She drew her gun and said, 'The lock was busted when we got here.'

It took Lake three swings to break the lock. Bloch hadn't seen another vehicle or another person on the street since they had gotten here and didn't imagine the noise would be too much of a problem either. There was no way to open the huge double doors. A dirt and gravel lot surrounded the building. On the side of the building, Bloch spotted a steel door, painted blue probably forty years ago. The lock on the door was good. And it was new. Shiny and oiled. The door had not been repainted. Someone wanted to make good use of this place but didn't want anyone to know they were here.

A walk around the perimeter of the building did not reveal an easy way in.

Around ten feet above them was a row of broken windows. About three feet high, three feet wide, going along in a row across the side of the building.

'Give me a boost,' said Bloch.

'You sure?' asked Lake. 'If you get in there and you can't open that door . . .'

'I'll be able to deal with whatever is on the other side,' she said, holstering her weapon.

The crowbar hit the dirt, Lake put his back to the wall, spread his legs, cupped his hands and held them low. Two steps to get her momentum, then Bloch stepped into Lake's grip, her hands on his shoulders. He pulled and pushed, and Bloch felt her way up the wall until she reached the window ledge. She'd thought the glass was completely out of this one, but there were a few old dusty shards still in the frame and she tore her calf as she threaded her leg through, then dropped to the floor below with a loud thump that echoed off the walls and the concrete floors.

Clicking on her mini flashlight, Bloch looked around.

The place had once been a warehouse. There were heavy iron shelves along the wall opposite leading up to the ceiling. There were plastic ceiling panels along the roof, interspersed among the corrugated iron roofing panels. The plastic ones were supposed to let in light, but they were way too filthy. Old pieces of machinery and tools littered the wide floor, and she had to be careful where she stepped. There didn't seem to be much else in the place, apart from a few stacks of wooden pallets. An area of the warehouse had been sectioned off into what looked like a foreman's office. The door was closed, but there was a window.

Bloch killed the light

Either there was a hole in the back of that office leading to the outside, which she hadn't seen on her perimeter inspection, or there was still power in the building.

Because she could see a dim light in the office.

It looked like it was coming from a lamp.

Or someone holding a flashlight.

CHAPTER THIRTY-EIGHT

BLOCH

There could be any number of explanations for the light in the little office. It wasn't strong, so it could be the light from a recently discarded cell phone, or a lamp, or something equally innocuous.

Or it could be the Sandman with a flashlight and a .45. Ready to shine the light into her eyes at the same time as he emptied the clip into her chest.

Bloch decided it would be better if Lake were in here. She made her way, silently, across the floor, never taking her eyes from the office window, until she reached a brick pillar. She quickly turned, just to get her bearings, and noticed she was only a few feet from the painted steel door. No latches. No bars. It was locked. You needed a key.

Lake must've heard her from outside as he gently tapped the door.

She wanted to tell him to be quiet. That she might have company. Her big advantage was that perhaps whoever was in the office didn't know that Bloch was outside the door. If it was the Sandman, she needed every inch of advantage. He was dangerous. Perhaps the most dangerous man she had ever faced, and she did not want to underestimate him.

There was nothing else to do but act. And act now, while she still had the element of surprise. Moving past the door, she circled the perimeter of the room, coming up on the office at an angle instead of head on. There was no window on this side. No way of him seeing her approach.

Her movement seemed louder than it should have been. Every breath a gale. Every step resounded like a stomp. Every heartbeat cracked like a drum. It was cool in the dark brick warehouse, and yet she had to blink streams of sweat away from her eyes. The weight of Maggie in her hand no longer felt reassuring as it had always done before. Now it felt cumbersome. As if she had brought the wrong weapon for the job.

Bloch recognized all of this for what it was – fear. She wasn't afraid of the Sandman. Bloch feared no man.

She was afraid of what she might find.

Afraid she might find the body of her life-long friend in a dusty old warehouse.

She was close now. It was just a few feet away.

The tip of the barrel began to shake.

It was not from exertion. When Bloch had selected the Magnum as her sidearm, she had trained with it every day for a year. An hour's target practice every morning, and then the gym in the afternoon. Every time that gun fired it was like getting punched in the palm. But she took it. Grew stronger. Ate those kicks up until there was a thick callus on her palm and it didn't hurt anymore. The weight and feel of the weapon were as natural to her as holding a knife and fork, or a pen.

But now, with her chest pumping oxygen and the adrenaline flooding her system, it felt like she was on sensory overload.

Bloch reached the door to the office and bent low.

No point in chancing a peek through the window. She was only likely to alert whoever was inside and maybe get blinded by their flashlight in the process.

There was only one way.

Go in hard and fast.

She reversed her grip on the flashlight, holding it now like a dagger in her left. The switch was on the base, and she could use her thumb to flick the power to the battery. She put her right hand over her left, her wrists on top of each other, keeping torch and aim aligned.

Bloch stood in front of the door. Gathered her breath. Rolled her shoulders. Cracked her neck. Put her foot through the door.

It gave easy. Bloch stepped over it, training her weapon around the dark room, following the flashlight beam with her sight.

Nothing in the corners.

No one straight ahead.

No one in the room at all.

She now saw the light was a pale green, and it was close to the floor. The flashlight illuminated what looked like a large white casket at one end of the room. Focusing on the light, she saw it was a power indicator. A white cable led from the casket to a plug.

It wasn't a casket.

It was a chest freezer.

Satisfied there was no one in the building, Bloch put away her weapon and approached the freezer.

Why would anyone have a freezer in an abandoned building? It didn't look like it was new, but it wasn't that old either. A layer of dust sat on top of it and as she got closer, she could hear the fans and motors purring.

Her hand reached out, almost by itself, and caught hold of the lever that sat in the center of the lid. Bloch didn't want to look inside. But she knew she had to.

She had visions of Kate inside the freezer. Still in her nightdress, dead inside this cold tomb. Her eyes misty with frost. Her lips broken and frozen black. Ice has a way of capturing the dead in a moment of life. She had seen dead bodies before, in all kinds of places.

She was not religious, but she found herself mouthing a silent prayer as the lever tilted up. Bloch pulled and heard that sucking sound, that smacking vacuum noise made when the rubber seal is broken on a cool box.

There was no light inside the freezer.

But there was something inside. A solid block of ice. It wasn't just normal ice formation – it looked as though thirty gallons of water had been tipped in to make sure whatever was inside was preserved.

The beam from her flashlight quivered as Bloch shone it inside.

She let out a breath. She recognized it instantly, even through the layers ice.

For a second, she thought she would lose it. She fought down her emotions, turned and ran to the door; the burner cell in her hand, calling Lake.

'You okay in there?' he asked. 'I've been going crazy out here.'

'Take cover and stand back from the door. Way back. I'm going to open it.'

'Understood,' he said.

Bloch strode confidently to the painted steel door, drew her Magnum, and standing six feet away she took aim – relaxed her arms, shook out the tension, then aimed again and pulled the trigger. The sonic rip from the gun was almost deafening in the old warehouse and she could suddenly taste the dust sucked into the air from the shot. Where the steel door had been solid, now the lock face was gone. She kicked the door and it swung up, the remnants of the mechanism falling onto the floor.

'Whatever it was you blew off the door went right through the fence over there,' said Lake. 'That gun big enough for ya?'

She said, 'Bring the crowbar.'

'What's going on?'

'We need to chip something out of a freezer.'

'What?'

'A body bag.'

CHAPTER THIRTY-NINE

EDDIE

All the way back to court, Peltier talked. He was giving Harry and me a lift in his Mercedes, so I guessed he got to talk all he wanted.

'This is all very clever, but how the hell are you going to get an acquittal without Carrie? She has to testify if she's going to have any kind of chance. I mean, shouldn't you be helping me look for her? Where is Kate? She could help me at least?' he asked.

I couldn't tell him about Kate. There was just no way I was taking that chance. Peltier was a straight-laced guy when it came to legal practice. I'm sure he would bend the rules as far as possible when it came to tax and inheritance law, but in the criminal field he was a baby, and babies get scared. If I told him about Kate I was sure he would tell the police, even if it was only to salve his own conscience.

'Kate's busy right now running down some leads. Look, I'd love to have Carrie here with us. I said it from the start, Carrie needs to look the jury in the eye and tell them she's innocent. If she is as convincing as she was with me, I'm sure the jury will take her at her word. But if she's not here it just looks like she's on the run because she's guilty. We've got a chance without her, but it's thinner than paper. You know her better than us, where might she have gone?'

'She hasn't contacted any of her old friends and if she uses a credit card the police will catch her right away. She's lying low somewhere and using cash, or she's found a way out of the country. Those are the options,' he said.

'Does she have any distant relatives anywhere she might trust, or friends in out-of-the-way places? Come on, Otto, we need something.'

He was quiet for a second, concentrating either on the road or the question, or both.

'She has no one,' he said. 'Her parents passed away. When it all came out about Daniel her friends abandoned her. She's been dealing with this all on her own. I can't think of a single person she would go to. They all hate her now. How sad is that? We're the only people she has.'

'Shit,' said Harry.

'Look, we've got a better jury and the prosecutor doesn't look so sweet to the judge right now. That might help us get some room when we cross-examine White's witnesses, but we don't have much to throw at them. We can't actually put it to any witness that Carrie is innocent. Because we can't do that without the firm knowledge that she'll be called to the stand to testify. All we can do is shake the prosecution tree and hope the roots are shallow enough for it to fall over,' I said.

'That's not going to be enough,' said Peltier.

I thought about Kate, gritted my teeth and said, 'We have to make it enough.'

My phone vibrated. Email from Denise with several links attached. They were all for news reports on the killings yesterday of Teresa Vasquez and the two FBI agents. I clicked on the *Times* report, read it. Then the rest. Most were syndicating the same story from Associated Press, but one wasn't. The *Post* had a little more detail as they'd managed to reach Teresa's family in Tijuana for comment. I read the article twice. Called Denise.

'I need you to get in touch with Mrs. Vasquez in Tijuana. You speak a little Spanish, don't you?'

'*Por supuesto,*' she said, in a good accent.

'The article says Mrs. Vasquez was due to move to Manhattan in the new year, how she was looking forward to it and she hadn't seen her daughter in years. I want to know everything about her plans. She'll need to make arrangements for her daughter; tell her we can help with that.'

'What's this all about?' said Denise.

'I don't know yet, it's a hunch. I want to help Mrs. Vasquez no matter what. Oh, and there's one more thing.'

'This a hunch too?'

'It is. I need an arrest record for Chester Morris, the doorman who was murdered the same night as Delaney. In fact, do a full background check, but the arrest records should be easy, it's all publicly available.'

'I've got our log-in details for the database. No problem. I'll get right on it. Is there any word—'

'No, not yet,' I said.

I hung up and turned to Harry. He had his elbow up on the door frame, his arm bent, and his fingers stroking his upper lip.

'Kate is going to be okay. We'll get her back,' I whispered.

'I can't go to no more funerals, Eddie. I just . . .'

Harry didn't finish the thought. Didn't want to say any more in front of Otto. The Mercedes pulled up outside the court building in Center Street. Before we got out, Harry gave me a look, said, 'It's all riding on the next few witnesses. You up for this?'

I took a deep breath, let it out.

Right then, I wasn't sure. I had a gut instinct I had to follow and that might help. There are some cases you just can't win. Otto was right – we needed Carrie Miller.

My phone rang again, and I answered as I got out of the car and stepped onto the sidewalk. It was Bloch.

'We're at the warehouse listed as the address on the old lease for Daniel Miller. It's empty apart from a freezer. Eddie, there's a body bag inside.'

She spoke plainly. Like she always did, but the fear inside her rippled through her voice. My legs suddenly didn't feel so steady. I closed my eyes, my mind reeling. I knew what I wanted to ask. What I had to ask, but I couldn't fill the dead air with it. I stared straight ahead at the crowd of reporters, photographers and camera operators at the courthouse entrance and begged that they wouldn't see me.

Harry came around the car, took one look at my face and reached out, grabbing my arm.

Right then, I wanted to lie down on the sidewalk, close my eyes and just wish for everything to go away. I wanted to fall asleep and wake up when this nightmare was over, and Kate was safe.

'Eddie, Eddie, come on. What is it?' said Harry.

I stumbled, his grip tightened on my arm. I listened, and Bloch said nothing. I wanted her to tell me that Kate was okay. That's all I wanted.

'Eddie, take a breath,' said Harry, and leaned in close, keeping me upright. I asked questions for a living. I was pretty good at it. There was a question I had to ask. There was no avoiding this. No wishing this away.

I had to face it. And take the pain.

'What's in the bag?' I asked.

'There's no way of telling. Not yet,' she said. I'd never heard Bloch this emotional before. Her voice quivered with it, like the fear was physically shaking her.

'It's not Kate,' I said. 'Tell me it's not Kate.'

Bloch said nothing. I heard her breath, working her way up to spitting out the words.

'It's completely encased in ice. Whoever dumped the body bag here must've poured gallons of water in after. Lake and I are digging it out, but it's slow going.'

'Bloch, you know who it is, don't you?'

'I can't tell. I-I c-can't tell. The ice is three feet thick. Lake . . . Lake said it could be a first kill.'

Here was some hope, at last, and I was going to grab it.

'What does he mean?'

'Some serial killers hide their first victims. They take care to dispose of the body or hide it so no one can find it. Usually because the victim has some kind of link to them.'

What Lake had told Bloch made sense, but I couldn't get the idea out of my mind that Kate was in that freezer, and Bloch was there with a guy I didn't fully trust, digging her best friend's body out of a block of ice.

Bloch said nothing. I said nothing. She thought it was Kate too. I could tell. I watched the reporters outside the courtroom making their way toward me. I listened to the faint static on the line. For one of the first times in my life, I felt utterly hopeless.

I knew Bloch was hurting. I'd heard it in her voice. There was a dam in her throat, holding back her fear. I didn't know what to say. She'd grown up with Kate. Bloch was closer to her than any other human being on the planet. If something happened to Kate, Bloch's world would end. I didn't know what to say. I pressed the phone to my ear. Really, there was nothing I could say to her. No comfort I could give.

Neither of us had any words.

Hope for Kate died in the silence of electrostatic.

The atmosphere in the courtroom had changed.

Judge Stoker looked like a man who'd had a tire blow out on the freeway during a rain storm, on the same day his wife left him and the stock market crashed. He looked punchy. Wary of a killer blow to come. The pale skin around his eyes from the sunbed goggles appeared even whiter than usual, making him look like a startled red panda.

The prosecutor, White, was on his feet, arranging papers on his desk and throwing a subtle side-eye at the jury. Or rather, the new juror. Clay Dryer was now ensconced on the jury stand in place of Ethel, who was on her way home with all that hate still in her heart, a hundred bucks in her purse, a good dinner, and no real idea what had happened that day.

'I call Professor Cal Johnson to the stand,' said White, standing up a little straighter.

Harry and I had discussed Bloch's call. He looked pained when I told him what she'd found. Then he shook his head.

'It's not Kate. The Sandman needs her.'

'What if she's already dead, Harry?'

'Then we have to go on defending her client. Look, for now, we have to think that Kate is alive. We have to hope. We have to get our head in the game, *right now.*'

I nodded, took a sip of water and tried to force all thought of Kate from my mind. I'd nearly lost it completely outside the court-house. All I could do was hope Harry was right. That she was still alive. And if she was alive, she needed us to win.

Professor Cal Johnson gave us a big problem. It was the only real forensic evidence tying Carrie Miller to the murders. In real terms, this was the prosecutor's ace card. The other witnesses were high cards, but they all had to stand together to make the straight flush. If we knocked one or two of them down, White was left with his ace.

Considering we were holding nothing in our hand, the ace could be enough to take the whole damn pot.

Forensic evidence is given holy-writ treatment in murder trials. The testimony of expert witnesses linking DNA to homicides was usually more than enough to send any defendant to a cramped, painted cell for a very long time. The defense has two hurdles to mount – the nature of the evidence and the jury's interpretation of that evidence. Even if you can make a great argument against the DNA evidence, it's not worth a damn if the jury doesn't understand your point.

I had to go slowly with this one, as would White.

Professor Johnson wore a thin, brown V-neck sweater under his navy suit jacket. I hoped it was an effort to hide his tie, which was mud-colored, to put it kindly. He was thin and tall, well dressed, I guess, but all of this contrasted with his bushy, scabrous beard. Thick tufts of white and dark hairs stuck out at odd angles as if he'd had a small animal living in there that had suddenly been evicted from its bristly home.

Polished leather dress shoes and a faded gold wedding ring completed his ensemble. I guessed the wife shopped for his clothes, she had some taste at least, and as a traditional suburban professional he always shined his shoes, but the beard spoke of a more manic personality – that eccentric part of the mind, which is such a creative boost for research scientists.

I was a little surprised his wife had let him leave the house with his beard in that state. He was sworn in, took a seat. He poured a glass of water and got himself comfortable in the witness box. I noticed him tugging at the beard, turning the strands over in his fingers. The good con artists can spot a tell. The great con artists can not only spot it, they can use it. This was not a complicated forensic case. It was easy. The same kind of testimony that Johnson had given over and over again, for twenty years. He'd testified in high-profile murder cases many times. This was his job. I'd even watched him testify before. And on those occasions, he looked better.

He'd been tugging at that beard all morning.

He was nervous about something.

That meant I had to find out what it was. And use it.

'Professor, we are all aware of your qualifications and expertise. You are well recognized in your field of DNA analysis. Let's start with your involvement in this case. Take a look at photographs eleven, twelve and thirteen, please.'

The screen facing the jury and the witness stand came to life. It showed the photograph of a white blouse hanging in Carrie Miller's closet. The next shot was a close-up of the cuff. There was a stain there. Rust red. Like a drop of ketchup had splashed on the cuff, dried and faded. The last photo was the same blouse in an evidence bag marked BS9.

'What can you tell us about these photographs?'

'I was given a data sheet with this exhibit, BS9, and these photographs. My data sheet said this garment had been found in Carrie Miller's closet and had been retained as evidence for examination. I was to examine and extract DNA from the stain on the sleeve fibers and compare that DNA with any known profiles on our systems,' said Johnson. His speech had the impression of clinical and deliberate thought. Every syllable of every word annunciated and spoken perfectly.

'What did you do with the blouse, exhibit BS9?'

'First, I examined the garment. It is a blouse, size six. White cotton and woven silk fibers. From the appearance of the stain, which had faded, it was clear that there had been an attempt to clean the garment, probably washed at a reasonably high temperature in a washing machine. Then dried, ironed and hung in the wardrobe. But even washing an item of clothing won't remove DNA completely. In this instance, I carried out a search for bloodstaining. May I refer to exhibit CJ3?'

White turned to his assistant DA, who used a laptop synced with the large screen facing the jury. The picture of the blouse hanging in Carrie's closet changed. What appeared on the screen was at first unclear. Most of the picture was too dark to see, but if you looked closely you could make out the shape of the white blouse and, on the sleeve and cuff, several spots of varying size and shape in metallic blue green.

'I treated the garment with Luminol and then examined it in a dark room to see if there were any remnants of blood staining that were no longer visible. As you can see in this picture there were quite a few more splashes of blood, but apart from the largest stain, which is around half an inch long, the remaining blood traces were not visible to the naked eye.'

'And having identified these traces, what happened then?'

'The identified traces were cut from the garment and applied to an Eppendorf microcentrifuge tube. DNA was extracted using the spin colon-based extraction method and the Phenol-chloroform Isoamyl organic method. PCR reaction and amplification process applied, and I used a spectrophotometer machine. The result was a successful DNA extraction and analysis. The DNA from the blood traces on the garment were a match with a profile on the system to a probability of one billion.'

'Professor, that last part. Your analysis. Can you explain the probability and the matching profile?'

'We can never provide an exact match of one person's DNA to another, but I can say that it is likely the blood on the garment came from the profile attributed to Stacy Nielsen on the database. The probability is one in a billion. That is to say, if I compared this DNA profile to one billion other profiles, it's possible it might match up with one other profile.'

'And how likely is that?'

'Like I said. One in a billion. It's as close to certain as I can scientifically be that the blood on the defendant's blouse came from one of the victims in this case – Stacy Nielsen.'

CHAPTER FORTY

EDDIE

When a skilled player really nails something, when all of their training, experience, craft and natural talent combines in a perfect moment of execution – there's a sound. It makes a noise. It's the sound of the nine-ball being *gulped* into the throat of the corner pocket; the *schnick* of the perfectly timed gear change; the *whisper* from a leather basketball kissing the polyester netting as it drops for three points; the *smack* of cowhide colliding with a maple bat for a home run that goes all the way out of the park.

Soon as you hear that sound you know something special happened.

It's different in court.

In fact, it's the opposite.

When something special happens – when an attorney commands direct examination of a witness, and everything goes perfectly – it's a goddamn symphony.

But one with no sound.

Courtrooms, especially those with a large public presence in the gallery, always carry noise. Someone is always coughing, whispering, shuffling their feet, or there's the ordinary court business of lawyers walking around, talking, shouting, chair legs scraping the floor – and all in a room designed to carry and amplify sound.

When that something special happens in court – there is silence.

Only it's a silence like you've never heard before. It's as if the entire thing was on TV and someone muted the volume. It happens that suddenly. It's not just *no* sound. It's *minus* sound. Like a cosmic vacuum sucked every acoustic particle right out of the room. It's so quiet, the silence itself has a weight.

If this majestic silence happens in a trial, there's only one thing to do – sit your ass down and enjoy it while it lasts, because it usually means you just won your case.

Harry wrote the word 'shit' on his legal pad.

We were toast.

'Professor, you described the bloodstains as splashes, early in your testimony. What did you mean by the word *splashes*?' asked White.

'The size and shape of the stains,' said the professor, 'they look like splashes of blood.'

'Thank you, Professor Johnson. No further questions.'

I got up slowly, my gaze focused on Harry's notes in front of him on the desk. I glanced once at Professor Johnson, then said, 'Your Honor, I just need one moment with my colleague.'

I leaned over, whispered to Harry.

'That went well for White.'

'How do you want to play it? You could grind this guy for hours,' said Harry.

One defense attorney tactic when it comes to DNA testimony is to grind out the details. To spend hours, going into every specific process of their work and examination of the evidence, checking that they are applying proper quarantine and cleanliness routines on biological evidence, making sure they use new or sterilized equipment, seeking to pick tiny holes in their recipe, which arrived at a one-in-a-billion shot that the blood didn't belong to Stacy Nielsen. It's a good tactic, and after the second hour the jury begins to hate the expert because they're bored and confused and some of them might even dismiss the testimony completely. But it's risky – the jury might turn on the defense attorney instead.

'We don't have time,' I said. 'We need to get this done as fast as possible, for Kate.'

Eddie Felson, a pool shark in the movie *The Hustler*, played best when he didn't grind out the percentages. When he played fast and loose, no one could beat him.

'Can I take a piece of paper and borrow your pen?'

Harry tore off a sheet, handed me his pen. I wrote down four words. Turned the sheet toward Harry. He read it, smiled.

Here we go. Fast and loose.

CHAPTER FORTY-ONE

EDDIE

When I got up to cross-examine Johnson I still had Harry's pen in my hand. It was a beautiful thing. A bright green barrel and a gold nib. A German fountain pen, renowned for its reliability. It was durable, too. It needed to be. Because I was holding on to it for dear life.

'Professor Johnson, you head up the crime lab in the Southern District, correct?' I asked.

'Correct.'

'May I approach the witness?' I asked, and Judge Stoker nodded.

'Professor, I've watched you testify before, some years ago, but I never had the opportunity to meet you until now. It's a pleasure, sir,' I said, then walked up to him and held out my hand.

Johnson smiled, rose a little off his feet and we shook hands, briefly. When he sat back down he had a look of relief. White had prepped him hard for this case, and probably told him I was a real tiger who would try to tear strips clean off his flesh. He was beginning to think he was in for a much smoother ride. For now, I wanted to keep it that way. Get him settled. Relaxed.

'Professor, you analyzed the stains on my client's blouse. Did you happen to find any of my client's DNA in the fabric?'

He leaned back in his chair, crossed one long leg over the other and folded his hands in his lap. He'd been prepared for this question. The trick was delivering the answer so that it didn't sound rehearsed or inauthentic.

'Your client's DNA would've gotten on the blouse if it had been worn. DNA from sweat can easily get into a fabric. However, the laundering of the garment may have removed your client's DNA.'

'But not the blood?'

'No, blood is a lot harder to remove from nylon and cotton than sweat. It stains badly, tainting the fibers, sometimes forever. A bit like red wine.'

'I see. And if my client had never even worn that shirt there would be none of her DNA on it either, is that right?'

'Probably.'

'You didn't test for my client's DNA, did you?'

He smiled at the jury, gave his answer, 'No, there would've been no point if the garment had been through the washing machine like this one.'

'But if you haven't tested for my client's DNA, then there's no way of telling if she'd even worn this shirt before, is there?'

He cleared his throat. Getting a little more uncomfortable. I didn't want to make him squirm. Not yet.

'I don't know if your client routinely washed her new shirts before wearing them.'

'Good, I'm glad you conceded that point,' I said, and quickly moved to another question as Johnson opened his mouth, about to say that he hadn't conceded anything.

'Professor, you are not a blood spatter analyst, are you?'

'No, I am not. But as you have yourself reminded me, I have testified in hundreds of felony trials in my career, most of them murders, and I have experience of examining blood. To me, the pattern of those stains looked like splashing. As if she was in the room when Stacy Nielsen was killed, or perhaps wielded the knife herself.'

'You are very far away from your lab and your machines now, Professor. You are aware that there is an ongoing justice department investigation into testimony from blood spatter analysts resulting in numerous wrongful convictions?'

'I'm aware of the investigation.'

'You haven't seen any blood spatter analysis reports in relation to the staining on the blouse you examined?'

'No, I have not. I don't believe such an expert was engaged.'

Now we were getting somewhere. White wanted someone to say that Stacy Nielsen's blood got on Carrie Miller's blouse because she was present during the murder. Unfortunately, every blood spatter expert east of the Mississippi was refusing to consult on cases until the outcome of the justice department investigation. They didn't want any exposure. Testifying in a high-profile multiple-murder trial might make their name a little more prominent and provoke the kind of thorough investigation that could lead to the Justice Department crawling over their entire careers. In the absence of a blood spatter expert, White had pushed the good professor here into uncomfortable territory, trying desperately to connect Carrie Miller to the crime scene.

'Professor, there is no biological or forensic trace evidence linking my client to any of the crime scenes in these cases, is that your understanding?'

'Apart from the blood, which I examined, no. No, there's not.'

It was time to put the professor down.

'What is primary transfer?' I asked.

'That is where material, usually biological material, transfers from the victim to the suspect. Like blood spatter.'

'What is secondary transfer?'

'It occurs where some forensic material passes from the primary transferee to another individual.'

I paused for a second. Letting Johnson know I was considering my next question carefully. I let my mouth curl into a brief smile. His shoulders tensed.

'Professor, before I ask my next question, is there any part of your testimony you wish to change or revise?'

He uncrossed his legs, put his feet firmly on the floor.

'No, I don't believe so,' he said. 'I am giving my professional, expert opinion as fairly as I can.'

My eyebrows shot up in a mock face of surprise.

Johnson swallowed, then tugged at his beard with his right hand.

That's what I was waiting for.

'Professor, you are aware that the prosecution is making the case that my client had a part to play in these crimes along with her husband, Daniel Miller?'

'I am aware.'

'You are aware, because you carried out the DNA extraction and analysis of the fingerprint found beneath Stacy Nielsen's arm. What was the result of that analysis?'

He stroked his beard, drawing his fingers across it and then pulling his chin hairs and twisting them into a point, which then unfurled as he let go. Before he spoke, he glanced at the jury, then back to me.

I heard some faint whispers from behind me. I turned. One of the jurors, a blonde lady in a red sweater, was nudging and discreetly pointing to the witness stand.

I knew what they were looking at, and pointing at.

Too bad Johnson didn't.

'Yes, I extracted the mixed DNA strands and was able to separate them. It was a fingerprint linked, independently, to Daniel Miller. Before I knew of that result, I had built two DNA profiles from the samples taken off Stacy Nielsen's body. One DNA sample strongly indicated it belonged to Stacy Nielsen herself. The other sample remained unidentified until I extracted DNA from a toothbrush found in Daniel Miller's bathroom. The DNA on that toothbrush gave a strong match with the other DNA strain from Stacy Nielsen's body.'

The whispering got louder. Now some folks in the gallery were picking it up, giving strange looks to Professor Johnson.

'There is DNA evidence linking my client's husband, Daniel Miller, to the victim, Stacy Nielsen. Touch DNA, from sweat?'

'Correct, the blood, which made the fingerprint, was from Stacy Nielsen. It shows that he touched her.'

'I see, so isn't it possible that the blood on my client's blouse got there via secondary transfer?'

'Possible. Not likely.'

'It's entirely possible that when my client's husband, the known killer of Stacy Nielsen, took off his clothes in his closet, which is beside Carrie Miller's, that some of the blood residue on his clothes got on my client's blouse?'

'Again, possible, not likely,' said Johnson, raising his voice now. He was beginning to notice the looks from the jury, and the people in the gallery, and now even Drew White was looking at him strangely and Johnson had no clue why.

I lit him up.

'Why do you say it's not likely?' I asked.

I knew his answer before he gave it. It's what all blood spatter experts say when a plausible sequence of events doesn't go their way. I'd heard it a dozen times before. So had Johnson, who had been involved in hundreds of trials. He was on the edge of his expertise, and he knew it. He was vulnerable, and so when he spoke, he was almost shouting the answer from the rooftops.

'Because I don't believe someone could get blood on them or their clothes, through secondary transfer, without noticing it.'

There it was. His explanation. Laid out exactly how I expected it.

'Really,' I said, holding up my palm, letting Johnson and the jury take a good look.

Johnson squinted, leaned forward.

'Professor Johnson, I should apologize,' I said, 'I had made a note with my colleague's fountain pen just now and I got ink on my hand.'

There was a circular, dark red stain on my hand from Harry's pen. From when I'd turned the piston knob on his fountain pen, squirting some into my palm. I then shook hands with Johnson, and before too long I'd made him nervous enough to stroke that beard of his. He held up his hands, saw the ink on his fingers and palm.

It was all over his beard too. The white tufts were now red. The jury had seen it. The people in the gallery had seen it. The prosecutor had seen it and now everyone had seen it.

Apart from Johnson.

'You have ink on you. Secondary transfer. What was that you were saying? That people couldn't get blood on their clothes without noticing it?'

He stared in disbelief at the ink on his hand and began shaking his head.

'Professor, you cannot say *when* that blood got on my client's blouse, *where* that happened, nor *how* it happened, can you?'

He just shook his head, staring at his palm and then looked at me like he wanted to beat some biological matter out of my face.

'It's okay, Professor. You don't need to answer that. The jury has seen enough. I'll just leave you there – with egg on your face. Sorry, I meant *ink*.'

CHAPTER FORTY-TWO

BLOCH

Bloch's shoulders burned.

Her hands were freezing. They were numb around the tire iron that she raised and smashed into the ice. Lake used the crowbar, and together they frantically chipped away at the thick casing surrounding the body bag. In this way they had removed the first foot of ice. There were plenty more feet to go.

She raised the tire iron, drove it down and as soon as it hit the block, she lost her grip and it slipped and crashed onto the floor. Panting now, Bloch blew into her hands, rubbed them together.

'My back is going to give out. I need a breather. Come on, sit down. We need a break or we're going to get hurt,' said Lake.

Bloch took up the tire iron, swung it again into the freezer. She lost her grip again and it ricocheted into the air.

'Come on, stop it. Take a minute,' he said.

Too exhausted to talk, Bloch sat down on the floor, put her back to the freezer.

'You really don't trust the feds, do you?' she said. 'Surprising, considering you used to be one.'

'Used to be. But I was never a fed. There's a certain mindset in the Bureau that meant I could never be one of them. Not really.'

'What's that?'

'Oh, you know. Obeying orders, respecting superiors, following policy. That kind of thing. I won't do it if it's wrong. The Bureau gets a lot of shit wrong, but they're never more wrong than in their pursuit of serial killers.'

'What do you mean?' asked Bloch.

'The entire approach. A serial killer profile is only as good as the profiler who wrote it. If they stick to Bureau policy it's probably worthless. They thought they could figure out who the man behind the crimes could be from examining their methods and the psychology of the killings – the theory that they can see the killer's personality traits in the way he kills, but that is not how human beings behave. A man who goes out at night and kills people isn't applying the same personality traits that define how he dresses, or how he speaks to his customers at the manager's desk at Walmart during the day. We adapt our personalities for different situations. My thinking is you don't look for the man in the crime scenes – you can only look for the killer.'

'Makes sense,' said Bloch. 'Hard to write a profile with that approach.'

'Profiles don't work anyway. In the history of the FBI, how many profiles directly led to the capture of a serial killer do you think?'

'I don't know. Fifty?' she said, then blew into her hands and rubbed them together, trying to get the blood flowing again.

'Two.'

'Two?'

'I won't ask how many profiles have wrongly excluded the perpetrator from a suspect pool, but it's known to be at least five, for sure, and probably more like twenty.'

'Then why maintain the BAU unit?'

'It's good for publicity, and of course they changed it all about fifteen years ago. Now profiles are written on the basis of statistical analysis of the crimes of ninety-two serial killers. It's a numbers game, and even more useless.'

'How does that work?'

'One of the big dichotomies for analysis now is whether the killer moved the body. For example, if the body has been moved, according to the Bureau's analysis there's a forty per cent chance either the killer or his father was in the military.'

'Bullshit.'

'Pretty much. This approach has lots of problems, not least that this metric is published by the Bureau. If I was a serial killer, I would look at how they categorize and extrapolate personal characteristics for their profile and change my MO to make sure it didn't come close to my personal history or demographic.'

Bloch said nothing.

'The other problem,' continued Lake, 'is that this analysis is based on a small study of the ninety-two serial killers that have been stupid enough to get arrested. General consensus among experts outside the FBI is that there could be between five hundred and two thousand serial killers operating in the United States right now. I don't want to use a statistical analysis method based on the guys we caught. I want to figure out how to find the men we haven't caught.'

Lake approached the freezer, took up the crowbar and hammered the ice with five quick strokes, scooped out more water.

'You know Seong talked to Eddie about what happened in that stash house incident. He said at one point you stopped defending yourself, and you went after every man in that house,' said Bloch.

He was breathing hard now. He put down the crowbar, rubbed his hands together to get some warmth into them.

'A lot of people have theories about what went on in that house,' he said. 'I was there because I was hunting a serial killer and I got a tip from one of the federally registered snitches. Turns out that about four hours after he gave me that tip the same snitch was found on a patch of waste ground under the Manhattan Bridge. He'd eaten the wrong end of a shotgun. His arms and legs were hogtied with cable loops. Kind of like how law enforcement secure a suspect – *federal* law enforcement, that is.'

'Jesus,' said Bloch.

'Somebody in the Bureau wanted me to walk blindly into that stash house, knowing the odds of me walking out again were slightly higher than the Milwaukee Brewers winning the World Series. Tell you the truth, I don't know how I survived. I got shot four times and almost bled out. Some part of me . . . I don't know how to describe it. At one point it felt like I wasn't there. I was just watching it happen.'

'Do you know who set you up?' asked Bloch as she rose to her feet.

Lake shook his head, said, 'Someday I'll find out. When I told my superiors why I'd walked into that building, and what had happened to the snitch, they got me pensioned out of the FBI straight away. They don't want scandal. They don't want trouble. They protect their own.'

She picked up the tire iron, hit the ice with three hard jabs.

'But *you* were one of them,' she said.

'Not really. I didn't play by their rules. I was an outsider even though I was the one putting results on the board. The brass don't really care about results if you're not playing their game.'

He swung the crowbar hard into the center of the packed ice. Bloch heard a loud crack.

She shone her flashlight inside.

Using the crowbar, Lake levered clear a chunk of ice that must've weighed forty pounds.

Now they could get access to the zipper around the center of the body bag. From her boot, Bloch pulled a switchblade and carefully cut open the portion of bag, about ten inches, that they could access through the hole in the ice.

With Bloch holding the flashlight, Lake prized the bag apart.

Bloch dropped the flashlight in the freezer. She felt dizzy. Grabbing the sides of the freezer to steady herself, she leaned over.

Tried to catch her breath.

Bloch had not cried in a long time. She felt that familiar wave of endorphins, the heave in her stomach, the sticky feeling in the back of her throat.

She shut her eyes tight, fighting every instinct to break down and cry.

Bloch stood up straight, took out her cell phone, hit the call button for Eddie Flynn.

CHAPTER FORTY-THREE

EDDIE

White had no more questions for the ink-stained DNA expert.

When one of your witnesses implodes on the stand, there are two responses. Try and patch up the damage, or get them out of there as quickly as possible and get a fresh witness in front of that jury. The prosecutor opted for the latter. It would need to be a good witness. One that is more or less unshakable.

'The people call Mrs. Daisy Broder.'

Perfect.

A small woman with white hair, wearing a smart gray suit and a blue and white pin-striped blouse, strode confidently along the aisle. She moved so well it reminded me of those prank TV shows where stuntmen were covered in prosthetics and make-up and passed off as an old guy until they got onto a skateboard and started pulling outrageous tricks. Mrs. Broder could've been a stuntwoman in disguise. Thin flesh hung from her bones as if all the muscle had been sucked out. Hands misshapen with arthritis. Age had written its story across her skin with fine wrinkles just about everywhere, and liver spots along the back of her wrists and forehead.

Seeing an opportunity, White rose from his seat and hustled around the desk so he could hold out an arm for Mrs. Broder. He was going to support her as she stepped into the witness stand.

She waved him away. Mrs. Broder didn't need any help. It made White look a little foolish, but he smiled at her as warmly as he could fake it, and then returned behind the prosecution table. Mrs. Broder swore on the Bible to tell the truth, the whole truth, and nothing but, so help her, God. I've lost count of how many people I've watched taking that oath. Most are nervous, getting mixed up what hand to put on the Bible, sweating and stumbling through that oath even while the clerk is helping them to recite it. All they have to do is repeat what the clerk says. Some take it seriously, or pretend to at least – trying to give off a sense of sincerity, when really all they're projecting is how much of a hypocrite they really are.

Mrs. Broder, though, she was serious. Repeated every word the clerk said, out loud, like she meant it. Like she was reciting the pledge of allegiance in the first game of the World Series from the pitcher's mound at Yankee Stadium. When she was finished and the judge invited her to sit, she thanked him like he was a stupid but much beloved grandchild.

'Mrs. Broder,' began White. 'Do you remember where you were on the night of June tenth last year?'

She nodded, said, 'Young man, I know exactly where I was, what I was doing and what happened that night.'

White smiled and threw me a glance to say that this witness wouldn't take any of my shit. I didn't need him to tell me that. Mrs. Broder was going to be a handful. Some witnesses you just can't shake. They're ironclad. Kate was relying on me. On Harry. On Bloch.

'Just listen,' whispered Harry. 'There's always an opening. Just wait for it.'

'Mrs. Broder, why don't you tell us where you were, and what you saw that night.'

'I was watching a movie. *Predator*, with Arnold Schwarzenegger. I was about halfway through, at the point where Hawkins gets killed, when I happened to glance out of the window and saw a couple on the other side of the street. They were walking past the Nielsen house, but they were taking their time about it.'

'What do you mean they were taking their time?'

'They were walking slowly past. It didn't look like they were going anywhere. That's what made them stand out. Everyone in New York is going somewhere. These people were not.'

'What happened then?'

'Well, I didn't think much of it. So, I went back to my movie. Maybe five minutes later, they came back. Walking past the house. Then they stopped, turned around and stood on the sidewalk just looking at the place.'

'How long did they stand there?'

'Maybe five, ten minutes?'

'Did you recognize this couple?'

'Not at first. I didn't know them. You see some strange things in this city, but I got a feeling from those two. It's hard to describe. This may sound strange, but I got a bad feeling watching them. I paid close attention. I got a good look at their faces.'

'When did you speak to the police, Mrs. Broder?'

'The next day I saw the police cars outside the Nielsen house. And the paramedics. They closed off a whole section of the street and I couldn't go out to my class. But I went down and spoke to a police officer. I told him what I'd seen the night before.'

'And what did he say?'

'He said they weren't looking for a couple. It was one man, alone, he said.'

I could sense that White wanted to move on swiftly from the police officer's mistake, but he paused. He thought it was more important the jury heard that Mrs. Broder had spoken to the police before Daniel Miller's face appeared on every news channel, news website and newspaper in the country.

'What happened next, Mrs. Broder?'

'Well, it was a couple of days at least, after that. The whole neighborhood was shook up. We knew that family. We saw those kids playing outside their house every day, coming home from school, going to the store. It was so shocking. I can't remember how long it was after that night when I saw the man's face again on the news. I called up the local precinct and by the time the officer came to my apartment there was another face on the news. It was the woman I'd seen. I didn't know who they were at the time. But I knew it was them the moment I saw their picture.'

My phone buzzed in my jacket.

An email from Denise, with attachments.

I clicked to open it and read the text.

'Mrs. Broder, I notice you're not wearing glasses. How good is your eyesight?' asked White.

'I'm longsighted. I need my reading glasses, but I have no problem watching TV, or reading signs that are far away.'

'One final question, Mrs. Broder. How sure are you that the couple you saw watching the Nielsen house the night of the murders was the defendant, Carrie Miller, and her husband, Daniel Miller?'

At first Mrs. Broder didn't answer. She looked around, seemingly surprised by the question.

'I have never been surer of anything in my life. It was them. I got a real good look at them that night, and there's no chance it could be anyone else.'

'Thank you, Mrs. Broder. I know that you have been under close protection at a secure location for the last day or so. That can't have been easy for anyone. I want to thank you for providing the jury with your testimony here today. Please remain in your seat, Mr. Flynn may have some questions for you.'

White sat down, pleased with himself.

I looked at the jury.

Sometimes it can be hard to read people. Most folks can't even read one person, never mind twelve. But I didn't need twelve people on my side. I only needed one for an acquittal. Looking over the faces of the jurors in that room, I couldn't see an open expression. Not one who looked even mildly skeptical. Mrs. Broder had delivered the gospel.

A trial can be like a rollercoaster – one minute you're riding high and the next you're plummeting toward the earth in what feels like a death spiral. A couple of jurors looked back at me. Their faces were either saying *go ahead, pal – take your best shot – Mrs. Broder is telling it like it is*; or they seemed genuinely curious as to whether I could shake the formidable Mrs. Broder.

I was curious myself.

Nothing to do except try.

Harry placed a hand on my forearm, said, 'Just do what you can. Keep it tight. Keep it short. We do not want to get into a battle with Mrs. Broder. She's got another ninety years in her.'

I nodded, got up, buttoned my jacket.

Eyewitness testimony is like an old Detroit muscle car: it looks and sounds amazing but run it for a while and you'll probably find it to be about as reliable as a twenty-dollar Rolex. The only thing a defense attorney can do is to try and stop the jury being dazzled by the body shape and the sound of the V8. I have to make sure they don't just kick the tires and jump in, they have to look under the hood at the faulty wiring, get underneath it and feel the rust, really listen to it so that they can hear that hole in the exhaust pipe. Some will look beyond the beauty of the thing, some won't. All I can do is pop the hood and fire up a flashlight.

I knew this witness had hurt us. The jury didn't just believe Mrs. Broder, they wanted to believe her.

'Good afternoon, Mrs. Broder. My name is Eddie Flynn. I'm very sorry to hear that you have had some troubles because of this case. It must've been very frightening.'

'It reminded me of a time long gone. But it wasn't as bad. I'm an old woman now, Mr. Flynn, and I am not afraid of this Sandman.'

I nodded, took a step forward.

'I admire your bravery, Mrs. Broder. Let's talk about what you saw that night . . .'

In cross examination there are three areas of attack when it comes to eyewitness testimony – distance, light and time. There are other vulnerable points, and I would need at least one more. For now, I went back to basics. Distance.

'How far away is your apartment window from the Nielsen house across the street?'

'Oh, I don't know exactly.'

'Let me help you. What floor is your apartment on?'

'The third floor.'

'So you're, what? Thirty, maybe forty feet up?'

'About thirty I'd say.'

'Okay, and you live on East 12th Street between 3rd and 2nd Avenue?'

'That's right.'

'Major cross streets in New York are a hundred feet wide. This isn't a major cross street so it's only what, sixty feet wide?'

'Yeah, I would say about that.'

'And given your elevated position, you were about seventy feet away from the sidewalk outside the Nielsen house that night?'

'That's right,' said Mrs. Broder, nodding.

Distance established.

Now for light.

'What time did your movie start that night?'

'Oh, around ten, I think.'

'And what time do you think you saw the couple?'

'Maybe ten forty-five, or eleven. Something like that.'

'It was dark out, right?'

'Right. But there's a streetlight,' she said.

It's often around this time the witness gets a sense of where they are being led. They try to push back, get ahead of the game. Only way to handle it is to let them know I'm in control.

'I didn't ask you about streetlights, Mrs. Broder. I asked you if it was dark outside. We'll talk about the streetlight in a second. Let's just try this again. It was night time. It was dark outside, isn't that right?'

She laced her fingers together, nodded, said, 'Yes, it was dark.'

'The streetlight you were so keen to mention, how far away is it from the Nielsen house would you say?'

Mrs. Broder struggled trying to estimate distance. A lot of people have the same problem. They can't think in feet or inches, they just can't visualize it. My job was to make Mrs. Broder as uncomfortable as possible.

'Oh, I don't know really. I can't think like that. It's close, though.'

'How far away is close?'

'I don't know, ten feet?'

'Let's make this easier. Is the streetlight on your side of the street, or the opposite side?'

'My side.'

'Is it outside your apartment?'

'No, it's down a ways.'

'We've already established your apartment is seventy feet away from the sidewalk outside the Nielsen house. That means this street light is not ten feet away from the Nielsen house, is it, Mrs. Broder?'

She clamped her lips together, raised her hands and shrugged in the way that people do when they just don't know what to say or what to do.

'I can see you're not sure, so let me help. The streetlight isn't outside your building, it's between your building and 3rd Avenue, right?'

Closing her eyes, she tried to visualize the street, said, 'Right, so if you're standing facing my apartment, it's to the left.'

'I understand, the question is how far to the left?'

'Again, I don't know exactly. Not far.'

'Does this help? Say you're outside your building right now. Use a reference point in the courtroom to show us where the light is located. It's not where I'm standing. Would it be all the way to the back of the courtroom?'

Gazing out across the room, she said, 'No, not that far. Maybe halfway?'

I turned, walked as slowly as I could damn well get away with. Letting the sound of my feet hitting the floor echo around the room as I made my way past the defense table, past the first row of the gallery, second row, third, fourth, fifth, slowing even further as I reached the tenth row, about halfway.

I turned back to Mrs. Broder, said, in a low voice, 'About here?'

Mrs. Broder cocked an ear in my direction, said, 'I'm sorry, I can't hear you.'

This time I shouted.

'Sorry, I'm so far away. Is this the rough distance between your apartment and the streetlight?'

She nodded.

I started walking back. Slowly. Letting the jury take in the distance. Making it feel further away than it really was. I stopped at the defense table.

'I estimate that's around forty-five feet?'

'I think so. Yeah.'

'And your apartment, as we've already established, is sixty feet away?'

She nodded.

'I need you to state an answer for the record, Mrs. Broder.'

'Yes,' she said, curtly.

'The streetlight you were so keen to tell us about is over a hundred feet away?'

Leaning forward, she opened her mouth. Shut it again, quick. Took a moment then said, 'I . . . well, maybe so. But I could still see them.'

'When Mr. White asked you earlier you said the couple walked past the house slowly, then came back and that time they stood there, watching the place for five, maybe ten minutes. It sounded like you weren't sure how long they were standing there, is that fair to say?'

'No, I saw them. And they stood there for a while.'

'A *while*,' I repeated. 'Mrs. Broder . . .'

I paused. Counted to ten in my head.

Taking the time to give it the full second. *One one-thousand, two one-thousand, three one-thousand . . .*

Mrs. Broder waited patiently, wondering what I was going to hit her with next.

'I just paused there for ten seconds. Felt like a long time, didn't it?'

'I . . . well, not really.'

'It felt like a lot longer than ten seconds.'

Silence. Especially expectant, anxious silence can make a second feel like a minute. Time is subjective.

'Maybe. It felt awkward.'

'Fair enough. Mrs. Broder, were you really watching the couple all that time, or were you kind of watching the street and watching your movie? What did you say it was again? *Predator*?'

'That's the one, with Arnold,' she said, with a smile.

'Do you like Arnold?'

'Doesn't everybody?'

'That's a good movie, I'll give you that.'

'One of my favorites.'

'So, am I right then? You were kind of watching the movie and looking outside?'

'I suppose so, but I saw them standing there.'

'Would it be fairer to say you're not sure how long exactly they stood there? It could've been a minute, or less?'

'Probably more,' she said.

One last topic – viewpoint.

'I take it you can see the street from your armchair? You didn't have to get up and look out the window?'

'No, I can see it from my chair.'

'And you had the lights on in the apartment?'

'My lamp, beside the TV.'

Now I had a choice. There were several ways to play this. Bloch had told me Mrs. Broder didn't have an unobstructed view of the street. There was a tree branch cutting her view. If I asked her whether the leaves on the tree outside her apartment obscured her view, she would just say no. Better to make it about the chair, and not the tree.

'Did you have to move around in your chair to see past the leaves and branches of the tree outside your building?'

'A little. I just had to lean forward.'

Time to wrap it up.

'Mrs. Broder you spoke to a police officer the day after the murders and told them you saw a couple standing outside the house the night before, but the policeman didn't think it was relevant because they were looking for one man, the Sandman, right?'

'Yeah, that's what I told Mr. White.'

'It was three days after the murder when the NYPD and FBI released pictures of the Sandman to the media and the manhunt began, do you remember seeing that?'

'I suppose so. I don't know when I saw it, exactly. I saw his picture first.'

'Two weeks later, right after the grand jury had indicted Carrie Miller, and her picture, alongside her husband's, was printed on the cover of the *New York Times* – that was when you contacted the police again, correct?'

'That's correct.'

'But you just told this jury you recognized them. Are you saying you didn't recognize Daniel Miller when you saw his picture on TV seventy-two hours after the murder across the street?'

'They told me they were looking for one man. Not a couple.'

'But you saw his face on the news and you didn't tell police.'

'No, I think I did. I'm not sure. I guess I thought they weren't interested in talking to me.'

I took a breath. Let it go.

Time to gather the threads into a ball. I felt sorry for Mrs. Broder, but Kate's life was on the line. I had to have hope. That meant I couldn't hold back.

'Mrs. Broder, that night, from a well-lit apartment, through leaves and foliage, you briefly saw a couple on the other side of a dark street seventy feet away. And when you saw the picture of Carrie and Daniel Miller in the newspaper or on TV weeks later you knew Daniel Miller had been identified as the man who committed the Nielsen murders, and you put two and two together, made five, and told the police you saw the Millers that night on the street, isn't that what really happened here?'

She stammered, stopped, took a breath, said, 'I don't agree with that.'

I didn't give her the chance to elaborate. And White wouldn't do that either. If he got into specifics, it might get worse. You never ask a question you don't know the answer to, so he stood, said, 'Your Honor, no re-exam. There is, however, a deeply troubling matter that I need to address right now.'

CHAPTER FORTY-FOUR

EDDIE

'Your Honor,' began White, 'two of the prosecution's eyewitnesses were murdered just days ago. I'm sure this has not escaped the notice of the court.'

'Your Honor, shouldn't we have the jury out for this?' I asked, before White got as far as prejudicing the twelve souls on my left.

Putting his elbows on the desk, Stoker clasped his hands together and said, 'I'm not sure what Mr. White is asking me to do. Maybe it would be safer to send the jury home for the day. It's just after four.'

White said, 'We would like the jury to read the depositions from those deceased witnesses.'

And there it was. Technically, he hadn't prejudiced the jury because he gave no hint as to what was in those depositions, but the jury would sure leave thinking the Sandman had removed two key witnesses from his wife's prosecution. That can't be good. I had at least got Denise to do my prep for me, and I had no choice now but play my hand.

'Your Honor, we would object to that course of action. Chester Morris, one of those alleged eyewitnesses, has had an assault and battery arrest on his record for a year now with no sign of a prosecution. In other words, he made a deal to save his license as a doorman in exchange for testifying in this case. Teresa Vasquez had agreed to testify on the condition her mother got a green card and fast-tracked through US citizenship. A representative from my office spoke to Mrs. Vasquez's mother just today. We can no longer cross-examine these witnesses on those points, so we would object strongly to their depositions being considered by this jury.'

As much of a creep as Stoker clearly was, he was a smart creep. As far as these witnesses went, I was pretty sure they had been lying.

'You heard Mr. Flynn. I'm afraid that's a perfectly valid point. We will adjourn 'til nine a.m. tomorrow morning. Have your next witness ready by then, Mr. White.'

The jury got up and were escorted back into their room to get their coats and bags. Stoker rose, and we all stood. Battle was over for the day.

Harry leaned over to me, said, 'You did well.'

I shook my head. 'Maybe one or two jurors will think Mrs. Broder is shaky. Maybe not. What do you think?'

Harry started packing up his pad and pens into a leather satchel, pretending like he didn't hear me.

'Harry, what do you think?'

'You raised doubt. That's all you can do.'

I moved in real close, making sure no one else could hear us.

'I'll tell you what I think, Harry. We have to win this case for Kate. And I'll do everything to make sure that happens. But on the flip side of this, we have a client on the run, a victim's blood on our client's shirt. Maybe Chester Morris and Teresa Vasquez were playing the DA to get what they want. Maybe they saw something, but I don't buy it. Mrs. Broder . . . well, I scored some points, but goddamn it, Harry, that woman is telling the truth. Daniel and Carrie Miller were outside the Nielsens' the night that family was murdered.'

He froze, his hand still in his satchel. Eyes closed.

'I know. I believed Carrie too. Now, like you, I'm not so sure. We don't have the full picture from our client, I know that. But we also don't have a choice. We've got to win this thing, for Kate.'

'There were two little kids in that house . . .' I said, but I couldn't finish my thought. I didn't want to. Some truths are too hard to face.

'So what are you suggesting? We drop out of the case? Leave Kate to the Sandman, if she isn't dead already?'

'No, of course not, but that doesn't mean I'm blind to this. Carrie is hiding something or carrying some kind of guilt. You could see it on her. Maybe she didn't actively participate in the murders, but she knew. I'm sure she *knew*. That's the only thing that makes sense.'

I wanted to say more, but I saw White headed over to us with a big brown envelope in his hand.

'As ordered,' he said. 'These are the phone records from the tap. None of the information we gleaned from this tap will be used in these criminal proceedings.'

I took the envelope, broke the seal and pulled out half a dozen or so pages of phone records. Calls, numbers, times, call duration – all set out in columns. There were separate bound pages for my phone, Bloch's, Kate's and Harry's. These were only a page long. They sure got onto us fast, but of course they wouldn't have found anything useful. In fact, I was pretty sure these records would help us.

Because I knew White had them, and he had not disclosed them prior, that meant there was nothing incriminating in any of the calls. There were only five pages of calls for Otto's phone, with numbers listed. I would need to sit down and go through it to check the numbers, but there were no transcript sheets. White was on his way out the door when I called him back.

'Where are the call transcripts?' I asked.

'There are none.'

'What do you mean?'

'Our warrant allowed us to monitor all calls, but we were only permitted to transcribe and exhibit incriminating calls. We didn't get anything. And she never spoke to her lawyer.'

'I don't believe you,' I said.

'Do you think if I had something on Carrie Miller that I would suppress it? I'd be waving it in your face, Flynn. Sorry, there's nothing. It was the biggest waste of time.'

And together with his assistants he left. There was something very wrong with this picture, and the calls. I could feel it, but I couldn't yet see it. I didn't trust White, and if he could hold an ace up his sleeve, ready to play at the perfect moment, he wouldn't hesitate.

I checked my phone. Two missed calls from Bloch fifteen minutes ago. Harry and I were the last people in the courtroom. I called her back.

'What's happening?' I asked.

'It's not Kate,' she said.

I closed my eyes, raised my head for a second and whispered a silent prayer.

Another Sandman victim. But who . . .?

Sometimes when you look at the world, nothing looks exactly right. There's something off, something out of whack, something just plain wrong. You can feel the problem, but it's hard to find the solution.

Sometimes the solution comes from another problem. It can feel like my subconscious has been working away on something for days, solidly, without me knowing it. And then suddenly, the last piece falls and *wham*!

It's like magic.

'Tell me about this victim,' I said.

'He's been chopped into several pieces in order to fit into the freezer. That's about all we can say. Still can't see his face . . .'

'Are there any pieces missing?' I asked.

A moment's pause. Dead air on the other end of the line.

Then Bloch said, 'How did you know that?'

We talked for ten minutes. Agreed a plan.

'What's going on?' said Harry.

'It's time to give the reporter her exclusive,' I said.

CHAPTER FORTY-FIVE

KATE

First, there was pain.

And then darkness.

Her head and neck were ablaze with agony. The most intense pain she had ever felt. As if someone had held an acetylene torch to her brain and cooked it until it was a hot, pink ball of boiling tissue.

She felt pressure on her chest, and realized it was from her chin. Slowly, she tried to raise her head. Agony whipped through the muscles in her neck. They had been strained and stretched as she'd been out cold with her head leaning forward for God knows how long. She had to fight through it. Had to lift her head. She tried to raise her arms, to help lift her chin, but her hands were bound behind her.

It was then she realized she was sitting upright in a chair. The sharp ties at her wrists were also fixed to the back of chair.

Her eyes opened. She blinked. There was still only darkness. No light at all.

Swallowing burned her throat. It felt raw and sore. She took two quick breaths, gritted her teeth, and pulled her head up, straightening her neck. The pain in those muscles quickly abated when her headache decided it didn't like any neck movement at all. The pain was so bad she cried out, and salty tears rolled onto her lips, stinging them. Her mouth was so dry her lips felt like they had been baked in the sun. They were cracked, and when she tried to wet them, she tasted blood.

She whimpered, almost overwhelmed with the pounding in her head.

Kate put her back against the seat, let her shoulders relax and concentrated on her breathing. She knew if she didn't, she would

be sick and then she would panic. And that would make everything worse.

Pain gave way to confusion. Why was she here? Was this a dream?

Confusion gave way to memory.

The hand on her mouth.

Breath on her neck.

The prick of the needle.

The song. That fucking song.

And now here.

But where was here?

Thinking helped.

Her old man had been an NYPD blue for over twenty years
before he hung up his badge. She remembered his stories – those
tight spots. That's what he called them. Tight spots. Not pinned
down behind his cruiser while some gangbanger turned it into
Swiss cheese with a Mac 10, not pulling a jumper off the top of a
ten-story building because he'd just smothered his baby by mistake
when he was high, not watching his partner eat the business end
of a shotgun when he knocked on the wrong door in the wrong
neighborhood.

Tight spots.

What her father told her was that people lived or died because
they were able to think things through and make good decisions.
That was the key to survival. Good decisions. There was always
something you could do to make things worse or make them better.

Kate's eyes slowly adjusted to the thick darkness.

Her breathing slowed.

She was able to listen, and smell and see.

There wasn't much to look at. She couldn't make out any shapes
in the dark, apart from what she thought might have been a ceiling
panel above her. How far above, she couldn't tell exactly, but it
was a lot closer than it should have been. She wondered if the chair
she was on had been put on a table, because it seemed that if she
stood on the chair her head would hit the ceiling.

Her breath sounded loud, even though she had it under control
now. She let out a small 'woo' and listened. The sound came back

at her almost immediately, and it was dense and muted at the same time. She guessed she was in a very small, narrow room with concrete walls. Maybe an ante room in a bunker.

Her bare feet moved over the cold floor. Definitely concrete. It was level, solid and smooth. There was something else underfoot. Something which made the soles of her feet slide. It wasn't grit.

It was sand.

For a second, the fear returned. Doubled, this time. But she suppressed the surge, breathed through it, got her nervous system under control.

The odor all around her was familiar and strong.

Grease. Motor oil. The metallic tang from tools.

It smelled like a garage, which didn't fit with the dim outline of her surroundings one little bit. She began to shiver. She was still in her nightdress, and now she felt the cool air biting at her skin. The small tremors, like an engine, started up the fire in her head. That pain had dulled somewhat, but cold, fear and the shaking brought it back to life with a vengeance. Like someone had replaced her brain with a wrecking ball and the slightest movement sent it crashing around her skull, ricocheting off bone, trying to burst right out.

With the pain, came sickness. She closed her eyes, tried to remain still.

Think.

She was alive. And she didn't know why. The Sandman did not take live victims hostage. There could be two reasons.

She was ransom. Something to hold over the cops, or Eddie. Something to bargain with. That seemed the most likely explanation.

There was another reason. One she didn't want to think about. But the thought came anyway and stayed with her. Like that smell. It was there, constantly.

He took her so that he could take his time killing her.

Kate decided right then she had to escape. She could hear no one, see no one. The Sandman was not in this strange room. She had time. No idea how much.

She had to think.

She had to plan.

She had to escape.

From shifting her body weight she'd guessed she was in a wooden dining chair. It squeaked if she leaned back, the way old ash or pine does when it's rubbing against other wood. Her hands were behind her, wrists bound together with cable ties. Using her thumb and fingers, she'd felt another tie, in the middle of her wrists, and this was attached to something beneath the chair, a central crossbar that had the cable tie attached.

She pushed down with her right leg, shifted all her weight over to the left, got both legs on the right off the ground, higher, and then, just when she thought she might tip over, she threw herself to the right. The legs on the right side of the chair crashed down, and she pushed up, until the left set of legs was in the air, and then flung all her weight in that direction.

This rocking motion made the chair legs screech and crack, and she pulled up with her arms, letting the cable tie bite into her flesh.

It didn't take long to dislodge the central bar as the legs threatened to come out of their housing and break the screws holding them in place.

Kate pulled, shimmied, and felt the cable tie slide free.

It had taken a lot of effort, and she was out of breath, but she almost smiled when she was able to stand up straight, now free from the bastard chair. Her back muscles ached as she straightened up. She took a moment to loosen up then bent over, slid her hands over her behind and down to the backs of her thighs. She bent down and let herself sit on the floor, then pulled her arms forward and tucked her legs and feet, one by one, through her arms.

Now her hands, still bound, were in front of her. And she could stand.

With the effort she had actually broken a sweat, and apart from her feet, she was no longer cold. And her teeth had stopped rattling.

Teeth.

She brought her wrists to her face, angled her head, and was just able to get her lower front teeth over the lip of the cable tie.

Kate started chewing.

The plastic felt sharp against her lower lip, and she tasted blood now as she worked her jaw, back and forth, tears streaming her face, stinging the cut, her wrists raw and bleeding, her whole body shaking.

The tie snapped.

When it fell to the floor her eyes followed it, instinctively, and it was then she saw a thin strip of light on the floor. The light wasn't coming from the floor, it was a reflection. She looked up, saw a small gap in the ceiling. At first, she couldn't understand what kind of place she was in. It was narrow, she was sure of that, maybe only five feet wide and ten feet long. The ceiling was low, as she had suspected. Very low. Kate wasn't tall, but she could easily touch the ceiling. She was surprised when she heard the *ting* of her knuckles on steel.

It felt like there was a huge metal plate that acted as a roof. She placed her palms flat against it and pushed. It didn't even budge. She moved forward, to the end of the narrow room, and it was here that she stood beneath the tiny gap. Wide enough to slip a paper towel through, but no more. She couldn't even get her fingernails through it. She tried again to shift the steel plate, but it was way too heavy.

Now she realized where she was.

The smell of oil, the sand on the floor, the shape and dimensions of the space. She felt the wall, the narrow head of the rectangle and found that the concrete gave way to wood, but not all the way. It was as if there was a gap cut out of the concrete and old mahogany placed there.

She was in an inspection pit.

This place, wherever it was, had once been an old garage, probably specializing in buses, trucks or long heavy vehicles. The wooden section of the wall was actually a stopper. If it was removed, there would be concrete steps leading out of the pit. It would have been specially made so that it would cover the steps when the pit was not in use. When it was in use, men would walk down into the pit, and the vehicle would be driven over it, so they could work at a comfortable height on a truck or a bus in the days when there were no hydraulics powerful enough to lift those vehicles.

The steel plate was now covering the pit. If she could move it, somehow, she could get out.

She heard a cracking, crunching sound. And then whatever was making the sound, made a different noise. She heard the cooing and the fluttering of wings from a rock dove.

Just a bird.

Just a fucking bird.

Kate took a moment to think. She had to get the hell out of here. And she had no idea how to do it.

CHAPTER FORTY-SIX

Extract from the Journal of Carrie Miller

June 5

There was only one person I thought I could trust.

My parents have passed on. I don't have siblings. Since Daniel and I had been together, I'd seen less and less of my friends. He always encouraged me to go visit them – have 'girly nights' as he called it, but they kind of petered out. Clare, Vanessa, Suzanne, they were all still in New York. Still in the same shitty apartments. With the same shitty jobs. When I pulled up in the Tesla, I could see their hearts sink. When I paid for dinner, or settled the bar tab, I saw it eating at them. They never said anything, but it was there in the corner of their forced smiles and thank-yous. There was a wedge between us. Money hadn't changed me, but it changed things. Soon, they stopped calling. I didn't want to make them feel uncomfortable, and I tried talking about it, especially with Clare. She said it made no difference, in fact, she was happy for me. But I saw it different. And it felt different.

Daniel didn't have a social circle. Not really. We went to movie premieres, charity balls, cocktail parties, gala dinners at the social club – the kind of parties, places and people I'd only ever dreamed about or seen on TV. None of them were friends of ours. People went to those events to be seen there and to make small talk with the people they thought were powerful.

There was no one I could call about this. No friends, anyway.

So, I called someone who I knew could keep a secret. Someone who told me I could reach out to them at any time. Someone who had to keep a secret because it was their job.

Otto's firm looked like a high-end art dealership. The furniture in the waiting room was old and very beautiful. I didn't have to wait long before his receptionist showed me into his office. It had oak paneling on the walls, antique book cases, green bankers' lamps scattered around the room and a beautiful walnut box on his desk filled with fine cigars.

At first, Otto was wary of talking to me without Danny being there. He said something about a possible conflict of interest as Danny was his client. I told him it was important that he knew this about Danny too. I told him I had to tell someone – that I couldn't go on keeping this bottled up inside.

Maybe it was something in the way my voice fractured as I spoke. Maybe it was the pleading tone. Maybe it was the look on my face. Whatever it was, Otto dropped the lawyer façade, reached his two hands across the desk and took mine.

He asked me if Danny was beating me. He'd probably heard enough stories from clients, done enough cases to know, almost instantly, the secrets people hold.

I told him. I told him everything. The late nights. The cop coming to the house. Danny lying to the cop, and then making me lie as well. The van I didn't even know existed. Taking showers in the middle of the night. The earrings he'd given me and the picture I'd seen of Margaret Sharpe wearing those same earrings. The two rings, and then him doing laundry for the first time at three a.m.

His mouth opened then, but no words came. I could see the possible responses tumbling across this face, like the reels of a slot machine, and for as long as he was unsure what to say, or how to say it, his jaw remained slack. He licked his lips as the slot reels slowed.

I could see that what I'd said had hit him, hard. But it hadn't sunk in. Not yet. Because he said he didn't believe Danny was a killer. I told him that a month ago I wouldn't have believed it either, but there was just too much here to ignore. I told him I could be living with a killer.

I took out this journal, showed it to Otto, and told him the dates that he gave me the jewelry after being out all night, it was the day after the Sandman had killed someone else. This caused Otto to pause again.

He asked if I wanted to go to the police about this. I asked him what he thought about that – I was here for his advice. He said he didn't know what do to, because of my prenup. Part of the prenup is a mutual-respect clause – basically, if I falsely accused my husband of anything, I would lose my right to a share of the marital assets.

I told Otto I was scared, and I didn't know what to do. I couldn't sleep, I couldn't think about anything else. This was driving me mad.

He got up and came around the desk. Put his hands on my shoulders and did his best to console me, whispering softly and gently rubbing my upper arms. There was an antique mahogany chair at the wall behind him, he picked it up, placed it beside mine and sat down.

He tried to calm me. I felt stupid. Stupid, afraid and selfish. I took a Kleenex from my pocket and wiped away the fresh tears. I said that I look at my husband now and I ask myself if he killed all those people, and I don't know the answer. I just don't know. I can't live like this.

I remember staring into Otto's face. The poor guy. He dealt with nice, wealthy people whose only problem was making sure they didn't have to give so much of their money to the IRS. He didn't need this. He didn't need me coming into this office, crying all over his desk. Being stupid. Hysterical. He seemed genuinely concerned. And I could tell he wanted to help. But he didn't know how to handle me.

He said he had a private investigator who would look into this, in secret. And if they found something he would come to the police station with me. He was concerned when I'd told him I'd lied to the police. He kept referring back to this, asking why I'd said that. I just told him I didn't know what it was about, and right then I didn't suspect Danny of so much as a parking violation never mind being a serial killer.

He got up and approached a steel filing cabinet in the corner. It was a large, heavy-duty, fireproof thing that looked like it weighed a ton. Probably used to hold property deeds and other important original documents. He took a key from the chain in his waistcoat, unlocked the file and opened the second drawer. He took out what I thought was a bright yellow toy gun.

He said he hated guns, but for insurance purposes they insisted he have some kind of personal protection, so he had this. It was a taser gun. He said he wanted me to have it, and that it might make me feel better. He also said he would feel better if I had it. I took the taser gun, felt the weight. It was surprisingly heavy.

I thanked him.

He said he would be in touch. I left Otto's office thankful that I'd taken the plunge. At least someone else knew. At least, if something ever happened to me, Otto would know I'd told the truth.

Someone would know.

CHAPTER FORTY-SEVEN

KATE

She sat on the floor in the dark. Catching her breath. It didn't matter that it was cold, that she was only in her nightdress. No shoes, not even socks. Her feet had gotten so numb from the freezing floor that she could no longer feel them.

Still, she was sweating.

For hours, she had tried to shift the steel plate covering the pit.

It had not moved. There was no way to lift it from the center because that would mean lifting most of its weight. Instead, Kate had moved as far forward as she could get, put her back against the wall and pushed upwards. Her arms couldn't do it.

She had then tried locking her elbows, bending her knees and using her legs to push.

No dice, and her wrists had started to hurt so bad that she feared they might break. Nothing seemed to work. Not a sustained push, nor short, explosive pumping pushes from her legs. When a pain shot through her forearm, she stifled a scream and collapsed on the floor.

When her mom died, Kate had gotten low. As low as she had ever been. Her parents had put her through college, then law school. What Kate didn't know at the time was that her mom hid her cancer diagnosis from her daughter. She didn't want her to waste those years with worry, with sadness and the anguish that came near the end. Also, she didn't want Kate to know of the choice that she had made. Insurance wouldn't cover all of her medical bills, so it was either pay for Kate's school, or pay for drug treatment that would have extended her life. Her mom decided it wasn't really a choice at all. She had her life, and it was Kate. Her father understood and supported her mother's decision. And every day Kate practiced law was a day that she paid back that debt to her mother. Every case she won for a victim, every morning when she put on her suit, every phone call to her father – the debt was supposed to get smaller; the guilt was supposed to lessen.

It never did.

Not once.

And now, she was caught in a pit by a monster.

Was this what her mother had sacrificed those years for? And they could have been good years. The best years. Because when time is precious, every moment, every smile, every hug and every kiss counts.

Kate wiped her face, ran her hands through her sweat-streaked hair. She gritted her teeth, and with her legs, arms and back aching – she stood up.

If she couldn't move it from the center, or on one side, she would have to try one corner. Lifting the chair, she set it in the right-hand corner of the pit, the square seat slotting more or less perfectly into the right angle.

Kate stood on the chair this time; knees bent. When she started to straighten up, she realized her head touched the steel plate a lot sooner, her legs at a forty-five-degree bend. She tucked her chin into her chest, spread her shoulders on the steel, hands on her knees.

Took three deep breaths.

Whispered a prayer to her mom.

And pushed.

The plate moved.

She dropped it down again. Took more air into her lungs. It had moved, but barely. She needed something else. Something to help prop it open so she could really get the plate tilting. She grabbed the strip of wood that was the backrest of the chair, put her other hand on the upright and started to work it free.

She was getting out of here.

She froze.

A metal door opened and then slammed shut. She heard footsteps on the floor.

He was coming.

CHAPTER FORTY-EIGHT

THE SANDMAN

The Sandman opened the five-pound padlock around the thirty-pound steel chain securing the double doors to the old bus depot in Coney Island. Before the bus routes came in 1955, streetcars carried passengers on the Coney Island Avenue Line. Those cars needed a lot of maintenance. When the streetcars gave way to buses, they needed work too – probably more than the streetcars.

As the buses modernized, the maintenance regime and practices had to modernize too. This depot wasn't part of the old MTA yard on Coney Island. It had been part of a private company. He had bought the old depot through a shell company on the pretense of buying up land for development. Only the company didn't develop the land. They sat on it and waited for the price of real estate to increase. And while they were waiting, the Sandman had a place all of his own. A private place, where it didn't matter what kind of noises were made, or who came in and what came out. There were no houses or people in this particular part of the neighborhood, just more industrial buildings and supply companies. After five in the evening, there were no cars or trucks on the street until five the next morning.

He went inside, shut the door behind him. The space inside the depot could hold four buses. Four inspection pits. The first one up ahead, on his left, had a steel plate covering the pit. On top of the plate was an iron tool trolley, right in the center, for added weight. The depot had been constructed in the 1880s, and timber was still cheaper than steel back then. The roof had huge wooden beams running in cross sections. Some had fallen down. They had just rotted away. Mostly on the right side of the depot, near the twin double roller doors at that end. The wood wasn't rotten. An infestation had done the damage.

Deathwatch beetles had all but destroyed the roof. He could see them, especially at night, like little black raindrops running over the old oak. Thousands of them.

He approached the covered pit. Tapped on the steel plate with the toe of his boot.

Listened.

He could hear her down there. Her breath, quick with fear. And something else. Her feet, moving.

She had gotten free of the chair. He expected as much.

From his bag he produced a bottle of water, a pastrami sandwich and a few candy bars. She would be hungry about now. Thirsty too.

He deepened his voice. Dropping it an octave. It helped when he was working. People responded to commanding tones.

'I'm going to give you some food and water. If you try to climb out, I will hurt you. Do you understand, Kate?'

After a short pause he heard her voice. The strange echo of it, distorted by the close concrete walls and steel enclosing the pit.

'Yes.'

He had left a gap between the pit edge and the plate. It was tiny, maybe only an eighth of an inch. Large enough to let air through, but not wide enough to allow anyone to get a pinkie finger out of that pit. First thing was to move the trolley. He stepped onto the plate, and with some effort, rolled the heavy iron trolley onto the floor. It was easy enough to move once you got it started, but getting it started took some doing. Each of the trolley's four wheels had its own symphony of rusty squeaks and squeals as they moved.

A long steel bar with a hook on the end lay on the ground. He picked it up, wedged the flathead end of it into the gap and started to work it back and forth. Soon as he had a gap wide enough, he stuck the bar down further into the gap, then used it as leverage, pulling down on the bar. The plate screeched and scraped against the concrete as it moved back a few inches.

He leaned the bar against a pillar, dropped the water, sandwich and candy into the dark pit. He couldn't see her in there. She was probably hiding in the opposite corner. No point in tempting her with thoughts of escape. He picked up the bar, swiveled it so the hook was pointing to the floor, and managed to attach it to the catch that was countersunk into the plate. Then it was easy enough to walk backwards, yanking the plate to get it moving at first and then pulling until it covered the pit.

Dropping the bar, he moved to the trolley and got it back into the middle of the plate.

No way anyone could get out of there now. Not with that extra weight on top.

He'd left a slightly wider gap than before. About an inch.

The Sandman sunk down, balancing on the balls of his feet, his elbows on his knees, fingers locked together.

'I told Flynn I would let you go if he got an acquittal for Carrie.'

No response.

'It went well today, by all accounts. He's good, Flynn. Very good. He just needed the right incentive. Case should be wrapped up by tomorrow.'

Silence.

'Carrie should come out of hiding when the case is over, don't you think? After all, she needs me.'

He waited this time for a reply. None came.

'Are you scared?' he asked.

Kate didn't say anything, but he heard her. A soft whimper. Then . . .

'I'm scared. Carrie is scared too. She's scared of you,' said Kate, her voice echoing in the pit, amplified by the space and the steel roof.

The Sandman drew his blade from the leather sheath strapped to his lower back.

'I know I told Flynn I'd let you go if he won . . .'

Rolling his wrist, he tossed the handle, flipping the blade in the air, catching it expertly.

'I meant it. If he wins Carrie's case I'll let you go. Whether you walk out of here with both of your eyes is up to you.'

He stood and turned, made his way to the door. Beside the entrance was a stack of hessian bags that stood at shoulder height.

He put the knife away, took hold of the top bag, hauled it onto his shoulder. Forty pounds of fine sand.

Ready for a new home.

He locked the building behind him, used the chain to secure the doors and the padlock to hold it in place. The sand he put in the back of the van, and then he rode out of the street, back toward the city.

It was almost six when he found a parking space in an open-air lot that had a building standing on it about a year ago. Construction had stopped for a long time in New York, due to Covid, but a sign on the chain link fence of the parking lot said it was closing permanently next week. Life had returned to the city, and it was slowly getting back to normal.

He passed a news stand and something caught his eye. Something that caused both of his feet to stall on the sidewalk like they'd just trodden in superglue.

The news section. Every single headline was about the case.

He pulled his phone. There were half a dozen notifications and emails for case news alerts.

#EddieFlynn was trending on twitter.

He clicked on the latest update on the *New York Times* website. The headline didn't make sense.

Eddie Flynn calls on Carrie Miller to expose her husband.

The *Times* had a statement from Flynn. A reporter called Betty Clarke had an exclusive with the *Sentinel*, and they'd syndicated the story to all the news outlets – print, online and TV.

New York Sentinel reporter Betty Clarke has an exclusive with the defense attorney at the heart of the trial of the Sandman's wife, Carrie Miller. The trial proceeded today in the absence of the defendant. Despite this setback, defense attorney for Carrie Miller, Eddie Flynn, made a spirited defense of his client in the face of forensic evidence, which Flynn challenges. At the end of today's proceedings, Flynn released the following statement.

'It's no secret that my client is not in court today. She has not answered her bail. She's running because she is scared. My client is afraid because she is another Sandman victim. The real murderer is still out there

and is still killing innocent people. It is about time the NYPD and the FBI stopped trying to persecute my client for her husband's crimes. This is what the justice system and the media does. Whenever there is violence against women – women somehow get the blame.

'*This has to stop. And it stops right now with me. This is a message for Carrie. I know you're frightened, and I know why. You need to trust someone. I know that's hard considering what you've been through, but you can trust me. I can't help you unless you come in. We will stand or fall together. Call my office tonight. Either you call me, or in the morning I'll come off record for you in the case. Then there will be no defense. The trial will proceed without you or me, and you will be convicted.*

'*You've got until tonight to call. This is your one chance. Don't waste it, because I can guarantee you one thing – I know you are a victim and so long as you trust me, I will never stop fighting for you, no matter what. But I can't do this alone.'*

The Sandman hit the side button on his phone, blanking the screen into standby mode. That message to Carrie was smart. She would call him. He was sure of it. Flynn was a clever son of a bitch. Turning, he headed back to the van.

Once he saw Carrie Miller with Eddie, he would kill the lawyer and take her.

There was a new life waiting for the Sandman and Carrie. Somewhere far away. He'd already made preparations. By the time it was all over, they would be safe. They could take long walks along country roads. Eat lazy dinners in front of a real fire. Talk all night, like they used to do when they first met, and then sleep late, wrapped in each other's arms.

Sleep.

That was what he craved. It didn't come easy, but holding her, or even just having her close, gave him a contentment that lulled the sharp teeth that gnawed at his brain in the dark. Everything would be perfect. As long as she was safe.

In truth, if he had to, he knew he would die for her.

But first, he wanted to live again.

All he needed now was the woman he loved.

CHAPTER FORTY-NINE

EDDIE

The phone handset for reception sat on my desk.

All calls to the firm go through this number. Denise, Harry and Bloch all slumped in chairs around my office. Lake didn't do slumping.

He was the opposite. Bent over in the chair, elbows on his knees, right foot tapping. Occasionally the tapping stopped long enough for him to take a bite out of the cuticles around his nails. Then the tapping would begin again.

It was annoying me. And everyone else, apart from Bloch, who was too exhausted to notice or care. She was engaged in a battle with her eyelids that she was losing, badly. Now and again, she drifted off into sleep, but only for a second or two. Soon as her head began to slump her eyes fired open and the war started all over again.

'Would you like some coffee, Mr. Lake?' said Denise.

'Do you have any lemons? I'd really like some hot lemon water.'

'We don't buy lemons,' said Denise, 'on account of how they don't fit in the coffee machine. We got coffee is what we got.'

He said, 'What kind of coffee is it?'

Denise had never been asked this before. She knew every one of the filing codes that had to be displayed on court documents for criminal and civil proceedings, she knew the entire criminal and civil procedure rules, basically she was the most over-qualified secretary in Manhattan. She knew everything. She didn't know what kind of coffee we had.

'It's ground coffee,' she said.

'Yeah, but is it organic?'

'It comes in a plastic pouch.'

'Where were the beans grown?'

'On a coffee plant.'

'Okay, but like, is it ethically sourced coffee? Where was the plant grown? Colombia, Brazil, Indonesia—'

'I think it was grown out of my asshole.'

'*Denise* . . .' I said.

'Do you want coffee or not, Mr. Lake? I buy it from Target with petty cash.'

'I'm fine, thank you,' said Lake.

'I'll have some coffee, thank you, Denise,' said Harry, and he straightened up. Clarence sat at his feet, gazing up at him. He stroked the dog, smiled.

A digital ring tone exploded from the phone, filling the room, and as if the noise itself was electric, everyone sat up, leaned toward the phone. Denise grabbed it off the table.

'Flynn and Brooks, attorneys at law,' she said, her expression filled with hope and expectation.

The hope fell out of her face as her shoulders sagged. She rolled her eyes, gave the phone to me and said, 'It's Mr. Peltier.'

I took the receiver.

'Eddie, I'm downstairs. Been buzzing your office door. Has she called?'

'Someone go let Otto in,' I said.

Then, into the phone, 'We're buzzing you in now. Sorry, we're sitting in my office waiting for her to call.'

Denise got up and left. A few seconds later I heard the buzzer, then the door. Then Otto's thousand-dollar suit and cologne filled the room.

'Sorry, I didn't mean to jam up the phone line. I didn't want to talk on the phone at all. Not after the FBI had their listening party,' he said.

'It's alright, grab a chair.'

'No, I'm not staying. I know I shouldn't really be here considering I'm a prosecution witness.'

'It's fine,' said Harry. 'Like we said before. As long as we don't discuss your testimony then there shouldn't be a problem. How are you holding up?'

It was only then I noticed the rings around Otto's eyes. You can't carry a case like this for so long and not have a personal connection to it. Lawyers, even the cynical ones, can't help but get invested when it's someone's life on the line. That's what I chose to believe about Otto. I'm sure the thought of the loss of a million dollars in fees was taking a toll as well. She wouldn't pay up if she was on the run.

'I'm okay. I just want to know what's happening. I chose you for the case. I need to know she has someone representing her. She placed her trust in me once. I don't want to let her down.'

I said, 'We're trying to help her. We really are. But we can't do that when she's in hiding. She has to come out and face this. We need her, Otto. We're gambling more than you know. It's not just Carrie's life at stake here.'

'I don't quite follow,' he said.

'Don't worry about it. We've got this. She's gonna call. Then I'm going to meet her and bring her in. It's all going to work out.'

'That reminds me. Be careful if you go to meet her tonight. The FBI are parked a couple of blocks from your office.'

'In marked cars?' asked Bloch.

'No, it's a surveillance team. There's a dark-colored van outside the noodle place just down the street. I was watching for them. At least I think it's them. That wire tap has me chasing shadows.'

Bloch, Lake and I got up and moved to the window. Sure enough, three blocks down. A dark panel van parked outside Ho's Noodles. There would likely be other cars on the street, ready to run a three-car tail, but every move would be coordinated from the two or three guys looking at screens in the back of that van.

It was hard to tell in the dark, and at this distance, but I thought I could just about make out a single figure in the cab of the van. A darker shape behind the wheel.

'If she calls, make sure you get the number and call her back from your burner phone,' said Lake. 'They could be listening to your land line in the back of that van.'

I heard Denise come through the door with coffee, and the phone rang.

For a second, we all just turned and stared at the screen on the handset flaring brightly. I picked it up, hit answer.

'Hello?' I asked.

There was a woman on the other end of the line. I could tell by the sounds. No words. Just breath rattling in a coarse throat, the effort taken to stifle the crying, the sheer wall of anxiety on the other end of the line.

'Can I really trust you?' asked Carrie Miller. This wasn't some asshole calling our office to fool around, we'd had two of those calls earlier.

'You really can. I want to make sure our call is private. Just you and me. I'm going to call you from a secure line. I've got your number on the screen. Wait by the phone. I'm going to hang up and call you right back.'

As I ended the call, I was typing the number into my burner.

I hit the call button. Everyone in the room was looking at me. I glanced out of the window at the van. No movement. No lights. It just sat there. Too late for any deliveries.

Carrie picked up the call.

'Here's the plan. We need to meet and talk. After that I will arrange your surrender to the NYPD tomorrow. You will be arrested and placed into custody, but you will be at the hearing. You will be with me, and you will be safe. I guarantee that. I can't guarantee you will win the case. It depends on you, but I think I know how to do it. It might take a day, or a day and a half to finish the trial. No more. This will all be over inside of forty-eight hours, starting now, as long as you meet me tonight.'

While I waited for an answer, I watched the van.

'I didn't kill those people,' she said.

'I know you didn't. But there's a lot more than the case to talk about. Meet me in DUMBO, in the park by the river in one hour.'

'I'll be there.'

I hung up, dialed another number. My call was picked up almost instantly.

'Eddie Fly,' said the voice of Jimmy 'the Hat' Fellini. Jimmy and I grew up together. We had a lot in common as kids. My father was a con man masquerading as a regular Joe. Jimmy's father, old man Fellini, ran the largest Italian crime syndicate in the country. Only difference was his old man didn't pretend to be straight. We both loved boxing, and we spent whole summers, and most of our winter nights, in Mickey's gym, pounding heavy bags, working our knuckles into the concrete with push-ups and chasing each other around the ring. We both followed in our respective father's footsteps, at least for a while in my case. We've always been there for each other, although lately it was me asking Jimmy for help, but I knew he was only too glad to give it. That's how things worked. And if he ever needed anything from me – I was right there, no questions asked.

'How are you?' I asked.

'I'm good. Busy. I see you are too. You need something?'

'I'm in the market for private hire but I'm on a tight clock.'

'How tight?'

'Like, thirty minutes tight.'

'Doable, depending on what you need.'

'Four wheelmen with their own rides at my office. I need a crew who have worked together before and know how to run a veneziana.'

'You hitting jewelry stores now?'

'In fairness, it would probably make my life easier if I went into that line of work. No, I need to be somewhere and I don't want the feds on my ass when I get there. Who is your best driver?'

'Wings is still the best.'

'How old is he now?'

'Nobody knows and nobody asks. I'm the boss and I don't have the balls to ask him.'

'Fair enough. It's thirty minutes' work. Tops. Fifteen hundred per car. Two grand to you. That good enough?'

'Forget the two large to me. The guys will kick back five hundred a piece. I'm good. They'll be out front in a half hour. Take care of yourself, fly man.'

'Thanks, Jimmy.'

CHAPTER FIFTY

EDDIE

Twenty-nine minutes later I waved Otto into his Mercedes, he was feeling better than he had when he first showed up. It was safer this way. This was out of Otto's league. All the while I was on the street, I couldn't take my eyes off the van. There was someone behind the wheel, but I couldn't make out a face. The more I looked at the van, the more I wondered if it was the FBI in the back, or whether it was just that driver up front. Maybe Otto was right and he was just spooked.

Better not to take the chance.

If we had time, I'd ask Bloch to do a walk-by and eyeball the driver. But there was no time, and it didn't matter really. Soon as we took off, the van would follow, I was sure of it.

Bloch, Harry, Lake and I stood on the sidewalk.

'Why can't I drive?' asked Bloch.

'Because you're great at driving fast, but you don't know how to work a veneziana.'

'What the hell is a veneziana?' she asked.

'You probably don't want to know,' said Harry.

A line of cars made their way past Ho's Noodle joint in convoy. The car up front was a new model Mustang in electric blue. Behind that was another Ford, a Focus RS, followed by a Dodge Hellcat and another Focus. It didn't matter what these cars looked like or what kind of engine had been fitted in the factory, every one had been remodeled to the driver's specification, because that's what wheelmen do. Most of them have their own shops, or they know a garage that is friendly enough to let them work at it all hours of the night and day.

They all pulled up outside the office. Harry got into the RS, Bloch the Focus, Lake the Mustang, and I got into the Hellcat. I knew the driver. Big guy who had a specially adapted seat to accommodate his stomach. He wore his hair in a tousled mop, and a leather jacket stretched over his frame tight as a super-hero suit.

His name was Anthony Lombardi – a cousin of Jimmy's. Everyone was a cousin of Jimmy's. I knew him only by his nickname – Tony Two Fucks.

'Eddie *fuckin* Fly, hey, how the fuck you doin'?'

Whatever Tony said, there were at least two fucks in every sentence, no matter how short. He could get two fucks out of buying a pack of cigarettes; ordering a cheeseburger; or picking up his dry cleaning. Even when he went on a long rant, you might think the 'fuck' you got at the beginning would be it, but sure enough, another surprise 'fuck' would come along when you least expected it.

'Tony, I'm good. You ready?'

'Fuckin A, motherfuck.'

He floored the accelerator, and we all took off in different directions. I could almost hear the FBI surveillance team on their radios now. They would be rivaling Tony for the sheer volume of fucks on that channel.

The veneziana is a traditional Italian folk dance. Couples part at the beginning of the dance. The men and women forming groups, and they come together and rotate. But there's one thing that is special about the dance – before it's finished, they swap partners.

'Okay, so we got the fuckin' Crown Vic and the fuckin' panel van on us. The fucks.'

I checked the side mirror. Tony was right. There were two other pursuit cars – a Chevy Sedan and a Honda pick-up. The Chevy had gone after Harry and the pick-up was still in a U-turn, no doubt it was going after Bloch. Lake was free. Like I expected. They would focus on the core legal team.

The computer console on the dash of the Hellcat was lit up with a four-way call, so the drivers could coordinate.

'Wings, I'm on fuckin' Hudson coming up on Canal in thirty fuckin' seconds.'

'I'm on Watts already, waitin' for ya,' came the reply.

Tony pushed the Hellcat, and whatever he'd done under the hood, the torque was too much for the steering because the car started to fishtail. He feathered the gas and had it under control in a second and then the grip kicked in and my head and back were welded to the seat as we took off.

'What did you do to this thing?' I asked.

'Fuck all. It comes out of the fuckin' factory a beast.'

Watts Street leads onto Canal, a major cross street with two-way traffic. Hudson Street is the intersection before Watts. Tony turned left onto Canal, headed for the Holland Tunnel, and said, 'Fuckin' busting onto Canal now. Where the fuck are you?'

A blue Mustang turned right out of Watts Street and pulled up by the central divider on Canal. Tony hit the brakes, stopped alongside the Mustang. The cars were pointed in opposite directions.

I already had the door open as Tony was braking, and I leapt out of the car, straight into the front of the Mustang. Lake bounced into the front passenger seat of the Hellcat, and I heard Tony swearing to fuckin' Jesus fuckin' Christ that Lake better hurry his ass up. Tony took off, then I heard Lake's door close. I stayed low in the seat, closed my door just as I heard two cars whizz after Tony, who was already halfway to the tunnel.

'That's the Vic and the van all the way up Tony's fuckin' ass,' said Wings as he pulled out slowly and we drove away in the opposite direction, with no cars on us.

That's the veneziana. The feds didn't see the switch. Far as they were concerned, they'd be following me and Tony around all night, not knowing it was Lake in the passenger seat. Wings and Tony had executed it perfectly. They had practice. The FBI had been on Jimmy the Hat's ass for years. If he had to meet someone in private, the veneziana was the easiest way.

'So where are we going?' asked Wings.

'Brooklyn Park.'

'No problem.'

Wings was a lot older than me and Jimmy. When we were little kids he always looked out for us. He was from Jimmy's neighborhood and when I went up there to visit, he would always make sure no one was bothering me. As the only Irish kid in Jimmy's solidly Italian neighborhood it could be intimidating. No one bothered Jimmy on account of his father, but plenty of the other kids would want to pick a fight with the mick. Unless Wings was around, of course. Back then Wings always had a black eye, or a big purple bruise on his face or arms. I thought it was from fighting rival gangs, but it turns out it was Wings' old man who was quick with his fists.

Back then everyone called him Tommy. When his old man pushed his mother out of the window of their second-floor apartment and Tommy leapt out after her, catching her in mid air and taking the impact of the fall on his back, people started calling him Wings. His mom said he flew out of that window, grabbed her and she landed on top of him. That day the doctors didn't know if Tommy would ever walk again due to the spinal injuries. Jimmy's father and Tommy's father had a talk that night, so they say, and it didn't go well. Tommy's old man didn't survive the fall from the top of the building. Tommy not only recovered, but he came under the protection of the Fellinis and started working for the family, boosting cars for one of the chop shops. He got good at it, especially driving. There was nobody faster behind the wheel than Wings.

We arrived in Brooklyn Park with time to spare.

'You want me to come with?'

'Nah, I should be okay. You alright to stick around til I'm done?'

'Sure thing, kid. I'll keep an eye on ya.'

I left the car, huddled into my overcoat and made my way to the shorefront in Brooklyn Park. This part of DUMBO (down under the Manhattan Bridge overpass) had been looked after and developed, especially when the East River ferry started moving foot passengers commuting to the city. There weren't too many people in the park at this time of night. The occasional jogger or an old man with a dog. The park abutted the East River, with a railing looking right into the water. The lights from Manhattan's sky scrapers glimmered on the chop of the river.

I put my back to the rail, stuffed my hands into my coat pockets for warmth and watched the paths that led up to here. An older couple with a small dog on a leash approached from my left. They stopped at the view finder, which looked out across the water, and the guy hunted for change in his pocket before giving up and passing me by.

I waited until long after Carrie was supposed to get here. And my anxiety and fear increased with every passing minute. I was cold and afraid that my gamble had not paid off. I took out my burner, dialed the last number and waited.

Carrie picked up.

'I'm sorry,' she said. 'I don't know if I can trust you yet.'

'There's no other way of knowing without giving me a chance. Just come and meet me, I'm still here. I'm still waiting.'

'You don't know what I've done,' she said.

For a moment, I didn't know what to say. I needed her and I was usually able to convince people to trust me. There was a reason why Carrie didn't know if I could be trusted. The reason was I didn't know the whole story. I guessed she had been keeping some things from me, but now I knew it for certain. And I had a pretty good idea what she was hiding.

'I know more than you realize. And I'm still on the phone. I'm still here to help you. Because no matter what happened, I don't think you're a bad person, Carrie. People make terrible mistakes, but they are still good people at heart. One mistake shouldn't define someone's life.'

'Okay,' she said. 'Can you see the view finder?'

I looked around for someone watching me. I couldn't see Carrie, but I guessed she had already been here. I turned my attention to the view finder.

'I see it.'

'There's a rail at the bottom that goes around it. You'll find something tucked in behind the base of the view finder.'

I walked over to it. Sure enough, in the base, there was a little black book.

'A book?'

'My journal. The rest of it. Read it. And if you still want to help me after that, then I'll trust you.'

She hung up.

I opened the journal and read as I started walking back to the car. By the time I reached the Mustang I knew why Carrie had run.

And the pieces of the story I wasn't sure of suddenly made sense. Gaps had been filled in. For the first time I had the real story, or most of it. The rest I could fill in on my own.

I called Carrie.

'I'm in. I know what happened. I know what you've done. I'm still here for you. We can win this case together. Truth is, Carrie, I need you. The Sandman has Kate.'

'What?'

'You have to come to court tomorrow. You will get arrested for jumping bail, but don't worry. Everything will work out fine. If you don't come in tomorrow, Kate is in real danger. He said he would kill her if you are convicted. He loves you.'

'Oh my god.'

'I won't let anything bad happen, I swear it. I think we can win. But I need you in court. Can I count on you? My partner's life is on the line, here.'

'I'll be there. And, Eddie – thank you.'

'I just wish you'd told me the truth sooner. I understand why you didn't, but we have to trust each other now.'

'I trust you. I'll be at court in the morning.'

I ended the call, looked out at the black river coated in swirling columns of light. There is something about water at night that calms me. Makes everything clearer. The half-truths and missing pieces of information had all come to me now. What I didn't know in that moment was what I should do. There could be no mistakes. Kate's life was on the line.

I gazed out at the East River, let things play out in my mind.

There was great risk to it all. Especially to Kate.

I closed my eyes and listened to the wind and water.

When I opened them, I'd made a decision.

First, I called Denise.

'You know someone in Company Records, right?'

'I know the manager, the assistant manager and two of the clerks,' she said.

'Could you get them to open up for Bloch in the next half hour?'

'Are you kidding me?'

'Let the manager know that if he helps us, we can make it worth his while.'

'Got it. He's a friend and I think he'll help.'

Next, I called Bloch.

'I want the original filings on that company Daniel Miller used to buy the warehouse for his freezer. You need to see the original documents. If I'm right, you'll find the start of a trail. Follow it. Take Lake with you.'

I took five minutes, told Bloch what Carrie Miller had written in her journal.

Bloch said nothing. I waited.

'Son of a bitch,' she said.

'Tell me you can do this.'

'I can do it.'

Two more calls to make. The next one was a breach of legal professional conduct and ethics. Not the first time I've fallen below those standards. It would not be the last.

Otto picked up right away.

'Carrie will be in court in the morning. And we're going to win this case with your help. I know I'm not supposed to talk to you about your testimony. Coaching a prosecution witness might get us both disbarred. Maybe even prosecuted. There's no other way of putting this, Otto, I need you to fight back against Drew White tomorrow,' I said.

He was silent for a time, letting this roll around in his head, then said, 'If I deny what I've already told White then he can ask Stoker to declare me a hostile witness. Then he can cross examine me and discredit me. I would lose everything I've spent my whole life building. My entire career wiped out. And for what? Soon as I'm declared hostile the jury won't believe a word I say anyway. I have to stick to what I've told the DA.'

'Maybe so, but you can put a favorable slant on it. She didn't know her husband was a killer, not for sure. She suspected but she had no proof. She was a victim, Otto. Come on, you can do this. I really need your help.'

'I really feel for Carrie, but I can't throw away my career on one case—'

'You won't have to throw it away. Just do your best, alright?'

'Alright,' he said.

Last call of the night was the most difficult. Bill Seong sounded pissed. I could tell by the tone of his voice, even over the noise from the car.

'You don't happen to be following a red Dodge Hellcat by any chance?' I asked.

'Yeah, some asshole named Eddie Flynn is tearing around New Jersey. Just tell me where you're meeting her. That would make things a lot easier.'

'I'm not in the car. It's Lake in that passenger seat. I switched cars.'

'Son of a—'

'Before you say anything you might regret, listen up. I'm going to bring in the Sandman tomorrow.'

All I could hear was the throb of the engine and the sound of tires squealing around a corner. Once he'd gotten hold of his tongue he said, 'Tell me that again.'

'I'm going to deliver the Sandman to you, but there's a price.'

'Isn't there always? What do you want?'

'I want two things and they are non-negotiable. First thing is you *don't* arrest him.'

'Say what?'

'You heard me. The Sandman is smart, and the media is all over this thing. There can't be another trial. No arguing over witness testimony, no disputes over forensics – you are going to get this guy red-handed. I'm wrapping this motherfucker in a bow for you. If you want that, you've got to wait until I give you the okay before you arrest him.'

'Jesus, Eddie, what's the second thing?'

We talked some more and by the time I hung up I was as satisfied as I could be that Seong would stick to his word. There were so many things that had to go right tomorrow, and so many people

I was relying on that any slip, from any one of them, would make the whole thing crumble. I'd seen jobs go that way before in my old profession. As a con artist, working with a team, sometimes even something so small as giving the mark the wrong look could blow the entire operation.

I was used to working on a knife edge. But not when someone I cared about had their throat at the end of that blade.

I blew into my numb hands and walked back to the car, got into the passenger seat.

'You okay, kid?' asked Wings.

'No, but I think this time tomorrow I will be. How would you like to make ten grand?'

'Sounds good.'

'You got a different car to this one that's just as fast?'

'I got one that's faster, a new Camaro. It won't do a quarter mile drag under ten, but it'll corner faster and tighter than most.'

'Bring it tomorrow. We'll need it.'

'Someone putting the squeeze on you? You want me to do something?'

'It's fine, Wings. You heard of Bloch? She's got a handle on it.'

His eyes widened and he said, 'That's one tough cookie. Don't sweat it, kid. Whoever she's going after, they're the ones who should be worried.'

CHAPTER FIFTY-ONE

THE SANDMAN

The Sandman had followed the car through the Holland Tunnel, and eventually lost it in Jersey City. It was crucial that he kept his distance as the FBI were also following, and he didn't want them to make him as a pursuit car. The chances of that were slim. He'd calculated them of course. In a pursuit situation, the feds are only interested in the target cars, not who is on their tail. All their attention is thrown forward. If he kept his distance, kept them in sight, he had a chance.

The target car, a Dodge Hellcat, started doing loops. The feds kept on it, and it made no real attempt to lose them. The Sandman pulled up. Turned off the engine. He sat for a while thumping the steering wheel. He should've known Flynn would pull some kind of switch. No way would Carrie hide out in New Jersey. This car was a decoy. Somewhere along the way, Flynn had switched vehicles.

He had been so focused on following the feds that he had not given much thought to the likely destination.

He turned around, came back through the city and across the bridge to Coney Island. In his rage he had bent the steering wheel, and he noticed the odd angle and contour with every corner. This did nothing to abate his rage. Anger sometimes felt like a pressure in his head. It needed to be released. If it was held at bay for too long his thinking would become clouded, his mind overtaken by the stresses of the fury.

By the time he got there, it was late and he was tired. The adrenaline from the chase and the anger at losing the chance to grab Carrie had not subsided. If anything, his fatigue had amplified his emotions. He thew open the door to the old bus depot and shone his flashlight inside.

The tool trolley had moved. Only one wheel remained on the steel plate covering the pit. He shone the light on the plate, saw a gap of an inch. Around that gap were fresh splinters of wood.

Clever girl.

'Kate, there is no way out,' he said.

He listened and heard her breathing hard. Either through fear, or more likely, the effort of trying to move the plate. It was clear Kate had removed the wooden back support from the chair, and had been working it into that gap, using whatever leverage she could generate to try and rock the plate up at the corner. It was working. The trolley was almost off the plate.

He turned and walked past the sandbags, into the small office in the back of the building that he used as a store. In here he had two passports – one for him and one for Carrie. Both in different names. Two hundred grand in cash, another two-fifty in gold bars. There was a refrigerator in this store too. In this one he kept his trophies in pickling jars. Seventeen jars.

Seventeen pairs of eyes.

Ignoring these items, he lifted his pack and hoisted it onto his shoulders. In the corner of the office were four jerry cans, each holding five gallons of gas. He picked up one in each hand and carried them out of the office to the pit. The gas sloshed around in the can, and they made a deep, but hollow, metallic *cloink* as he placed them on the concrete floor.

'You hear that? Recognize that sound?'

He took the steel bar in his hand, levered open the pit about a foot. He unscrewed the cap of the first can, opened his pack and found the plastic spout, which he clipped and then tightened in place at the mouth of the can.

'Can you smell it yet?' he asked.

Tipping up the jerry can, he poured the gasoline into the pit.

'You smell it now?'

The scream that came first was pure pleasure. As the gas *glugged, glugged*, into the pit, and the aroma filled his nose, and Kate's screams filled his ears, it felt like he was taking a hit from a powerful drug. The more he poured, the louder she screamed.

And the pressure eased.

It didn't take long for the can to empty. Less than a minute. He tossed the can into the pit, then reached into his pack.

His hand came out holding a ground flare. A red tube with a cap. Once that cap came off the flare would ignite and burn at two thousand degrees. Gripping the flare tightly with one hand, he placed the other on the cap and it was then he noticed his chest was heaving, sweat dripped from his face and he had a fluttering of pure excitement rippling over his body.

He paused. Got control of himself.

If he tossed the flare into the pit now, it was anyone's guess if the fumes would ignite before the flare hit the small reservoir of gas on the floor. The gasoline itself is not flammable, it may actually extinguish the flame. The fumes, however, were highly flammable.

The Sandman had never burned anyone before. Certainly never burned anyone alive. He imagined Kate in the pit, probably standing on the chair, getting as much distance between her and the gasoline, perhaps wondering how long the chair would hold out before it caught fire, and then her feet, her legs and then . . .

But it wouldn't work that way. Not quite.

If he let the fumes build up in the pit first, then tossed in the flare, the air itself would ignite in a fireball. The plate would keep him safe, as long as he stood back after he tossed it in, but Kate would be instantly engulfed in an inferno. The air all around her, in her mouth and in her lungs, would instantly burn.

The thought occurred to him again – *Keep her alive. You might need her.*

He knew it would be foolish to kill her now.

Pure joy, but foolish all the same.

'If you try to escape again I'll burn you alive, do you understand?'

He put the flare on the ground, then used the hook on the bar to drag the plate to the edge of the pit, leaving a small, two-inch gap. He lifted one of the sandbags he had piled high and tossed it onto the plate. Then another. And another. Making sure she had no way out.

CHAPTER FIFTY-TWO

KATE

The boom from the plate above her head made Kate's teeth rattle every time she heard it. Something was raining down into the pit, but it wasn't gasoline. Not this time.

It was sand.

He was throwing sandbags on top of the plate to weigh it down.

Kate balanced on the chair. Her feet on the seat, bent over, hugging her knees, keeping as far away as possible from the gas. She was shaking so much she'd almost fallen a couple of times.

Now the fumes were making her gag. Her eyes were watering and sore. Her throat burned and the smell was already making the headache come back with a vengeance. She wanted to be sick, but didn't want the retching and convulsion of vomiting to throw off her balance.

Her tears seemed to burn her eyes.

This man was going to set her on fire. If not now, then soon.

And there was no escape.

The deafening boom of the sandbags landing on the plate stopped, and she heard his footsteps retreating into the distance. A familiar sound of the door slamming shut brought silence in its wake.

Kate stepped down off the chair, her feet instantly wet in the small pool of gasoline on the floor. She moved the chair into the right corner, stood on it, put her shoulders to the plate and pushed.

No give.

Not this time.

The chair back, a simple strip of hard wood, an inch thick, which she had removed from the uprights, slipped into the gap between the plate and the lip of the pit. She pushed again with her shoulders, tried to push down with the strip of wood trying to lift the plate and lever it open, widening the gap.

The plate didn't move.

The chair back snapped in two and fell to the puddle on the floor.

Kate screamed again. And cried. She had missed her chance to get out. It would take a small crane to move that plate with all that extra weight piled on top of it. The Sandman was completely unhinged. Even if he let her live, he wouldn't ever let her go. She would die in this pit. The only question was when. He wasn't trying to scare her just now with the gasoline, it was just dumb luck that he didn't set her on fire right then.

Her life was perched on the head of a match.

She sat on the chair and gazed up at the gap. Her strip of moonlight returned and she knew, right then, that this was probably the last light of the moon she would ever see.

CHAPTER FIFTY-THREE

EDDIE

The courtroom had no natural light. A concrete box filled with loss, hate, betrayal, murder, corruption and lies. It was the great theatre of human weakness.

Harry and I sat at the defense table.

The client chair that sat on the end of our table was empty.

It was just past nine in the morning. I hadn't slept for two days and Drew White was about to put on a show in our little theatre.

'The people call Otto Peltier,' he announced.

Harry opened a fresh page on his legal pad, primed his fountain pen and sat ready to make his notes.

The jury liked the look of Otto. That suit, the hair, the physique – it screamed wealth and authority. This was someone the jury would listen to.

He took his oath on the Bible and sat down with Judge Stoker's permission.

'Mr. Peltier, how did you come to know Daniel Miller?'

'My firm represents elite clientele, Mr. White, in all matters of wealth management including tax law, trusts, wills and estate planning. Mr. Miller was a successful hedge-fund manager and formerly a broker. We represent a good deal of Wall Street clients, and he came to me from a referral.'

'You were at one time representing Carrie Miller in this case. How is it that you know her?'

He cleared his throat, said, 'I met Carrie when Daniel introduced her as his fiancée. He wanted to make sure she was taken care of financially in terms of spreading the ownership of some of his property. I advised that a prenuptial agreement would be sensible, and they both agreed. I carried through the agreement, and the asset splits.'

'Mr. Peltier, there came a time when the defendant, Carrie Miller, sought your advice regarding her husband, correct?'

'Correct,' he replied.

Harry tutted.

That was a missed opportunity. If Otto had been sharper, he could have elaborated on that answer, painting Carrie as the concerned, innocent partner. I moved my chair back, scraping all four feet on the tile floor. Peltier, drawn by the sound, looked in my direction. I flared my eyes. He looked away.

This theatre also shows one of the great failings of our species, cowardice.

'The jury have had an opportunity to read Carrie Miller's journals, which she left with your office for safe keeping, just tell the jury your impression of those journals.'

'They are an account of how she was feeling and thinking at the time. The conversation she recounts with me is accurate as far as my memory serves . . .'

Peltier wanted to say more, I could see his gaze drifting to the jury, his tongue coating his lips. He opened his mouth . . .

'Thank you,' said White, cutting him off before he could say anything helpful to the defense.

'In those journals, she talks about her husband coming home late at night and showering, that he gave her gifts of jewelry that had belonged to the victims, usually the day after they were murdered, and putting his clothes straight into the washing machine in the middle of the night. Isn't it clear from the journals that Carrie Miller knew her husband was the Sandman?' asked White.

Before Otto could answer, his train of thought was interrupted by the doors opening at the back of the courtroom. He stared down the aisle, and when the judge noticed who it was, he leaned forward on his elbows to take a long look.

Carrie Miller looked thinner than she had been a few days ago. Her make-up couldn't hide the dark rings around her eyes, nor the strain on her features. Bloch came through the doors behind her carrying a pile of papers, which she placed on the defense table before she took a seat in the gallery. Harry and I stood up as Carrie came over to our table and took a seat at the end. Everyone in the courtroom held their breath and stared at the one person who mattered most. The person this whole story revolved around. They all wanted to take a good look at her and judge her for themselves.

'Your Honor, if I might interrupt Mr. White for a moment to inform the court that my client will be surrendering to the police at the end of today's hearing in relation to her breach of bail conditions. I have spoken to the detectives involved and this is agreed.'

'We can deal with that at the end of the day. Back to you, Mr. White.'

White seemed to have grown an inch. He stood very straight, his back almost arched as he thrust out his chest. Some prosecutors lose sight of the law early in their careers. For them, the job becomes about getting convictions, racking up victories, winning, winning, winning – that's all they care about.

'Mr. Peltier, I'll repeat the question. From the journals, Carrie Miller noticed her husband exhibited strange behavior. He was out late at night, most nights. He gave her jewelry that she knew came from the Sandman's victims. And more. She came to you, and she *knew* her husband, Daniel Miller, was the Sandman, correct?'

'She suspected him, I would say. But she didn't have any real evidence.'

'That's not what the journal says, is it? She knew and she came to you for advice, right?'

Peltier licked his dry lips, said, 'You can interpret the journal anyway you want, but suspecting something and having knowledge of a crime are two different things.'

'In the last entry, which the jury have had time to read in advance, she tells you her husband is the Sandman. Not only that, but she tells you that she gave a false alibi for her husband to the police.'

'I think it's clear she was pressurized into giving that alibi,' said Peltier.

'She doesn't claim that her husband threatened her in order to get that alibi, does she?'

'No, but—'

'She backed up her husband's lies to the police. She told the officer her husband was at home the night of Margaret Sharpe's murder, didn't she?'

He sighed, said, 'Yes.'

'Once you told her about the penalty in the prenuptial agreement for making false allegations she didn't go to the police, did she?'

'She didn't go to the police.'

'The evidence she presented to you wasn't enough to convince you that Daniel Miller might be a person of interest to the police?'

'I'm not saying that. I'm saying there wasn't enough to prove he was the Sandman. We looked into Daniel, but we never found anything more. Had we made further discoveries, well, then I might have advised her to go to the police.'

'Did she tell you, at any point, about the bloodstains on the sleeve of her blouse?'

This was a turning point in his testimony. White wanted to use Peltier to paint Carrie as dishonest.

'No, she didn't.'

'She told you that she had in her possession the silver rose earrings that belonged to Margaret Sharpe and the rings that belonged to Penny Jones and Suzanna Abrams. Did she ever mention the cameo brooch that had been taken from Lilian Parker? Because that item has never been recovered.'

'No, she didn't mention that.'

'Did she, at any time, mention her husband giving her the black pearl necklace that was stolen from Stacy Nielsen?'

'I think that item was found in her closet, but no, at no time did she tell me about that item.'

'Mr. Peltier, is it clear to you now the purpose of Carrie Miller coming to you, and giving you these journals?'

'I don't know what you mean.'

'*You* and the journals are *her* alibi. She knows that eventually she and her husband will get caught, and she wants to paint a contemporaneous picture that she suspected her husband, maybe even believed he could be the killer, but she never had absolute proof. She was attempting to forge that narrative, in order to disguise her complicity in her husband's crimes, is that what really happened here?'

Clearing his throat, Peltier reached for a glass of water. He took a sip, composed himself before he said a word – always a bad sign. It looks like you're searching for an answer that helps you, instead of just telling the truth.

'I can only explain to the court what Carrie Miller told me, and her journals are an accurate reflection of our conversations. She merely suspected her husband – she had no proof and she was *never* sure that he was the Sandman.'

'And yet she kept important information from you that implicated her in the murders?'

I stood up to object, 'Your Honor, Mr. White is cross examining his own witness . . .'

'I'm aware of how these questions are being phrased,' said Judge Stoker. 'Mr. White, do you wish to have this witness declared hostile?'

'That was my last question, Your Honor.'

'Well, ask it. But rephrase.'

'Mr. Peltier,' said White. 'Did Carrie Miller keep information from you that implicated her in the murder of Stacy and Tobias Nielsen?'

'She didn't tell me about the blood stains, or the black pearl necklace. And she never mentioned him giving her a brooch, but you have to understand, he gave her a lot of gifts, and the police never said that those items had been taken from the Sandman's victims until after he was identified. Just because she was given some jewelry doesn't mean she's involved in any crimes carried out by her husband.'

White nodded, then walked back to the prosecution table with a swagger in his step and sat down.

'No further questions.'

There are moments in a trial that are lever points. Moments when everything changes and starts to go in one direction. This was that point. And this was that moment.

I stood up, approached Peltier. His shoulders sagged a little, and he took another drink from the glass of water in front of him. For Otto, the tough part was over. Now, I would lob softballs at him and he could try and repair some of the damage he'd caused to Carrie. He was starting to relax. He felt safer.

'Mr. Peltier, you said that Carrie Miller was never sure that her husband was the Sandman, is that right?'

'That's right,' he said.

I paused, took a second to look at the jury. Most were alert and following the testimony. Some looked a little distracted – they were staring at Carrie Miller. The next few seconds would grab their attention and keep it with me.

'Mr. Peltier, I would remind you of your professional commitment as a lawyer and officer of the court, and to the oath you just took, to tell the truth, and with that in mind I will ask you again – prior to the FBI identifying Daniel Miller as the Sandman, did Carrie Miller have actual knowledge her husband really was this killer?'

'No, she did not.'

The jury expected this answer.

They weren't expecting the next question.

'Mr. Peltier, that's a lie, isn't it?'

The air in the courtroom seemed to solidify.

'I'm sorry? I don't understand?' he said.

'Well, it's simple. Carrie Miller knew her husband was the Sandman before the FBI found him, and she covered up that fact, isn't that what really happened?'

'What?'

'Answer the question.'

I couldn't resist glancing at White. He'd pushed his chair away from the table, stretched out his legs, put down his pen and folded his arms. A huge smile spread across his face. I was doing his job for him and as far as he was concerned, any hope of an acquittal for Carrie Miller just flew out the window.

'That's an outrageous accusation,' said Peltier.

'Really? Your Honor, I'd like to submit this last journal entry from Carrie Miller as Defense Exhibit 1.'

CHAPTER FIFTY-FOUR

Extract from the Journal of Carrie Miller

Undated

This is the rest of my story. The part that I hadn't written down, until now. The part that matters.

After I left Otto's office, I didn't hear from him for a few days. Danny was away on business that week and I found myself ignoring his calls and texts. I didn't want to talk to him. I couldn't until I knew for sure what he was really doing when he said he was working or entertaining clients. Even though part of me felt guilty, I was glad he was away. I knew I shouldn't be feeling like this, but I couldn't get the thought out of my head — my husband might be a killer.

I got a call on Thursday evening, around six-thirty. At first, I let my cell phone ring, and it was only at the last second I checked the caller ID and noticed it wasn't Danny — it was Otto. He told me his investigator called him to say Danny was exhibiting some strange behavior. Otto wanted me to come take a look for myself.

I asked him if he wanted me to get a plane to Seattle. He said Danny wasn't in Seattle. He'd never left New York.

I met Otto in the parking lot of a new apartment development in Queens. More and more people were looking for somewhere decent to live outside of Manhattan and these condos were being bought up by investors hoping to flip them for a healthy profit. Otto said Danny and a woman had gone into that building, up to the third floor second apartment. I asked him where his investigator had gone, and he said he had left to find out who was living in that apartment. Otto hadn't told the investigator what to look for. At that moment I started to panic.

I told Otto Danny might be going up there to kill that woman. I could tell by the way he looked he'd had the same thought. Otto said I shouldn't call the police. I wanted to, there's someone's life in danger, but he said it would take too long for them to get here and we should go up and take a look first.

I felt sick climbing those stairs, Otto behind me. We reached the third floor. A bright hallway freshly painted white. We counted along two doors and stopped. Listened.

I could hear something. A woman. It sounded like she was in pain. And then.

A scream.

Otto heard it too.

'He's killing her!' I said.

Otto pushed me out of the way, stood back, and leapt forward kicking at the door. It took three kicks to bring it down. This time we heard the woman screaming for her life.

I ran inside, Otto behind me. I was expecting to see the walls covered with blood. And Daniel standing over the corpse of another victim.

There, in the bedroom.

Daniel and the woman in bed. Both were breathless.

Both were naked.

He wasn't killing her.

He was having an affair.

Danny looked at me with a mix of embarrassment and shock.

The woman got up and pulled on her underwear. She had bone white skin, apart from something black and shiny around her neck – a black pearl necklace. She flipped a top over her head and stepped into her jeans. She took care to flop the necklace over her white shirt.

She said this was so embarrassing for her, but she didn't apologize, I remember that.

I couldn't cry. I couldn't think.

I had made a complete fool of myself. Danny wasn't a killer. The lies and the late nights, the clothes in the laundry machine . . . He was sleeping with someone else.

He wasn't killing anyone.

Now that I got a good look at the woman, she didn't appear embarrassed in the least. She just looked pissed that I'd interrupted them. She asked no questions when I came in. Daniel had called me by my name, and she wasn't curious . . .

She knew who I was. She knew he was married.

I was standing in the doorway, shaking.

'Out my way,' she said.

I had been going quietly crazy for weeks. Afraid to be around my husband. Questioning myself over and over as to why he chose me, and then went out and killed innocent people, and I would think this for hours and then tell myself I was being stupid – that Daniel was a good man. I was utterly lost. Doubting my husband and my own mind.

And now I was betrayed and hurt.

And she wanted me to move out of her way?

Before I knew what I was doing, my hand lashed out smacking her in the face. I lost it and I hit her again. In the mouth this time.

Danny screamed at me to leave her alone.

I was suddenly very frightened. I was unmoored. The world was spinning around me. My mind was disintegrating. What he had put me through just hit me all at once and I started crying. I ran out of the apartment. Otto said something to the woman, I couldn't hear what, but I thought I heard a name. Then Otto chased after me. I got into my car and I just drove away. Otto called me seven times, but I didn't answer. I needed time to think. To get myself together. I don't know how long I drove around, but it was dark by the time I pulled in and parked by the side of the street and called him back.

I felt like such a fool.

He told me I had been betrayed, that it wasn't my fault.

God, I felt so awful for hitting that woman. I'm not a violent person. I'd never hit anyone before in my life. The thought of it just made me feel worse.

Otto said he was sure she would understand. But that's not exactly what he said. He kind of stumbled over his words and I got the impression he was about to say her name, then caught himself before he said too much. Then he went very quiet on the other end of the line.

He knew her. Or recognized her. I was sure of it.

This at least was one thing I could do to make myself feel better. I could go and apologize. Danny had made me hit that woman. Yeah, she was sleeping with my husband, but Danny was the one who had put me through this hell. It wasn't her fault. Not really. I bet he was lying to her too.

I begged Otto to tell me who the woman was.

At first, he didn't say anything. Then he admitted he did know her.

After a few minutes, he told me what I needed to know.

He gave me Stacy Nielsen's address. It was fifteen minutes away. I drove onto her street, parked and stood outside her house. I wanted to talk to her. Tell her I was sorry, and I guess I wanted her to say sorry too. She had hurt me, deliberately. Neither of us deserved a man like Danny. I wanted to tell her we busted into that apartment to save her because we thought he was hurting her. It wasn't to confront her.

I was standing on the street. Her house in front of me, when someone spoke. Someone asked me what the hell I was doing. I swung around to see Danny walk up beside me. He said he'd just dropped off Stacy, and he saw my car pull up.

I couldn't quite believe it, but he started to bitch about me. He wanted to know what the hell I was doing here? Was I really going to confront Stacy about her affair, in front of her family?!

Her family.

I moved forward, slowly, Daniel kept in step beside me, and I gazed through their front window. Two young kids curled up on the couch beside her. A husband in the big armchair in the corner as they watched TV.

Stacy Nielsen looked like mother of the year, sitting in her living room with her family around her.

I turned, started walking back to the car.

Danny said he needed to talk to me. To explain all of this. I told myself I wasn't going to be lied to again, and I told him no. I didn't want to talk to him. I never wanted to see him again.

I didn't want to have an argument on the street. I saw Daniel glance up at the lit windows. It distracted him enough to let me put some distance between us. I got to my car, got in and locked it as he approached the passenger window.

He looked different. Outside my window, his face had changed. There was an anger inside of him.

I put my foot on the gas and drove straight home.

The house felt empty and cold. It was a hostile place – somewhere I couldn't trust. It didn't feel like home anymore. I stripped off in the bathroom, the shower running. I was about to put my clothes in the wash basket when I noticed blood on my sleeve.

Jesus, I must've split her lip when I lashed out in the apartment.

I showered, put on my night things and went to bed. I was hungry, but I couldn't face eating. I couldn't sleep either, but I lay in bed, willing myself to drift off into unconsciousness. I just needed that day to be over. Somehow, at some point that night, sleep took me.

The sound of my phone ringing woke me just after one a.m. I checked the display. Answered it.

It was Otto.

For a blissful second, in the moment of waking, I was not the foolish woman who had shamed herself, who had been betrayed, who opened the door and stepped into another life that was burning me up inside.

Then, I remembered.

I told him I was alone.

What he said next frightened me.

'Do you still have the taser I gave you?'

A cold feeling spread across my back.

He said he was on his way to my house. Stacy and Tobias Nielsen had been murdered. His investigator had heard about it through a police contact. Otto was sure Danny had killed them.

He told me not to answer the door until he arrived, to get the taser and then find somewhere to hide.

He hung up.

That's when I heard the front door opening.

I leapt off the bed and ran into my closet. My purse was hanging on the coat rail behind the door. I opened it, took out the taser Otto had given me. I switched off the light and sat on the floor in the dark.

And I waited.

The stair with the loose floorboard creaked. He was coming up.

Sweat made my grip on the taser gun slip. I had to keep switching hands, my breath catching in my throat, and pointing it into the hallway. My hands shook, and I couldn't aim it properly.

A figure, in shadow, stood in the doorway.

'Carrie, we need to talk,' he said, and came toward me.

I yelled at him to stay back, but he kept coming.

I pulled the trigger.

A blue flash of electricity shook the air and Daniel collapsed to the floor. His body shook violently like he was having a terrible fit, his limbs thumping against the floor with such force that he was at times lifting off the ground. A bloody red foam erupted from his mouth.

I dropped the taser and the convulsions stopped. He lay still. Then, his hands spread out on the floor and he began to lever himself up. I was in the closet. He was right there in the doorway. I pulled one of the drawers out, a heavy, solid oak drawer. As I raised it up, socks spilled out, and I threw it down on top of his head. He lay still and I stepped over him and ran, down the stairs, and there was Otto coming through the open front door.

I told him Danny was upstairs.

I'd shot him with the taser.

Otto told me to go outside. He said not to call the police, not yet. Just to wait for him and if he wasn't back in five minutes then I should call the cops.

Tears streaming down my face, my hands shaking, I stepped out into the cold. Daniel's car was in the driveway. The driver's door lay open. I went to sit down on the driver's seat just to take a moment and try to calm the fuck down, but then I saw it.

A knife and a pistol sat in the door pocket. I didn't dare touch it or go near it. In the backseat were a set of black clothes, shiny with blood. I went around the back of the car and opened the trunk. Inside were two sandbags, rope, screwdrivers and a leather bag. With trembling hands, I opened the bag. Inside were women's necklaces, rings, watches. There was something else in the bag that made it heavy. Two jars. At first, I didn't know what they were, but one rolled over as I tilted the bag.

I clasped my hands over my mouth to stop the scream.

A pair of eyes stared out of the dark liquid in the jar.

I heard Otto calling me.

I ran toward him and hugged him tightly. It was right then Otto told me my husband was dead.

I'd killed him.

I couldn't say anything. It felt like a hole opened in my chest. My legs gave way, but Otto held me.

He looked in the car, and then he half carried me inside. He was so pale and shaken-up. He told me we had to think about what to tell the cops, because right now it didn't look like self defense.

I sat in my living room, my teeth rattling in my head, shaking and crying for almost half an hour while Otto tried to calm me down.

He told me Danny's head was caved in, and we went through what had happened, Otto firing questions at me. Did I give him a warning? Did he threaten me?

No, he didn't threaten me. And I didn't give him a warning. And there's not a mark on me.

Then, the false alibi came up again.

Otto thought there was a few ways this might play out.

I could be a hero who stopped the Sandman.

Or I could be a murderer. One, for killing my husband, and two, for covering up his crimes by lying to the police. Otto said they could implicate me in all of the Sandman killings.

We talked and talked and no matter what way I turned things around in my head, I came back to the police arresting me. There was no way out of this. Everything had gotten so much worse, and I wished I had just left Daniel. Just took off and never looked back.

I'll never forget what Otto said next.

'What if there was another way?' he said. 'What if he just disappeared? I could put him in his car, drive him to a quiet spot on Hempstead Lake and make him and all his evil just go away for ever.'

I agreed to keep the jewelry, in case he was ever linked to the Sandman murders and I could say he gave them to me before he disappeared. Hide it in the house so there's something linking him to those murders. After a year, I could have Daniel declared dead, and inherit his money.

The plan was to stay quiet and stay clear of a murder charge for killing my husband. And if the police linked him to the murders, I was to say I suspected him, but I never had any proof.

Otto said it would be okay.
It would be our secret.
In the days that followed, I trusted Otto. We became close.
We became lovers.

CHAPTER FIFTY-FIVE

EDDIE

'This is just lies,' said Peltier, coolly, having read the journal along with the judge, DA and jury. He poured himself another glass of water, took a sip and set the glass back down. He didn't need a drink; he was just taking a moment to calm himself.

'You're saying there are inaccuracies and lies in that account?'

'I am.'

'I think you're right. You've been lying to Carrie Miller since the day you met her.'

'No, I have not.'

'You didn't put Daniel Miller's body in Hempstead Lake, that's for sure. His car might be there, but he isn't, is he?'

Peltier's eyes narrowed, he said, 'This is a total fabrication.'

'The police know the Sandman rented an apartment across the street from Lilian Parker's building. My investigators were able to link a company to that lease, and at that company's registered address they found a freezer. This freezer,' I said, pointing to the screen.

I had shared Bloch's photographs with Bill Seong and the DA last night. I had given no explanation, simply said Bloch would testify to having taken the photographs.

The picture on screen showed a chest freezer in a dark, dusty office. A series of close-ups showed a corpse inside a body bag, frozen in ice.

'That's Daniel Miller, isn't it, Mr. Peltier?'

'I don't know who it is, I've never seen these photographs before.'

'FBI forensic support are at that scene right now. They will, in time, confirm it is Daniel Miller, and that he died from a knife wound to the throat – not electric shock, not a stroke or cardiac arrest from the taser, and not a blow to the head. Anything you'd like to say about that?'

He said nothing.

'The other important factor from these photographs is in photo three. See here, Daniel Miller is missing his right thumb. Professor Johnson has already testified that the fingerprint lifted from Stacy Nielsen's body came from Miller's right thumb—'

He interrupted me, said, 'I don't know what any of this has to do with me.'

'The Nielsens' bodies were discovered just after seven a.m. by two patrolmen, not one a.m. when you called Carrie Miller and told her they were dead. At that time, the family were very much alive. You knew Daniel Miller was going home to see his wife. You scared Carrie half to death – told her to pick up the high-voltage taser you had given to her. You set up that whole thing so you could kill Daniel and frame him as the Sandman. You cut off Miller's thumb, then murdered Tobias and Stacy Nielsen and planted his thumbprint at the scene. You wanted to frame Daniel Miller for *your* crimes, Mr. Peltier, because *you* are the Sandman.'

DA White was on his feet and objecting, but Stoker waved him down.

'That's ridiculous,' said Otto.

'The Sandman is alive and active, Mr. Peltier. He's already murdered two witnesses in this case, sent a note to the FBI and killed two of their agents. But you already know about that.'

'I don't know anything about this. And I've never seen that freezer before in my life.'

'And yet your firm registered the paperwork for that company,' I said. 'It's stamped on the original document filed at companies register. You knew that address, and it's not like Daniel Miller or anyone else is using that property.'

'That was Daniel Miller's company.'

'He's not in a position to kill anyone. But there's still so much we don't know. Why did you frame Miller for your crimes and then stop? What happened? What changed you?'

His gaze flicked to Carrie, and then back to me.

'Soon as the Sandman became active, Carrie's world imploded all over again and she ran. She knew then her husband was not a killer. That you planted the evidence in his car that night when you got to her house, didn't you?'

'No, of course not.'

'You had already taken steps to distance yourself from ownership records for the van you used in your crimes. It's registered to a company owned by Daniel Miller. That company hasn't traded in years, hasn't filed any accounts either. It's a front.'

'No, I have nothing to do with that company. The van belongs to Daniel Miller.'

'It sure does, but your firm filed all the company paperwork and you are the company secretary. Would you like to see the paperwork?'

'Your Honor,' said Otto, 'I won't stand for this spurious attack—'

'You'll answer Mr. Flynn's questions,' said Judge Stoker.

'This was your perfect opportunity to frame someone for your crimes, make Carrie believe she had killed her husband and cover the whole thing up. Then, you could get what you really wanted. You wanted Carrie all along, didn't you? You wanted her from the first moment Daniel brought her into your office. And you framed him for your crimes so you could have her.'

His jaw muscles flexed as he bit down. His expression changed. A flare of anger. Of pure rage. He ran a hand across his face, perhaps aware his emotions were showing, wiping his face into a neutral stare.

'Lies, Mr. Flynn.'

'In the diary entry we just read, Carrie doesn't mention seeing the black pearl necklace in her husband's car, does she?'

'No, but—'

'She doesn't mention it being there, because it wasn't there at the time, was it?'

'I don't know what she saw.'

'It wasn't there at the time, but it found its way into that bag later, didn't it? After you took it from Stacy Nielsen's house?'

'Lies.'

'You knew Stacy Nielsen?'

'She and her husband were well-known socialites. Of course I'd met them.'

'And you'd been in their house . . .'

He grimaced.

'I don't remember,' he said.

'You were in that house, Mr. Peltier. You knew that the only way to force entry would be the front door, not the back door with the deadbolts, right?'

'I didn't kill Stacy or her husband. Nor anyone else.'

'Was it you who introduced Stacy to Daniel? Their affair is very convenient to you. It allowed you to gaslight my client into believing her husband was a killer. You planted that seed, didn't you?'

'Lies.'

'Really?' I said, and Harry gave me a brown envelope. I opened it, held up the contents.

'These are your phone records, I won't say how I got them, but they log all your calls with Carrie Miller. In the months leading up to her trial, you never called her, and she never called you. That's unusual, isn't it? She didn't call you because you were with her. You were in constant contact. You were in a relationship with her by then. Carrie Miller will testify to this.'

'She's a liar.'

'Her diary entries, they are all accurate, aren't they? You said so yourself earlier.'

'I told you, she's lying. Your client is desperate for an acquittal and she's trying to frame me for her crimes. It's my word against hers. I'm a lawyer with a sterling reputation and your client is a failed actress who married a serial killer for money. I think this jury knows who is telling the truth.'

For a man in his situation, he was remarkably cool. He lifted the glass of water to his lips, sipped and set it down.

I approached him, reached up and took the glass of water from the witness stand, then placed it on the defense table.

'It's not just your word against Carrie's, is it? The Sandman abducted a young woman in Manhattan, two nights ago. He's getting sloppy. He left behind a plastic syringe cover. It has been tested for fibers and other trace evidence . . .'

As I spoke, I saw his neck bloom into a red blush that spread out of the top of his shirt collar. He swallowed, and I got the impression he was making a great effort to stay calm.

'The lab that examined the syringe is now sharing its results with the FBI. Turns out the DNA on the syringe doesn't belong to Daniel Miller. My client's DNA is already on record. It doesn't match her profile either . . .'

I paused, stared down at the glass on the defense table.

'What are the odds it matches the DNA you left on this glass?'

'This is preposterous,' he said, and then took a breath, puffed out his chest like he was going to say a lot more.

He didn't. His eyes fell on Carrie and there was a longing in his gaze that was better than a hundred DNA matches.

'I have nothing further for this witness,' I said, and turned to White.

He looked like he'd just been run over by a flatbed truck full of horseshit. The judge asked him if he had any questions on re-direct. He shook his head.

'Mr. Peltier, you are free to leave the stand,' said Stoker, eyeing him warily.

Otto got up, buttoned his jacket and walked past the defense table on his way out the door. His eyes never left Carrie, who in all this time had her head bowed. She couldn't look at him. Carrie had questioned her sanity, wondered why she hadn't spotted the signs from her husband long ago, why she hadn't known before she married him that he was a killer. The irony was she hadn't married a killer. A killer had seen her, and wanted her, and manipulated his way into her life, made her believe she had killed her husband, made her carry all that guilt, and then stepped in as her savior.

It was only when the Sandman killed agent Delaney and started up his killing spree again that Carrie realized she had been played. Many people wouldn't have put it all together as quickly as Carrie. But she was wary after her experience with Daniel. She knew how easily her trust could be broken. And so, she had run, not knowing what else to do and unable to trust anyone, even her new lover and lawyer, Otto.

Just as he was passing the defense table, Otto took a step toward it, raised his knee and bumped the edge of the desk, tipping it up.

The glass of water toppled over, fell to the tiled floor and smashed into a million pieces. Peltier smiled and walked out of the courtroom.

Soon as Peltier left, I asked Harry to take over, get an adjournment for the day while the FBI carried out further investigations on the body in the freezer to confirm its identity, and then I turned and ran for the door.

The sound of boots running after me made me turn.

Bloch was right behind me.

Behind her, Bill Seong started to move toward us.

CHAPTER FIFTY-SIX

THE SANDMAN

As Otto Peltier stepped out into the crowd of reporters outside the courthouse, he waved them away with one hand, and with the other, he pushed through the heaving mass of questions, cameras and microphones all being shoved in his face. He lunged forward, pushing a female reporter to the ground and then shouldered another man out of the way. The cameras swerved from him to the fallen reporter, but by the time they came back to him he was through the crowd and running at speed toward his Mercedes parked across the street.

Otto opened the car with the fob as he ran. When he reached the car, he heard the crowd of reporters start up again. He turned, saw that Flynn and Bloch were now caught in the crowd.

They would try to follow him. This is how they would find Kate. They wanted to expose him, provoke him, and then follow him to where he was holding their friend.

He got in, fired up the engine and slipped on his seat belt. He revved the twin turbo V-12.

They would fail.

There was no way they would catch the Sandman, not in this car. Otto still thought of himself by that name. The Sandman gave him power. Made him invincible. Sharpened his wits and his cunning and his ruthless nature. If he thought long and hard about it, there was no Otto Peltier. That pedestrian name was a mask. A character he played.

There was only the Sandman.

He had been convinced that after the trial, once Carrie was acquitted, she would be with him forever. She had betrayed him. She had spoken against him, to Flynn, to that fucking smartass lawyer. That's why he'd chosen him when he realized he couldn't make a deal with the DA to save Carrie. Flynn was exactly the type of lawyer she needed.

Getting Flynn on this case was his worst mistake.

He glanced to his left, saw, somehow, the crowd of reporters parting for Flynn and Bloch. They saw Otto in the car and started sprinting toward him.

As he spun the wheels, letting the rubber bake into the blacktop, he enjoyed the look on Flynn's face as he realized he was too late. That the Sandman was about to take off and that they had no hope of catching him. And, of course, the certain knowledge of the consequences of that failure were there on Flynn's tortured features for all to see.

The Sandman was heading for the bus depot in Coney Island. Before he left the USA for good, with his fake passport and money from the depot office, he would have his revenge on Flynn. The lawyer had taken his woman. Turned her against him. This could not go unpunished. Ideally, he would love to kill Flynn, maybe even take his eyes while he was still awake. But he knew there was no time. And there was something else he could do. Another way to have his revenge on the smartass lawyer.

He would burn Kate Brooks alive.

CHAPTER FIFTY-SEVEN

EDDIE

I ran through the open, glass double doors of the courthouse and straight into a sea of reporters that swam around me and Bloch, enveloping us.

'Harry Ford is right behind me, he will be making a statement,' I said, and with that, the oceans of media parted like I was Moses, jostling each other to be the first ones to get to Harry, who, unbeknown to them, was still in court.

I leapt the three steps to the sidewalk, heard a huge engine across the street hitting the redline on its rev counter – Peltier behind the wheel of that Mercedes, staring at me with a terrifying grimace on his face. He took off like a bolt, hooked a left onto Leonard Street.

Another sound. A car horn. On my right.

Wings was leaning out of the driver's window of an orange Camaro, patting the side of the door with his hand and calling us. Bloch got in the back, and I jumped into the front.

'Come on, come on,' said Wings.

Before I could close the door, Wings hit the gas and we shot in front of a Semi loaded with concrete that had to swerve into the other lane to avoid us. The sound of the Camaro was deafening. I put on my belt as Wings turned onto Leonard Street, said, 'There he is, the son of a bitch.'

My phone rang. I picked up.

'Bill, we've got him. He's on Leonard. Looks like he's gonna loop around Lafayette and Federal Plaza. Probably headed for the Brooklyn Bridge. You mobile yet?'

'I've got three cars on you. I'm in the fourth and we're way back. I've got the tracker online so we won't lose him, but I don't want to give him a chance to change vehicles. Stay on him. I still can't believe I let you talk me into letting him go.'

As an insurance policy, the feds had fitted a GPS tracker to Peltier's wheel arch while he was in court.

'We're not letting him go. I told you. He's gonna lead us to where he's been keeping Kate. We'll stay with him, and I'll keep you on the phone. Like I said, you're going to get him giftwrapped. There will be no argument about who is telling the truth. You're gonna catch this guy in the act. I don't want any part of it – you'll take the credit for this.'

'I don't want credit. I want the bastard that killed my agents.'

CHAPTER FIFTY-EIGHT

THE SANDMAN

He spotted the Camaro on the Brooklyn Bridge.

In his rear-view mirror. Five cars back.

The other cars behind him were no threat. He could tell from the make and model. Two old Japanese SUVs. Both a dull gray. Both battered. Behind those he saw an electric car with a guy wearing a long beard behind the wheel. The fourth was a soccer mom in a sedan rocking along to her stereo, tapping the wheel in time to the music and singing along theatrically.

The Camaro was the only possible. Too far back to see who was driving. It was the only possible tail, and not a likely one. The feds don't tail suspects in a car you could see from a mile away.

He lost one of the SUVs and the soccer mom on the Belt Parkway. The electric car and the other SUV went off on the cloverleaf on Shore Parkway, but the Camaro stayed with him.

The power in that car could easily keep pace with his own, but whoever was driving showed no intention of pushing that gas pedal. There were at least two people in the car. Both men. The driver was older. Wisps of white hair shot through his dark curls.

He put his foot down, hard. Left the Camaro way behind and slipped off the highway. He wound through streets to Coney Island, and the old depot. He parked outside, killed the engine and popped the trunk. He picked up his backpack, flung it open and removed a pistol, which he slipped into the waistband of his pants. He then took the ground flare from the bag, closed it and hoisted it onto his shoulder while he shut the trunk and then ran to the locked gate. He got through it and was at the door of the depot when he heard the Camaro coming up fast.

He opened the door, closed it behind him and moved quickly to the pit. A late November sun filtered through the fiberglass panes in the ceiling, giving the depot an orange glow, as if the sun were sitting right on top of the building. Slanted columns of sunlight poured through the holes in the roof.

He would soon light the place up even more.

The sandbags and tool trolley were still on top of the pit, just like he had left them. He had to work fast, kicking the bags off the steel plate, he ran at the trolley, used his momentum to get it rolling and then with one mighty push he shoved it off the plate. Lifting the steel bar, he slipped it into the gap he'd left at the concrete lip of the pit and pulled, levering the plate back to create a two-foot-wide opening.

Tossing the bar, he heard the door being kicked in behind him.

No time for more gasoline.

Now that he was here, he knew it wasn't needed. The smell coming from the pit told him it would go up like a tinderbox.

He turned to face the door, cracked the flare.

'Don't move,' said a voice.

One of those columns of pure sunlight separated him from the door. It was thirty feet away, but he had to tilt his head, shield his eyes to see who had spoken.

Bloch stepped into the sunbeam, pointed her hand cannon at him, said, 'Don't move.'

Flynn was beside her.

The flare in his hand burned fiercely.

'Don't move!' screamed Bloch, again.

Only she was armed. And no doubt she was good with that weapon. He heard another sound now.

Sirens.

In the seconds that followed, he made many calculations. There was only one move.

Toss the flare into the pit.

The ignition would cause an explosion, probably blow the steel plate into the air. It would be enough of a distraction to let him get his gun out and put two rounds in Bloch while she was still recovering from the shock of the blast. He knew it was coming, so he could duck and cover. Then shoot.

Yes, this was the way.

'Down on the floor,' said Bloch.

'You should do the same,' said Otto as he dropped to his knees and tossed the flare into the pit.

At first, he thought nothing happened. And then, he heard the scream. A wild sound that was followed by a huge *whomp*!

The force from the gas fumes igniting threw the plate right off the pit. Otto stumbled, fell over onto his side.

He glanced up, saw Bloch and Flynn ducking and covering their heads.

He reached behind for his pistol as the fire screamed into life and flames erupted from the pit in a plume of oranges and reds and a solid wall of heat came with it, burning his lips and singeing his hair.

He drew his pistol.

CHAPTER FIFTY-NINE

KATE

Every breath was an effort of pure concentration.

She stood on the chair. Her eyes tightly shut. Her lips were clamped around the funnel she'd taken from the jerry can and forced through the gap between the plate and the pit. Breathing gasoline fumes would burn out her lungs or give her carbon monoxide poisoning. The funnel allowed her to take in clean air.

If she shut her eyes they didn't sting so bad. Yet she had to half-crouch, standing on top of the chair in order to get her mouth close to the funnel, and the funnel through the gap. Her back and legs were aching. Muscles cramping and trembling.

But it was the only way to stay alive.

She didn't know how long it had been since he'd left her like this. Hours. Many hours. And she wasn't able to hang on much longer. She knew it. She would have to hold her breath, duck down and give her legs a break.

The sound of the door opening and shutting. It echoed throughout the building and her eyes popped open with the shock of it. She shut them again, soon as they started to sting. They were already swollen and the skin around her mouth was burning too.

Footsteps running toward her.

She took a deep breath. The most air she could hold, and ducked down, pulling the funnel with her.

She knelt in the dark, eyes shut. Lungs bursting.

Knowing this was it.

This was how it would end.

He'd come to burn her.

The footsteps were overhead now. Stomping around on the plate. She opened her eyes, just for a second, and saw sand dribbling down into the pit.

He was moving the bags.

The heavy trolley on wheels. That made a distinctive sound. The wheels squeaked and rumbled on the steel, and then banged down onto the concrete floor.

The steel bar dipped into the pit, then it was pulled back. Kate backed away as the plate was levered open.

Voices.

She couldn't hear what they said. Her head was roaring and she felt dizzy with the fumes. A lurch from her stomach brought vomit into her mouth, and she had to let go of the air she'd been holding.

As the plate was ripped back, she glanced up into a light. It burned brighter than anything she'd ever seen, scorching her eyes.

Kate's whole body began to shake, and she forced herself to look up. To look at him. If this man was going to kill her, she wanted him to look her in the eye before he set her alight.

She stood and forced her eyes open.

The torch shut off.

In its place was darkness. But not the all-encompassing blackness of the pit.

It was moonlight.

And there, in the moonlight, in front of her face, was a hand.

She took it. Another hand grabbed her and hauled her from the pit. Only now did her eyes adjust to low, soft light. Through the blotches from the torch, she blinked, and looked into the face of her friend, staring back in the dim darkness.

Bloch took hold of Kate and wrapped her arms around her. Kate's body was shaking, and it felt like her brain was shaking too. She couldn't understand what was happening. Was this a hallucination from the gas fumes?

'I got you,' said Bloch.

Moonlight poured through the fiberglass roof of the building, and behind Bloch she saw a man in an ill-fitting suit. He must be Gabriel Lake.

Kate couldn't stop shaking, and then realized Bloch was shaking too.

They held each other and Kate cried harder than she had ever cried before. And when she caught her breath, she looked at Bloch, and said, 'Thank you.'

'The Sandman is Otto Peltier,' said Bloch.

Kate shook her head, still confused and dizzy from the gas.

'We traced the companies he'd set up for Daniel Miller, and himself, and found a bunch of old properties. Mostly old warehouses and depots. This is the third place we tried tonight. Jesus, Kate. I'm so glad you're . . .'

Bloch choked up, couldn't finish the sentence. She grabbed Kate again and held her.

'Where is he? Where's Otto?' asked Kate.

'He's at home. Eddie has one of Jimmy the Hat's men watching him. Some big guy who says fuck a lot. Don't worry. We're going to nail Peltier tomorrow. Carrie told us everything. Eddie's going to confront him on the stand in the morning. That will provoke him to come back here and try to finish you off tomorrow afternoon. The Sandman is going to lead half of the New York FBI right to this place and then they'll have proof it's him.'

'I want to be here,' said Kate.

'What?'

'I want to be here when they catch him. I want to look that motherfucker in the eye.'

Kate glanced around the warehouse, saw the office in back.

'I can wait in there, in that office, if you stay with me. I just need some clothes and water to wash my eyes.'

'I don't think it's a good idea,' said Bloch.

'Neither do I. But if I don't watch this asshole being taken down, I know I'll regret it every day of my life.'

'I need to help Eddie tomorrow. Lake will stay with you tonight.'

'Hi,' said Lake. 'I'm so glad you're okay.'

'I'm not okay,' said Kate. 'But I will be tomorrow.'

CHAPTER SIXTY

KATE

After the gas explosion, dressed in Bloch's spare clothes, which she kept in the Jeep, blue jeans, boots and a sweater, Kate walked out of the old depot office beside Gabriel Lake. They were behind Peltier, who was on the ground.

He drew his knees up, into a crouching position.

Lake raised his right hand. He was holding Bloch's back-up piece. A Glock. He aimed it at Peltier.

Moving fast, Kate swept up the steel bar from the floor. She raised it above her head, stepped forward, in front of Lake, and using all her strength she brought that steel down on top of Peltier.

As it curved toward him, he raised his gun, pointed it at Bloch and Eddie just as the bar made contact with his arm between the wrist and the elbow. The impact was savage. His forearm bent in two, the gun shot into the ceiling and fell from his grip to the concrete floor as he howled in agony.

Peltier turned and saw Kate.

The sight of her made him fall back onto his side, his face a perfect picture of shock and confusion.

Kate bent down and picked up Peltier's gun, pointed it at him.

'Kate, no!' screamed Bloch.

Her finger was on the trigger, and the pistol shook in her hands. Her body flooded with anger and adrenaline at the sight of Peltier. The man who was going to burn her alive. The man who tortured her in that pit with the gas and the darkness.

Eddie and Bloch ran toward her, stopped a few feet away.

'Kate, put down the gun,' said Eddie.

'No,' she said. 'He was going to kill me. He's evil. He should die right now. Right here.'

Lake stepped in close. She could feel him beside her.

His voice was soft and full of sorrow.

'You don't want to do this,' he said.

'I do,' said Kate, gritting her teeth.

She heard the sirens getting close now. The cars that came with those sirens were pulling up outside.

'Trust me. I've been down this road. I know what it's like. You pull that trigger and you're changed, forever. You'll always see his face as it is now. Afraid and in pain. You'll see it every night before you go to sleep. It'll be waiting for you in the morning, first thing when you wake up. That face will haunt you forever. You don't need that. You don't need that man in your head.'

And he reached out, gently.

Tears stung the red, inflamed rims of her eyes. Her chest heaved. Lake's hands touched her own, and with great care, he held onto them. Until the sobs came bursting from her chest, and she relented, and let Lake have the gun.

Kate stepped back.

Lake turned toward the Sandman. His face was passive. There was no anger there. No judgment. No emotion whatsoever.

He pointed Peltier's own gun at him and said, 'Kate's better than me. She's going to be just fine. I'll be fine too. Because you killed my friend, and one more face in the dark won't make any difference to me.'

Kate covered her ears at the sound of the shots. They were rapid. Muzzle flash flaring from the barrel. It didn't even sound like multiple shots. They were so quick, so close together, it just sounded like one long roll of thunder as Peltier's chest burst with small, scattered eruptions of blood until all was still and his dead eyes gazed up at the ceiling.

The door to the depot burst open and Bill Seong, followed by a dozen agents, ran inside shouting instructions.

Then he saw Peltier, dead on the floor.

'What happened? Lake? Why is my suspect dead, Lake? You did it again. Didn't you. You mother—'

'He saved us all,' said Eddie.

Seong turned to him, gave him a skeptical look.

'Peltier was going to kill us, Lake wrestled with him, and Peltier's gun went off. Lake saved everyone in this building. That's how it went down.'

Seong stood over Peltier's dead body, bent low to look at the gunshot wounds. Then looked at the empty gun in Lake's hand.

'A struggle? Are you shitting me? This guy's been shot like ten times.'

'Well, there was a lot of struggling,' said Eddie. 'Come on, look in the depot office.'

Kate watched Eddie go inside the office where she and Lake had hidden earlier that morning to wait for Peltier. She knew what was in there. The jars of eyes. Unblinking.

Never to sleep again.

Kate got down on her knees and wept. Bloch knelt beside her. Lake too. And they huddled together as she cried.

'Thank you,' said Bloch.

Lake, nodded, said, 'You found this place. You saved Kate. We did this together.'

FBI agents swarmed around them. The fire burned low in the pit.

'Let's get out of here,' said Kate. 'I have a client that needs me.'

BREAKING NEWS – SHOCKING SCENES IN MANHATTAN COURTROOM.

CNN NEWSHOUR

DANIEL MILLER IS INNOCENT. LAWYER OTTO PELTIER NAMED AS THE SANDMAN.

The New York Times

DISTRICT ATTORNEY WITHDRAWS ALL CHARGES AGAINST CARRIE MILLER.

The National Enquirer

FBI ISSUES PUBLIC APOLOGY FOR NAMING DANIEL MILLER AS THE SANDMAN.

The Washington Post.

CHAPTER SIXTY-ONE

GABRIEL LAKE

He was already late when he left his apartment.

The delay had been caused when he had to tape up the pocket of his suit jacket, after he had caught it on the door handle and ripped the fabric. Six months of rehab to recover from the gunshot wounds he'd suffered in a shootout in a heroin stash house had caused him to lose forty pounds. He still hadn't bought new clothes, even a year after finishing his physiotherapy. Lake liked his clothes, even though they no longer fit. And in truth, his medical pension didn't give him a lot of spare cash to throw around.

He took the subway, exited at Grand Central and found the little Irish bar two blocks away, just off the corner of Lexington Avenue.

They were huddled around a table in the back of the bar. They'd kept him a seat.

Kate looked good. After taking a little time off, she was back in court. Back in the office and she had regained a little of the color in her cheeks. The haunted look that sometimes comes with trauma was still there, just in the corner of her eye. He caught it as she looked at him coming through the door. He hadn't seen her since that day in the old bus depot, but Eddie had kept him informed of her progress over the past month.

Beside her, Bloch stretched out her legs. She sat close to Kate. Eddie had told him Kate was staying with Bloch in her house in New Jersey, temporary, while she looked for a new apartment. Bloch and Kate were drinking beers.

Harry Ford had a bottle of bourbon in front of him, and two glasses. Beneath his feet was a friendly looking dog. Lake couldn't tell the breed.

Eddie said hello, took a drink from a glass of cola.

'I didn't think they allowed dogs in bars,' said Lake.

'They do if you buy bourbon by the bottle,' said Harry. 'Besides, this is an Irish pub. There has to be a dog in here somewhere.'

'How are you doing, Kate?' asked Lake.

'I'm okay,' she said. 'I'm getting better and better. It takes time, you know?'

Lake nodded, said, 'If you ever want to talk to a professional, I know some good people.'

'Thank you. I'll see how it goes, for now.'

Taking the spare glass, Harry poured a large measure and put it in front of Lake and said, 'Here, take a drink, why don't you.'

'I'm not a big drinker,' said Lake.

'Neither am I,' said Harry, draining his glass and pouring another.

Lake stared at the drink in front of him.

'It's entirely ethically sourced,' said Harry. 'It's made in Kentucky and it's really, really bad for you. Drink up.'

Lake said cheers, and they all acknowledged him. He took a sip of the bourbon and was surprised how smooth it tasted.

'Here comes Denise,' said Eddie.

He turned and saw Denise walk up to their table. She took off her coat and Eddie fetched another seat. A brown envelope stuck out from her bag. She gave it to Eddie, who thanked her and placed it on the table in front of Lake.

'This is for you,' said Eddie. 'You earned it.'

Lake waved a hand, said, 'That's not necessary. I didn't do this for money, I—'

'We know,' said Eddie. 'I never said you asked to be paid, I said you earned it. Now take it, or I might be offended.'

Lake opened the envelope. Inside was a check made out to Gabriel Lake for two-hundred thousand dollars. He stared at it for what seemed like a long time. He had never had money like that before in his life. He read the check again. Checked the spelling of his name. Checked the amount.

The scotch tape holding his jacket together started to come away.

'Take it,' said Bloch. 'Get a new suit. Just make sure it's not double-breasted and you don't have to button it.'

Lake nodded.

The others looked at Bloch, quizzically, not getting the reference. Lake didn't have any friends. And he never really had a good enough friend to share a private joke.

Bloch smiled at him.

Right then, it felt good to be here among this crowd. They were good people. He liked them. He liked being around them. And they were smart, too.

He put the envelope in his pocket, and thanked Eddie and Kate. 'I feel bad taking this, there's still so much to clear up.'

'Carrie Miller paid her legal bill. You earned some of that. Otto was the Sandman and he's dead. What else is there?' asked Harry.

'Well, we know some of Carrie's diary was obviously true. Giving the bad alibi. I can buy that completely. I can see Daniel, the Wall Street guy, just dropping a white lie to the cops to take himself out of what could be a lengthy investigation, plus he didn't want to tell the cops he wasn't at home, he was really out having an affair. And Otto got Carrie to lie about her husband giving her the jewelry and then disappearing. She was vulnerable. Otto was a lawyer, and he was telling her she could go to jail. But I don't know the real link between Otto and Stacy Nielsen.'

'Why is that important?' asked Harry.

'The deadbolts on the back door of her house,' said Bloch. 'Only someone who had been inside the Nielsen house would know they were there. Peltier didn't even try the back door. He went in the front.'

'Wasn't it that they ran in the same circles? I remember Otto saying something like that on the stand. The Nielsens were socialites. They probably met at a party,' said Eddie.

'Probably, but Peltier was lying his ass off on the witness stand, denying everything after Carrie sold him out. Maybe he knew Stacy some other way. I know Seong is re-examining every murder to look for links between the victims and Peltier. I don't know, I just have a feeling that if we knew the exact link between Peltier and Stacy Nielsen it might open up the whole thing. It might help to establish if there is a link to any of the other victims. Could be she was the only victim known to him.'

'He's dead, and the feds are chasing all of this down. Seong is working his ass off. If he finds something, he'll keep us in the loop,' said Eddie.

'I know, I know. It just feels too loose at the moment. Peltier could've been lying about the connection. This reminds me, did they find Lilian Parker's cameo brooch yet?' asked Lake.

'Not yet,' said Bloch. 'Seong says that they're still running down all the properties that were associated with Peltier and Daniel Miller. They may still find it.'

'I hope so,' said Kate. 'It may give her mother some small comfort.'

Lake nodded, said, 'Are you folks going to the memorial next week?'

'Kate, Bloch and Harry are going,' said Eddie. 'I can't, it's my night with my daughter, Amy.'

The city had planned a memorial service for the victims of the Sandman. During the ceremony the FBI were going to give back to the families the personal items Peltier had taken from the victims. Some of which they recovered from the office in the old bus depot.

Lake was still thinking about what Eddie had said. The Nielsens were well known in the city. Tobias was a successful restaurateur. And they were known for throwing annual parties.

He downed the bourbon, coughed, then stood.

'I gotta get going. Thanks for the drink. And for the check. I'll see you folks at the memorial.'

He said his goodbyes, went outside and hailed a cab.

'The public library, please,' he said.

It was two in the afternoon when the cab dropped him off at the New York Public Library. Lake had spent a lot of time here. Libraries were the great cathedrals of knowledge. He loved spending time in the study hall, or just walking the racks and taking in the building. Most of all, he loved books. He remembered coming to this building for the first time, with his mom, and getting his library card. And was then further staggered when he learned the card entitled him to pick any books he wanted, take them home, read them and then bring them back. For free. Unbelievable.

The records office still hadn't converted everything to a digital format. Some archives were still on microfiche. The records officer took Lake's note, then showed him to a viewing machine and loaded up the first microfiche.

There were several publications which covered society in New York. Before the turn of the century, there were about a dozen. Now, maybe three or four. He focused on those magazines and began his search.

Many reels and many hours later, he pinched the bridge of his nose, then stretched and checked his watch. It was coming up on six o'clock.

He moved the controller, swiping through the images, then stopped. Rolled it back.

The picture was not in color. Black and white. A photo from a local magazine that covered arts and culture in the city, and the movers and shakers in the art world. Every artist showing at every gallery, every Broadway play opening-night party, every red carpet – they had a camera there.

He had found some pictures earlier of Tobias Nielsen hosting parties at his restaurants, but this one was different. The photographs were from a fundraiser they had thrown for a mayoral candidate in 2013. They had the party at their home. Lake recognized the living room and dining room.

On the next page he found it. He recognized the Nielsens' lounge straight away.

And there, standing in a crowd behind Stacy and Tobias Nielsen, wearing a tuxedo and holding a glass of champagne – Otto Peltier.

Lake's shoulders sagged. He had found the link for sure. Something that explained how Peltier knew the layout of the Nielsen house.

He was about to go ask the archivist for a copy of this page when he hesitated.

Leaned in closer to the screen.

Peltier had the champagne in his left hand. His right arm was linked around the slender arm of a woman.

Lake's breath rushed from his body. He stared at the screen. Unblinking.

The young woman linking arms with Peltier was Carrie Miller.

CHAPTER SIXTY-TWO

CARRIE MILLER

'Would you like me to top up your glass, Mrs. Miller?' said the flight attendant.

'Actually, could you get me a fresh glass,' said Carrie, the strawberry at the bottom of her champagne flute had begun to look a little mushy.

'Of course,' she said, and as she leaned over to pick up Carrie's glass, she noticed something.

'Oh, that's a gorgeous cameo brooch you're wearing,' said the flight attendant.

'Thank you. It's a family heirloom,' said Carrie.

The flight attendant left, and Carrie gazed out of the window at the blue Atlantic beneath her. Another four and half hours to London and a new life.

Part of her felt bad for Otto. No one had loved her like him. Not even Daniel.

Ever since she was young, Carrie had longed to be someone else. Perhaps that's why she had tried to become an actor. She had no idea who she was, but she liked the idea of being other people – now *that* was intoxicating. It had been her dream to be on Broadway. She had given it her best shot and failed. The money she had from the sale of her parents' house had only gone so far in the city, and she had to work a lot harder at menial jobs to make her rent. In some ways, all the effort she had made to subtly sabotage the brakes on her father's pick-up, which resulted in the crash that killed her parents, wasn't really worth it. The house hadn't fetched much on the open market and New York was expensive.

Things were difficult, until she met Otto.

He had looked after her. Helped her. She knew he was special the first time she met him. He wore the same kind of mask as she did – pretending to be human. She knew his heart was as cold as hers when they first kissed.

And when Otto told her of his fantasies, the power he could have from taking life, from becoming the Sandman, he had expected Carrie to be terrified. He had not expected her to ask if she could watch. But Otto's appetites exceeded her own. And she worried. Even though he was careful and clever, one day he would make a mistake.

When Otto introduced Carrie to Daniel Miller, she knew this was someone who could take the blame for them. If they were careful, they could set this man up for their crimes, and even take his vast fortune for themselves in the process. Otto had money, but not real money. Not the kind that brings total freedom. Of course, Otto hated Daniel.

Everything would have worked out fine, except for that day when the cop came to their house, and she had been forced to give Daniel an alibi. The other mistake was the last killing. Carrie had failed to notice the blood on her sleeve from the Nielsen murders. She had been excited, and stood too close to Stacy Nielsen as Otto stabbed her. Daniel's fingerprint was already on Stacy's body. Carrie had washed the shirt, and hung it in her closet, not realizing Stacy's blood had been on it.

That led to her arrest. And trial.

And she could have weathered that storm if Otto had simply left the trial to take its course. Carrie had written out the journals implicating Daniel, all apart from the last entry. She had warned Otto not to interfere. When he killed Chester Morris, and the agent, she knew he could not be controlled. That's why she had fled. She was worried he would make another mistake. And he did, leaving a syringe cover with his saliva on it in Kate Brooks' apartment.

She felt bad about betraying him. Felt bad about inventing the story of Daniel's affair with Stacy Nielsen, and subtly dropping Otto into the frame for the murders. She knew, even though she had betrayed him, he would not accuse her while he was testifying.

He loved her too much, and he was willing to sacrifice himself for her. While she had lived with Daniel, Otto was insanely jealous. He never said so, but she saw the relish with which he cut Daniel's throat. And then he took the watch, the Panerai she had given to Daniel as a gift, and asked her to place it on his wrist. She did so. For him.

The investigator, Lake, had murdered Otto. In some ways, Lake had done her a favor. If Otto had been captured, there was always the risk he could have changed his mind about Carrie and told the FBI the truth. Now he was dead, and the truth would never be known.

After she had paid her legal fees and the FBI had removed their monitoring and alert system on Daniel's accounts, Carrie had thirteen million dollars to show for her efforts. Now *that* was freedom.

'Here you go, fresh champagne,' said the flight attendant, handing her the glass.

Carrie sipped her champagne, put her headphones on, hit play on her laptop to resume the movie she'd downloaded.

It was her favorite part.

Mitchum sat on the tree stump in the dark, watching his victims in the house. He was powerful and unafraid. Not just watching the woman and children he planned to murder – he was serenading them.

In her light falsetto voice, Carrie settled back into her seat and softly sang along.

'*Leeaaannning, leeeaaaning, leaning on the everlasting arms . . .*'

CHAPTER SIXTY-THREE

GABRIEL LAKE

Lake sat at the small dining table in his meagre apartment.

He had no memory of the thirty blocks he'd walked home from the library. All he could think about was Carrie Miller, and how she had played and manipulated Eddie, Kate, Harry, Bloch, the FBI, and ultimately even her lover – Otto Peltier.

His foot tapped out a beat on the floor. Staring at the cell phone on the table in front of him, he tried to calm his breathing. A murderer had gotten away. And in some small part, Lake had helped that happen.

He picked up the phone, dialed Eddie.

The lawyer picked up.

'Hi, it's me . . .' said Lake.

'You okay? Don't tell me you've lost that check,' said Eddie.

Lake opened his mouth to speak, hesitated. His lips moved but he couldn't find the right words. What he was about to tell Flynn would hurt. There was no easy way to say it. There is no gentle approach here. The knowledge was a bullet to the stomach, and there just wasn't a way to soften it.

He heard Kate and Bloch laughing in the background at something Harry had said. They were still in the bar. Relaxing, and enjoying the company.

'I haven't lost the check, it's something else,' said Lake.

In the background, Kate let out a peal of laughter. She sounded happy.

'What is it?' said Eddie.

'It's . . . it's nothing,' said Lake.

'You called me up to tell me nothing,' said Eddie. 'I'm not

sure you understand how this whole human conversation thing is supposed to work.

'It's just . . .'

'It's what?' said Eddie.

'If you ever need another investigator, you know you can call me.'

'I know. Now get some rest.'

Eddie hung up.

There was nothing Eddie could do about this. There was nothing the police could do about it, either. The charges against Carrie Miller had been withdrawn.

It wasn't likely she could be tried again. The breach of bail came with a warning and a two hundred dollar fine, which she was happy to pay. Carrie Miller was free now. In the wind.

He opened the drawer in the kitchen where he kept his cutlery and some of his hand tools. Inside was his personal protection carry. A Glock. He removed the gun from the box along with a loaded magazine. He dry-fired the pistol to get it open and the slide back. He slotted in the magazine, racked a round into the chamber.

Someday he would find Carrie Miller. On that day he would explain to her that there would be no second trial, no media circus, no months of waiting on a verdict.

Sometimes what is right and what is legal are not the same.

He was going to find her. No matter how long it took.

There was a bullet in this gun for her.

Someday, he would deliver it.

ACKNOWLEDGEMENTS

Like all of my books, this one would not exist without my wife, Tracy. This book is dedicated to her, but really they are all written for her as my first reader, and the one person in the world that I want to impress.

My thanks to Shane Salerno, Don Winslow, Steve Hamilton, Adrian McKinty and all at The Story Factory. I don't know what I would do without you.

My thanks to Francesca, Sarah and all at Orion Books for their work and for bringing Eddie Flynn into the world.

To my family, friends and my dogs, I thank you for your support and kindness.

My biggest thanks, like always, has to go to you.

Yes, you.

The person who is reading this now. Thank you for reading my books. Without dedicated, intelligent readers like your good self, I would be at a loss. For a book is not really a book without a reader and I have some of the very best readers in the world. I can't thank you enough for buying the books and spreading the word about Eddie Flynn. I hope that I can keep you entertained for many years to come.

Let's hope they are good years for all of us.

Tense, twisty, unpredictable –
a masterclass in misdirection:

Don't miss a single Eddie Flynn case.

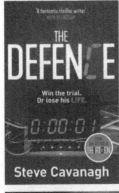

'Books this ingenious don't come along very often . . .'
MICHAEL CONNELLY

And if you just can't get enough of Steve Cavanagh, don't miss:

'This guy is the real deal. Trust me.'
LEE CHILD

TWISTED

Never let **MURDER** get
in the way of a good story

FROM
THE AUTHOR OF
TH1RT3EN

Steve Cavanagh

BEFORE YOU READ THIS BOOK
I WANT YOU TO KNOW THREE THINGS:

1. The police are looking to charge me with murder.
2. No one knows who I am. Or how I did it.
3. If you think you've found me. I'm coming for you next.
After you've read this book, you'll know:
the truth is far more twisted . . .

'A powerhouse thriller'
IAN RANKIN